"POLITICS?" TURRIN ASKED

"Over," the head Fed said as he settled himself. "At least for the moment. We're ahead of the game."

Turrin started the Jeep and headed back along the trail leading to the main house. "We get a green light?"

"Yeah. You been keeping up with the news?"

The look on Turrin's face was all the answer necessary. "We have targets now."

"That's how the Man feels. But things over there are going to get bloody. I don't know if we're going to try for full insertion yet, or work it covertly."

"Any way you want it handled," Turrin said, "Striker's going to cut himself a big piece of the action."

DON PENDLETON'S
MACK BOLAN®
STONY™
MAN

TERMS OF
SURVIVAL

A GOLD EAGLE BOOK FROM
WORLDWIDE®

TORONTO • NEW YORK • LONDON
AMSTERDAM • PARIS • SYDNEY • HAMBURG
STOCKHOLM • ATHENS • TOKYO • MILAN
MADRID • WARSAW • BUDAPEST • AUCKLAND

First edition January 1996

ISBN 0-373-61904-9

Special thanks and acknowledgment to
Mel Odom for his contribution to this work.

TERMS OF SURVIVAL

TERMS OF SURVIVAL

To the UN peacekeepers. God keep.

PROLOGUE

Cape Anansi, Walukagi
7:52 a.m.

"Stop that girl!"

Nerves frayed from an all-night stint reconning for snipers in the steamy jungle surrounding the port city of the tiny African nation of Walukagi, Sergeant Tyrell Craigie of the U.S. Army brought up his M-16 in a purely defensive maneuver and waved his team into partial cover against a boarded-over store. Bullets had taken the windows out a long time ago, and black soot showed the effects of firebombing.

"She's a damn thief! Stop her!"

Craigie looked across the war-torn street as he flicked the safety off the assault rifle. Cape Anansi's citizens were already making their way clear of the situation, fading into every shadow and gap between the bullet-scarred buildings.

An eight- or nine-year-old girl wearing a faded pink dress and no shoes darted from in front of a parked British jeep and raced across the narrow street with the agility of a running back. A barrel-chested man with dirty-blond hair waved a 9 mm pistol menacingly as he chased her.

"Hey, Yank," the blond man yelled at Craigie, "want to give a fellow soldier a hand here? She picked my damn pocket and I just drew pay."

"Ouch," said Connolly, the recon team's communications officer, then he chuckled. "I understand how the poor bastard must feel."

After only a moment's hesitation, Craigie stepped into the street ahead of the girl, causing her to freeze in her tracks. She looked wildly around, seeking an escape route.

"Burris," Craigie called out, spreading his hands to show the girl he meant no harm.

"Yo."

"You keep our back door covered here, buddy."

"Like a blanket, Sarge," Burris replied.

During the past few months of duty in Walukagi, the squad had become like the fingers of Craigie's hand. He knew without looking that Burris had taken up his rearguard position at the back of the recon team. He turned his attention to the girl and her pursuer.

He upped his age estimate to twelve. She was just thin for her age, like a lot of the kids in the impoverished nation. Her skin was blacker than his, but she reminded him of his baby sister back home in Fort Worth.

"Just take it easy, girl," Craigie said in a gentle voice. "No one has to get hurt here." He tried a smile as he slowly slung his rifle over his shoulder, muzzle pointing down.

"Don't let her get away," the man with the pistol said. He pointed the gun at her and continued to move in slowly. "Little bitch isn't going any farther. This I promise." The guy's English was heavily accented.

Craigie knew there were a number of UN troops operating in Walukagi to stem the current violence, but he couldn't identify what country this guy was from. "Hey, partner," he said authoritatively, "you just hold up there. There's no reason to be shooting her."

"Get out of the way!" the man ordered.

"Johnson!" Craigie snapped, his stomach rolling slightly at the thought of the girl getting killed. He believed in the efforts his country was putting forth to help the people of Walukagi, but there was no way he was going to shoot kids. Or allow them to be shot.

"Yeah."

"You got him?"

"Oh, yeah."

The man gazed over Craigie's shoulder and froze. Craigie knew the man was looking down the barrel of Johnson's M-16. "Your call, partner."

The invective that came from the man wasn't recognizable except in a general way. Reluctantly he raised his pistol until it pointed straight up.

A horn blasted from behind Craigie. Jerking his head around, he spotted the rusted-out hulk of a decades-old station wagon bearing down on him. The driver made no attempt to slow or change directions.

Craigie brought up his M-16 fluidly. Three different warlords were fighting over the living corpse that was Walukagi. The influx of food and goods from the United States and Western Europe had become the latest target of their efforts. A soldier who took chances didn't get to take them long.

On the other side of the bug-spattered and cracked windshield, the driver hunched behind the steering wheel and kept coming. The other passengers folded down, as well, offering no threat.

"Stand down!" Craigie barked to his squad. During the night, with the possibility of gunners diving out of the bush or picking them off from safe vantage points, trigger fingers had gotten itchy and tempers had flared.

The heat and mosquitoes had put the finishing touches on a night carved from darkest hell.

The station wagon roared by, swerving from side to side.

When Craigie glanced back to the girl, she was once more in full flight, running down an alley.

With a curse, the armed man took off after her.

"Move out!" Craigie commanded as he took the point himself.

The alley was a thin, twisting artery that bled between two- and three-story buildings. Grass and weeds had grown up between cracks in the blacktop. Rats and cats fought over the fresh garbage piled on top of old garbage in crushed and overturned trash cans.

The girl twisted around the next corner and disappeared. The man with the gun was less than a half dozen steps behind.

Craigie pumped his feet harder. He slammed up against a garbage Dumpster for momentary cover, almost gagging on the stench. Glancing back to check his team, he caught sight of a shirtsleeve sticking out of the Dumpster. Then he noticed that the sleeve was partially filled with a skeletal arm that had been almost completely stripped of flesh by animals and birds.

"Jesus," Connolly said as he fell in beside the sergeant. He stared hypnotically at the corpse's arm.

"Johnson," Craigie called out.

"Yeah, Sarge."

"You're on the guy with the gun. I want him safely out of the way, but not hurt. Unless you have to."

"Affirmative."

Less than sixty yards farther on, the girl ran out of places to flee. She drew up short against a wooden fence easily twice as tall as she was, framed by buildings on both sides.

The man waving the pistol showed no hesitation about closing in on her. Even at the distance, Craigie saw the gleam of sharp metal in her hand. He gripped his M-16 in one hand. "Burris!"

"I've got you covered."

Craigie and Johnson converged on the man with the pistol. He became aware of them and swung his weapon warily.

Without warning, heavy-caliber machine-gun fire erupted from above and blanketed the alley.

Craigie tried to turn and yell his team into cover, but a round struck him in the hip and smashed him to the ground. His right leg went numb immediately. He managed to keep his grip on the M-16 as he rolled weakly to one side. Scanning the alley, he spotted the machine-gun nest mounted three stories up on a fire-escape landing. Two men worked it. At least three other men were part of the ambush raining death on his team.

Most of the recon squad didn't have a chance. Fifty-caliber rounds chopped them down and sprawled their bodies across the alley. Craigie was hit twice more, again in the same injured leg and once in the back. He lost motor function almost at once and knew he'd taken the round somewhere in the spine. His cheek came to a rest on the rough, heated blacktop facing his attackers and the girl. He moved his eyes and tried to make his gun arm work.

The man with the pistol had taken refuge behind a pile of wooden crates. The machine-gun rounds ripped through the wood and plucked him from hiding. He was a corpse before he hit the ground.

The silence that followed the last echoes of the machine gun were as eerie as any Craigie had experienced in the jungle. Four men, all dressed in the sandy tan uniform of Geoffrey Masiga's hardforce, climbed from hiding and dropped from the fire escape.

No one from the street had come to investigate the outbreak of violence.

Paralyzed, Craigie watched the first of the men close in on the girl. She seemed confused, but came forward hesitantly. The gunner lifted a pouch from his belt and offered it to the girl. She shook her head and drew back. Wordlessly he offered it again, a look of anger on his face. Hesitantly she took a couple steps forward and reached for it.

Although unable to move, Craigie could feel his life-blood emptying out of him. There was no doubt in his mind that they'd all been set up and the small girl had been nothing more than a stalking horse for the ambush. Masiga and the other warlords were going to make the peacekeeping mission costly in American lives.

Before the girl could take the proffered bag, the gunner shoved his pistol barrel into her face and pulled the trigger. She dropped to the ground at once.

An animal noise escaped Craigie's lips.

"Hey, American GI Joe," the gunner said as he walked over to the paralyzed sergeant with a leisurely gait, "you don't have the stomach for this, huh?"

"Go to hell," Craigie growled. There was some movement in his arm now, and he willed his hand toward his rifle. His fingers moved a few inches.

The man squatted beside him. Perspiration dripped down his ebony features and stained the wrinkled uniform blouse. Behind him, his comrades moved among the dead Americans and spoke in their tribal dialect as they prodded their victims. One of them was slicing Johnson's ears off with an ivory-handled knife. A string of wrinkled and mummified ears hung from a belt at his waist.

"Americans don't have the hearts of warriors," the man said. "You come to our country, you die easy." A cruel grin bared filed white teeth. "No good for people you say you here to protect. But you bring nice things." He brandished the Colt Army .45 automatic he held.

"This isn't over," Craigie promised. "You assholes have gone too far. We're not going to back off now."

"Brave talk. But the time of long dying come, I bet you people leave by the boatload and leave many of your toys behind. People of Walukagi, they know. That why they stay away from you except to take table leavings you bring."

Craigie's fingertips touched the heated metal of his assault rifle. He forced them around the pistol grip.

"Beg, American," the gunner taunted, "and maybe I let you live."

"No." Craigie pulled the M-16 toward him, but he knew he was going to be late. He saw the pistol spit fire in front of him and felt the dulled impact against his skull as superheated air kissed his face. He stared up at the bright blue African sky until scarlet extinguished it. He'd never planned to die so far from home.

CHAPTER ONE

East London, South Africa
11:57 p.m.

"You're not exactly standard CIA issue, are you?"

Mack Bolan tracked the speeding Cadillac ahead of him through the bullet-riddled windshield of the full-size Chevy Blazer he was driving as the fleeing car wound through the night-darkened heart of the city. Sirens screamed in the distance behind them, but none of the police cars was close enough for the lights to be visible.

He looked at the beautiful black woman in the passenger seat. Molly Rifkin reloaded a clip for her SIG-Sauer P-226 with hands that shook only slightly. Her dark vest showed plenty of the cleavage that had been distracting to their quarry only minutes before. A rip showed frayed white edges over one delicate shoulder. Slim hips were encased in dark blue bicycle shorts that left her knees and calves bare. The warrior had to admit that it wasn't exactly battle dress, but he'd given her the option of pulling out when the violence had erupted back in the Ivory Vineyard Tavern. Instead, she'd stuck.

"No," he said, knowing she deserved the truth. "Not exactly standard issue."

"Didn't think so." Rifkin shoved the clip into her weapon. "The guys I usually work with would've backed off when Dewbre started making ugly noises.

But not you. Hell, no! You up and shoot two of the most dangerous guys he hangs out with right there in the bar.''

"They'd have killed you," Bolan said. "They had you made." He downshifted, double-clutched and floated the Blazer around a tight turn, closing the distance on the Cadillac.

"How do you know they didn't make you?" Rifkin protested.

"There's nothing to make." The Stony Man Farm mission controller had dropped him into the play with barely enough legal documentation to last him twenty-four hours before the CIA tripped to the fact they had a wolf in their fold. Ansell Dewbre had fallen into the Executioner's sights on his own merit, but the Stony Man cybernetics team had been operating on the fringes of Dewbre's operations even before he'd arrived on the scene.

Rifkin clung grimly to the overhead bar and slouched in her seat as sporadic fire flared from the big luxury sedan. "Standard operating procedure says we should file a report and forget it. The locals are in on the scene now."

"Somewhere out there," Bolan said, nodding east toward the coast, "is a ship full of munitions bound for some of the Walukagian warlords. If it doesn't get stopped, more American lives are going to be lost in the next few weeks. By the time the locals can take action, that ship will already have made its delivery."

A bullet slammed into the windshield, then whined away. A fresh maze of fractures intersected the ones already there.

"You're military intelligence," Rifkin said.

The Cadillac lunged around the corner less than fifty yards ahead of them. For a moment the driver lost it, oversteering, then overcorrecting and losing ground.

"Something like that," Bolan replied. He gripped the wheel in both hands and dropped his foot heavily on the accelerator. "Hold on."

The Cadillac fishtailed for a moment, then he was on it. Yanking the steering wheel forcefully, he rammed against the big car. The Blazer shook with the impact. Big as the four-wheel-drive was, it was still dwarfed in weight by the luxury sedan.

A man stuck the barrel of an assault rifle out the side window. A stutter of bright muzzle-flashes darted at Bolan, the side mirror ripped away in a blaze of sparks.

Pulling on the wheel fiercely, Bolan rammed the Cadillac again. Both vehicles shuddered and swept across the two lanes of traffic. A westbound taxi braked to a sliding stop only yards ahead of them. Bolan pulled away from the Cadillac and slipped around the taxi with inches to spare.

The man in the rear seat of the Cadillac thrust the assault rifle out again, firing on full-auto.

"Clear!" Rifkin said as she freed herself from her seat belt and leaned across the warrior, holding the SIG-Sauer P-226 in both hands.

Bolan made room for her and calibrated his chances of stopping the Caddy in the next few seconds. The local law-enforcement people would arrive in less than a minute. He had no protection here, and he had to know the name of the freighter carrying the munitions to Walukagi.

Rifkin's weapon banged out a deadly tattoo, and hot brass rebounded from the inside of the windshield. She backed away when the slide locked back empty.

Glancing at the Cadillac, Bolan saw the gunner drop his weapon through the open window and slump back inside the car.

Rifkin buckled up again and reloaded.

Choosing his moment, the Executioner yanked on the steering wheel again. This time he'd gained a little more ground, nosing just ahead of the Cadillac. The impact crumpled the Blazer's front fender on the driver's side. Miraculously the tire remained intact.

But the driver took the Cadillac onto the sidewalk, metal screeching as the sedan hurtled through a small sidewalk café. Wrought-iron tables and chairs and gaily colored umbrellas scattered before the rushing juggernaut. Brick and mortar exploded as the sedan rammed through a flower box, then mowed down a support post for the canopy hanging over the café area.

The driver tried to make for the street again, but Bolan was waiting. Before the Cadillac had time to clear the sidewalk curb, the warrior rammed the Blazer into it again. The fender crumpled further, and the headlight on the driver's side shattered and went out.

Out of control, the Cadillac jerked back toward the line of buildings behind it. Careening wildly, it smashed through the huge glass pane fronting an English department store at the bottom of a five-story building. Racks of clothing bounced from the car's front bumper, and a desk splintered. The cash register spun crazily until it smashed through the window on the opposite wall overlooking a cross street. The Cadillac halted abruptly against a support pillar as security alarms went off.

Bolan tapped the brakes and brought the Blazer around in a skidding, tight turn. Unbuckling the seat belt, he reached behind the seat for the double-barreled

Ithaca 12-gauge hunting shotgun he'd gotten from the black market in Cape Town and chopped down. He'd arrived in South Africa totally unarmed. Stony Man Farm hadn't been able to get any diplomatic pouches to him, and there hadn't been time for him to arrange his own munitions drop.

He flicked off the safety as he shoved the Blazer's door open and stepped out. He'd dressed for the night, from the black silk sport shirt to the black denim jeans and biker boots. Spare shells for the shotgun hung in a pouch clipped to his belt, just in front of the paddle holster holding a Smith & Wesson .357 with a four-inch barrel.

Rifkin's door opened with a screech of protest, then she was at his heels.

Bolan advanced on the stalled car at a jogging run. The numbers had nearly run out on the play, and he knew he was already treading in no-man's-land as far as time for his escape went.

A shadow jumped free of the Cadillac and stepped through the broken frame of the huge plate-glass window. Bolan recognized the figure as one of Dewbre's hardmen just as the guy brought up an Uzi in clenched fists.

Bolan triggered the shotgun from waist level. The tight pattern of double-aught buckshot knocked the man from his feet and stretched him out across the rear of the Cadillac. A bullet whipped by Bolan's head, warning him of another gunner near the front of the sedan. He swung around and touched the second trigger, putting the other man down.

"God, God," Rifkin said as she stumbled along in the Executioner's wake.

Bolan broke the shotgun open. The expended cartridges jumped free of the barrels and spun over his shoulder. He took two shells from the ammo pouch at his waist, dropped them into the shotgun and closed the breech with a harsh click. Without breaking stride, he pulled back the double hammers with his thumb.

The driver was struggling to start the Cadillac's engine when the Executioner laid the Ithaca on the open window. The guy froze, then slowly raised his hands to the top of his head.

"Out," Bolan commanded. "Slowly."

The door popped open with some difficulty. Immediately Rifkin stepped forward and screwed the barrel of her pistol into the back of the driver's neck, guiding him out and away from the car.

Ansell Dewbre sat in the back seat with a dead man in his lap. The munitions dealer had gone pasty white, making his pencil-thin mustache prominent. He wore an expensive suit and a modish haircut that didn't quite go with the nickel-plated .25 automatic in his shaking hands.

Bolan shifted the business end of the Ithaca toward the munitions dealer. He kept his gaze flint-hard and unflinching. "Your call," he said in a graveyard voice.

The screaming sirens of police cars sounded close.

"Are you a cop?" Dewbre asked.

"No. Drop the gun now, or someone's going to have to scrape you off that seat."

"What do you want, you son of a bitch?" Dewbre tossed the .25 over the front seat onto the floorboards.

"The name of the freighter carrying the arms shipment to Walukagi."

"I don't know what you're talking about."

Bolan pulled the first trigger and blew out the Cadillac's back windshield. Trapped inside the sedan, the noise was deafening.

Dewbre clapped his hands over his ears and yelled in pain. His tearing eyes remained fixed on the shotgun as the barrel shifted to focus on him.

"That piece of information is the only thing keeping you alive," Bolan stated, "and you're about to hit the expiration point."

"The ship's name is *Seahorse Moon*," Dewbre replied.

Bolan filed the name as he stepped back from the wrecked Cadillac, keeping the shotgun trained on the munitions dealer. Whirling blue cherries painted long shadows over the street. He glanced at Rifkin. "Staying or coming?"

The CIA agent finished cuffing her prisoner to a toppled dress rack. "I'm definitely not staying," she answered. "Whatever cover I had in place evaporated the first moment you shot one of Dewbre's guys." She kept her pistol in her hands. "I'll be persona non grata to the local law and they'll have my deportation papers waiting first thing in the morning. When it comes to leaving, I'd rather it be my idea."

Bolan filled the shotgun's empty chamber and took off for the back of the building at a trot. He broke a window in the back and guided them away from the battle zone while the law enforcement people were still trying to cordon off the area.

The *Seahorse Moon* had at least a three-hour lead on him, but the Executioner was burning up the freighter's back trail now. Dozens of American lives had been lost in the peace effort in Walukagi in the past few weeks, but Bolan had determined to mount his own effort after learning about the shipment while in the Netherlands.

Bolan cut across the alley. Rifkin kept up with him, but her breathing was labored. He slowed. All that remained was taking the munitions out of the play. After the thin trail he'd followed to South Africa, he was now working with concrete facts. Then he'd see what kind of pressure he could alleviate in Walukagi. The Executioner had never been one to leave a job half-done.

Dulles International Airport, Washington, D.C.
3:33 a.m.

"WHO IS THIS GUY?"

Carl Lyons turned in the captain's chair behind the console of the Ford van, passing out the color fax he'd just received over the on-board computer system. "Name's Henry Kalimuzo."

"So who's he to me?" Hermann Schwarz asked as he glanced at the fax and passed it on to the remaining man in the van.

"The guy we're here to help Hal bring in safely," Lyons replied. He settled back in the captain's chair and looked out over the maze of landing fields that made up Dulles International. During his years with the Los Angeles Police Department, Lyons had learned how to wait during the tense times. Now, as part of Stony Man Farm's elite domestic counterterrorist group, Able Team, he'd fine-tuned that ability.

"He's more than that." Rosario Blancanales barely glanced at the fax before handing it back to Lyons. Like Schwarz, Blancanales had gotten his start back with Mack Bolan in Vietnam as part of Pen-Team Able. Whereas Schwarz's deadly ability with things mechanical and electrical had earned him the sobriquet of Gadgets, Blancanales was called Politician because of his facility with people, words and emotionally charged situations. "You've heard about the UN peacekeeping effort in Walukagi?"

Schwarz nodded. "Yeah. Brought to you by the same type of idiots who triggered the Somalia action."

"Right. Henry Kalimuzo is the leader of the Unity Liberation Front. Six years ago he was being called a guerrilla leader by *Time* and *Newsweek*. Now he's a hero and a media darling."

Lyons glanced at the fax sheet again. Kalimuzo looked as if he'd once been a guerrilla leader. His smooth brown skin was marred at his right eyebrow, and at his neck where it joined his shoulder. The ex-LAPD cop recognized the white and pink splotches as burn scarring. The ULF leader looked to be in his mid-thirties, but the dossier that Stony Man Farm had sent listed him as two years shy of fifty. Despite the hours of research that Lyons knew went into every document Stony Man Farm sent out, Kalimuzo's background was sketchy at best. CNN and the other media hadn't been much better at digging up new facts, Lyons knew, but they didn't have lives depending on what they could dig up.

"So what does Hal want with him?" Schwarz asked.

"Hal" was Harold Brognola, director of the Sensitive Operations Group based at Stony Man Farm and unofficial liaison with the White House.

"The President asked Hal to give Kalimuzo an escort in from Dulles," Lyons said. "Hal wanted us on hand in case anyone decided to try for him before he reached the White House. There's a police motorcade waiting on the other side of the gates. They aren't inside because the Man's trying to keep this operation strictly low-profile.''

Lyons leaned forward, trying to ease some of the tension from his big frame. He'd developed a way to handle the waiting, but hadn't figured out a way to short-circuit the stress. He scratched at an itch under the chafing weight of the shoulder holster carrying his .357 Magnum Colt Python. A Colt Government Model .45 was on his hip.

Dulles International was rife with possibilities for violence. Brognola had also fielded a special blacksuit unit from the Farm. Snipers were already in place on tops of hangars, and others were secreted away for the time being as a support group.

Brognola was in the sleek burgundy limousine sitting less than fifty yards away. Leo Turrin and John ''Cowboy'' Kissinger were with him. Turrin, an ex-Justice Department organized-crime agent who'd used his family ties to fight the Mafia, was the wheelman. Kissinger, Stony Man Farm's armorer, rode shotgun.

All in all, Lyons figured Kalimuzo was in good hands. But his cop instinct wouldn't stop picking at the scenario. He knew the other members of Able Team were busy with their own dark thoughts, as well as the men in the limousine. All of them had fought in the jungles against the cannibals who crawled out of the darkness. They were too seasoned to think there were any safe bets.

The radio squawked. ''Redball, this is Convoy.'' The voice was Brognola's.

Lyons scooped up the hand mike. ''Go, Convoy, you have Redball.''

''ETA on Pigeon is two minutes.''

"Roger, Convoy. Redball copies. Two minutes."
Lyons hung up the mike and glanced back at his teammates. They were already shrugging into their Kevlar
vests. He pulled his own vest on, then freed the Steyr
AUG from its clips on the dash.

"Got it," Blancanales said as he took the passenger
seat.

Lyons keyed the ignition, and the Ford's engine
started smoothly. He swept the potential battle zone
with combat-trained eyes. The lights along the landing
strips kept most of the night at bay and created a shim-
mering lake of illumination.

"We've got contact," Brognola confirmed. "That's
our bird at ten o'clock."

Lyons saw the lights on the big Learjet as the sleek
aircraft dropped toward the airport on final approach.
He fisted the mike. "Got him."

"One determined man with a bullet," Schwarz said
quietly, "can change this whole night."

Lyons nodded. He'd worked security assignments
while on the LAPD, everything from political figures to
criminals to Hollywood stars. The main lesson he'd
learned was that no one was safe from an assassin's
bullet. Blancanales and Schwarz had worked with Mack
Bolan; Lyons had worked against the big man as part of
the LAPD's Operation Hardcase effort. The Executioner had taught them all the value and threat of a
skilled marksman.

In the distance, the big jet made first contact with the
landing strip. Rubber shrieked and smoke billowed out
from the wheels. The nose came down slowly and without apparent effort.

Lyons raked the roofs of the nearby hangars with his gaze. The Stony Man snipers were in place, but the thought wasn't as comforting as he'd hoped.

Without warning, a comet streaked out of one of the hangars, flying less than ten feet off the ground as it homed in on the approaching jet.

"Oh, shit," Lyons said. He picked up the mike and keyed the frequency. "Rocket, dammit! Somebody launched a rocket!"

Before he had the words out, the speeding missile slammed into the Learjet's landing gear. The jet was crippled at once by the explosion. Off balance, the aircraft fell over like an ungainly bird. A wing broke off and spun away until it smashed into a parked fuel tanker. Liquid poured out for a moment, then a spark ignited the fuel. Extremely flammable, the high-octane fuel went up in a whoosh. Yellow flames licked over the ruptured tanker like carnivorous will-o'-the-wisps.

Even from where he was sitting, Lyons could feel the sudden splash of heat. He dropped the van's transmission into Drive and pinned the accelerator to the floor. The Ford's augmented power plant pushed him back in the seat as he came around in a tight circle. He switched on the lights, including the high-intensity fog lights, as he headed for the suspect hangar.

A second missile leapt straight for them.

"Another one!" Blancanales yelled.

Lyons pulled hard right, throwing everyone off balance inside the van.

"Missed," Schwarz called out a heartbeat later. "Us and them."

Sparing a glance in the rearview mirror, Lyons saw the limousine racing for the downed jet, which had burrowed up against a parked 747 that provided some shelter from the attackers. Then he turned his attention toward the hangar.

The fog lights cut through the shadows filling the structure. A group of men scrambled for shelter. Small-arms fire banged out at the van, but the bulletproof glass and armor kept Able Team from harm.

Lyons brought the Ford to a screaming halt inside the mouth of the hangar and left the lights on. He kicked the door open and dropped out. The Stony Man black-suits would be able to identify the team from the specially marked Kevlar vests they wore.

Two abandoned LAW rocket launchers lay in the middle of the grease-stained floor. A six-passenger Cessna occupied the center of the hangar.

Lyons went left while Blancanales and Schwarz went right. A bullet smacked into the Able Team leader's vest, but he ignored it as he drew target acquisition on the bearded man standing in front of him with an Uzi. A triburst from the Steyr tracked across the man's upper body and sent him spinning away.

An object clanked heavily in front of Lyons. He glanced down in time to recognize the spherical shape. "Grenade!" he yelled as he dived over a rack of airplane parts and tools.

The grenade went off a second later. The concussive wave was hot and insistent, but the light was incredible.

"Ironman!" Blancanales yelled out.

"Here." Lyons dug out from under a pile of parts and tools, feeling like he'd gone ten rounds with a heavyweight contender. "It was a damn Thunderflash."

The grenade was Special Forces issue, akin to the British SAS's flash-bangs, and not easy to get hold of for a garden-variety terrorist. The discarded LAWs indicated the same thing—that the attackers were definitely some kind of specialty team. Lyons knew from the dossier that he had a selection to choose from. There were contingents in Walukagi, South Africa, England and Germany that all had reasons not to want Kalimuzo to solicit further aid from the American President.

A man lunged from hiding behind a row of lockers and fired a big handgun at Lyons.

Responding immediately to the threat, Lyons triggered a short burst that chased the man back behind the lockers. With a roar that echoed inside the hangar, the ex-LAPD sergeant charged the freestanding lockers, hitting the metal wall like a linebacker going for a quarterback attempting a sneak.

Bolts popped free of the floor and the locker unit toppled over. Gunfire punctuated the rattling of the metal as it collapsed.

Spying a crowbar lying on the floor near the upended tool rack, Lyons grabbed the bar and shoved it under the edge of the lockers. Lifting one-handed but putting plenty of back into it, he levered the lockers free of the man.

The guy was disoriented and flailed weakly, his hands empty.

Lyons slung the Steyr over his shoulder and knelt beside the man. He freed a pair of handcuffs from the back of his belt and quickly secured his prisoner. As he started to get to his feet, he saw another man peering at him over the barrel of a 9 mm Ruger pistol.

"Get up nice and slow, buddy," the man advised. "Otherwise I'm going to blow your ass away."

"You're American," Lyons said, spreading his hands out.

"As apple fucking pie," the man replied. "And I ain't about to see this country piss away time and money on another third-world country in Africa."

Lyons gathered that social consciousness wasn't exactly high on the man's agenda. "You're not going to get out of here."

"Wrong," the guy replied, a trace of the Deep South in his voice. "You're my ticket out of here. Get up."

The sounds of gunfire had died away for the most part.

"You like wearing sheets?" Lyons asked as he stood up. "Bet yours are all lavender. And I bet you come from a part of the country where the men are men and the sheep are scared."

"Shut up!" the guy snarled. He pointed the pistol more forcefully.

Knowing he'd bought himself a brief respite, Lyons flicked out a big hand for the crowbar and brought it around in a sweeping arc. A bullet lanced the air scant inches over his shoulder. The curved end of the crowbar caught the man on the side of the head with a meaty crunch, dropping the gunner to the floor like a pole-axed steer.

Dipping a hand into his Kevlar vest pocket, Lyons took out the ear-throat headset and quickly put it in place. The handcuffed man had been trying to crawl away. Lyons shook the bloody crowbar in warning and the man froze. He tapped the transmit button. "Convoy, this is Redball."

"Go, Redball, you have Convoy." Brognola sounded as unflustered as ever.

"Our guy?"

"Too soon to say."

"Get back to us as soon as possible." Lyons hooked his prisoner's handcuffs with the curved end of the crowbar and yanked him over to the corner, where a chain winch hung from the steel rafters. Cinching the plastic restraint between the cuffs over the S-hook of the chain, Lyons pressed the green button. In response, the winch motor ground to life and pulled the prisoner up off his feet. Satisfied the man couldn't escape, the Able Team warrior returned to the battle.

He slipped a small penlight from its place on his gun belt and played it over the interior of the hangar. The Steyr swung easily before him, covering the immediate vicinity.

"Ironman," Schwarz called over the headset.

"Go." Lyons stepped over the body on the floor and headed for the metal stairs that led up to the second story of the hangar.

"We're done here, guy. Me and Pol took three prisoners."

"I got one."

"Talk English pretty good, don't they?"

"That's what I was thinking." Lyons looked toward the rear of the hangar and saw his teammates approaching, herding three men in front of them.

"I figure KKK or some other white-supremacist group," Blancanales said.

"Sounds good to me," Lyons replied. "We find out who supplied them for tonight's raid, we could be on to something." He retreated to the van, then switched frequencies on the headset to cover what was going on with the blacksuits.

Out on the tarmac, emergency vehicles were converging on the wreckage of the Learjet.

Lyons took a set of night glasses from the van's glove compartment while Blancanales and Schwarz escorted their prisoners into the rear of the vehicle.

Focusing the night glasses, Lyons trained them on the jet. The aircraft looked demolished, but Lyons knew people had walked away from worse. He hoped he was going to see a miracle again. If Brognola was right—and it was the head Fed's job to be right—the fate of the people of Walukagi might be dependent on Kalimuzo's survival.

Then he heard airplane engines screaming overhead. He looked into the sky, spotting the small plane with difficulty. There was no doubt that it was in attack mode or that its target was the downed Learjet.

CHAPTER TWO

Berlin, Germany
9:39 a.m.

"You are a very attractive man."

Yakov Katzenelenbogen looked across the table at the beautiful woman he was having a late breakfast with. The attentions of attractive women weren't new to him. He enjoyed them from a variety of females whenever he got the chance. But usually not with any who were as dangerous as Sara Handel. He smiled.

"If you'll forgive me my indiscretion, you don't seem properly flattered by my observation." Handel was a cool brunette in her late thirties with delicate eyebrows, a sharp chin and gray eyes that looked like they'd been chipped from the Arctic depths. The plunging neckline of her dove gray dress revealed a generous expanse of warm, tanned flesh.

"Perhaps," Katz admitted, "I'd be more flattered if the words weren't coming from such a consummate liar. Albeit a pretty one."

Handel raised her eyebrows in feigned shock. "Why, Mr. Kreit, that's an affront to my dignity. You'll be lucky if I don't have you drawn and quartered at this very moment."

"My dear lady, no insult was intended. I tender my apologies." The restaurant was on the tenth floor of one of the city's more elegant buildings in what used to be

East Berlin. Posh and expensive, the restaurant wasn't listed anywhere, depending solely on the trade from the higher-class criminal element that flowed through the country.

She gazed at him from under lowered lashes. "I accept." She reached into her purse and withdrew a slim cigarette from a gold case. After tapping the butt against the table, she put it between her full lips and waited expectantly.

Katz knew three men were watching him intently as he reached inside his jacket for his lighter. All of them were Handel's bodyguards. She never traveled anywhere without them. They were spread around the room, triangulating Katz in a deadly cone of waiting violence. They were dark and violent, their gazes predatory. Although the restaurant security staff had quietly taken the Israeli's pistol, Handel's three guards still carried their weapons under carefully tailored clothes.

The lighter flared and Handel leaned forward. Katz shook an unfiltered Camel cigarette free of his own pack and lit up, as well.

Handel leaned back comfortably in her chair and gazed at Katz over the trio of red roses occupying the vase in the center of the table. "I like you. It would be a pity if you don't turn out to be who you say you are."

"Then I guess we're both hoping I turn out to be who I say I am," Katz replied.

She laughed. "You understand my caution."

"Not only do I understand it," Katz said, "but I applaud it. I had you checked out, as well."

And according to the Intel from Stony Man Farm, the lady had a veritable heritage on the black market in Europe. Both her father and grandfather before her had held similar posts in the criminal community. But Sara

Handel had turned the small family business into a budding dynasty in the last ten years. However, whereas her forebears had kept bloodshed to a minimum, she seemed to revel in it. Unofficially Interpol agents and officers of a half dozen international law enforcement departments had gone down under her guns over the years, as well as competition and small dealers too weak to defend themselves. And the profits had kept mounting.

She rested her chin on her folded hands and regarded Katz. "And what did you find out?"

"That you drive a very hard bargain."

"Absolutely."

"And that you were the only person to talk to these days regarding gold coming out of South Africa."

"There are others."

"None who seem to be as connected as you."

"Perhaps."

Yakov Katzenelenbogen was the leader of Stony Man Farm's international counterterrorist arm. Phoenix Force was a five-man team of specialty warriors designed for covert work. Their assignment in Berlin had been to start shutting down the pipelines into Germany from Walukagi.

"You never have stated to what amount you wanted to invest."

Katz spread his left hand. The other was a prosthesis, sheathed in a black glove. He'd lost the hand and part of his arm in Israel's Six-Day War. Barrel-chested and fit despite the iron gray hair that announced his years, he knew he made the woman's guards nervous. There was no way to disguise the threat that was inherent in him. "Let's say it's considerable."

Her eyes were sharp. "I think we should say how considerable."

"I have a computer-accessible bank draft on a Swiss account."

She held out her hand.

Katz produced the draft, knowing his team was going into motion now. He'd filled enough time. The waiter approached the table with a large round tray. Taking advantage of the distraction, the Israeli reached up and tweaked his left ear. A microcommunicator was disguised as a hearing aid, and the tweak sent a beep over the frequency.

"It's okay, mate," David McCarter replied in a near whisper. "We're 'go' here." The Briton was an ex-Special Air Service commando, and was stationed two floors above in a hotel room on the same side of the building. He was accompanied by Rafael Encizo, who was working the satellite link with Stony Man Farm.

The waiter placed several dishes of food on the table and excused himself.

"That is considerable," Sara Handel said, closing the draft. "Still, forgeries are known to exist. You don't mind if I call and confirm this?"

"No. If you don't mind that I don't wait to eat breakfast."

"Not at all." Handel reached into her purse and took out a compact cellular phone. She flipped open the mouthpiece with a pen, punched a number in and sipped her coffee. She sounded sweet as she talked to one of the bank's assistant managers. She put Katz on long enough to validate an impending electronic transfer of funds through the account. There were no problems. Stony Man Farm had arranged for the money to be there.

Handel broke the connection, then dialed again. "I'm going to take care of the business end of things first, then we can move on to the more pleasurable aspects of this meeting."

"Of course."

Across the room, two men entered the door, and Katz knew them both. Gary Manning was a six-footer with gray eyes, light brown hair and broad shoulders. He was Canadian and the team's explosives expert. Calvin James was black and taller, though more lanky. He was an ex-SEAL from the American Navy. Both of them wore suits and carried briefcases. The restaurant's security staff closed on them immediately.

Handel spoke in clipped sentences. "Bismarck, confirm voice check."

The microreceiver in Katz's ear picked up the other end of the conversation, patched through the satellite link Encizo was monitoring through Stony Man Farm resources. "Bismarck confirms voice check, subject prime." The reply was in a tinny voice that sounded as if it was coming from the bottom of a barrel.

"Stand by to access."

"Standing by for access code."

Handel gave it in a calm voice, her eyes locked with Katz's. The Phoenix Force leader knew the moment of truth had arrived. Handel was part of a murderously efficient network that was funneling Walukagian diamonds, gold and illegal ivory out of the country through undisclosed contacts, draining the country to near poverty. Law-enforcement people had gotten close to her and whomever she worked with, but no one had made a connection. He wasn't surprised that computers figured into the scenario in a big way. Handel had specialized in cybernetics while at university.

"Processing," Bismarck answered calmly.

James and Manning were drawing stiff resistance about entering the restaurant without proper ID and without surrendering their briefcases. Their envelope of protection was almost played out.

One of the three bodyguards left his position and came to stand beside Handel. The woman glanced at him in mild annoyance until he nodded in the direction of the door. He stood with his hands crossed, the right one tucked quietly under his open coat.

"Warning," Bismarck intoned without histrionics. "This system has been breached. Repeat, this system has been breached."

Handel's eyes focused on Katz and blazed suspicion. "Abort program," she said, then folded the phone and addressed the bodyguard beside her. "Kill him."

"We did it, mate," McCarter called over the micro-receiver. "The Bear's logged on to her computer. Me and Rafe are on our way."

Handel didn't hesitate about leaving the table. She was on her feet as her bodyguard's hand started out from under his coat.

Gripping the steak knife that was part of his place setting, Katz erupted from his seat. He caught the man's wrist and pushed it upward. The pistol banged twice, chips of glass flying from the unlighted chandelier in the center of the ceiling. Then the Israeli slashed the knife across the man's throat in a glittering arc. Even with his lifeblood pumping out of him, the man struggled to retain control of his pistol. Three more rounds cracked amid the screams and sudden exodus of the patrons, but only dug into the soundproofed walls.

The security staff immediately pulled back from the door, and more guns appeared as if by magic.

Shadows dropped across the huge windows looking out toward Checkpoint Charlie only a heartbeat before the glass shattered inward. McCarter and Encizo came off the rappeling lines as though they were part of a circus act.

After a brief paratrooper's roll to get to his feet, the Briton came up with his Browning Hi-Power clenched in his right fist. The gun boomed four times and Handel's surviving bodyguards went down, each with two hits directly over the heart.

Only a few feet away Encizo unleashed a short burst from a Heckler & Koch MP-5 that sent the restaurant clientele diving for cover. Brass spilled over the floor. The Cuban reloaded as the thunderous roar died away.

Manning backed the security staff away from him with a Beretta 92-F he'd retrieved from the back of his waistband. James opened his briefcase and took out an H&K MP-5, then covered the big Canadian while Manning did the same.

A waiter at the far end of the room, in the periphery of Encizo's vision, slipped a pistol from a shoulder holster.

Wresting the pistol from the man he'd slain, Katz fired three rounds that knocked the waiter back against the wall. He turned toward Handel.

"No one else has to get hurt!" Manning roared in German over the confusion. Three of the waiters didn't listen. The Canadian and James showed no hesitation as they took the men out with short bursts from the submachine guns. Manning repeated his warning.

Movement in the restaurant came to an abrupt halt. Katz didn't feel bad about the violence. The restaurant catered to a clientele formed almost entirely of the city's international criminal element. There were very few innocent souls inside the establishment, if any.

Sara Handel moved with a suddenness that made her dress whirl. A small silver pistol from her purse barely showed beyond her fist as she cut in behind a cocktail waitress who'd stood in frozen terror. The short muzzle of her Walther PPK was lost in the flesh behind the waitress's jaw.

"Please," the woman moaned in fear. "Don't shoot."

Katz held up his hand and his team fell quietly into place, waiting for him before making their next move. He locked eyes with Handel, finding no remorse and no mercy there

"I'll kill her," Handel warned. "You can bet she'll die before I do."

"No one else has to die," the Israeli said in a calm voice. He knew they had extra minutes to work with. In a legitimate operation, the police would have already been called by the staff. In this place, there would be others to call, people who would be more lethal than the Berlin police, but it would take more time for them to respond.

"That's your choice," Handel snapped. She yanked the waitress's hair, making sure she remained as small a target behind the other woman as possible.

Katz opened his hand and let the captured pistol fall. "Take me."

"I don't even know who the hell you are," Handel argued.

"A better shield than she is," the Israeli promised.

"Don't," McCarter said. His grip on the Browning Hi-Power was firm and sure. "We don't need her." His meaning was clear to the rest of the Phoenix Force members. McCarter had been an Olympic medalist in pistol shooting. The range and angle were all his.

But Katz didn't want to take the risk. There was every chance that the cocktail waitress was an innocent. She looked no more than nineteen or twenty. Tears trickled down her face.

"Me for the girl," Katz said. "Otherwise you're not going to make it out of the building."

"I don't trust you."

"Trust this," the Israeli stated in a hard voice. "The way it is now, you're a dead woman. I can keep you alive."

Encizo fell back and surveyed the situation through the broken windows. "Upstairs we found an alarm patch on the phone lines leading to an interior office. We disabled it, but you can bet it wasn't the only one."

"Choose now," Katz said to Handel, "or I'll choose for you."

The woman's features hardened. "Get over here, and tell your friends to point their weapons away from me."

Katz waved the team into compliance.

Slowly the Phoenix Force commander moved toward the woman.

"Stop," Handel ordered.

Katz did.

"The knife. Get rid of it."

Without taking his eyes from hers, Katz dropped the knife to the carpeted floor.

"Now come on."

Katz crossed the distance. Handel grabbed him roughly and turned him around. Not moving her pistol from the cocktail waitress, she expertly patted him down. Satisfied that he was unarmed, she shifted the Walther's barrel to the side of his neck with enough force to hurt. She shoved the waitress away, and the young woman dropped to her knees and started to sob helplessly.

"Now," Handel said, "you're going to get me out of here." She stayed close behind the Israeli, her body against his. "Put your hands behind your head."

Katz did as she requested, estimating where her head was behind his shoulder. He laced the prosthesis inside his left arm, allowing the stiff fingers to point at her face. Two of the restaurant's security staff attempted to get up, but Manning and James kicked them back down into prone positions.

"Move," Handel shouted into his ear.

The men of Phoenix Force stood their ground, holding in check the pent-up violence waiting to explode in the room.

"Fräulein Handel," a voice called.

Katz felt the Walther's barrel bury deeper into his neck. He allowed the woman to turn him slightly.

A dozen men in business suits and carrying automatic weapons charged out of an elevator at the end of the corridor. Their leader was a man with chiseled features, a hawk's beak of a nose and slicked-back hair. Katz recognized him from the rogues' gallery Stony Man Farm had assembled as Juergen Schatz, the restaurant's chief of security.

"There are four men inside," Handel said. "Kill them."

Schatz nodded and waved his men into motion, taking the point himself.

"Copy that, mate," McCarter said over the micro-receiver. "Hope you can shake yourself free in time to make the big breakout."

Katz had no way of answering.

Pulling him more tightly, Handel stood up tall enough to breathe into his ear. "It seems to me," she said in a harsh voice, "that you're no longer necessary."

Head turned so that he could peer into her cold gray eyes, Katz knew the woman fully intended to kill him.

Dulles International Airport, Washington, D.C.
3:48 a.m.

"LET ME AT THE DOOR for a minute."

Hal Brognola stepped back from the flames wreathing the Learjet's jammed door and continued to hold the chemical fire extinguisher at the ready. He didn't know how much of the contents were left. Acrid smoke from electrical wiring stung his nostrils as John Kissinger whipped past him to work on the jammed door.

The heat was intense. Perspiration dripped from Brognola's face as he turned toward the knot of rescue workers racing on foot for the downed jet twisted in the wreckage of the empty 747. The head Fed reached inside his jacket, then unfolded his wallet to reveal his ID.

"Brognola," he barked with unflinching authority. "Department of Justice. We've got a man inside, and until we get him out, you people are to stay back."

"You can't do that," a burly man bellowed. His ID tag identified him as Airport Fire Chief Joshua Clements. "Till we get these fires out, they're a danger to this whole airport."

"Try me," Brognola said. "Cross me, and I'll have you busted down so far that the most demanding thing you work next is a Cub Scout weenie roast."

Clements glared but came to a stop, his men stopping in a ragged line behind him.

Leo Turrin, a short, stout shadow in a dark suit and white shirt, stood his ground with an Airweight Bodyguard .38 pistol in his right fist. His stance made it clear that the fire chief would first have to cross him to get to Brognola. Five blacksuits had fanned out in a half-moon behind him.

Whirling lights from the emergency rescue trucks and ambulances played over the wreckage. Shrill warning Klaxons screamed across the airstrip. In the distance, silhouettes could be seen pressed up against the lighted windows of the air terminal.

A sheet of flame curled over the Learjet. During the sliding wreck into the 747, the jet had turned over on its side. The stub of the wing left from the rocket blast had scored deep scars into the tarmac. Kissinger ducked under the fire and continued pushing a thin worm of putty into the crack of the door.

"Somebody's in there banging on the door," the Stony Man armorer said.

Brognola nodded. There'd been no way to know if Kalimuzo or his escort had survived. A sour bubble of anger and frustration burned his stomach. The situation in Walukagi had been volatile for months, but there was no way to expect such a blatant attack.

"They're going to need to know before I blow this door," Kissinger went on. Despite the flames nearly licking down the back of his shirt, he worked without hesitation.

Brognola dropped the fire extinguisher, reached into his coat pocket for his cellular phone and punched in one of the Farm's numbers.

The call was answered immediately by Carmen Delahunt, one of Kurtzman's cybernetics people.

"This is Farmer Brown," Brognola said. "Patch me through to Pigeon."

"Connecting you now," Delahunt responded smoothly.

The phone stuttered and whistled, then started to ring. Brognola counted them out of habit. There was every chance the cellular phone connections aboard the jet had been too damaged to work.

The third ring halted midway and an anxious voice answered in a clipped British accent. "Hello."

"This is Brognola," the head Fed said without preamble.

"Thank God," the man breathed. "I thought we were going to die in here." The words were broken by racking coughs and wheezes.

"The door is jammed." Brognola cupped his free hand over his ear to block out the sharp reports of autofire. Able Team and the other blacksuits were still busy with the rocket-launcher support squads. "We're going to have to blow it."

"Blow it?" The voice sounded incredulous.

"Yeah. To get you out of there in time, the door's going to have to go."

The coughing sounded more painful. "Okay, but we're going to need a moment to get ready. We have two men down in here."

"Let me know," Brognola said, glancing at the fire creeping down the side of the jet. "Use the free seat cushions to protect you from the concussion."

Ducking from the plane, his rugged face a mask of sweat, Kissinger said, "She's ready." A remote detonator box gleamed in his gloved hands. "I think I got it measured right, but there's only one way we're going to know for sure."

Brognola nodded. He put his free hand over one ear to block out the sharp reports of gunfire coming from the hangar.

Turrin rushed over to the big Fed, one hand pressed to the earpiece of his headset. "Just flagged a communiqué from the Ironman. We got company." He pointed upward.

Brognola scanned the dark sky beyond the bubble of light streaming from the airport. Just as he caught sight of the small plane, the ground started shaking from cannonfire. Dual lines chopped through the tarmac, digging potholes as they swept toward the crippled jet.

"Shit!" The emergency people went to ground in a wave of movement. Brognola lifted the cellular phone. "Take cover! Now!" Then he dodged to his left, taking refuge behind the armor-plated limousine.

The cannon's rounds slammed into the ground with the consistency of a metronome, sounding like an approaching torrent of thunder. The destruction washed over them. Rounds thudded into the jet near the bent tail section, tearing holes in the metal and causing it to jerk. A few feet beyond the tangle of wreckage, the gunner stopped firing.

"He's coming back for another pass," Turrin yelled over the confusion.

Brognola fisted the cellular phone. "Are you ready in there?"

There was no immediate answer.

"This time," Kissinger said as he reached into the limousine's trunk, "the guy's going to have the range. He'll turn that Lear into a goddamned sieve."

The airplane made a tight circle in the sky, a swift shadow streaking through the scudding black clouds almost lost against the starless night. Brognola glanced at the jet's jammed door.

"We are ready," the British voice called over the telephone.

Brognola glanced at Kissinger. The armorer was taking an H&K PSG-1 sniper rifle from a case in the limo's trunk. "Blow it." He dropped the cellular telephone into his pocket and swept his Delta Elite 10 mm pistol from a paddle holster at the back of his waistband.

A bright flash ignited around the jet's door a heartbeat ahead of the explosion. The aircraft shivered, then lay still. The oval door flipped out of its moorings like a tossed coin and crashed into the cab of an ambulance, tearing off the light bar and shattering it against the tarmac.

"Go!" Brognola bellowed. "Get those people out of there!"

The waiting team of blacksuits rushed forward with the head Fed leading the way. Leaping flames illuminated the jet's interior, and charcoal electrical smoke curled out in creeping tendrils.

Brognola avoided the superheated metal framing the door and made his way inside. His lungs rebelled almost at once, and he had to hold his arm across his face as he choked back tears.

"Help me," someone croaked.

Glancing at the man, Brognola recognized Henry Kalimuzo straining to lift the body of another man. The Unity Liberation Front leader was disheveled, and his once-immaculate tan suit was charred and tattered.

Two of the blacksuits used backpack fire extinguishers to hose down the inside of the jet. The other three moved among the pilot, copilot and other passengers.

Kalimuzo had one of the unconscious man's arms across his back and struggled to his feet with difficulty.

Brognola took the man's other arm and together they stumbled for the doorway. In the distance, he could already hear the cannonfire coming for them.

Kissinger had assumed something of a prone position across the limousine's trunk, the sniper rifle a hard steel bar in his hands. He squeezed the trigger methodically, and the brass spun out to the side and away.

Cool air rushed over Brognola as he steered Kalimuzo and the injured man toward the limousine. Turrin caught the door and held it open.

Abruptly the cannonfire died away, then the small plane's engines sounded strained.

"He's hit," Kissinger said grimly as he shucked the empty clip from the sniper rifle and recharged it. "I don't know how bad. But I got lucky."

Brognola glanced up at the plane. It was trying to climb now, but one of the engines was streaming smoke. "He won't get far. Let's get the hell out of here."

Kalimuzo helped the injured man into the rear seat while the blacksuits aided two more men into the limousine. Both were ULF representatives. Kissinger took the shotgun seat, still holding the rifle, while Turrin slid behind the wheel.

"Let's move," Brognola said, closing his door.

Turrin put his foot to the floor and the limousine responded with shrilling tires. Glancing out the back window, Brognola watched the emergency squad regrouping themselves. The fire department shook out the hoses, and streams of water leapt at the wreckage of the jet and the 747.

"Son of a bitch hasn't given up," Turrin said, hunched over the steering wheel to stare through the windshield.

"What?" Brognola asked, leaning forward. The unconscious man was bleeding profusely in Kalimuzo's arms, and it didn't look like he was going to make it.

"The plane," Kissinger said. "Evidently it can't get away, so the pilot's decided on a suicide run."

"Or try to get away in the confusion if he can finish the hit," Turrin said. He kept the limo aimed at the gates they'd arranged to pass through, almost three hundred yards distant.

Brognola watched the plane as it rapidly lost altitude, the damaged engine streaming smoke. Bullets still drilled into the limousine, letting them know the ground troops hadn't been totally routed.

"The guy must have a death wish," Kissinger said.

"All we can do is find out," Turrin growled. He kept the heavy sedan rolling toward the exit.

Brognola saw the plane touch down ahead of them, riding on its front-wheel system like a dancer, the tail twisting as the pilot brought it on course. "May not be a death wish at all," the head Fed stated. "The guy may just be feeling lucky enough to take us out and make his way clear."

"Either way," Turrin said, "we're for damn sure losing running room quick."

The plane was a hundred yards away, skating on the forward wheels, when it opened up with the cannon. One of the rounds smashed into the limousine's windshield, and Brognola lost sight of everything in the sudden flash of light.

CHAPTER THREE

Berlin, Germany
9:52 a.m.

There was an edge to impending death. Yakov Katzenelenbogen knew that from years spent as a warrior. Once a soldier accepted death, there was no fear. He returned Sara Handel's gaze full measure as she held the small pistol against his neck. Then he flexed the muscles in the stump of his right arm and triggered the .22 built into the index finger of his prosthetic hand.

The round punched through the thin plate of bone covering Handel's temple. Her gray eyes froze at the impact and life drained from them.

Moving quickly, Katz caught the dead woman's arm as she fell away from him and plucked the Walther PPK from her grip.

Alerted by the shots, Juergen Schatz wheeled, bringing up his pistol. He managed to get off one shot that dug into the wall beside Katz.

The Phoenix Force leader snap-aimed the Walther and fired three quick shots, all of which took the German security chief in the face. Schatz staggered several feet, then dropped, his features a torn and bloody mask.

Rather than try to stand his ground, Katz rushed his nearest opponent. The man swung his submachine gun toward the Israeli, who lashed out with a vicious savate kick that sent the subgun flying. Confusion reigned in the other security men because they were afraid of hitting their team member.

Without pause, Katz ran his prosthesis under the man's neck and stepped behind him, taking him as a human shield. He shoved the Walther PPK over the man's shoulder and fired two rounds, both bullets drilling through the nearest man's forehead and dropping him.

Instantly the security team started to return fire. Bullets chopped into tall ferns and leafy bushes that sat behind the Phoenix Force commander.

Katz was well aware that he had few rounds left in the Walther. He fired another round that entered a gunner's armpit—above where Kevlar armor would be worn—and streaked unerringly for the heart.

"Katz!" McCarter yelled from inside the room.

"Yes." Katz swung his prisoner and felt the man shiver as at least two bullets crashed into him.

"Flash-bang, mate."

"Do it!"

An instant later a spherical object bounced into the corridor. One of the Germans tried to scream out a warning, but the explosion covered it. The flash was like a miniature supernova inside the hallway, and the crash of thunder deadened all sound.

Katz dropped his dying prisoner and raced for the door to the restaurant. "Coming in."

"Come ahead," McCarter called out.

Once inside the room, Katz saw that his team still had control of the immediate environment. Encizo was readying two rappeling lines hanging out the shattered windows.

"It appears we'll be on Plan B," the Briton said with a mirthless smile. "The woman?"

"Dead." Katz pulled the restaurant door shut behind him and locked it. Bullets instantly thudded into the ornate oak surface. He shoved the Walther into a pocket and glanced at Calvin James. "Grenade."

The lanky ex-SEAL tossed over an antipersonnel grenade.

Katz quickly worked it into a booby trap on the door. "Let's go." He raced across the room to the rappeling lines. "How far?"

"Three floors," Encizo said.

Stepping into the window frame, Katz worked himself into the rigging, aware of the frightened eyes of the restaurant staff and the clientele. "Where will that put us?"

"Private offices. Today's Sunday. Most of them will be empty according to the Bear's Intel."

"The police?" Katz glanced at Manning, who was monitoring the law-enforcement bands on a radio.

"On their way. They're already setting up plans for roadblocks to cordon off the area."

"Rafael and I go first," Katz said. "Then Gary and Calvin." He looked at McCarter. "You can cover us. After that it gets tricky."

"Assures me of a good adrenaline flow, laddie buck." McCarter grinned.

"All the same, lash on with the other rappeling line and we can cut down on immediate pursuit."

The Briton nodded.

After accepting an Uzi from James, Katz walked backward out of the building, then pushed himself out in a big swing to begin the descent. The street ten stories below looked like a narrow concrete river with a child's toys scattered across it. The breezes trapped between the tall buildings were still cool, not yet warmed by the morning sun.

The rope sizzled in his hand as he used his prosthetic arm to take up slack. He made the seventh floor in two jumps and balanced on a narrow ledge. Through the window, an empty office sat in silence, the walls decorated by posters advertising sports equipment.

"I've got it," Encizo said, arriving a moment later. He produced a diamond-tipped stylus from a pocket and swiftly inscribed a large oval in the glass. Taking a firm grip on his rappeling line, the Cuban kicked out hard.

The oval section of glass popped free of the window and landed on the carpeted floor, spiderwebbing from the impact. Katz ducked inside and freed the rappeling rigging. Encizo finished at almost the same time.

Seconds later James and Manning arrived and hustled out of the gear, as well. One of the rappeling lines arced out into space, then James started hauling it in.

"Gary," Katz instructed, "belay David's line. He's going to be coming down fast."

The big Canadian wrapped the ends of the remaining rappeling line around his waist. Breathing deeply to focus himself, he set himself against the wall, one leg raised to use his muscles as well as his weight. "I've got him."

"Calvin, you and Rafael scout out our escape route."

The two men nodded. James shot out the door lock because it couldn't be unlocked from inside without the key. They moved out in tandem.

Katz used the diamond-tipped stylus to cut another opening in the window, beside the one they'd entered through. Then he took the SIG-Sauer P-226 from the equipment pouch James had dropped on the nearby desk. He leaned out the window and looked up just as McCarter leapt out the window in an Australian rappeling maneuver that left him facing the drop to the street. Knowing he was working on borrowed time, the Briton tried to make the distance.

A man stuck his head over the window frame and followed it with a handgun. McCarter was twenty feet away and closing.

Leaning out slightly, Katz dropped the open sights of the 9 mm pistol over the gunner's head and chest, and fired six shots as fast as he could squeeze the trigger. Hammered by the shots, the gunner jerked and went slack, then tumbled out the window, narrowly missing McCarter.

When the Briton was ten feet away, someone in the restaurant got the idea of cutting the rappeling rope. There was no warning. McCarter went from being a well-coordinated flesh-and-blood machine to an out-of-control one in a heartbeat. The slashed end of the rappeling rope trailed him like a failed umbilical cord. He scrabbled for the building surface but couldn't make it.

"Gary," Katz called.

Manning braced himself, both gloved hands tight on the rope around his waist. "I've got him, Katz, I've got him." His words sounded as if they were intended more for self-confidence than communication.

The Israeli fired four more shots, driving a man back into hiding three floors above them. Sirens screamed from below, cutting into the city noises.

The rappeling line snapped taut, and Manning grunted with the effort of holding the deadweight hitting the other end of the line.

McCarter slammed into the office window one floor below, disappearing for a moment before penduluming back out into view. He clung to the line grimly for a moment, then climbed up to join Manning and Katz.

"Bloody hell, mate," the Briton said as he shucked out of the rappeling rigging. "I thought I was a goner for sure." He clapped Manning on the shoulder.

"Before we do that again," Manning said, "you're going on a diet." He dropped the rope and took up rearguard position as Katz and McCarter sprinted through the office door, trailing behind James and Encizo.

Katz moved the team up to a trot once they reached the hallway. James took the point and guided them down to a locked mail room. A 9 mm parabellum round cycled through the silenced Beretta the ex-SEAL carried and shattered the locking mechanism.

With the primary plan out of their reach, Katz was satisfied to see that their backup was holding. No one was in the mail room. They made their way through it quickly, easily breaking into one more office before they found the mail chute that twisted through the building and allowed the postal sacks to slide down to the underground maintenance level.

James took the lead and Katz followed. The chute was dark and slick. He heard the whoosh of his clothing against the metal surface. The first corner knocked the breath from his lungs, and he continued gaining speed. His mind was already whirling ahead, working out the next phases of the operation.

Sara Handel had been cut out of the loop that was bilking millions of dollars from the people of Walukagi. But the Israeli knew that was a void that would quickly be filled. Nothing grew as swiftly as greed. Whatever files Kurtzman had managed to raid from Handel's computer would give Phoenix Force the next cog in the black market existing in Germany, and probably Europe. But until the roots were pulled out in Walukagi itself, the pillaging of the country would continue.

For himself, Katz was ready to take on the Walukagian warlords in their own domain and put them down. But with UN and American efforts in the country, they'd need the backing of the White House. So far that hadn't come.

James's grunt of contact at the other end of the slide was the only warning Katz got of the abrupt ending. Even though he'd curled himself up into a ball, he was still severely battered when he hit the varnished wooden floor. He scrambled to his feet only seconds ahead of Encizo's arrival.

Playing a penlight about, James took in their surroundings. "This way."

Katz nodded and reloaded his pistol, then kept it in his fist. Besides servicing the mail room, the maintenance level also had a manhole leading into the sewer system. The tunnels were large enough for the team to run through. Kurtzman had turned it up in his research of the building. By the time the German police realized what they'd done, Katz and his warriors would be long gone.

Dulles International Airport, Washington, D.C.
3:57 a.m.

THE COLT .45 Government Model in Carl Lyons's hand came up automatically as he raced for the van. One of the attackers was moving toward it, as well, swinging a 9 mm subgun in the Able Team leader's direction.

Lyons fired three shots as fast as he could, not bothering to space them. At that distance it didn't matter. All three rounds slammed into the man's chest and bounced him from the van's open door.

His attention riveted on the airplane circling toward the limousine, Lyons vaulted over the corpse and swung himself behind the wheel. The ignition caught on the first try. He tossed the .45 into the passenger seat and dropped the transmission into gear, pinning the accelerator to the floor.

The airplane had touched down, flying toward the limousine in a direct approach. The cannon flared to life without warning, and one of the rounds slammed into the luxury car's reinforced bulletproof windshield. Miraculously the limo surged through the black smoke, weaving only slightly.

Lyons tapped the transmit button on his headset. "Leo."

"Go, Ironman," Turrin responded.

"Stay with it," Lyons advised. "Take it right down the bastard's throat. I've got you covered."

"Affirmative."

The limousine reeled again as another round exploded against the front end, ripping the grillwork away. The airplane came straight at it.

Lyons reached up and secured the seat belt across his chest and hips. His path lay at a ninety-degree angle from the airplane and limousine, and he was closing the distance damn fast.

"Ironman," Schwarz called over the headset, "what the hell are you—"

"No time, Wiz," Lyons said beneath his breath. He was certain the airplane pilot never saw him coming.

There was time for the guy to have attempted lift-off, maybe even have made it. Then there was no time at all.

The van intercepted the airplane less than seventy yards out from the limousine. Lyons remained behind the steering wheel all the way to the bitter end, gambling his life on the van's armor and safety systems. With two wheels barely touching the tarmac, spreading friction over a few sparse inches of rubber, the airplane had no chance at all.

With speed and the added weight of the armor on its side, the van slammed into the airplane and sent it skidding like a hockey puck skating across the ice. Not designed to withstand the impact it was suddenly subjected to, the airplane came apart, driven before the van like a snowman before a snowplow.

Lyons was enveloped almost instantly by the air bag that sprouted from the steering column. He knew the seat came loose, torn free of its moorings by the collision, but wasn't aware of anything that happened afterward.

Then he came back to the quiet that rang like wind chimes in his ears. Something hard was pressing against his chest. He took a deep breath, and realized for sure that the weight was against his chest, thank God, and not through it. He seemed to hurt all over when he struggled to get free.

"Hold on, Ironman," Blancanales said.

Lyons tried to peer through the loose mass of the air bag smashed up against his face but couldn't. He smelled gasoline, but he didn't feel any heat.

"You okay?" Schwarz asked.

"I think I'm in one piece."

"You shouldn't be after a stunt like that."

"Figured the air bag and the armor would take the brunt of it."

"I bet you figure an inside straight is a good bet, too," Schwarz said.

Lyons didn't try to summon the strength to argue. He felt a warm trickle of blood over his right eye. It seemed to take forever for the rescue team to free him, but he knew it was only minutes. Then Blancanales was smiling down at him, a wrecking bar still in one fist.

"Hell," the Politician said, "you look like shit."

Lyons managed to stand on his own two feet even though he felt woozy. A trio of blacksuits stood nearby, their M-16s up and ready as they stood guard. Lights whirling, an ambulance and a fire engine sat idling within a few feet, their crews looking at Lyons in amazement.

The airplane was scattered in front of the wrecked van. One broken wing was wrapped over the crushed top of the vehicle, like another layer of metal that was supposed to be there. A pair of blacksuits had already dragged three bodies out of the wreckage and left them on the pitted tarmac.

"Yeah," Lyons said, "but you should see the other guys."

Outside Cape Town, South Africa
10:27 a.m.

"WHERE IS KALIMUZO now?" Wilhelmus Kamer demanded as he watched the CNN broadcast. A man in a pale gray trench coat stood in front of a pair of wrecked planes at Dulles International Airport detailing how Department of Justice agents had spirited away a mystery entourage less than two hours earlier. The audio reception was sporadic due to the rainstorm that had swept into Washington, D.C.

"I don't know."

Kamer pinned the woman with his gaze. He knew he was intimidating, standing almost six and a half feet tall, with Germanic blood that gave him white-blond hair and eyes the color of pale sapphires, and a physique made broad and muscular by hours of physical discipline.

But Sonnet Quaid regarded him without emotion. "If he was wounded, one would assume they'd take him to Walter Reed." She was five-nine, with generous curves that would turn any man's head, and her hair was short-cropped brunette curls that fell over her head in controlled disarray. The woman was beautiful.

"Can you find out?" Kamer demanded.

Still sitting in the office chair in front of the big desk topped in veined black marble, she waved toward the open laptop computer before her. "I've hacked my way into the hospital's records. If Kalimuzo shows up there, I'll know about it. But I don't think he will."

"Why?"

"I've already tracked four of the Justice agents through the hospital's ER."

"ER?"

"Emergency room."

Kamer walked closer to the woman to view what she had on-screen. Her ease with languages and computer skills fascinated him, and made him desire her even more. But that hadn't happened yet. For once Kamer found himself wanting a woman to give herself to him rather than simply taking her. But the time would come, he was sure. Quaid was attracted to powerful men. It was what had brought her to him in the beginning.

"Show me," he said.

In minutes she took him through the tangled skeins of hospital bureaucracy she'd unraveled. One man had died from his wounds, two others were still in the hospital and one had been released after getting a couple of sutures in a forehead wound.

"Who are these people?" Kamer asked.

Quaid shrugged. "I don't know yet, but I'm working on it. I don't think they're conventional Justice Department agents. Their movements were too quick, too decisive."

Kamer remembered that from the field reports his people had sent in. "A special force?"

She nodded. "I'd bet money on it."

"Who managed the pickup?"

Quaid's fingers flew over the computer keyboard for a moment. The lists from Walter Reed vanished, replaced by color footage of the CNN broadcast. "These are from security tapes CNN got from Dulles Airport, although they didn't name their sources."

"Somebody gave it to them."

"I think so. Otherwise the Justice Department would have squelched them."

"They wanted to show the danger that kaffir is in."

"Public sentiment is a powerful weapon," Quaid said.

Kamer nodded. He knew that because he'd manipulated it to his advantage every chance he got.

"But I think they gave away more than they intended." Quaid stopped the feed as Henry Kalimuzo was being hustled into the waiting limousine. A bright lime circle appeared around a man's head, then the screen rippled and the man's face was blown up to several times the original size.

"Who is this?" Kamer asked.

"His name is Harold Brognola," Quaid answered, her hands rubbing together, working the fingers against each other as she stretched them.

"And who is he?"

"Officially he's part of the Justice Department. Unofficially I can tie him to some extremely delicate missions of a covert strike force."

"What force is that?"

She shrugged. The small half smile that played on her full lips meant she was more than a little annoyed. "I don't know, but he's definitely been involved with some behind-the-scenes trouble that's faced America. No matter how good an agency is, it can't cover up everything. Especially not in the United States. I'll find out his every little secret. In time."

"The shorter, the better," Kamer said.

"I know."

"What about the kaffir?"

"He didn't show up at Walter Reed, so I have to assume he wasn't injured."

Kamer crossed his arms over his chest, more annoyed than worried. Events were reaching fruition in Walukagi at a faster pace than he'd expected. The threat that Kalimuzo posed was only a small one at best. Even throwing himself on the mercy of the United States and the UN, the ULF leader wouldn't be able to halt the economic machine waiting to gobble the country up.

"How can you know he wasn't injured?" he demanded.

Relaxing in her chair, Quaid steepled her fingers in front of her, her elbows resting on the chair arms. "Kalimuzo's blood type is AB positive. That's a very rare blood type. Of the fourteen emergency surgeries that have taken place in the last hour at Walter Reed, none of the patients required an AB-positive blood transfusion." She paused. "If he was injured at all, it wasn't seriously."

"The dead man?"

"I believe he was one of Kalimuzo's people. The report I was able to track down listed him as a black male, late forties, then the rest of the physical particulars."

"No name?"

"No." Quaid turned back to the computer. "However, I think I know who he was." She tapped the keyboard.

Kamer watched as a face took shape on the screen. A black man with a thin face, a ghosting of gray in a fringe around his head and a salt-and-pepper mustache came into view. "Martin Adeben."

"Yes. According to the reports, the dead man was a diabetic and only had one kidney, which fits Adeben's profile. He lost the other kidney seven years ago due to renal failure before the diabetes was diagnosed and treated."

"The dead man is Adeben?"

"Has to be." Quaid studied the picture. "I'll know more as soon as all the reports and X rays are logged into the hospital computer files."

Turning away from the desk area, Kamer crossed the room to stand in front of the floor-to-ceiling window filled with thick bulletproof glass designed to refract an image eight inches to his left. Even if a sniper managed to get a bullet through the glass, the refraction would put him off target.

Beyond the glass, the fertile woodlands had been turned into a lush garden filled with flowers and trees. The surveillance and security devices had been skillfully hidden in the sculpted landscape. Two of the armed guards inside the ten-foot wall were visible, carrying Russian-made AK-47s as they made their rounds.

The savanna fell away on all sides from the hilltop where the mansion estate was located. To the east was a short landing strip and hangar that housed a Learjet and a Bell helicopter. Two Land Rovers were parked there, part of the independent security over that area. Farther north was the two-lane highway that led back to Cape Town. As he watched, Kamer saw a silver Mercedes appear, going well over the posted speed limit.

"If it is Adeben," Quaid said, "then the attack on the airport wasn't a total washout."

"I agree." Stepping to the built-in shelves lining one wall opposite the elegant stone fireplace, Kamer took down a pair of field glasses. He uncapped the lenses and trained them on the approaching car. "How did the attack team fare?"

"Fourteen dead," Quaid replied. "Eight wounded. Twenty-three in custody."

Kamer took in the figures stoically. None of the men who'd been taken prisoner could hurt him. The white supremacy group he'd contacted in Atlanta and "donated" money to for the strike against Kalimuzo didn't know enough to connect the effort back to him. And he doubted any of them would roll over on him, anyway, because they hated the accursed kaffirs as much as he did.

The Mercedes braked to a halt at the main entrance gates. A guard jogged out from the armored station house and checked out the car. A minute later the telephone inside the den rang.

Quaid answered it immediately, then looked up at Kamer. "It's Vanscoyoc. He says he has the person you wanted to talk to."

"Have him come ahead." Kamer watched through the field glasses while Quaid relayed the message. A few seconds later the Mercedes glided through the heavy gates and sped toward the main house. Kamer put away the field glasses and found Quaid glancing at him expectantly.

She really looked out of place in the den, feminine and fragile against the collection of leather-bound books, kaffir knives and spears taken in battle as trophies and placed on two walls, colored vases and bottles that spoke of the heritage of the land and Kamer's own ability to take what he wanted and the crossed elephant tusks behind the massive main desk to one side of the plush chair. The tusks were yellowed with age, and carved ideograms made intricate patterns across the surfaces. Once they'd belonged to a tribe in the northwest corner of South Africa, where Kamer had some business developments. The ideograms contained the written history of the tribe, some six hundred years in the making.

The tribe had guarded an elephant graveyard that held a wealth in ivory just waiting to be gathered up. That had been ten years earlier, when Kamer had usually had to work with his own two hands and do most of his own killing. He'd taken a team of handpicked mercenaries into the jungle, armed them with automatic weapons and mortars and descended on the tribe without warning on the heels of a bloodred dawn. In less than an hour he'd stolen the tribe's past and robbed them of a future, killing them to the last child so no one could identify him later. The fortune in ivory had been cut up and found its way into the black market, helping to lay a cornerstone that founded White Tiger Investments, his company. He'd kept the tusks as a souvenir.

He walked behind his desk and took his seat. Opening a drawer, he found the Webley Mk VI resting comfortably in a paddle holster. He drew it out, thumbed back the hammer to make sure the cylinder was full, then laid the weapon in his lap.

"Are you going to kill him?" Quaid asked.

Kamer laughed. "You *are* bloodthirsty, aren't you?"

"I can be. But you didn't answer the question."

"He could be a dangerous man. I asked Vanscoyoc to get him here. After that, the decision will be his."

"Are you frustrated?"

He glanced at her. Of any woman over the past twenty years, she'd been the only one he let in close enough to begin to see how his mind worked. "Bored," he replied. "Some days I miss the up-close-and-personal action."

She laughed, and he liked the genuine sound of it.

Then the foyer door opened. Meier, the houseman, talked briefly, and the Dutchman's voice was low and clear—no hurry at all. Footsteps tapped across the Italian marble tile leading to the den.

Kamer used the remote control to mute the television. CNN news had moved on to sports, picking up the action with hockey playbacks. The Webley felt comforting in his lap, even though he trusted the Dutchman's skills.

Jakob Vanscoyoc knocked politely at the door and stood framed inside it. Six feet two inches tall, he was built broad and lean like a swimmer, looking dapper in the black turtleneck, cobalt blue slacks and matching jacket. His long copper-colored hair was pulled back in a ponytail that reached just past his wide shoulders. Slightly darker, his beard was trimmed short and neat, parted only a little on the left side to reveal a knife scar that scored the jawline.

"Spare a moment?" the Dutchman asked with a twinkle in his hunter-green eyes.

Kamer waved him in with two fingers.

Reaching back, Vanscoyoc grabbed the man's lapels and dragged him into the room. Ansell Dewbre offered little resistance and came to a stop only a few feet from the massive desk.

The munitions dealer had certainly seen better days. Despite the fancy suit and the expensive hairstyle, Dewbre looked worn and nervous. His left eye ticked severely.

Vanscoyoc took up a position next to the door and closed it. Still seated at her desk in front of the computer, Quaid surveyed the man with a small smile. Kamer knew she'd never liked the gunrunner.

"You had a bit of excitement during the night," Kamer stated.

Dewbre shrugged. "Walked away from it, though."

"How?"

"Guys on the police force. I keep them paid off. Plus, that bit of action didn't have anything to do with my business. My guys figure it was attempted robbery."

"Attempted robbery?" Kamer couldn't keep the smile from his face in spite of the anger he felt. Over the years Dewbre had been useful, even dependable, but he'd never been an overly brave man.

"Yes, sir." Dewbre stroked his mustache nervously. He rubbed at his eye, but the tic didn't stop.

"The way I hear it," Kamer said, "you were the only one left alive after the attack."

"Yes."

"I'm mystified." Kamer leaned back in the chair, keeping the Webley hidden.

"The police arrived too quick for them to get to me."

Kamer heard the resonance of truth in Dewbre's words. Evidently the man had spent all morning telling himself that very thing until he almost believed it himself. "There were two people."

Dewbre nodded.

Kamer opened a manila folder on his desk. "One of them was this woman." He pulled out the picture of the woman and laid it on the desktop.

Stepping forward, Dewbre glanced at the picture. "I think that's her."

"Oh, I'm sure it is." Kamer dropped other pictures on the table, showing the woman seated at different restaurants with Dewbre. "She's very pretty, for a kaffir."

Dewbre didn't say anything.

"You've shown an interest in this woman for three weeks. She's shown an interest in you for even longer than that. Yesterday Sonnet discovered she was an American CIA agent named Molly Rifkin who was here on assignment, investigating illegal arms shipments. It was Sonnet who let your people know the woman was trying to penetrate your organization." Kamer paused. "And she almost succeeded."

"He was thinking with his little head instead of his big one," the Dutchman commented.

"Mistakes are unavoidable," Kamer said in a sharp voice, looking squarely at Dewbre. "But I will not allow stupidity to exist within this organization."

"Yes, sir. I know that, sir." Dewbre actually looked contrite. "It won't happen again."

"I'm sure it won't," Kamer replied. He let his words hang in the air just long enough for the double meaning to register. "Tell me about the man."

"His name was Michael Rideout. She said he was her bodyguard."

Out of his peripheral vision, Kamer saw Quaid tap the name into the computer and archive it away for later reference.

"And it was he who started the trouble in the club last night?" Kamer asked.

Dewbre nodded. "I had a couple of my boys ready to move in on the CIA woman. Rideout threw off their timing. Before they could outflank them, Rideout had his gun out and started blasting away."

"So you escaped during the confusion."

"Yes, sir."

"And Rideout and the woman pursued?"

"Yes." Dewbre dropped his eyes and made himself cough into his hand.

"They caught up with you," Kamer said flatly. "What did you tell them?"

"Nothing. They didn't have time. The police were right there."

"Goddammit!" Kamer roared, slapping the desk with his left hand. "One thing I will not tolerate is a liar. Mistakes happen. As long as I know about them, I can fix them. I can't go mucking about in the dark here."

Dewbre swallowed hard and made himself speak. "Rideout knew about the shipment to Walukagi."

"What about it?"

"He knew it was going out, but he didn't know what it was going out on."

Kamer stared at the man, forcing the eye contact. "So you told him."

"I didn't want to, but the bastard had me cold. He killed everyone else, just shot them down where they stood. After seeing him do Thorvald and Kinney in the bar, I knew he wouldn't waste any time with me."

Kamer relaxed. Now he knew what kind of damage to expect, and it might not be too bad. If Rifkin and Rideout were working for the CIA, they wouldn't be able to do much in the way of stopping the *Seahorse Moon*. Information would have to be routed through the U.S. military and UN forces in Cape Anansi. It could take days before an operation would be in place to act against the freighter. By then delivery would have been made. He glanced at the Dutchman.

Vanscoyoc nodded imperceptibly, agreeing that they'd gotten all the pertinent information out of the munitions dealer.

"I've invested a great deal of time and money in the operation in Walukagi," Kamer said. "So have a number of other people. You risked it all tonight when you talked to the CIA agents."

"He would have killed me," Dewbre protested. "You weren't there. You could see it in his eyes. God, he had death written all over him."

Kamer ignored the outburst, feeling the adrenaline thrill through him. "I've got a meeting with a number of the other people involved in this operation in less than two hours. I'm supposed to debrief them on the current situation and let them know we're on track. They're already going to know about you. Do you know what kind of fool it makes me look like when they realize how much I trusted you?"

The hollow look in Dewbre's eyes let Kamer know the man had admitted to himself that he wasn't going to walk back out of the room without a fight. Dewbre's right arm shook as he brought it up. A concealed derringer flipped forward into his waiting palm, hooked into a riverboat gambler's spring.

Acting on instinct, Kamer swept the Webley from his lap, eared the hammer back with a thumb and squeezed the trigger, aiming for the center of Dewbre's chest. The revolver boomed, followed almost immediately by two more rounds as Kamer rolled the hammer back and fired again and again.

The big .455-caliber slugs drove Dewbre backward. The corpse shuddered against the wall, then sat down on the floor with a harsh bounce, blood streaking the paneling behind him.

Kamer glanced up and saw Sonnet Quaid sitting at her desk with a somber look on her face and a Charter Arms .44 Bulldog clenched in both fists. The Dutchman hadn't shifted from his position at all, and a broad smile split his beard.

"Reflexes are all still there," Vanscoyoc said as he casually moved forward. He made a show of looking at Dewbre's ruined chest. "So is the killer instinct." He reached inside his jacket pocket and dropped a pair of bullets on top of Kamer's desk. Kamer stared at them.

"Found the gun earlier when we brought him in," the Dutchman said. "Figured it might make him feel more talkative if he felt like he had an edge, so I unloaded it and slipped it back into the wrist holster without him knowing it. Bastard died figuring he had you cold." He thrust his hands in his pockets and grinned.

Kamer broke open the Webley, removed the empty shells and put in fresh rounds. Then he slid the revolver back into the leather. "What if I'd missed and hit you instead?"

"I knew you wouldn't," Vanscoyoc said. "I've seen you shoot, remember?"

And Kamer realized the man was right. The Dutchman had been with him before the real money had been within their grasp, back when the blondes had been peroxide, the beer had been domestic and decent meals had been hard to come by.

"Give you a chance to reclaim your salad days," Vanscoyoc said.

"Maybe something more, as well," Kamer replied, gazing at a long knife he'd taken forcibly from a Zulu warrior. "Sonnet."

"Yes?"

"Stay with trying to trace Kalimuzo in Washington, D.C., and get me a line to Masiga as soon as you can. He's out in the bush, so it may take awhile. When you get it, boot it to me downtown on the scrambler frequency. And see what you can find out about this Michael Rideout guy."

"Right." The woman turned her attention back to the computer.

Kamer took the Zulu knife from the case and crossed the room to the dead body. He grabbed the corpse by the hair and pulled the head back, exposing the throat. Looking up at the Dutchman, he said, "Give me a hand with this."

CHAPTER FOUR

Durban, South Africa
11:01 a.m.

Mack Bolan placed the overseas call on a card with an account number that wouldn't trace back to anything connected with him or Stony Man Farm. He sipped old, weak coffee from a foam cup as he waited for the connections to be made. Extra cutouts along the way made sure the call wouldn't turn up anywhere near the Blue Ridge Mountain hardsite in Virginia.

The glass in the phone kiosk was dirty and smeared, providing an uninspiring view of one of Durban's back streets drifting back away from the industrial area. Molly Rifkin sat behind the steering wheel of the tan Dodge sedan they'd swiped after quitting the scene with Ansell Dewbre.

Barbara Price caught the phone on the second ring.

"Me," Bolan said, knowing she'd recognize his voice. "We're on an unsecured line at this end." A garbage truck rattled past, the back door beating against the hopper.

"Okay," the Stony Man mission controller said, "where are you?"

"Durban."

"The cargo?"

'I've got a fix on it.'' The warrior quickly explained about the *Seahorse Moon.* ''But I don't know where it's headed.''

''Maybe I can help you out with that. Phoenix made a call this morning and came across some background that might fill in your blanks. The client they saw had some investments in the same area, basically handling some of the profits afforded by the delivery of the merchandise you're checking into.''

''They were seeing investment people?'' Bolan repeated.

''Right.''

''Where?''

''Turned up a number of them in Germany, but it's not over-the-counter stock.''

''I'd have guessed South Africa,'' the warrior said, putting the angles together in his mind. ''That's where most of the pressure is coming from.''

''Yeah, but with the current political situation going on there, economics are risky.''

Bolan sipped more coffee and glanced at Rifkin. So far the CIA agent was hanging tough.

''The portfolio we got a chance to look at here listed a delivery point, if you're up to it,'' Price said.

''No choice. If that product gets released into the market, it's going to hurt for a long time.''

''Agreed. I can arrange air transport. I can get you inside, but I'm not sure about getting you back out.''

''If the territory's right,'' Bolan said, ''I can see my own way out.'

''It's definitely undeveloped.''

Bolan took that to mean a jungle delivery. It made sense because all three warlords vying for power were from tribal backgrounds. Only Essien Kwammanga had spent any time in the metropolitan area. "Do you have any idea who's supposed to take delivery?"

"Geoffrey Masiga," the mission controller responded without hesitation. "Recent Intel suggests that he's the primary product broker in Walukagi."

"He has competition in that market," Bolan said. He knew from related news stories concerning Walukagi that Masiga was in a death struggle with at least two other warlords seeking to take over the toppling government.

"Right," Price said, "and he's not above taking part of their profits. The way he probably looks at it now, American interests are the chief competitors. They can work out the details between themselves later."

Bolan threw out the rest of the coffee. Just thinking about drinking it was enough to keep him wide awake. "How soon can I expect transport?"

"Two hours max. G-Force is in the area waiting for me to drop a coin."

"Get it done."

"As soon as I finish up here. One other thing."

Bolan waited.

"The Man is seeing someone this morning," Price said. "I think the Farm's about to be activated. We've been holding a yellow light on an operation in that area for three days."

"I'll get back to you," Bolan said, "as soon as I'm able. Either way it goes, I'm going to recon the situation and see what I can do. Even if I have to go it alone."

"Understood. But I'm betting it's going to be a team effort." Price quickly gave him the coordinates where he could meet Jack Grimaldi, G-Force, who was the Farm's ace pilot.

Bolan broke the connection and walked back to the car, where Rifkin was waiting. He'd made his split with Stony Man Farm some time back, knowing his time with them had slowed his War Everlasting, but he'd never passed on a specialty play when asked by Brognola. If the Stony Man warriors were given a go-ahead, the big man knew it would be nothing less than a hell-fire-and-thunder effort. American lives had already been given in Walukagi, and the cannibals bent on ransacking the country were about to get the butcher's bill.

"We got a problem," Rifkin said as he slid behind the wheel.

"Besides the coffee?" Bolan asked, keying the ignition. He scanned the small grocery store's parking lot. Signs advertising specials and bargains littered most of the store's windows, but he could see the clerk who had waited on them standing near the counter, a telephone in his hand as he talked and gestured forcefully.

"I think we've been made," Rifkin said. She held her SIG-Sauer under her thigh.

"The car?"

"I'd bet on it." Rifkin looked at him, a half smile on her face. "It's these damn computers. Everybody's getting more efficient. Somebody back in East London probably found out about the stolen car, put two and two together and logged the information with an American salt-and-pepper hit team. The guy in there heard us both talk. And despite the months here, I still don't sound local."

Bolan pulled out onto the street. "So we'll lose the car a few blocks from here. Feel like walking?"

"A lot more than I feel like sitting in a jail cell hoping the State Department can cut a deal." Rifkin poured her coffee out the window and dropped the cup in the back seat. "Did you arrange a ride?"

The warrior nodded. "If we make the docks in two hours, there'll be a plane waiting on us."

"You got connections."

"Sometimes."

"Then what?"

"We make contact with your people and get you out of here."

"What about you?"

Bolan glanced at her, then checked the rearview mirror. He didn't think anyone was following them. He made two hard lefts to make sure, then was satisfied. "There's still the *Seahorse Moon*."

"Do you plan on taking it down all by yourself?"

The warrior didn't reply, his mind already touching on the various aspects of what he needed to accomplish over the next few hours.

"You probably would if you got the chance," Rifkin said. "After seeing you in action, I wouldn't put anything past you."

Three blocks from a mass-transit stop, Bolan pulled the car over to the curb and cut the engine. "Get the maps out of the glove compartment." While the CIA agent was doing it, he opened the trunk and took out the gym bag that held the cut-down shotgun and the spare munitions he had. He'd picked up a 9 mm Ruger pistol for a hideout gun and carried it in his waistband under the tails of his shirt.

Drum brakes issued a squealing protest behind them. When Bolan looked, he saw a battered gray-and-green bus lumbering toward the stop. Five people drifted out of a small café and formed a line.

"The local law," Rifkin said as she shouldered her bag.

Bolan took the maps from her and tucked them into his pants pocket. He slipped a pair of sunglasses from his shirt and slid them into place as he watched the police car cruise around the corner ahead of them. Two uniformed officers sat inside, gazing at pedestrians. The passing bus blocked their view of Bolan, Rifkin and the stolen car. If it hadn't, the Executioner had already marked the maze of alleys behind the café. They could have faded in minutes. The police car went on.

"Geez," Rifkin said as she took her place in line, "that was close."

Bolan dropped money in the fare box and asked the driver for a copy of the bus routes. Midway back, there was an empty seat and they took it.

"What's the plan?" Rifkin asked.

Bolan leafed through the bus-route schedule, thankful that English was one of the languages it was printed in. Working by landmass orientation would have required more effort. The routes were also color coordinated. "I'm going to find our way to the docks."

"What am I supposed to do?"

Bolan looked past her and grinned at the kids at the back of the bus who'd stopped playing and started watching them. "Start acting touristy and not so much like a fugitive."

The Oval Office, The White House
5:23 a.m.

HAL BROGNOLA STOOD on the other side of the room from Henry Kalimuzo and stayed silent. He knew the man was hurting, and he also knew there were no words he could say that would take away the pain. Warriors—good men, with families and dreams—died in every battle. The head Fed nursed the cup of coffee he held and waited. The President was on his way.

The ULF leader gazed through the blinds over the bulletproof windows. He kept his hands behind his back and maintained a rigid posture.

Brognola glanced at the TV-VCR built into one of the walls. A CNN reporter was doing an update on the violence in Walukagi. Footage rolled, showing UN tanks burning as locals threw Molotov cocktails over the heads of the crowd held back by ground soldiers. One of the tank commanders took the full brunt of a fire-bomb, and flames immediately wreathed around his body, turning him into a human torch. The cameraman who'd caught the action on film was obviously shaken by the incident because the camcorder wavered visibly.

The tank commander had tried to beat the flames out for an instant, then abandoned the tank altogether, leaping off the vehicle and landing in the crowd. By the time ground soldiers reached him, he was already dead. It was one of the scenes most associated with the police action in Walukagi, relayed over and over again in the media.

Brognola fished in his pocket for a roll of antacids and took two. For weeks the killing had escalated. The delivery of American soldiers was supposed to take the edge off the fighting, and at first he supposed it had. The Walukagian government officials became more protected. Then the local forces became more organized and went after the U.S. and UN soldiers and the people themselves. The goods and medicines that were being delivered became prizes to be captured.

The scene cut to the trio of recon Marines who had been found less than a week earlier. Brognola remembered the story. The Marines had turned up missing on their patrol, and search-and-rescue teams had been sent into the bush. They'd found the men within hours, hanging from trees, their throats slit, nude and disfigured.

The footage continued to roll—all images Brognola knew he and the rest of America had branded into their souls. He unwrapped a cigar, stuck it in his mouth and started chewing.

The anchor moved on to Henry Kalimuzo, who was starting to be hailed as perhaps the only thing that stood between Warikagi and total anarchy. Brognola thought the man looked more relieved in the footage.

"What kind of man do you think I am?" Kalimuzo asked.

Brognola turned to face the ULF leader. He returned the frank gaze full measure, then took his cigar out of his mouth to speak. "Some say you're a good man. Some say you're bad. Personally I don't know."

"Every man makes mistakes, Mr. Brognola." The whites of Kalimuzo's eyes were almost parchment yellow, veined with red, looking hollow with the dark circles under them.

"I've made some myself," the head Fed replied. "Don't look to me to start throwing bricks at glass houses."

Kalimuzo nodded. "No matter what you think of me, Martin Adeben was a good man."

"I'd heard that." And Brognola had. The research Price and Kurtzman had provided had been extensive, going well beyond the efforts the media had proved capable of. Adeben had been a government official for a number of years before switching camps to the Unity Liberation Front.

"They murdered him." Kalimuzo raised his hands before him and clenched them into shaking fists. "Just as they will murder everyone in my country who doesn't give in to them. And the ones who do will only be granted a slow death."

Brognola remained silent.

Kalimuzo forced his hands down again. "Even if I am not perceived to be a just man, it must be recognized that my cause is just. If I could, I would gladly walk into those jungles and kill the enemy where I found him, until I had no more blood to give. But I am only one man."

The words took Brognola back to a time when he'd first met Mack Bolan, at a time when the Executioner was launching his one-man war against the Mafia. As with Bolan, he felt the words weren't hollow. Kalimuzo meant what he said.

Before the head Fed could respond, the door to the Oval Office opened and the President entered, looking harried and worn.

"This place is a madhouse," the Man said as he approached the coffee service and poured a cup. "My office has been fielding phone calls from the media since the incident at Dulles." He glanced at Kalimuzo. "How're you doing, Mr. Ambassador?"

"Fine."

Brognola listened to the exchange with renewed interest. As far as he knew, Kalimuzo had never been referred to as a Walukagian ambassador.

"Coffee?" the President asked.

"Thank you, no."

The Man stood behind the desk, waved Kalimuzo into a red leather chair in front of the desk and took his seat. He took out a notebook and pen from one of the drawers and dropped it on the desk. "Hal, what can you tell me about the people behind the attack at the airport?"

"They're part of a white-supremacist group from in and around Atlanta, Georgia. They're called the Brotherhood of Aryan Defense."

"BAD?"

"Yeah. Witty little bastards, aren't they?"

"What's the tie to the situation in Walukagi?"

"As far as we've been able to find out, there isn't one. The local papers carried a few stories on the protests rising up in Atlanta regarding American intervention in Walukagi, but none of them involved violence."

"They certainly didn't show any hesitation this morning." The President watched the silent footage of the burning airplanes on the television.

"No, sir." Brognola flipped through a notepad. "Most of the guys we turned up at the site had priors for assault with a deadly weapon, armed robbery or rape. There were a few with clean records. Some of them are already trying to cut a deal, saying they were paid to shoot down the jet. They say they didn't know who was in it."

"What's your take on the attack?"

"I think they knew who was on the jet. But I don't think they were told it was going to be as heavily guarded as it was. Most of them feel like they were used."

"Can we deal with these people?" the President asked.

Kalimuzo sat up straighter in his seat. "These men killed Martin Adeben. They can't be allowed to get away with that!"

The President looked at the ULF leader. "Mr. Ambassador, I'm prepared to do everything I can for your country at this point, but I need a lever to get things working. I'm kind of like Archimedes, the guy who said that if you could give him a lever long enough, he could move the earth. If these killers can give me what I need to get the American public behind me, then I'm going to let them. It doesn't mean they're going to get away scot-free. Let's try to save lives here, not go into the vengeance business."

Kalimuzo's mouth became a thin, hard line as he forced himself back in the seat.

"We can cut a deal somewhere along the way," Brognola said. "How much good it will do is another matter. The FBI interrogation teams I've got working with them have relayed that they didn't know much. They were paid by someone in Atlanta, but that person hasn't shown up on any records so far."

"So it may turn out to be a dead end?"

"Probably will."

"I hate the idea of going to those media people and telling them we can't find out who paid off a white-supremacist group to kill Mr. Kalimuzo. That makes it appear more like the attack was a domestic problem instead of one related to the insurrectionist forces in Walukagi."

"Then don't," Brognola suggested.

The other two men looked at him.

"Tell the press you can't disclose who hired the Brotherhood of Aryan Defense," the head Fed said. "If you don't give them the answers—"

"They'll draw their own conclusions," Kalimuzo said in appreciation.

"And it's probably going to be the truth," the Man said.

"Or close to it," Brognola agreed.

"Are your people ready to roll on this in Walukagi?" the President asked.

"They're only hours away," Brognola answered. The Man had been vague about whether there was going to be any insertion of the Stony Man teams.

"What about Striker?"

"He's already anted up on a related front."

"He's in?"

"Once he gets the call, I think so."

The President nodded. "If this goes the way I believe it will, I wouldn't want to do it without him."

Brognola knew the feeling.

The intercom buzzed, and the Man punched it into operation.

"Ambassador Henley is here to see you, Mr. President," a male voice said.

"Send him in," the Man said. He and Kalimuzo stood and turned to face the door.

Intrigued, Brognola watched. Other than outlining his needs for military tactical advice and information, the President had been keeping his cards pretty close to his vest regarding Walukagi.

Henley was a youthful forty-something, with chestnut-colored hair and hazel eyes. His chin was cleft and his dark gray suit was immaculately tailored. A yellow carnation decorated his lapel. "Mr. President," the ambassador said, extending his hand.

The Man took it for a moment. "Ambassador Henley, I'd like you to meet Ambassador Kalimuzo, of Walukagi."

Henley shook Kalimuzo's hand but looked puzzled. "I'm afraid I didn't know you were elected ambassador." His accent was definitely British.

"He hasn't been," the President said. "At least not yet. Have a seat."

Puzzled, Henley sat.

"I'm backing Mr. Kalimuzo for an ambassadorship," the President said. "In light of all the problems in Walukagi during the past few weeks, and the fact that the government currently in place doesn't appear willing to talk to me while American soldiers are over there dying for them, I've decided to open negotiations with someone I feel is qualified to speak for the Walukagian people."

"And that person is Mr. Kalimuzo," Henley said.

"Yes." The President didn't flinch from his stance. "Tea?"

"Please."

Brognola got the impression Henley was accepting the drink only to buy time. The Man served it himself.

"Exactly how do I—or more particularly, the British government—figure into this?" Henley asked.

Kalimuzo looked at the ambassador. "Speaking on behalf of the Walukagian people, we wish once more to become a British protectorate and renounce our independence."

Henley glanced at the President, then back at Kalimuzo. "Bloody hell," he said in stunned surprise.

Brognola figured that didn't say the half of it.

Outside Cape Town, South Africa
12:17 p.m.

RIDEOUT, MICHAEL, DECEASED.

Blinking her eyes to clear blurred vision, Sonnet Quard reread the line. It didn't go away.

"Shit," she said in disgust. After a number of attempts to track the name down by hacking her way into different sets of CIA files, this was all she could come up with.

The revelation cut no ice with her, and she knew it would have the same effect on Wilhelmus Kamer. Personally two other names she'd worn in previous incarnations were dead. Others had simply disappeared over the years just as easily as they'd appeared.

Rideout, Michael, deceased.

It was possible the man really was Michael Rideout, and it was just as possible that he'd merely borrowed the name. The files she'd turned up on Rideout weren't very flattering.

Either way, he had penetrated the munitions end of the Walukagian operation and now posed a threat.

She leaned back in the chair and thought. She was out on the patio now because the house maintenance people were replacing the carpet and the bloodstained paneling in the den. It wasn't the first time it had been done.

Her agile mind wrapped itself around the problem. She'd been on her own before, carrying out an agenda in enemy territory. She intimately knew what Rideout's mindset would be. During her rifling of CIA files, she'd discovered the other agent, Molly Rifkin. Rifkin's handler in South Africa was busy beating the bushes for his agent, while the SAC—the Special Agent in Charge—demanded phone calls every thirty minutes. The South African authorities were also watching the

CIA handler, waiting until he linked up with Rifkin so they could seize them both. And maybe Rideout, as well.

Getting up, she walked into the huge kitchen and made herself a Finlandia vodka, neat. She took her drink and went back to the garden behind the den.

For a moment she tried to lose herself in the beauty of the garden. But it was no use; she was an alien thing to that kind of life. Still, if it was possible later, she fully intended to go down to the beach, bake, drink vodka and possibly bed one of the young men from out of country looking for adventure. She needed something to work the kinks out of her back.

She fixed another drink, then returned to the computer. When she glanced at the screen she saw a line of asterisks, indicating that something had come through on one of the other programs she was running.

Placing her drink on the table, she cracked her fingers and opened up the file. She was working off the mainframe inside the mansion, plugged into phone lines that would be extremely hard to trace because they were joined to satellite relays.

The file contained a report from the Durban police, reporting that the stolen car from East London had been found. The report also confirmed that a white male and a black female had been together in the car, and that the male had placed a long-distance telephone call from the pay phone. As yet, the police hadn't been able to get the call sheet from the telephone company.

"Yes," Quaid said. It wasn't success, but she was quickly vectoring in on her prey. All she had to do was drop the cross hairs over Rideout and Rifkin.

She reasoned that if Rideout had used the telephone, he had to be setting up a way out of the country. Whoever he was, he suspected that the CIA's operation was vulnerable. He was right, though Rifkin had slipped through the net. If only Dewbre had called in to check her out, she would have been busted.

She hacked her way into the telephone company's logs. She didn't need a warrant the way the police did. Within minutes the information was hers. The number belonged to Knitpicking by Olson, a craft shop in Minneapolis, Minnesota. A quick background check assured her the number had been in existence for seven years.

She called. A flustered feminine voice answered after eleven rings. A brief conversation followed, and Quaid learned that the shop didn't open until eight and that the manager was there only to put inventory away.

Hanging up, Quaid realized the number had to have been cut out somewhere along the way. Rideout had his own resources, then, and wasn't dependent on the CIA, or was operating from a smaller, more covert unit within the Agency.

Figuring on that, she guessed that Rideout would go for air transport out of South Africa.

She pulled up maps of Durban on the computer and immediately seized on the docks. A seaplane could easily put in there and unite with the American forces in Walukagi to the north. Then she contacted the port authority, finding out that a Grumman Goose seaplane was expected to land at any time.

Satisfied, she called Kamer, reaching him on the cellular phone in his Bentley. "I think I've found your missing CIA agent," she said.

"Where?"

"Durban." She explained about the stolen car and the Grumman Goose.

"You've done well," Kamer said when she finished.

"Thank you."

"Have you contacted Masiga?"

"I'm still waiting for him to return my call."

"Okay. For now give Vanscoyoc a call and let him handle Rideout."

Quaid cradled the phone, then dialed again from memory. The Dutchman sounded as if he'd been waiting for the call. When she hung up, she looked at the computer screen. It had gone back to the original line: Rideout, Michael, deceased.

"Not yet," she said, "but soon."

Capitol Hill, Washington, D.C.
6:27 a.m.

CARL LYONS SURVEYED the Senate seats spread out around him. He'd been in the Senate before, on different assignments, but it never failed to fill him with awe. It was one thing to see a police squad room in action— the issuing of assignments in an investigation—but quite another to realize that only a hundred people had so much to say about the fate of a nation.

Pushed in behind the senators' seats and in the upper deck, a veritable parade of media personnel nursed coffees and hurriedly wrote down questions they intended to ask. From the bits of conversation Lyons had overheard, the reporters hadn't been given many clues as to the subject matter of the emergency press call. Everyone seemed aware that Henry Kalimuzo had been brought to the White House, but no one appeared certain of what direction to take the speculation.

"I feel like I'm in a zoo," Schwarz complained over the ear-throat headsets the Able Team members were wearing to maintain their own private channel. Brognola had asked them to be present during the questioning though the big Fed hadn't had time to discuss it with them.

"There's so many reporters jammed in here," Blancanales said, "that I feel like I need the trading-card set just to keep up. ABC, NBC, CBS, CNN. Not to mention the papers and magazine people."

Lyons felt the same way. The White House security people hadn't been happy about the decision to call the impromptu meeting, and the Secret Service wasn't thrilled, either. The ex-LAPD cop searched the crowd, relying on his honed instincts to guide him through the flesh-and-blood maze. He was certain the forces behind Kalimuzo's attempted assassination hadn't given up.

He stood next to the wall where Secret Service agents kept a path open for their use. Dressed in a suit, he blended in with the security staff but not the media people.

"So what's your story?" a feminine voice asked.

Looking down and slightly behind him, Lyons discovered the speaker was a petite woman with short, snarled, ash-blond tresses. Her punk-cut turquoise leather jacket and matching jeans allowed her to stand out from the rest of the media crowd. Her eyes were violet and magnetic.

"I don't know what you're talking about," Lyons answered.

"Bullshit." She handed him a cup of coffee and kept one for herself.

Lyons didn't turn down the offer. Drinks and doughnuts had been assembled on racks in a service area that had been set up in the back. Braving the line would have meant a considerable investment of time, and the scent of coffee had been driving him crazy. "No bullshit," he replied. "Do I know you?"

As an answer, she pulled back the lapel of her jacket and revealed her ID card. Her press pass labeled her as Emma Creighton of *Global Realities*. "I'm Emma."

"Of *Global Realities*. I can read."

"That's something, anyway. I like interviewing someone who's educated." Her eyes roved over the podium area, where sound people were still hooking up the microphone equipment.

"Why would you want to interview me?"

"You were at Dulles when they tried to whack Kalimuzo."

"You think so?"

Creighton rolled her eyes and dug in her pocket. She came out with a stack of pictures. After flipping through them for a moment, she handed one to Lyons. The big Able Team warrior saw a picture of himself outside the van, frozen in midrun.

"Where—"

"Where did I get that?" Creighton asked, snatching the picture back. "From the security cameras at the airport."

"Those haven't been released to the press."

Creighton covered her mouth as if she were stifling a yawn. "And?"

"No one has those pictures."

"*Global Realities* does." The reporter glanced around and looked at a scruffy camcorder operator. The guy wore denim cutoffs, thong sandals and a Hawaiian print shirt, and he stood only a few feet away. "Hey, Billy, get over here. When I do this story, I'd like our audience to hear my voice, too."

"The hell with it, Emma. You got a recorder. We can dub your voice in later."

"Sure, but it kind of adds weight when a reporter's asking hard-hitting questions and her camera guy is standing in her shadow."

Billy grinned at her. "Tough. Cowlings hired me to get good pictures, so I'm going to get good pictures. You want to look tough when you brace the Prez, stand close to one of these other guys. You got plenty to choose from." He moved through the crowd, angering a number of people but not seeming to care.

"Artists," Creighton said. "What the hell can you do with them?"

Moving quickly, Lyons reached inside the bulging pocket of her jacket and removed the microcassette recorder inside. It was running. Without a word, he switched it off. "When you interview someone, you should at least give him the courtesy of saying 'no comment.'"

"Screw 'no comment.' That's not a news story. Can I have my recorder back? Please? It comes out of my pay, and I damn sure can't go back to Cowlings with no words for Billy's masterpieces."

"Keep it off?"

"Sure. Can't blame a girl for trying, can you?"

"I can," Lyons replied as he gave the recorder back, "and then some."

"Tough guy." Creighton gazed at him speculatively.

"Yeah."

"It's okay. I like tough guys."

In spite of himself, Lyons was warming up to the woman. He smiled and some of the nervous tension went out of him for a time.

"So how about a quote?" Creighton asked.

"No. And for the record, I've never heard of *Global Realities.*"

"You will. We're going to be the biggest news outlet on the I-way."

"The I-way?"

A disbelieving look crossed Creighton's face. "Haven't you ever heard of the information highway?"

"Something about computers, right?"

"No shit. You must be living in a mushroom garden." She shook her head. "*Global Realities,* where the news bytes. It's a computer-generated news magazine, complete with digitized film footage that can be altered or amplified any way a subscriber wants. You want the news as headlines only, three-paragraph stories or the whole detailed ball of wax, you just punch it up the way your little heart desires. Want to see footage of a news story again? Just run it back. Want related stories published by *Global Realities* or another source, we've got reference archives like you wouldn't believe. This is going to be a must for the info-junkies of the world."

"Does the truth still exist in there anywhere?" Lyons asked.

"As much as you can stand. And, anyway, with the avalanche of information we've gotten accustomed to these days, you can take your choice of truths. People will, you know, as long as you make it entertaining. That's the key."

"I'll remember that."

Increased action around the podium drew their attention. "You sure you don't want to be quoted?" Creighton asked. "Andy Warhol figured everybody got their fifteen minutes in the spotlight, but I could maybe stretch it if you know enough."

"I'm sure."

Creighton pulled up the lapel of her jacket. "Then I'm out of here. I'll get your story from another source, Mr Mystery Guy. But first I got to go ask the President embarrassing questions. Ciao." She made her way through the crowd with deceptive ease, managing to stand close to a deeply suntanned man holding a camcorder over his shoulder near the podium. She apparently tried working her charm on him, but he ignored her for the most part.

"So who was the babe?" Schwarz asked over the headset.

"Talent scout," Lyons said. "Said she thought she could get me bit parts on 'America's Most Wanted' playing the heavies."

"Hold out," Schwarz said. "You can do better. The way Hollywood's recycling all the old sitcoms and cartoons as movies, you're a cinch for the lead in *Dudley Do-Right.*"

Blancanales laughed into his headset.

Lyons ignored the good-natured banter that followed and kept his cop radar trained on the people in the room.

The Senate majority leader stepped up to the podium. Quiet settled over the reporters.

"Ladies and gentlemen," the Senate majority leader said, "I give you the President of the United States."

On cue the Man emerged from stage left and walked to the podium, waving to the media representatives. Secret Service men, dressed in dark suits and outfitted with hidden radios, maintained a loose cordon around him.

Lyons's eye still hurt from the two sutures that had been necessary to close the cut he'd gotten when he rammed the airplane with the van. He had a headache and his cheekbone throbbed, but he ignored the pain. Glancing up, he saw Blancanales and Schwarz along the second-floor railing. They wore ID tags similar to the one he had.

Heads turned to the President, and Lyons followed. Brognola and Kalimuzo had just become visible within the ranks of the Secret Service men. A third man Lyons didn't know was with them, being guarded just as closely. The head Fed hadn't had a chance to talk to them since their arrival at the White House, so they still didn't know what the agenda was.

"Senators, and ladies and gentlemen of the press," the President said, "we've really got a lot of ground to cover here this morning, and I'd like to get down to it if I could." He shuffled his notes on the podium. "As most of you are aware, Henry Kalimuzo, the head of Walukagi's Unity Liberation Front, arrived at Dulles International Airport this morning and was almost assassinated."

Lyons sipped his coffee and kept tracking.

"Mr. Kalimuzo was here by my invitation," the President said, and his declaration sparked a round of conversation. He paused to let it die down before going on. "In light of the current political situation in Walukagi, and the fact that American troops are in the field there on a mercy mission, I felt it necessary to have someone in Walukagi whom the American government could deal with. So I have accepted Mr. Kalimuzo's offer to be an ambassador for his country. From this point on I'll open the floor for discussion, but I warn you, our time here this morning is extremely limited."

Lyons followed the questions automatically. They were the same ones a cop would ask, and the reporters seemed to work in tandem, unearthing a foundation to build on, then weaving a web of other truths that overlapped.

"A question, Mr. President." The speaker was Emma Creighton, who showed no qualms about stepping forward to challenge the Secret Service agents. The camcorder operator beside her shied away from the extra attention.

"Sure," the Man said, pointing at her. "I'm afraid I don't know your name. I know most of the people here."

"Emma Creighton, with *Global Realities.*"

"Yes."

"Is it true that the attack on the airport this morning was by a white-supremacy group that calls itself the Brotherhood of Aryan Defense?"

The President bought himself some time by leaning over to one of his advisers and listening to whatever the man said. When he got back to the microphone, the Man said, "I'm afraid I don't know the answer to that question at this point. As soon as I do, I'll get it out to the media."

Lyons was aware that Price and Kurtzman had turned up the Intel at the Farm, and he also knew that Brognola was keeping that information from the press until Justice agents could act on it.

The President moved on to other questions, then Creighton broke into the conversation again. "Mr. President, isn't it true that James Howert is the regional head of the Brotherhood of Aryan Defense in Atlanta, where most of the suspects taken into custody at the scene are from, as well?"

Spreading his hands and grinning good-naturedly, the President said, "Again, Ms. Creighton, if this is true and you can confirm it, your resources must be better than mine."

A small ripple of laughter floated through the assembled crowd. A number of reporters pulled back from Creighton. The questioning continued. Creighton raised her hand patiently and waited, but the Man never called on her again.

Lyons watched as the reporter's shoulders knotted in frustration.

"Mr. President!" she shouted over the other reporters. "Mr. President!"

Shaking his head, the Man turned to address the *Global Realities* reporter. "Ms. Creighton, surely you can proceed at this meeting with a more democratic attitude."

"That won't get me the front page."

Lyons's hackles rose all of a sudden, and he didn't understand the cause. He tapped the headset's transmit button. "Look alive," he said as he scanned the room again, "something doesn't feel right."

"What's your question?" the President asked.

"It's not so much a question as it is a request for an explanation."

"You've got my attention, Ms. Creighton."

"I'd just like to know what you and Mr. Kalimuzo plan on doing with the cooperation from Great Britain, if there is any cooperation."

Obviously the question took the President by surprise. He stepped back to confer with his advisers again.

Then Lyons saw what had been troubling his subconscious. There, near Emma Creighton's feet, was an abandoned camcorder. The guy who'd been holding it had left at a time when Lyons's attention had been elsewhere. He started forward, tapping the transmit button. "Pol, Gadgets."

"Go."

"Go."

"There's a camcorder lying on the floor next to Emma Creighton."

"Hey, buddy, look where you're going," a reporter said in anger.

Lyons ignored the angry protests, shoving his way through the crowd until he reached the camera. Secret Service agents surged toward him, forming a phalanx around the President as they moved on an intercept course. Pandemonium was threatening to erupt inside the room.

Lyons knelt beside the camcorder and ran his fingers along the case.

"What's going on?" Creighton asked.

"Where'd the guy go who was operating this?"

"I don't know. I've been kind of busy."

Lyons hit the transmit button. "Pol, did you get a look at the guy?"

"Yeah. I'm looking for him now."

"Let me know if you find him." Lyons found the camera's housing latches and popped it open. Inside were bricks of C-4 plastic explosive and a sophisticated timer that was showing one minute and forty-seven seconds. The Able team leader knew there was no way to get everyone clear before the bomb went off.

CHAPTER FIVE

Cape Town, South Africa
1:33 p.m.

After the Bentley limousine glided to a halt at the curb in front of the tall building in Cape Town's most modern business sector, Wilhelmus Kamer waited and let the chauffeur get the door. He got out of the car, aware that dozens of eyes were on him. Since it was Sunday, the crowd wasn't business related. Still, his picture and name had been in the papers and on television a number of times over the years. He was known to the community.

His two bodyguards got out of the car, as well, dressed in similar suits and wearing dark, wraparound sunglasses. They moved in concert, immediately flanking Kamer as he headed for the door. One of them carried the decorated hatbox he'd brought from the mansion.

Kamer raised his voice and pulled on the chain he held. "Sharde. Come."

With a regal, feline stretch, a black-and-gold leopard padded from the limousine in Kamer's wake. The animal was well trained and immediately fell into step with its master on the left side. The jeweled silver collar glittered. A little boy darted from the crowd that had gathered near the building's entrance. Excited, he reached a hand toward the great cat.

Kamer watched with a slight smile as the leopard spit and snarled and raked a claw toward the boy, missing by inches. The boy's mother shrieked and grabbed her child by the shirt collar, yanking him out of the way. Holding her son in her arms, the woman yelled obscenities at Kamer.

The bodyguards pushed the crowd back as they closed in.

"That animal should be shot," the woman shouted, standing behind a black man who'd moved in protectively.

"On the contrary," Kamer said in a harsh voice. "This cat is better trained than your brat, and she's not a showpiece, nor is she a pet." He stopped and reached down for the leopard's collar. The chain came away in his hands. "Sharde, guard." He gave the hand signal she would recognize.

Immediately the cat's demeanor became more aggressive. Kamer signed again, instructing her to speak. She gave voice to a full-throated, bloodcurdling yowl that sounded even more intense because it was trapped under the canopy of the building's main entrance.

The small crowd that had gathered pulled back and began to break up. The leopard ranged farther out, totally menacing.

"Mr. Kamer," the doorman said in a strained voice, "please."

Chuckling, Kamer signaled to the leopard and she came back to him, pushing her broad head against his thigh. As he reattached the chain to the collar, he said, "Damn yokels wanted a circus show. They got one."

"But the police—"

"Have never been a problem for me." Kamer slipped a business card from his inside jacket pocket and gave it to the doorman. The card was a dark jade and heavily embossed in gold foil. "When someone arrives, give them this."

"Yes, sir."

Kamer walked on through the revolving glass doors and stepped into the air-conditioned foyer. The lower floor of the building held two restaurants, a small branch of an international bank, a mortgage company with holdings that included some of the more palatial homes in Cape Town and a brokerage. In one form or another, White Tiger Investments—and Wilhelmus Kamer—owned them all.

Kamer made his way to the private elevator located inside the building's security office, keyed the lock with a magnetic card and rode the cage up to the penthouse offices. The leopard growled and stood swaying. She had never liked elevators.

"I'll take that," he said to the bodyguard holding the hatbox. "You guys can stay here for the time."

The two men nodded and went down the hall in the opposite direction. The floor's private security station was located at the end.

Carrying the hatbox, Kamer walked through the ornate double doors leading to the corporate headquarters of White Tiger Investments. A pretty receptionist sat behind the desk in a waiting room that resembled a nineteenth-century drawing room. Nautical maps done in sepias and browns hung on the walls in glass cases. The two couches, coffee table and end tables were hand-carved Victorian pieces done in dark woods. An organ was against the wall to the left, and sheet music was on the rack. First editions of books from around the world occupied the modest shelves built around models of sailing ships, cut crystal decanters and dueling pistols.

A brass telescope sat against the floor-to-ceiling glass wall overlooking Cape Town and the Cape of Good Hope.

"Good afternoon, Mr. Kamer," the secretary said brightly. She was made up to fit the room. A throat-to-ankles lace dress that was an antique rather than an imitation—with slight alterations to show off the curves beneath—combined with the correct jewelry to make her seem elfin. Her dark hair was pulled back, accentuating her pale, translucent skin.

"Good afternoon, Clarice. Are they inside?"

"Waiting, sir."

"Was anyone late?"

"No, sir."

Kamer took a final look around the room as he put his hand on the door handle. "The Age of Imperialism. God, you have to love it."

"Yes, sir."

He passed through the door, letting Sharde range ahead of him now. He felt good, despite the miss on Kalimuzo. Things were on track regarding Walukagi's future.

The hallway was long and dim, and the offices were soundproofed. Before he reached the conference room, though, Sharde's interest had turned to the box he carried. The leopard nosed the package and purred. Kamer tapped her nose in mild rebuke and she grudgingly turned away.

At the door, he fisted the pistol-grip doorknob, fired the latch and passed on through.

Nine men and two women waited inside the room, seated in plush chairs around a rectangular chrome-finished table. Their ages ranged from midtwenties to late sixties. They were all white, and in one way or another, Kamer knew he owned them all.

"Gentlemen and ladies," the CEO of White Tiger Investments said as he walked around the room and took his place at the head of the table, "I hope I haven't kept you waiting."

"Wil," Clyde Raines said from the right side of the table, "those people you hired in Atlanta made a proper mess of things in the U.S."

Kamer set the box on the desk and remained standing. The opposite end of the conference table never held a chair, and everyone in the room knew not to sit there. Anyone who entered the room would never be confused as to where the power resided. "Did they now?"

Raines was sixty-four, with sandy gray hair and muttonchop side whiskers that were his trademark, and heavyset. As Kamer's right-hand man in the organization, Raines often played devil's advocate for the rest of the group. But never without giving Kamer a call so he could arrange a suitable defense. "What would you call it?"

"A missed opportunity," Kamer replied. "Nothing more."

"Nothing more?" Lauren Severin repeated. In her early fifties, still slender and beautiful, she was a shrewd businesswoman. She'd started out as a prostitute on the docks of Cape Town, then became a leading figure in the nation's escort business, servicing the rich and famous and visiting business and political figures. She still maintained a hold in the old business, but these days she made most of her considerable fortune with shipping companies. "You've made sure every eye was focused on the plight of Kalimuzo."

"And how many people can stand up to such a scrutiny?" Kamer demanded. He signed to Sharde and the leopard seated herself on the other end of the table with a lithe coil of muscles under sleek fur, making almost no noise at all.

"But Kalimuzo is not an ordinary person." The protest came from Vic DeChanza, the thirty-year-old computer expert who'd made his money selling computer systems and specialized programming.

"Thank you, Vic," Kamer said, pacing and putting his hands in his pockets. "Exactly my point. Henry Kalimuzo is *not* an ordinary person. Henry Kalimuzo has been a terrorist, a murderer and a thief, which is not behavior the Europeans or Americans would look upon with any amount of fondness."

"We're dealing with the Americans," Raines said, puffing around a meerschaum pipe he held a lighter to. Gray smoke clouded around his head. "They take people like that to their hearts and make heroes of them. Jesse James, Bonnie and Clyde, the Shah of Iran, Manuel Noriega, Ferdinand Marcos. They were even in bed with Saddam Hussein for a time before he sold them out. In America the media makes and breaks heroes at its leisure. If the politics are right."

"And you think the politics are right in Walukagi?" Kamer asked. He looked around the room, knowing Raines would be speaking for them all. They'd had time to discuss things before his arrival; he'd seen to that.

"We have to face the possibility," Raines said.

"I see." Kamer put his hand on the hatbox. By now all of their minds would be partially occupied with what the contents were. He touched it only to remind them, then walked on. A small keyboard was built into the wall behind him, almost hidden by one of the five original watercolors Kamer had commissioned for the room. All of them were of nineteenth-century German militia.

"You've been watching the news?" Severin asked.

"Yes."

"You know the President of the United States has called a special press meeting?"

"Of course. Whether the assassination attempt on Kalimuzo had been successful or not, I was expecting him to do this." Kamer punched buttons on the keypad. Immediately the track lighting overhead dimmed, and a four-screen television monitor descended from the ceiling. All the screens came on with splashes of color and audible pops.

Henry Kalimuzo's picture filled the screen.

"This is our enemy?" Kamer questioned sarcastically. "This is the man you people are afraid of?"

No one said anything.

"You're looking at the face of a dead man," Kamer promised. "Whether it had happened earlier or it occurs later, that fact does not change."

"It's not Kalimuzo that seems to be the threat," DeChanza said. "It's the Americans."

"They've been there for three months," Kamer replied, "and they control less of Cape Anansi now than when they started. The American soldiers are afraid to walk the streets of the city for fear of being shot down like dogs."

"But if they make more concerted efforts—" Raines began.

"Then they'll die that much faster." Kamer pressed more buttons, and his prepared video started.

On-screen, scenes of American soldiers coming in on landing craft from Navy ships went into motion without sound. The Marines ran into a blistering barrage of fire, and soldiers dropped along the sandy beaches yards short of the jungle. More scenes followed, all depicting the losses suffered by American and United Nations forces.

When it finished, DeChanza said, "This display is more than a little slanted."

Kamer smiled. "True. But a good coach never dwells on his team's losses or foul-ups."

"We don't need a good coach," Raines protested. "We need something more along the lines of good damage control."

"In what form?"

"Kalimuzo has to die," Severin said. The others all nodded in agreement.

"You people are losing your focus here," Kamer said. "Kalimuzo may be the enemy, but he's not invincible."

"He may be if he gets the Americans to back him," Raines said.

"Say they do," Kamer said. "Say they agree to back him to the hilt. First they have to do something with the government in place in Cape Anansi."

"Everyone knows Pernell Spraggue is a joke," Hubble Weinholdt said. Tall and lantern-jawed, he'd made his fortune in manufacturing.

"Yes," Kamer agreed. "But to put Kalimuzo in his place? A kaffir replacing a white man?"

"Seems to be a popular trend," DeChanza pointed out.

"They might make it happen, but can they keep him there?" Kamer asked. "One bullet, and they have to find a new kaffir. You go through a few of them, how many do you suppose would even want the job? No, at present there's no power base in Walukagi. Even if he lives, which he will not, Kalimuzo would at best only have a few months in office. Even if the Americans were able to go in and take over the country and unite it under Kalimuzo, what the hell would they do with it?''

No one had an answer.

"Do you know what kind of debt load we're talking about here?" Kamer asked. "I do. Because I've had it researched. It's exorbitant. And should the necessity arise, I've got lobbying groups already in place in Washington, D.C., to remind the House of Representatives how much of that cost would fall onto the American people."

"Walukagi is not without resources," Weinholdt said.

"Gold and diamonds," Kamer said. "And that's only part of what we're in this for, remember?"

"They could pay the Americans," Severin said.

"If they would." Kamer looked at all of the people in the room, knowing it was their greed and fear that held them together. Most of them didn't have his vision or his drive to succeed. But managing them gave him extra resources. "Keep in mind that you're dealing with a very backward country that has had trouble with its independence since it was granted in 1980. There never has been a unified presence in Walukagi. And there won't be. Not until we're ready to make our move. If the United States makes a deal with Kalimuzo—or anyone else they think can hold that country—they're fools."

"What assurances can you give us toward our investments?" Raines asked.

"I can't predict everything," Kamer answered. Now was the turning point. Raines had brought up the most crucial question at just the proper time. He moved in for the closure of the deal. "But I can predict this—if you people think you're going to be able to continue your current way of living here in South Africa with that damned kaffir government in power, you're sadly mistaken."

Their stares were quiet and desperate. All of them had visions of their various empires dying over the next few years.

"Our future, if we're to have one," Kamer said, "lies in Walukagi." He knotted a hand into a fist. "I'm going to take what I want from that country because it's there. It's accessible to a man or woman who's brave enough to seize the day.

"You want to know what you can do to improve your chances and speed up the timetable on this operation?" Kamer continued. "Put up some more money. Masiga's people are turning in ears for bounty. They've been doing that for weeks now. Let's double it for the amount of American ears they bring in."

"How will we know if they're American ears?" Weinholdt looked uncomfortable asking the question.

"Who cares?" Kamer asked. "We're paying Masiga's people pennies for a life, anyway. What's a few more pennies when we stand to gain a country where we can make the rules?" He reached for the hatbox. Taking a pocketknife from his pants, he slit the ribbons and turned it upside down on the desk. Ansell Dewbre's head rolled out awkwardly, then tumbled three-quarters of the table's length.

Sharde looked up excitedly. The leopard's tongue was pink and shiny as it ran across her white teeth. Kamer froze her in place with a word.

"Some of you knew Dewbre," Kamer said. "I found out he betrayed us on a munitions shipment I'd arranged, so I killed him. I'm not afraid to get my hands dirty when it comes to getting something I want. There isn't a risk I won't take."

All eyes were riveted on the head.

"Now," Kamer said, "do you people want to remain wealthy and powerful? Or do you want to beg and scrape before the kaffirs and hope they let you stay in business?"

Slowly they began agreeing with him. First was Raines, but that was to be expected because he was paid to agree.

Kamer gave another sign to the leopard. With a lithe jump, she crossed the intervening distance on the table and sank her teeth into Dewbre's head. A few of the men gathered around the table looked away, while the others seemed hypnotized by the sheer savagery of the feeding. Lauren Severin watched with bright interest.

Working the keypad again, Kamer switched to a live CNN broadcast showing the interior of the Senate just as the President of the United States approached the knot of microphones. Henry Kalimuzo stood in the background next to the federal agent Sonnet Quaid had identified earlier.

"I've arranged a little party favor for the press meeting," Kamer said. "When this is finished, I'll tell you about a man named Dr. Linus Maaloe and the work he's done for us. Either way, the American soldiers who do attempt to help stabilize any government in Walukagi are going to end up dead, and they're going to take that death home with them." He let his words hang in the air as the action picked up on the television screen.

A broad, blond man pushed his way through the crowd of reporters and ran to an abandoned camcorder sitting on the floor. The CNN camera operator had to have been thinking it was an assassination attempt, because the focus was entirely on the big man, who worked the closures on the camcorder and revealed the explosives.

Wheeling quickly, Secret Service agents already bearing down on him, the blond man yelled, "Bomb!"

Durban, South Africa
1:36 p.m.

"WE'VE GOT COMPANY," Mack Bolan said as he took Rifkin by the upper arm and pulled her into the nearest warehouse fronting the Durban piers. Two forklifts at the opposite end of the warehouse rattled and squeaked as they lifted skids filled with crates bound by nylon cord. A guy in orange coveralls saw them and started toward them, his clipboard slapping against his thigh.

"Where?" Rifkin asked, her hand already dropping into her purse.

"Along the docks." Bolan pointed.

Five men in casual clothing fanned out through the docks, blatantly combing the area and drawing the attention of the dockworkers. The hot sun beat down on the emerald waves coming in slowly from the Indian Ocean. Beyond the ragged line of piers of differing heights, ocean-bound freighters and cargo ships waited to be loaded or for crews to return from shore leave. A small marina occupied an area farther north. Multicolored sails cut triangles against the broad expanse of blue sky.

"They'll have your picture by now," Bolan said.

"Then I'll make it harder for them to be sure," Rifkin replied. She pulled a red scarf from her purse and quickly tied it around her head, altering the shape of her hair. Turning her collar up changed her neckline from slender to short. Dark glasses hid her face. Working with a compact, she took a bright red lipstick and did her lips, bringing them out.

"You look different," Bolan told her.

"Every woman's secret," Rifkin said, glancing into the compact one last time. "Damn, I hate this color. Why do men like it on a woman?"

"I'm not one of those guys." Bolan turned to face the approaching warehouse foreman.

"What are you people doing in here?" the foreman asked as he stopped in front of them.

"Hotter than hell out there," Bolan said with a friendly smile. "We thought we might find a soft-drink machine inside here."

"This is a restricted area," the foreman said. He looked them over more carefully, then apparently decided they were safe. "Go on south about another block and you'll get to a place called Hakim's Tavern. It's not a place for tourists to get souvenirs, but the drinks are reasonable."

Bolan thanked him and moved on, gripping his gym bag more tightly. Rifkin followed closely.

The five men were less than a hundred yards behind. Two of them were showing pictures now. A guy leaning on a hand truck studied the picture for a moment, then pointed toward the warehouse. The guy who'd shown the picture waved to his comrades and directed them toward the structure.

"We're running out of options," Rifkin said as she picked up her stride.

Bolan nodded and scouted the available terrain. Going back to the parking lot wasn't an option because they'd miss the connect with Grimaldi, who was only minutes away. Staying on the docks would leave them exposed to attack. "Got to narrow the field," the soldier said, glancing over his shoulder.

The warehouse foreman stood outside the building now, and he threw a finger in Bolan and Rifkin's direction.

"We're made," the woman stated.

"Yeah." Bolan unzipped the gym bag and fisted the shotgun, leaving the cloth bag in place to disguise what he held. He had the Ruger 9 mm pistol snugged in his waistband under his shirt. Stepping up the pace, he ran toward the three-story building ahead of them.

Hakim's Tavern occupied most of the lower floor, leaving room for a shoe repair business and a barber shop. The building was wooden and was in dire need of a coat of paint. Spindly wooden stairs led up the back of the building, barely visible from the Executioner's position.

Shouts rang out behind them. Shots followed almost immediately, tearing into the wooden building beside them, smashing out windows and scarring the planks beneath their feet.

"Shit," Rifkin said. The SIG-Sauer was in her hands, held at shoulder level.

Movement through the plate-glass windows of a supply store warned Bolan a moment before a shot crashed through the glass. "Down!" he yelled, grabbing Rifkin by the wrist and pulling her behind a huge tub of coiled ropes of varying thicknesses and lengths beside the supply store's main entrance. Bullets riddled the tin tub but didn't penetrate the ropes.

Only three people and a clerk were inside the store as Bolan and Rifkin got to their feet.

"Get down!" the Executioner ordered as he charged between the racks of goods. Rifkin fired a shot into the ceiling, chipping one of the overhead fan's blades with a metallic shriek.

Three men had started through the hole in the plate-glass window. Without hesitation, the Executioner fired through the gym bag, ripping the cloth away as the double-aught buckshot took flight.

The blast took one of the men in the chest and dumped his corpse into the arms of his teammates.

"Can you swim?" Bolan asked as he surveyed the shop.

"Like a fish," Rifkin answered. She placed four rounds through the door, holding their attackers in position from that end.

"You're going to have to." Bolan spotted a green four-gallon container of gasoline beside the counter, neatly stacked with others. Obviously the store helped supply the pleasure boats. He slipped the Ithaca free of the shredded gym bag.

Bullets chopped into the interior of the store. Coffeepots jumped from the shelving. Burlap bags of beans, sugar and salt exploded and spilled their contents onto the hardwood floor.

One of the two survivors on the side of the building facing Hakim's Tavern fell into position beside the window frame and loosed two rounds.

Raising the shotgun, the Executioner fired the other barrel. The buckshot charge smacked into the window frame, tore the wood loose and slammed the gunner out into the narrow street.

"Have you got a plan?" Rifkin asked. "I'm beginning to feel like Butch and Sundance here."

Bolan broke open the shotgun and popped out the empty casings, dropping in two more loads from his pants pocket. "Yeah, but I'm having to improvise here."

"I hope you're an expert."

"I've had some experience." Bolan scanned the aisles and found boxes of detergent. He trotted forward and grabbed the biggest one he could find, then ran to the stack of four-gallon gas containers. As he'd expected, the cans were already filled and ready to go. He ripped the top off the detergent box, opened the gas can lid and poured. The white soap flowed around the opening, but most of it went inside. He recapped the lid and grabbed the handle.

Rifkin was watching him as she reloaded. So far she'd been able to keep their attackers from entering the store. "I've got one more magazine."

Bolan nodded. "Let's go." He took the point, sprinting for the back door of the store with the gas can in his free hand. Although it was heavy enough to throw his stride off slightly, he managed, concentrating on movement rather than speed. There was a panic bar across the rear entrance. He set it off when he went through, the 12-gauge raised at his side.

The harsh, insistent buzz of the door alarm startled the remaining gunner. He came around fast, already firing before he had his target in his sights.

Bolan dropped the shotgun into target acquisition and squeezed the trigger. The double-aught blast slammed into the guy's face and threw him backward. Without breaking stride, the warrior headed across the street. Pedestrians scattered before him, but he had to dodge a tan Volkswagen Bug that ignored him.

He paused beside the corner of the building, breathing hard and covered with perspiration, and took a fresh grip on the shotgun. "Go," he yelled to Rifkin as she came abreast of him. "Up the stairs."

Ignoring the handrail, she rushed up the steps. Bullets slammed into the building over her head.

Bolan fired the shotgun's second barrel at the doorway and caught the exposed leg of one of the gunners. The buckshot knocked the man around. Then the Executioner fisted the shotgun and ran after the CIA agent. The steps shuddered under his weight and the gas can thudded against the building, the contents sloshing.

The three flights of stairs passed in a blur. Bolan's breathing was labored as he charged toward the roof and his knees protested the awkward extra weight.

On the last flight of steps, a bullet penetrated one of the wooden planks and tore the heel off Rifkin's shoe. She fell, sprawling the rest of the length of the stairs.

"Come on," Bolan said. "Don't quit on me now." He looped an arm under her and helped her to her feet. Below, the first of the two remaining gunmen had reached the bottom landing.

At the rooftop, the warrior broke open the shotgun and dropped in fresh loads. He touched off both barrels at the first-floor landing while leaning over the railing. The buckshot hit the gunner in the upper body and blew him through a paned window that held a neon beer sign.

When he glanced back at Rifkin, she had her pistol up. She ripped the scarf free and it fluttered away in the breeze. The woman fired twice, causing the gunman below to take a defensive position. "I'm going to be out of ammo soon."

Bolan didn't say anything. He'd loaded the last two shells he had for the 12-gauge, and there were only two magazines for the Ruger.

The rooftop was unadorned, a blacktop-and-gravel surface that was a magnet for heat waves. In seconds he felt as if he was suffering from oxygen deprivation. Walking to the front of the building, he peered over the edge. The dock was eight feet out, well within jumping distance, and the water was surely deep enough, judging from the way the freighters sat in their assigned areas.

Something jumped from the edge of the building, and the flat crack of a high-powered hunting rifle sounded a split second later.

Bolan went to ground automatically, then searched for the source of the shot. To the left, less than twenty feet out, was a forty-foot motorsailer. Two men with rifles were on the bridge, flanked by another man on the main deck. The motorsailer floated free, the sail furled and put away.

Hunkering down below the edge of the building, Bolan made his way to Rifkin. "Change of plans," he said. "They've got backup in the water."

"Don't tell me we have to go back down," she said, pulling back from the landing to drop the empty magazine out of her pistol. A renewed flurry of bullets scored the building and tore free long splinters that spun over the railing.

"Not hardly." Bolan took up her empty magazine and filled it as much as he could from the extra one he had for the Ruger. "Make your shots count. They want to gain a flight of stairs, let them pay for it."

She nodded. "What are you going to do?"

"Get our evac team in and see if there's something I can do about the boat."

"What about the gas? I figured that you were going to use it on the stairs."

"I was. Now I've got something else in mind." Bolan moved off, peering out over the building at the motorsailer. The men were still in place, obviously expecting their quarry to leap from the building.

The dock had almost shut down. Warning sirens screamed in the distance.

Bolan took the compact radio handset from his belt and keyed it to life. "G-Force, this is Striker."

"Go, Striker," Jack Grimaldi's voice came back. "You've got G-Force."

"What's your ETA?"

"Minute, minute and a half. I can see the harbor now."

"Where are you?"

"Coming in from the northeast, buddy, clean and green."

Bolan scanned the clouds and saw the unmistakable lines of the Grumman Goose flying at low altitude and low speed. "We're going to have to time this one a little finer than we'd thought," the warrior said. Quickly he outlined the situation with the gunners.

"Call it," Grimaldi said, "and I'm there."

"I'll send you a signal," Bolan promised. He leaned the shotgun against the rooftop wall and hefted the gas can. Mixed with the detergent, the fuel was an imitation napalm that was dangerously effective. He looked down at the motorsailer.

"I'm down to three rounds," Rifkin called out.

"Get ready," Bolan said. He slid the Ruger free and flipped off the safety. Peering over the edge again, he fixed the position of the motorsailer's fuel tanks in his mind, making them his chief target.

Rifle shots cracked and bullets tore into the tarmac-covered wall only inches from the warrior. Steeling himself, becoming the gunsight, he brought the Ruger over and around in a loose fist. He fired as quickly as he could and still remain on target.

The gun crew aboard the motorsailer took cover, thinking they were being shot at. As the last of the rolling brass tumbled free of the Ruger, Bolan pulled back. He'd seen the bullets bite into the exposed tanks and knew he'd scored. He moved ten feet along the roof line and exposed himself again for an instant. Behind the gunners, the fuel quietly splashed over the motorsailer's deck.

"I'm done," Rifkin said. "If you have any aces up your sleeve, now's the time to show them."

Bullets from the rifles aboard the motorsailer chewed into the low wall along the rooftop.

Returning to the corner nearest the motorsailer, Bolan swept up the container of gas and detergent. He picked up the 12-gauge with his free hand. Setting himself, he threw the gas can in a high arc. As it hit the apex of the throw, it started plummeting for the motorsailer.

A quick glance showed the Executioner that his throw was on target. His mind functioned smoothly, drawing on years of handling guns and marksmanship that was driven by instinct. He took up trigger slack and waited until the gas can was less than six feet above the deck. When he fired, leading his target, the 12-gauge blast caught it less than three feet from ground zero.

As the buckshot struck the gas can walls and ruptured them, a spark ignited the fuel-detergent mixture. The imitation napalm dropped across the deck in fiery waves, setting off the contents of the leaking fuel tanks. A heartbeat later the motorsailer erupted in a rising fireball of orange and black. The explosive concussion made the building under Bolan's feet vibrate.

The Executioner swung back to cover Rifkin and the stairway. A man with an Uzi stepped up on the landing and fired short bursts. The 9 mm parabellum rounds chewed tracks in the tarred surface of the roof.

"I've got you, Striker," Grimaldi called over the radio frequency. "I'm coming in."

Bullets chopped toward Bolan's position. The warrior jumped away, landed in a shoulder roll and came up on his knees with the shotgun pointed before him. He stroked the trigger and fired his last round.

The 12-gauge blast spread across the man's body and knocked him through the fire-escape landing.

"All right, Rifkin," Bolan said, "it's time." He glanced up and saw the Grumman Goose pulling up steeply, pontoons hanging under the wings. Grabbing the woman's hand, he started her toward the edge of the building. She didn't hesitate, running as hard as she could until she reached the low wall, then putting a foot on it and vaulting out as hard as she could.

Bolan followed an instant behind. He jumped to the low wall and shoved himself outward with everything he had. Smoke from the burning motorsailer filled the immediate vicinity and provided cover for the dive. Flaming debris floated on the water.

Gravity overcame the Executioner and he dropped to the waiting sea. Rifkin plummeted feetfirst and disappeared into the murky water. Bolan had time for a deep breath before he hit, cleaving the water cleanly. His lungs were aching for air by the time he stroked for the surface.

He came up less than ten feet from where he'd entered the water. People on the docks were still confused about what had happened, but someone had started a bucket brigade to put out the burning motorsailer, though it would be long moments before the fire was anywhere near under control.

"Rifkin," he yelled. "Here."

He treaded water and turned, spotting the CIA agent to his right. Beyond her, Grimaldi brought the Goose around in a semicircle about seventy yards out. "Go."

The woman swam well. Bolan was hard-pressed to keep up with her. They were almost to the amphibious plane before some backup gunmen found them. Bullets splashed against the ocean surface around them as the gunners tried to find the range.

The Grumman's twin props kept churning as it drifted along in its position. Presented port side, Bolan saw the door kicked open and Grimaldi standing just beyond. The pilot grabbed the woman's arm and helped her aboard.

Bolan was just behind, managing his own way while Grimaldi went forward. Water dripped from his clothing and spilled all over the carpeted six-seat cabin.

"Button it up, Sarge," Grimaldi said as he slid into the pilot's seat. "Then get buckled in. There's a harbor patrol boat already headed this way."

Bullets smacked into the side of the Goose as the Executioner reeled in the door and latched it. The engines were roaring. As the amphibian gathered speed, it listed slightly from side to side, like a boat cresting the ocean swells. Then the lift kicked in as the wings bit into the air, smoothing out the ride until it launched into full flight.

As Bolan took his place in the copilot's seat, he glanced out the window and saw the sea fall away. But the masts of a large sailboat were coming up entirely too fast.

"Oh, shit," Rifkin commented from one of the rear seats.

Grimaldi reached over his head for the throttle and applied more power. "Come on, baby, you were born and bred for situations like this." He steered with his other hand. Abruptly, at what looked like the last possible instant, he pulled the Goose into a steep climb that took them over the threatening masts with only inches to spare.

"Yes!" Rifkin exclaimed with heartfelt enthusiasm.

"Piece of cake," Grimaldi said as he banked the plane sharply and took a north-northeast heading.

Bolan clapped his friend on the shoulder. "Good flying, buddy."

Grimaldi nodded. "That package Barb sent you is under the seat. She faxed me some new sheets and pictures at my last stop so the file would be up-to-date."

Checking the windows, Bolan found there were no signs of pursuit. He reached under the seat for the accordion file, taking time out to make introductions between Grimaldi and Rifkin, giving the pilot the alias that matched the license clipped to the visor overhead.

"So where'd the heat wave come from?" Grimaldi asked. He kept the amphibian low, hugging the coastline to lessen the chance of being traced by the harbor authorities.

"I don't know," Bolan replied. "We shook down a munitions handler in East London, but I don't think he could muscle up this kind of action."

"No," Rifkin agreed. "The only way we could have been traced here would have been through the car. Dewbre didn't have the connections for that. Harbor authorities, maritime shipping—he had people in those areas in his pocket. But no one who could have interfaced the police agencies. Things out here are more along the frontier lines. Sometimes police agencies don't even know they have someone wanted in another jurisdiction."

"So someone bridged the gap." Bolan glanced through the collection of photos and printouts.

"I think so. And those people back there weren't amateurs."

"Dewbre had a silent partner," Bolan said.

"We hadn't turned one up," Rifkin replied, "but that operation was run close to the vest. It's possible."

"Whoever he is," Grimaldi said, "the guy's got a lot of juice to move on his Intel that fast."

"Yeah," Bolan said. "Let's see how much juice he has when he starts getting squeezed." He dug the Walukagi maps out of his map case and started putting the mission strike together in his mind. Price had been able to come through with more hardware than he'd believed possible, even with the American forces in the area. Whoever was picking up the munitions drop was in for a hell of a surprise.

CHAPTER SIX

Capitol Hill, Washington, D.C.
6:38 a.m.

The Secret Service agents threw themselves at Carl Lyons, putting their bodies between him and the President of the United States while other teams hustled the Man and Kalimuzo offstage. Other bodyguards covered the senators.

Lyons caught the first Secret Service agent by the coat lapels, head-butted him in the forehead to stun him, then used him like a scythe to clear some of the other agents away. Most of the reporters had faded from the immediate vicinity, but some of the camcorder operators were still filming.

Free for the moment, Lyons hit the transmit button on the headset. "Gadgets."

"Yeah."

"We got a bomb down here, and I doubt there's much time left."

"Detonator?"

Lyons threw another Secret Service agent back, took a quick look at the open camera and got hit in the side of the head hard enough to stagger him. "Yeah." He hadn't been able to read the LED readout.

A Secret Service agent pointed a Colt Delta Elite at him, but Lyons knew the guy wouldn't use it. The Senate building was too close quarters and anything could happen.

"Back off!" Hal Brognola's rough voice grated. "He's Justice, and he's with me!"

There was a moment of confusion, but the Secret Service agents parted like the Red Sea before the big Fed.

Shrugging free of two agents who'd gotten hold of him, Lyons knelt beside the bomb. The blocks of C-4 looked clean and deadly. Wires ran across them like an arterial map stemming from the electronic heart of the bomb. The LED display counted down the seconds— 58, 57, 56...

"Damn," one of the Secret Service agents said, "that's a bomb."

"No shit, Sherlock," Lyons returned. "Have you got any bomb guys in the building? A detonating chest so we can try to contain this thing if we can't stop it?"

"Johnson," another Secret Service agent ordered, "find Travers with building security."

"Yes, sir." Johnson took off like a track star late for the starting gun.

"Get these people out of here," Brognola commanded, waving at the media personnel. The other agents moved out at once, shoving the men and women ahead of them when they didn't move quickly enough.

"A bomb this size," Lyons said, gazing at the maze of wiring in quiet frustration as the LED dropped to forty seconds, "could maybe level this building."

"One side, sonny." Schwarz pushed his way past a Secret Service man standing in the aisle and giving orders to his men over a thumb-mounted microphone. He glanced at the explosive. "Bomb squad?"

"They're checking," Brognola said.

"Isn't this the part where you reach in and simply cut a wire with fingernail clippers or something?" Lyons asked.

"If I knew which wire," Schwarz replied, "I'd do that very thing. Must be a couple dozen there. You want to pick one?" Before Lyons could answer, Schwarz sprinted for the soft-drink area. "Hal, you and Carl ought to shag ass."

"Not without you," the head Fed replied.

Lyons joined Schwarz at the soft-drink area and helped free a CO_2 bottle from the collection chained to a cart. Schwarz cut the attached nylon tubing nearly five feet from the hookup. "Get another one. These things don't last long."

Lyons grabbed another canister and ran after Schwarz. The timer was down to seventeen seconds.

Working quickly against the killer deadline, Schwarz opened the valve and held the tubing toward the timer. The CO_2 gas came out in frosty gray clouds and hissed over all of the C-4.

Lyons watched as the timer slowed, dropping to eleven seconds.

"The cold's freezing up the timer," Schwarz explained, shoving the empty canister away. "It'll buy us a little more time. Where the hell's that bomb squad?"

"Coming, amigo," Blancanales called over the headset frequency.

"Hit it, Ironman," Schwarz instructed, moving off to get another canister.

Leaning in, Lyons opened the valve and sprayed the CO_2 over the explosives. The timer had frozen again, this time at ten seconds.

"Did you get a look at the guy that dropped the camera here?" Brognola asked.

Lyons gave the description and listened to the big Fed relay it, cupping his mouth so the whooshing of the canister wouldn't interfere with his words. In seconds the canister ran dry.

"I've got it," Schwarz said, "but we're down to our last tank." He opened the valve and the gray mist frosted the lens of the LED display. The bright red numbers dimmed slightly under the thin layer of ice.

"Here."

Lyons turned toward Blancanales and saw his teammate pushing a safe that looked like a three-foot black cube on casters.

"Spotted this earlier in one of the secretaries' offices," Blancanales said as he wheeled the safe over. "Figured they used it to store eyes-only paperwork temporarily in different offices rather than put a safe in every room. Make it harder to get in and take whatever was being secured."

Looking into the depths of the empty safe, Lyons said, "It looks big enough. How'd you get it open?"

"Caught the secretary before she jumped ship." Blancanales turned toward Schwarz, who was still holding the tank hose. "Think it'll work?"

"Maybe. Damn, there's a lot of explosive here. But it'll cut it down."

"There's a bathroom down the hall," Brognola said. "The walls should be reinforced, maybe buy us a little more margin."

Schwarz nodded. "Let's do it. Ironman."

Lyons grabbed the camera and shoved it inside the safe. Handling wasn't going to detonate it. Schwarz partially closed the lid, leaving enough room for the tank's gas line. Once it was secure, Lyons got behind it and pushed with every bit of strength he had. The safe moved easily, gaining speed as his legs powered it toward the door, where a knot of Secret Service agents stood uncertain guard.

"Eight seconds," Schwarz called out, matching Lyons stride for stride as he carried the CO_2 canister and kept the hose in place.

"Bull riders do it," Lyons said. "I can manage this hunk of iron." He skidded around the corner, hanging on to the edges of the safe with his fingers as he brought it around. Behind it once more, he muscled it toward the bathroom, the way marked by Secret Service agents. The door was less than forty yards away.

"Seven seconds," Schwarz said. The canister hissed empty. "You're going to lose it fast now." Dropping the tank, he closed the safe door and raced ahead of Lyons and got the door open.

With the time factor working against him, Lyons went for broke, discarding finesse. He jockeyed the rolling safe in the general direction, banked it off the door frame with enough force to rip the wood from the entrance and crack the plaster and guided it into the bathroom. His feet slipped on the tiles as he built up speed again.

"Carl!" Schwarz yelled from the door.

With the last of his reserves, Lyons sent the safe spinning toward the stalls. He managed a sudden stop, reversed directions and sped for the door. A backward glance showed him the safe crashing into the first stall with enough force to rip the metal wall from the floor, then go off on a tangent and smash into a white porcelain urinal. Water immediately gushed out from the pipes.

Lyons had just made it through the door when the explosion ripped through the Senate building.

The dulled roar rolled out of the bathroom, then echoed down the halls. Plaster was ripped from the walls. Lyons went to ground and felt the floor shiver under his palms. It took a few seconds for him to realize the ringing in his ears was from the detonation and that the concussion was over. Grimly he pushed himself to his feet and surveyed the damage.

The hallway had filled with security staff and Secret Service agents. Torn from its hinges, the bathroom door had bowed inward and slammed up against the opposite wall in the corridor.

"Geez," Schwarz said, brushing plaster fragments from his clothing, "that was a serious bomb."

Lyons walked back into the bathroom to check the damage. A huge hole had been blown in the ceiling, and the floor beneath his feet had cracks running in all directions. Warped and ripped from the explosion it hadn't been able to contain, the safe was tipped over on its back against the wall to the right. All the stall walls had been knocked down like a stack of dominoes and left twisted and ruined.

"What about the guy who left it here?" Lyons asked.

Brognola had entered the room, an unlit cigar clamped between his teeth. "They're closing the Senate down now, cordoning it off with help from the city PD and SWAT teams, but it doesn't look like we're going to get him."

"I should have seen it sooner," Lyons said.

Brognola faced him. "Every person in that room is fortunate you saw the bomb when you did."

"Yeah, but how long is it going to be before these people try again?" Lyons eyed the big Fed, knowing he spoke for all of Able Team. "This isn't going to be counted a win until we put these bastards down. Hard."

Cape Anansi, Walukagi
9:21 p.m.

THE COOL, QUIET DARK of the jungle stayed with Geoffrey Masiga even though the big man was deep within the city now. His face was sticky beneath the paint he wore on his face and upper body. Dressed in a loincloth, his only concessions to the civilized world were the sandals, the waist sling that held a Colt .45 automatic and a heavy-bladed hunting knife and the shielded dive watch on his right wrist.

He and his band of warriors moved silently through the streets, intent on their destination. Besides himself, eleven other men closed in on the converted hotel where their quarry waited unaware.

Tightening his grip on the Viking submachine gun, he watched a U.S. Army jeep speed by in the street. When it reached the corner, it turned and was gone.

He jogged across the shadow-shrouded street and stepped into the alley. Rats moved in the heaps of refuse that overflowed the garbage Dumpster, their eyes glowing red as moonlight slid over them.

After his warriors joined him in the alley, Masiga used hand signals to split them into two groups. They obeyed quickly, moving like the parts of a well-oiled machine. Like their leader, they were painted in lurid greens, blues and reds, tribal symbols that promised war and death.

The hotel was less than forty yards away. Yellow rectangles, blunted by window curtains and shades, poked holes in the scarred walls of the building.

Moving at a trot now, Masiga led his part of the group to the rear of the hotel and gathered them around the service entrance. The steel door was securely locked,

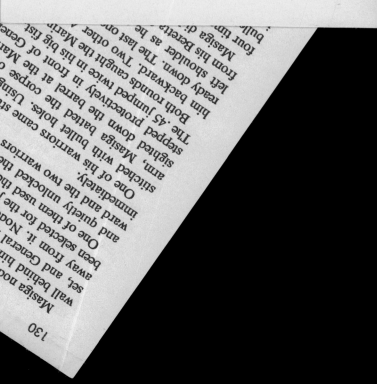

with no external knob. If the arrangement hadn't been made, there was no way Masiga could have gotten in quietly. He glanced at his dive watch, then banged on the door with the butt of the subgun.

A few seconds later the bolt was thrown inside and the door swung open. Cool air wrapped itself around Masiga as he walked inside. The young man holding the door was one of the tribe, hardly more than a boy, dressed in the crisp white uniform of the hotel.

"He is inside, Daudi?" Masiga asked.

"Yes, O King," the young man responded. "Perhaps as much as ten minutes ago."

Masiga led the way to the service elevator. Two of his warriors drew their knives and slashed Daudi's clothes from him. White cloth gathered at his feet and one of them handed him a loinwrap. Another gave him a mini-Uzi.

The service elevator, like the hotel's receiving area, was unadorned and smelled of pine cleaners that barely masked other odors. Once inside, Daudi pressed the eighth-floor button after the doors closed. With a jerk, the cage started swaying upward. The winch motor growled in protest. With Daudi's key in place, the service elevator wouldn't stop at any other floors.

At the eighth floor Masiga held the doors open and peered out. As king of the Kawalusa tribe and ene the American and UN military, his ca would be a coup to the invadin lying in wait, he move

With the
try. th

"Fool!" Masiga roared in English. He grabbed the American general's gun with his free hand and yanked it away.

Undaunted, McClendon went for the knife sheathed upside down along his combat harness.

Bringing his ham-size fist from his side and across his body, Masiga backhanded the general. The impact was dull and meaty. McClendon dropped into a stunned heap against the wall, the side of his face red from temple to jawline.

Masiga's warriors crowded into the room, with five left to guard the hallway and the elevator. Auta, his second, pointed to the woman who stood cowering by the bed. "What about the woman?"

Masiga looked at her. He didn't even remember her name. In her late teens, she was one of the prostitutes he used to gather information from the American and UN soldiers. Her tribal tattoos stained her dark skin, and her forearms and upper arms showed knife and cigarette-burn scars where her clients had sometimes tried to get information from her. Nothing she knew could hurt him.

The woman came across the floor tentatively, then draped her arms around Masiga's neck. She offered her mouth silently, her eyes liquid with fear.

"Traitorous bitch," McClendon growled as he forced himself unsteadily to his feet.

Masiga grinned. "You're right," he said in English.

He glanced at Auta. "Strip her."

"No," the woman gasped in her own tongue as Auta started for her, a knife in his hand. "I've done everything you've asked me to."

"You'll continue to do so," Masiga said.

Auta's blade flicked out expertly, and the wrap the woman had been wearing fell in gentle waves to her bare feet. She covered her breasts with her arms and tried to stand as small as possible.

Masiga thought she looked like a child, vulnerable and almost innocent. He glanced at the general, then waved to the aerial reconnaissance pictures on the bed. "Maybe you weren't just content with coercing this poor girl to cooperate with you," he said. "Maybe you wanted to satisfy your own hungers, as well."

"Fuck you," McClendon said. He lunged from the wall.

Masiga easily avoided the man, then pistol-whipped him to the ground.

The general struggled to get up, but his arms failed him. Blood trickled from one torn ear.

"Take her to the bed and tie her," Masiga commanded.

Auta grabbed the woman's wrists and dragged her to the bed. She kicked and screamed and fought him every step of the way, managing to rip three bloody furrows along his neck before one of the other men tied her hands to the post.

Masiga ignored the screams. He knew the hotel was already coming to life beneath him. Out in the hall, gunfire rang out.

"There were other soldiers parked in front of the hotel," Daudi commented.

Nodding, Masiga said, "It won't matter. They will come to die."

"You son of a bitch," McClendon said, rising slowly. He balled up a fist.

"Tie him," Masiga instructed, "and rope him."

Two warriors moved instantly to do his bidding. A grenade sounded out in the hallway, but he was certain it had come from his own men.

Looking down the side of the hotel, Masiga smiled when he spotted the American flag waving in the cool night breeze two stories below. He turned and saw McClendon held between the two warriors. The general's hands had been tied behind his back.

"Strip him."

Knives flashed. In seconds the American officer's clothes lay in shreds on the floor.

"The girl?" Auta prompted.

She gazed up from the bed. Her eyes were pools of hate and fear. Tied spread-eagled, she struggled against her bonds but couldn't get free.

"Kill her," Masiga said.

"No!" she screamed, then the word became a bubbling hiss as Auta reached out and deftly sliced her throat. Blood spattered the sheets and rained over her nakedness. In seconds she stopped moving.

"Bastard!" McClendon yelled. In spite of the armed men who held him, he tried for Masiga again.

Knowing that the man realized he was only seconds from dying, Masiga reasoned that it was fear, not bravery, that brought him to attempt an attack. The general was easily restrained by the two men guarding him.

Masiga took a rope from the warrior nearest him, knotted it into a noose and dropped it over the general's head. He yanked it tight, stopping short of cutting off the man's breath. He grinned. "When they find you naked, they'll believe you were taking more from the woman than just whatever information she might have about the Kawalusian tribe."

"Son of a bitch!"

Yanking the rope, Masiga pulled the man from the two warriors who held him. McClendon stumbled free. Before his captive could recover, Masiga opened the double balcony doors and hauled the general through.

The sounds of the street came up at him—voices, squeaking tires and gunfire. The breeze whipped over Masiga's sweat-drenched body and cooled him.

Looking down the building, Masiga saw the American flag jutting out from the hotel. It flapped in the wind, seeming to take wing. He smiled.

The sudden slack in the rope warned him, and he turned in time to slam his gunbutt into McClendon's skull. The general dropped in dazed defeat, half turning on his side.

White light blazed from below. Staring back down, Masiga saw that the newsmen had spotted him. He enjoyed the prospect of an audience.

"Where is it?" he demanded.

One of the warriors brought forward a small can, then doused a rag with the contents. The strong smell of gasoline filled the balcony. When the rag was thoroughly drenched, he handed it to Masiga.

It took Masiga only a moment to judge the length of rope and tie it to the railing at the top of the balcony. He reached back for the rag, then roughly shoved it in the general's mouth. He took a piece of paper with the word *Invader* written on it. Slipping a slim-bladed stiletto from the belt of a man standing nearby, he held the paper against McClendon's left shoulder, then thrust the knife through the paper and flesh.

The general groaned and responded weakly to the new pain.

Masiga used a lighter to ignite the gasoline-drenched rag. The flames caught instantly, wrapping the general's features in fiery fog. Catching McClendon by his neck and one thigh, Masiga easily lifted him. At the balcony, he stood for a moment, holding the defeated man over his head. The flames kissed his wrist as he held the struggling American officer.

Then he threw McClendon over the balcony rail.

Below, some of the reporters scattered from the presumed impact area, not seeing the rope around McClendon's neck.

Two stories down, the general came to an abrupt stop. Bone snapped as the neck gave way, the sound audible even over the crowd noises. The corpse extended its full length, pulled the rope tight and bounced once from the wall. When it came to a rest, McClendon's body hung just below the American flag.

Taking the gasoline can, Masiga poured a stream down over the man. The flames caught it, then consumed it, spiraling up the falling stream as Masiga pulled the fire over the U.S. flag. The material started to burn immediately.

Gesturing two of his warriors forward, Masiga stepped to the edge of the balcony and gazed down fiercely at the crowd gathered below. A fresh wave of flashes rushed across them. Taking in a deep breath, he started to speak, knowing he was making history.

Leipzig, Germany
7:42 p.m.

"ENJOYING THE FAIR, mate?" David McCarter asked.

The hardman glowered at the Briton. He was three inches taller than the Phoenix Force warrior and perhaps fifty pounds heavier. He wore a heavy coat that made him look even bigger. "Do I know you?"

"Nope." McCarter shrugged. "My bit for being sociable." He ducked his head and lit a Player's cigarette. The fall winds swept through the Leipzig Fair, advertising approaching winter.

"Beat it."

McCarter raised an eyebrow. "That's not being very festive."

All around them the Leipzig Fair was a walking, talking neon sign announcing that free enterprise had entered what used to be East Germany with a vengeance. In the medieval period, the fair had been used for an exchange of ideas. Royalty had held court there. For a time, things had seemed bleak for the carnival. But with the fall of the Berlin Wall and the advent of new trade as a unified Germany once more became an economic threat, the spirit of celebration had again taken over.

The center of the fair was the carnival and crafts show, as it had always been. The amusement rides were more sophisticated now, scabbed over with bright lights and the hum of electric motors and diesel engines.

But even as much as the carnival had expanded, the trade shows had become positively cancerous by comparison. Rings of industrial designers and packagers were set up in modular buildings that sprouted up like mushrooms and would be gone within days of the fair's end. Everything was represented, from computers to software and heavy industrial machines and investment opportunities.

The man took a step forward and reached under his coat.

McCarter, dressed in a trench coat and street clothes, had his silenced Browning out first and leveled it at the guy's face. "I think not."

"Okay," the man said easily.

McCarter could tell by the guy's accent that he was Hungarian. "We do this by the numbers," the Briton stated, "and you don't get hurt."

The man blinked and didn't look as if he believed him.

Reaching into his coat, McCarter pulled out the ear-throat headset and slipped it on. "Keep your hands at your sides. Slow. I want to be able to see them." Looking beyond the man, the Briton studied the modular building that was the target.

Finished in an off-white, the building was built in a square, formed by the joining of two rectangular shapes. The seams were easy to spot. Yellow light filled the windows. In front of the main door, a hastily built wooden stairway went up three short steps. A maroon welcome mat was on top, greeting in three different languages.

Tapping the transmit button, McCarter said, "I got him."

"Mine, too," Calvin James radioed back. Manning agreed.

That accounted for the three floating perimeter guards the team had spotted. McCarter looked at his prisoner. "How many inside?"

The man didn't reply.

"I'm on my way," Katz radioed.

"Come on, mate," McCarter said. "I can be a real ballbuster if I need to be. I know Fortunato's inside." He returned the hardman's stare full measure, letting the experiences he'd been through show as icy threat.

"Three more," he replied reluctantly.

"Fortunato's men?"

The guy nodded. "Two men, one woman."

"Good man. Let's walk this way." McCarter spotted Katz making his way toward the modular unit, an expensive briefcase in his hand. "Two men," he said into the mike, "and a woman, plus Fortunato."

"Affirmative." Katz didn't look in McCarter's direction. Neither did Encizo, who drifted in the Israeli's wake.

Manning and James had already reached the small empty building Phoenix Force had staked out for prisoners. James held the door open, waiting.

The Hungarian didn't hesitate to enter the building. His dark eyes looked like bruises in the shadows, and his approach to the situation seemed fatalistic. McCarter figured the man was surprised that he hadn't been shot.

"One team down," Manning said as he shut the door and locked the prisoners inside. "Let's see if we get as lucky on the second."

McCarter leathered the Browning, took a final drag on his cigarette and crushed it underfoot. "Luck's got nothing to do with it. These guys were ripe for a picking."

They took up the positions of the perimeter guards they'd removed. McCarter was extremely conscious of what might be transpiring in the modular unit but refused to look in that direction.

A few minutes later Katz said, "Everything's squared away in here."

McCarter settled in for the wait. Variables had already been introduced into the play. Although the perimeter guards had been jailed, there was still the possibility that Katz's prisoners could cause problems.

They were operating on Intel Price and Kurtzman had gathered from the files stolen from Sara Handel's computer. Evidently Handel had been quite aware of who had been competing with her stolen items from Walukagi.

Casimir Fortunato was the German anchor for the goods liberated by Essien Kwammanga. Although the Walukagian warlord's business hadn't been as brisk as that offered to Handel by Geoffrey Masiga, Kwammanga and Fortunato were still making a fortune while the wars raged.

"Look alive, David," James said over the frequency. "I think you're about to be approached."

"Got 'em," McCarter replied, catching sight of the four men headed in his direction.

They were an evenly balanced salt-and-pepper team. All of them looked well dressed and not the least bit interested in the activities offered by the fair.

"Fortunato?" the lead man inquired as he stepped up to McCarter. He was tall and lean, and his breath smelled of alcohol.

"Inside," McCarter answered.

One of the black men stared hard at the Briton.

"Take a picture, mate," McCarter said. "It'll last longer."

The man was undaunted by the remark. Thick and heavyset, his gnarled hands looked like extensions for heavy equipment. His hair was cut short, showing a network of scars beneath. "I don't know you," the man said in an accented voice.

"No reason you should," McCarter replied. "I don't know you, either." He moved his gaze back to the first man who'd spoken. "Now, do you want to do business, or do you want to stand out here freezing your arses off?"

"What happened to the regular guy?" the first man asked, looking around.

McCarter grinned. "Very upset brother of a past girlfriend knifed him in a bar last week. He'll be back. The brother won't."

The man looked at the second man. "Back down, Savalou. We're here to do business, not work on our paranoia."

The guy's eyes were totally dead, no response at all, and he didn't take them from McCarter. Seizing the moment, the Briton guided them to the modular unit. He opened the door and wiped his feet as if the prefab building was home.

Fortunato didn't resemble the photographs Kurtzman had forwarded from Interpol files. Evidently the trafficking business from Walukagi had led to some prosperous times. The man was probably forty pounds heavier than he'd been in the pictures.

His dark eyes flicked nervously past McCarter as he stood. Only five and a half feet tall and pear-shaped, smelling of cologne, Fortunato moved quickly.

"Please, Jake, Savalou, have a seat."

Katz sat to McCarter's left as the Briton took up a position beside the door.

A sofa and three upholstered chairs sat in front of Fortunato's desk. The interior of the prefab building was better than McCarter had expected. A few expensive prints of Renaissance artists' work hung on the wall. The office area took up most of the inside room, leaving enough space for a couple more rooms, McCarter guessed.

The two men who hadn't said anything took their seats on the couch. Jake sat in front of the desk, his briefcase across his knees and his right hand out of sight inside his coat.

"Can I get a drink?" Savalou asked, still on his feet.

Fortunato nodded toward the wet bar in the corner and sat down.

"Who's he?" Jake asked bluntly, nodding toward Katz.

"My partner," Fortunato replied. But he looked at the Israeli when he said it, and McCarter knew the man in front of the desk was too knowledgeable to miss it.

"New?" Jake asked.

"Yes."

"How do you like the stuff we're bringing in?" Jake asked.

"It makes money," Katz replied.

McCarter could feel the tension in the room, coiling restlessly like a live thing.

Jake tossed a carved figure onto the desk. "What do you think about that?"

Leaning forward in his chair, Katz picked the object up. It was solid ivory, with the raised features of a leaping lion. "Pretty bauble."

Jake grinned in disbelief. "You're not even aware of the culture behind that thing. It's seven hundred years old, seen kingdoms rise and fall and generations go to their graves."

Katz tossed it back, his face composed. "Then I suggest you quit throwing it around so easily. We're not going to buy damaged merchandise."

"What the hell are you doing with this guy?" Jake demanded.

McCarter fitted his hand smoothly around the butt of the Browning. The plan, once they got the delivery team inside the prefab building, had been pretty loose.

"Mr. Fortunato ran into a little cash-flow problem," Katz replied. "I volunteered to help tide him over for a time."

"I don't think I need your business that badly," Jake said, pushing himself to his feet.

"Wait," Fortunato said, jumping to his feet, as well. But he moved too quickly, too desperately.

At the wet bar, Savalou produced a Makarov 9 mm pistol and pointed it at McCarter's midsection. Without flinching, the Briton pulled the Browning, knowing he was going to be too late. Then Savalou's pistol spit fire and banged noisily, trapped in the small space of the modular unit.

CHAPTER SEVEN

Leipzig, Germany
7:58 p.m.

The 9 mm round hit David McCarter directly over the heart and knocked the wind out of him. Despite the Kevlar vest under his coat, the bullet hurt. He lifted the Browning, concentrating on his target rather than the gun sights. When he had target acquisition, he fired three rounds even as Savalou was firing his second.

Two of the parabellum rounds took Savalou in the face, knocking him back across the wet bar and sending liquor bottles flying. The third bullet was off target, deflected by the bullet that caught McCarter high on the body armor, just under the collarbone. For a moment the Briton thought the collarbone had broken.

Spinning, he tracked on the other men in the room. The crash of Savalou's pistol had almost deafened him.

Katz had swept his SIG-Sauer from under his jacket with speed. He fired at Jake four times before the other man could properly unlimber his weapon, hitting him with every bullet.

One of the men on the sofa brought a Beretta 93-R from shoulder leather and loosed rounds on full-auto. Parabellum rounds thumped into the walls, exploding the glass from the window beside McCarter.

Still struggling to regain his breath, the Briton leveled his weapon and fired a pair of rounds that caught the gunner in the face and throat. He swiveled toward the remaining man but watched him go down. Looking over his shoulder, he saw Encizo standing in the hallway, his Beretta casually pointed into the room.

"Sit," Katz commanded Fortunato.

"Please," the broker said. "I did everything I could. You saw me. I tried to protect you."

"Quiet," the Israeli ordered. He glanced up at Encizo expectantly.

"Got it," the Cuban said. He lifted a satchel that bulged. "Figure maybe a couple hundred thousand once we convert it into American dollars."

James and Manning were anxious at the other end of the radio frequency. McCarter brought them up to speed, still sucking air painfully. He glanced through the window, the breeze slipping in through the broken shards of glass remaining in the frame.

"You people are going to have to evacuate," James warned. "Unless you plan on talking your way through fair security. They've already fielded an emergency rescue squad."

"Get him up and out of here," Katz said to McCarter, pointing his pistol at Fortunato.

Nodding, McCarter made himself move. He screwed the barrel of the Browning into the broker's neck and half pulled him from the seat. Fortunato cringed the whole time, eyes screwed up as he prayed and crossed himself.

Katz led the way out of the building, then along the chosen path of escape. The carnival aspect of the fair lent itself to a hasty disappearance.

"You okay?" Encizo asked McCarter.

"Yeah. Bloody shoulder hurts like hell, though."

"Have Calvin take a look at it when he gets time. I saw you take that bullet high up. If it broke something, you don't want to take the chance of shattering it later and really ending up with a mess."

McCarter nodded. James was the medic of the team. And as a team, each man knew the importance of relying on the other. If the injury was more debilitating than McCarter thought, the whole team could suffer as a result.

Another hundred yards farther on, Katz brought a stop to their flight. With stony features, he turned back to Fortunato.

"You know you're not going to die," Katz stated. "Not this time. Otherwise you'd already be dead."

"Thank you," Fortunato whispered hoarsely.

"Don't thank me," Katz said in a harsh voice. "I left you alive for only one reason."

Looking up the rows of buildings, McCarter saw Manning and James in the distance. Back in the direction of the prefab building they'd left, a Volkswagen minivan rolled along the tents and buildings with flashing blue cherries on a light bar. By the time security and police units got coordinated, McCarter knew Phoenix Force would be long gone.

"I want you to carry a message for me," Katz said. "Are you listening?"

"Yes." Fortunato nodded to show how well he was listening.

"Tell everyone in this business that you know that Masiga and his people are the only ones to deal with. No one else. Not Kwammanga, not Nanpetro, not anyone. Got that?"

"Yes."

Katz left the man standing there.

McCarter brought up the rear, his Browning still a visible threat. He wasn't sure where the mission would take them next. Price had mentioned that they might take a more active part in the events unfolding in Walukagi, but nothing definite had been given. But with the attack on Fortunato—making it look like it was instigated by Masiga—Katz was hoping to turn up the heat between at least two of the warlords struggling for control of Walukagi.

Glancing back at the man crumpled on the ground, McCarter figured Fortunato had become a true believer.

The Oval Office, The White House
2:11 p.m.

"ALL THE FOREIGN SOLDIERS are going to die. None of them can stand against us. We won this land over the years. Took it from the creatures of the jungle, from the Europeans who sought to steal our riches and control our lives, from the whites as they held on to this land so desperately."

Hal Brognola stood beside the President in bleak silence as he stared at the television set.

"My God," the Man said softly, his glass of iced tea frozen halfway to his lips.

Brognola knew he was referring to the burning corpse hanging beside the flaming American flag outside the Cape Anansi hotel.

The phone rang.

The President scooped it up without looking away from the television set. "Yes."

Brognola dropped his hand into his pocket and brought out two antacid tablets. He knew about death, and the cruel ways other humans sometimes chose to do each other in, but he'd never accepted it. Even a mission sanction was something to be carefully weighed. Once a life was gone, there was no replacing it.

But as he stared at the huge, dangerous figure of Geoffrey Masiga, he knew a man with the guts and skill could alter a future of hurt with a single bullet.

The Man cradled the phone. "That's Arthur McClendon."

"The general?" Brognola asked.

"Yes. I played golf with him just a couple months ago. My God."

"What was he doing at the hotel?"

"According to his aide, he went there to meet a woman who was supposed to give us the location of Masiga's stronghold. We've lost three jets over that jungle trying to find out where he is."

"It was a suck," the head Fed said.

The President made no reply.

Masiga still shouted on the television screen. "We arrived too late to save the woman this man was torturing, but we have our vengeance. Those of you still loyal to this land, rise up and strike back at these foreign oppressors. They confuse you with their gifts of food and clothing and medicine. These things are only given to you to make you weak, to make you dependent on their generosity. Once you are, they will strip you of everything. It's not too late to be men. Pernell Spraggue was given to us by the South African government that shoved us into independence in 1980. He never represented this country, never represented the black people whose home this really is."

Abruptly machine gun fire rattled along the balcony and drove Masiga to cover. Two of his warriors, glazed in reds, greens and blues, stood firm and returned fire with assault rifles. One of them was cut down where he stood, then the other dropped out of sight.

The camera perspective suddenly changed as the photographer focused on the Huey UH-1D helicopter hovering over the street. For a few seconds the picture was blurred as the camera was brought into focus. But the bright yellow flame spitting from the door gun was unmistakable. When the video camera operator had his picture clear again, sparks jumped from the helicopter's fuselage as Masiga's warriors returned fire.

When the camera focused back on the balcony, Masiga had vanished.

"Dammit," the Man said, lifting the phone. He punched a two-digit code and waited only a few seconds for a response.

Brognola listened to the one-sided conversation as he continued watching the news story breaking on CNN. The cameraman was a courageous guy, not showing many qualms as he broke free of the crowd in the street and dashed into the hotel.

The camera jounced and bucked as the guy carried it across the seedy main foyer of the hotel. A small phalanx of U.S. soldiers plunged into the building and tried to wave him off.

A voice-over by the CNN anchorman identified the camera operator as Curtis Diego, out of the University of Southern California and with CNN only four months. The head Fed figured the studio was putting the cameraman's past history together for a special later that night—if things cooled off in Walukagi before the audience forgot Diego.

Obviously Diego had some experience with the hotel. He slipped through the kitchen in a blaze of stainless steel and white Formica, and streaked up a darkened stairwell. The footage lasted for minutes. Brognola was riveted, and he was aware the Man was watching, as well. The anchor kept up a running commentary.

Then Diego reached the top of the stairs, burst through a steel door that had bullet holes ripped into it and stumbled over the bodies of two American soldiers. For a moment, even the CNN anchor fell silent. The blood was graphic and dizzying.

"Masiga's not there," the President said. "Marines have taken the hotel room."

On the television, Diego turned and brought the camera probing into the room. He swept it across the area as a Marine started for him, yelling at him to get the camera out. Diego retreated, but he had some footage of the carnage that had been rendered in the room.

Brognola knew the blood-spattered violence would live on in the minds of Americans and the world for months to come. The woman had been naked, bound and slaughtered without a chance to defend herself. That had been clear. Masiga's accusation would carry some weight.

"Jesus, Mary and Joseph," the President said in a low, stunned voice. Then, barking into the telephone, "Tell those men to get that cameraman out of that hotel. Now!"

But Diego was already on the move. He was speaking now, his words rushed and fragmentary, but pulsing with emotion and emergency. "The guys who did this have got to be somewhere." He rounded a corner, stumbling now because his reflexes were worn. "There's an outside fire escape at the back."

He passed through another door, then stood on a metal landing looking down on an alley. The darkness made the visuals difficult, but there was no mistaking the movement of men along the steel framework.

"Christ, kid," Brognola said, taking an involuntary step forward, "shut off that damn camera. It's going to light you up like a Christmas tree."

Abruptly the CNN broadcast shifted to a second camera that showed Diego at the eighth-floor landing as he photographed Masiga's escape. Diego's camera steadied, targeting one of the warriors at the end of Masiga's group.

"They're on him," the President said. "They'll have him any minute now."

Brognola watched in stony silence; his stomach was tight.

The camera view from the ground showed a Marine reaching for Diego in an attempt to pull him back inside the building. However, the other view showed the Kawalusian warrior suddenly lift his assault rifle and point it at Diego. From that perspective, it made Brognola feel as if he were in the gunner's sights. Then the muzzle-flash loosed miniature lightning.

Just as Diego's camera went dead, the other video camera's view showed the young CNN photographer go reeling backward as the bullets took him high, driving him back into the Marine's arms.

Before the Marines had a chance to organize and shoot at the killers, a small bus roared into the alley, one light out and the other burning like a fiery eye. It hardly slowed as Masiga and the kill team clambered aboard. Bullets from the Marines' weapons sparked from the armored top but couldn't stop it. Within seconds it charged out onto the street at the opposite end, smashed into two cars parked at the curb and drove away without pursuit.

"They got away," the Man said, cradling the phone. Brognola nodded.

On the television, the story started cycling again as the network began to layer in additional details about the assassination. The image of McClendon burning over the flaming American flag became a constant, filmed from a number of angles.

"However this goes with the British," the President said in a hard voice, "I want your team over there."

"Yes, sir."

"I don't care if this mission has the blessing of Congress or if we have to black bag it. The people responsible for this madness are going to be held accountable."

Brognola looked the Man in the eye. "I'm glad you feel that way, sir. If you didn't, I think you'd have a mutiny on your hands before nightfall. Hell, I know you would. It would start right here in this room."

The intercom buzzed and the secretary announced that Kalimuzo and Henley were waiting to see the President. The Man had them sent in.

Brognola could immediately tell the news was good. There was a lift to Kalimuzo's shoulders that he hadn't seen since he'd met the man, and there was a weight on the British liaison's shoulders that hadn't previously existed.

"Well, gentlemen?" the President prompted.

"We're in business," Henley said, running a hand through his carefully coiffed locks but still looking haggard and wary.

"Reluctantly, and with considerable trepidation," Kalimuzo added.

The British liaison didn't argue.

The President nodded. "Good."

He glanced at Brognola. "If you'll attend to that other matter, I've got some heavy politicking to do in the next couple hours."

"Do you need me here?" the head Fed asked.

"No. You'll do more good there."

Brognola nodded, shook hands all the way around and left. Using the cellular phone in his pocket, he arranged for a helicopter to be waiting on him at Dulles. Within minutes he'd be at Stony Man Farm and at the helm of another touch-and-go hellfire mission. But the big Fed was in his element there. Already his mind was filling with logistical problems of an infiltration by the Stony Man warriors.

Vengeance was going to be done in Walukagi, and it was going to be terrible and swift.

Cape Town, South Africa
10:13 p.m.

"IN THE BEGINNING," Wilhelmus Kamer told his audience, "I relied heavily on physical strength to achieve the goals I established for myself. Now that's not true."

All of the other interested parties were still with him from the afternoon meeting. They'd broken for an early dinner and he'd picked up the tab. Then they'd each had a couple hours to take care of personal business. None of them had been far from a television as events continued to unfold in Walukagi. Kamer had even known when Masiga would kill General McClendon, though he hadn't counted on the event being so widely televised.

They'd been in the conference room at that time, held spellbound by the CNN cameraman's daring.

Now it was time to show them one of the weapons they hadn't known they were going to have in their arsenal. He took them down to the basement level in his private elevator, then directed them to a secret door none of them had known about and revealed another two floors he'd had built beneath the structure.

The lighting was impressive, and security was so tight that the guards in gray coveralls held their weapons on Kamer as he was retina printed before being allowed past the first massive steel door. The guards worked in pairs. No one was left unattended. Kamer had impressed that point by killing the first two guards he'd found apart from each other. That had been twenty-six months earlier. It hadn't happened since.

He turned to face his coconspirators and smiled. Sharde coiled around his leg, her fangs bared as she flattened her ears back at a guard who had gotten too close. "Once you go past this door," he warned, his voice clear above the hum of air conditioners and computer equipment, "you're with me one hundred percent."

"Or what?" Clyde Raines demanded.

"Or I have you killed."

Their faces revealed no emotion, and they were completely focused on him.

"I'm not joking," Kamer said softly. "What I'm about to show you is something that will give us Walukagi on a silver platter, and make all of us much more rich than we currently are."

No one said anything.

Kamer took the lead, passing down the hallway with a sure step. Lauren Severin took his arm and squeezed it.

"There's something about a man who knows how to be in control that I find simply irresistible," the woman confided.

Kamer smiled at her, knowing she'd slit his throat in a minute if there was enough money in it for her. But he'd almost reached the point where none of them were necessary anymore.

"What is it you think we have to fear the most at this point?" Kamer asked.

"American military involvement," Vic DeChanza answered without hesitation.

"That may happen," Kamer said, "and there's nothing we can do to prevent it. In fact, it might be to our benefit if the Americans did decide to pull another of their John Wayne actions over here."

"But the time we'd lose on this operation," Clyde Raines argued. "I think we've waited long enough."

Kamer ushered them into an elevator. "We've waited long enough for Warukagi," he agreed. "But how long would you be willing to wait for half of all Africa? Or more?" He ran a magnetic key card through a slot and the elevator doors closed.

The cage dropped while the group dealt with the new question.

"We can't even hang on to South Africa," Hubble Weinholdt responded.

The elevator cage stopped and the doors opened on the opposite wall. With Severin still on his arm, Kamer led them through another corridor to a room with two thick Plexiglas walls that reached from ceiling to floor.

They remained standing outside them, peering in at the white room beyond.

"Earlier I made reference to my good friend, Dr. Linus Maaloe," Kamer said, gently disengaging his arm from Severin. The group formed a half-moon around him. "Dr. Maaloe is a brilliant man, a research scientist I discovered in Copenhagen when I was looking for outside properties for White Tiger Investments to diversify in." Kamer stared expectantly into the empty white room.

In seconds the others had joined him, pressing close to the Plexiglas walls.

"I'm afraid Dr. Maaloe's genius hasn't been well received in other countries where he's worked," Kamer said. "His specialty is DNA and viruses. I could let him talk to you and explain what it is I hired him to develop, but I think I have a quicker, more understandable way to show you what I'm talking about." He reached over his head and pressed the button set into the ceiling.

Across the white room, a door opened, revealing a yawning black rectangle beyond.

"Dr. Maaloe has worked with several intelligence agencies around the globe, as well," Kamer continued, "most of them free agencies, because that's where his political beliefs lie. But he did some work in Russia, too, before the fall. Once democracy set in, they gave him short shrift and hustled him out the back door."

"Why?" DeChanza asked.

"Dr. Maaloe's specialty has always been of a combative nature." Kamer watched the open door, knowing he had them.

"Bacteriological warfare," Severin said.

"Of a military nature," Kamer agreed. "And, of course, as illegal as nuclear arms in the possession of North Korea. At the time I found him, there had been no less than seven attempts on his life by various agencies." He paused. "Dr. Maaloe lost a leg as a result of one of them, but managed to stay alive. Overall, a most remarkable man."

Abruptly a naked man was shoved through the doorway. He was bearded and unkempt, white because Kamer figured that would make more of an impact on his coconspirators. Many blacks had been subjected to other deadly versions of the virus during the past few months.

The naked man ran at full speed at the Plexiglas wall where they had gathered. He never slowed. All but Kamer stepped back defensively. Without a faltering step, the man slammed into the wall and came to an abrupt halt. Blood poured from his mouth, nose and one ear, smearing the Plexiglas. He yelled and smashed the wall with his fists. Every scream sprayed more crimson on the see-through plastic. The skin over his knuckles split, then he started the attack with knees and feet, as well.

"Given somewhat to theatrical presentation," Kamer said, "Dr. Maaloe calls this the Apocalypse Virus." He paused to let them watch as the man inside the white room raced around the walls, seeking a way out. He snapped at Severin like a dog, but the eyes belonged on a piranha, greedy, dark and hungry.

"Will this kill him?" Raines asked.

"Sure," Kamer said. "But the average cycle takes twenty-eight days. Maaloe has another name for the virus, as well, but I can't pronounce it."

"Can this be spread?" DeChanza asked, appalled and hypnotized at the same time.

"Yes." Kamer knew he had them. "Usually through a fluid exchange between two people."

"Sex," Severin said quietly.

The naked man was back to beating on the wall with his fists and knees, his gaze hot and demanding on the woman. His howls were pain filled and stirring.

"Yes," Kamer answered. "Or a blood transfusion. Or exposure through an open wound during the contagion cycle."

"How long is that?" Weinholdt asked. "The contagious cycle?"

"Four months. There's a delay that's been programmed into the virus."

"Why four months?" Raines asked.

"Because it can be introduced quietly, without anyone knowing for some time." Kamer looked at them. "Let's say the American military starts taking a firmer stance in Walukagi. We could take a lot of losses and perhaps become targets ourselves during that time. This could be our option."

"Bullshit," DeChanza said. "Who'd want a country of sociopathic killers? Our problems here in Cape Town pale by comparison."

"Do they?" Kamer demanded. Sharde coiled next to him, as dangerous as a sword at his side. "The Apocalypse Virus could be introduced into Walukagi..."

"Then what?" DeChanza asked. "We go over and wait to die there, too?" He waved a hand. "Sorry, but I have no intentions of ending up anything like that."

Kamer reached over his head and pressed the button again. The door on the opposite wall reopened, then a gray-suited guard stepped through. The naked man rushed at his intended victim, broken-nailed hands curved into claws before him.

Dispassionately the guard raised his side arm and fired. All seven shots rolled together like thunder. Incredibly the infected man stayed on his feet even after being hit with the .45 slugs. All of the bullets hit their target and tore through, coming to a rest in the Plexiglas wall.

Then the naked man dropped, smearing blood over the white floor.

"They get to be amazingly hard to kill," Kamer commented.

DeChanza snorted.

"There is something I've neglected to mention," the CEO of White Tiger Investments said. "Dr. Maaloe also has developed an antidote for the virus. If we introduce the virus, we can also be protected against it."

"But the spread," Weinholdt said. "Once you get something like that going, how do you contain it?"

"Walukagi is pretty much cut off from the rest of the world. There are plenty of natural barriers, and political ones are going up every day. I feel that it can be done. If it even becomes necessary." He looked at the dead man in the center of the floor. "However, there is something I want you to think about."

They looked at him.

"The United States has set itself up as policeman to the world. Now that Russia is no longer a world power of the magnitude the free world had feared, the American sphere of influence has expanded. I think that their very nature will see them drawn into more and more violence—partially because they are finding it profitable. The allies in the Gulf War paid off their agreed amounts, and a large section of the world was suddenly opened up to American trade, American ideas. Eastern Europe is a good example. The people living there are picking up clothing, television shows, books, everything they can that originated in America. That is going to leave its mark. And once we take over Walukagi, how long will we have before the Americans decide to take action against us?''

''What are you suggesting?'' Raines asked.

Kamer nodded toward the room. ''That we use the virus without fail if it becomes necessary. Imagine the American soldiers over here that get exposed to the virus. In a month, when the violence quells, they'll start going back to their country, already infected.''

''And once they get there, they'll want to celebrate,'' Severin said with a knowing smile. ''The infection will spread across the United States.''

''Hopefully at an alarming rate,'' Kamer agreed. ''And the virus is virtually undetectable in its advanced stages. It marries within the DNA strands themselves, becoming almost indistinguishable.''

Inside the white room, the gray-suited guard brought out a hose and started sluicing the blood toward a sunken drain in the center of the room.

''The American public's faith in its government will be shattered,'' Kamer continued. ''They'll lose their stomach for 'police action' of any kind. And when that happens, it'll open up markets for us here.'' He paused to look at them. ''And possibly in Europe.''

''You've gotten more ambitious,'' Severin said.

''Yes, I have.'' Kamer stood his ground, moving into his full pitch now. ''Look, the kaffirs intend to take over this whole continent if we let them. The Arabs will hold their own in the north to a degree, but they haven't stopped fighting long enough to become a consolidated threat. And peace in the Middle East has never been a sure thing, despite how well things seem to be going at the moment. With the right hands on the wheel, this continent could become a prime mover and shaker in the political and economic arenas. Do you think the Americans are down here out of the goodness of their flag-waving hearts? Hell, no! They're down here because they're laying groundwork for potential markets for goods and services. And because they see Africa as a source of cheap labor. American businesses, after the NAFTA agreement between the U.S., Canada and Mexico, have shown a willingness to trust foreign countries with manufacturing plants. African countries will fill the employment rosters and be the consumers."

"They'll take the profits," Raines said on cue.

"Yes." Kamer challenged all of them with his eyes. "Imperialism isn't dead. It's been waiting, mutating. It's not about land anymore. It's about economic markets. With the population and resources we have, with countries that get away from centuries of bloodshed, this continent could be a veritable juggernaut. And I want part of it. If it's achievable in my lifetime, I want the biggest part I can get."

When he looked into their eyes, Kamer knew he'd closed the deal.

CHAPTER EIGHT

Stony Man Farm, Virginia
2:43 a.m.

From the air, the change in the countryside was subtle. If Hal Brognola hadn't been looking for it, he doubted he would have seen it. But Stony Man Farm had been the centerpiece of his professional life for a long time. He shifted his unlighted cigar to the corner of his mouth as he gazed through the helicopter's bubble cockpit and monitored their approach.

Once part of the Civil War battlegrounds, Stony Man Farm had a history of violence. If searched for, scars could be found on the land where even more recent firefights had occurred. Mercifully Virginia's Blue Ridge Mountains concealed their secrets and their wounds well.

The Farm didn't look like America's premier hard-site for counterterrorist forces, with recon satellites webbed into cybernetic circuitry that spanned the globe. Apple and peach orchards provided cover for the electrified fences and security devices that kept watch over the grounds. The denim-clad farmhands who worked the soil, tilling, plowing, pruning, seeding and harvesting, never went anywhere without weapons or communications gear. Dressed alike, it was hard for anyone who actually got close enough to observe them—provided they weren't picked up by the roving teams of man-and-dog—to get an accurate idea of how many men were actually housed on the Farm.

The main house was three stories tall aboveground, and had considerable basement space. Built on a ranchhouse frame, it nevertheless was constructed to withstand military assaults. Steel plating could drop over the windows in a heartbeat, and electronic locks slipped into place with the press of a computer-key combination. The two outbuildings held secrets of their own.

After making sure the airspace was free, the pilot expertly juked toward the disguised landing field north of the main house. Sections of the camou netting were pulled back as they approached, clearing enough space for the landing.

When the chopper thumped gently against the ground, Brognola disembarked and trotted toward the waiting Jeep. The helicopter lifted off at once, and a dozen men moved to resecure the camou netting.

Leo Turrin sat in the driver's seat of the vehicle and gave him a crooked smile. "Politics?" he asked laconically.

"Over," the head Fed replied as he settled himself. "At least for the moment. We're ahead of the game."

Turrin started the Jeep and headed back along the trail leading to the main house. "We get a green light?"

"Yeah. You been keeping up with the news?"

"CNN?"

Brognola nodded.

The look on Turrin's face was all the answer necessary. "We have targets now?"

"That's how the Man feels. But things over there are going to get bloody. I don't know if we're going to try for a full insertion yet, or work it covertly."

"Any way you want it handled," Turrin said, "Striker's going to cut himself a big piece of the action."

"I know. Any word on where he is?"

"There's an arms shipment headed for Walukagi. Supposed to land within the hour. Barb's moved some heavy equipment into the area for him."

"Any contact from him?"

"Not since Jack dropped him into the LZ."

Brognola checked his watch out of habit. When Turrin parked the Jeep in front of the main house, he led the way inside, moving through the main room, kitchen and hallway until he reached Kurtzman's lab. Palming the ID plate at the side of the reinforced door, he heard it stutter through the identification process, then passed through.

Despite the number of times he'd seen the room, every time he stepped into it, Brognola felt as if he entered another world. Even the air seemed to come from a different altitude, crisp and cool.

Aaron Kurtzman, confined to a wheelchair by an assassin's bullet, sat at a huge horseshoe-shaped desk on a raised dais in the center of the floor. He was a big man, with broad shoulders, looking totally out of place at the keyboard in front of him. His gaze constantly wandered over the three monitors in front of him, as well as the huge wall screen at the opposite end of the big room.

Approaching quietly, Brognola stood beside the cybernetics expert.

"Hello, Hal," Kurtzman said without looking up. He tapped the keyboard rapidly, then reached up and adjusted the headset he wore, making sure the mouthpiece was in position.

"What's up?" Brognola asked, staring at what looked like a carnival of confusion. People moved across the huge screen, propelled by security staff and police or military forces. There was no audio.

"Leipzig Fair," Kurtzman said. "Phoenix made a stop there after the Berlin assignment, establishing a fire break of sorts for the movers and shakers profiting from contraband coming out of Walukagi. They got away clean after accomplishing their objective, but I'm having the footage sorted through in case there's anything we can use."

Brognola looked around the room. Kurtzman's top three computer experts were at their workstations in a flying wing formation.

To the left was Carmen Delahunt. Red-haired, feisty and extremely capable, Delahunt was old-line FBI. Kurtzman had liberated her from Quantico after he'd discovered her.

Next up was Akira Tokaido. Although lacking in formal training in cybernetics and computers, Tokaido was a natural hacker, understanding the machines and software on a level that was almost supernatural. He wore a black concert T-shirt of a group called Alice in Chains, and on his right thigh was a small CD player that had a plug leading up to one ear. Tokaido's head bobbed in time to a fast beat, and he chewed bubble gum vigorously.

Dr. Huntington Wethers, late of U.C. Berkeley where he was a professor in cybernetics, occupied the last chair. His hair had started to go gray at the temples, standing out against his ebony skin, but fitting in with the way he carried himself. Dressed in a suit, sitting with perfect posture, his thin mustache neatly clipped, he chewed his unlighted pipe with grim enthusiasm as he flipped through various documents on-screen.

"Where's Phoenix now?" Brognola asked.

"On their way to Potsdam," Kurtzman answered. "Barb arranged a safehouse there through the CIA." He grinned. "They're not using it, so we are. She knew about it, but they don't know she knows. She figured after seeing the CNN footage that we're going to be in-country in Walukagi soon. One way or the other."

Turrin handed Brognola a cup of coffee he'd poured from the coffee maker at the rear of the room.

"Did you get anything from the Brotherhood of Aryan Defense?" Brognola asked.

An evil grin twisted Kurtzman's face as he looked over his shoulder at the head Fed. "Do you mean, do I have any BAD news?"

"Oh, geez, Hal," Turrin groaned. "You should shoot him. Drop him right here in his tracks."

"Well," a feminine voice said, "first off, it's not all BAD."

As they turned to face the speaker, Turrin said, "How do you like playing the straight man?"

Standing in front of them, Barbara Price gave them a smile that had once graced magazine covers when she was putting herself through college. Tall and honey blond, she was wearing jeans, boots and a white blouse. A cellular phone rode in a hip holster at her side. Extremely insightful and able to work on the fly, she was the Farm's mission controller.

"We tracked the money back," Price said.

"And?" Brognola prompted.

"We scored." She glanced at Kurtzman. "Let's have it."

The big man tapped the computer keyboard, and bank accounts opened up on the three screens in front of him.

"Screen one features an account in the name of Rick Carrey," Price said. "He's the front man for a lot of BAD's underground activity. He handles the monthly newsletter, collects dues, meets with the new recruits and basically manages BAD's PR in the media."

"So he's somebody to get to."

"Oh, yes. That's why Aaron and I started working him as soon as we figured out BAD pulled the hit at Dulles. Look at the date on that deposit."

Brognola looked more closely. The amount was for a half million dollars, and was dated almost two weeks before the attack on Kalimuzo's jet. "This is his personal account?"

"Yes. And look here."

Another line on the screen was highlighted when Kurtzman worked the keyboard.

"He drew it out three days ago," Brognola said.

"Right. I figure that's when he disbursed it to the rest of the group."

Brognola put it together easily enough. "Someone hired BAD for the hit and went through Carrey to do it."

"It plays. I've got federal marshals en route to pick him up now." Price glanced at the screen. "The group has other accounts, I'm sure, that would be harder to access. They've incorporated themselves, so it might take more time to turn up those accounts."

"But Carrey put the money in his personal account. Why?"

"Nine days of interest," Kurtzman replied. "He's a greedy little bastard."

"But it gave us our lead," Price said. "Carmen was able to work through the tangled web that led back to the Caymans. The money came from WildStar Communications, a lobbying group on the Hill."

"Who owns them?" Brognola asked. "With them in the vicinity, it could also tie into the bomb that Lyons found."

"So far that's still a mystery. They're licensed to a holding company in Germany that apparently has no history, no money, nothing it sells in the way of goods or services. For all intents and purposes, it's a ghost."

"But we have WildStar?" the head Fed asked.

Price nodded. "I've already assigned Able Team and armed them with federal paper that will get them into the company's offices. Maybe we can pick up the trail from there."

"What about Striker?"

She glanced at her watch. "I haven't heard, but he should be on the arms shipment now. Phoenix is standing by in Potsdam while I stage the transportation. I've got two alternatives. If we go overt, Aaron has a package identifying them as military personnel and they can make use of the base in Berlin. If we're going to be covert, I've got a jump arranged in forty-five minutes, but it'll take twice as long."

One of the phones beside Kurtzman rang. "The White House," the big computer expert said, checking the caller ID.

Brognola set the instrument on speakerphone function. "Brognola."

The Man's voice was tense but wearily elated. "We're go on the operation," he said. "Your people are going to have the full backing of the U.S. military forces. How do you want to work the insertion?"

Without a word Price handed over one of two manila folders waiting in a slot on Kurtzman's desk. Brognola flipped it open and scanned the one-sheet summary on top of a stack of paper and military documents that were almost two inches thick. All the details of Stony Man involvement with the U.S. and UN military were outlined thoroughly and succinctly. Much of it the big Fed was already familiar with because he and Price had reasoned out the various scenarios, constantly updating them with the addition of new Intel that indicated necessary changes.

When he finished some minutes later, promising to fax the entire strategy to the President, with copies going to the Pentagon, Brognola looked up at the frozen image on the wall screen at the other end of the room. Geoffrey Masiga stood on the balcony holding McClendon above his head while the general's face burned.

"That bastard's about to find out what hell on earth is really all about," the head Fed promised grimly.

Kawalusian Jungle, Walukagi
12:57 a.m.

THE SCENT OF ROT and decay clung to the underbrush. The canopy formed by the trees was dense and blotted out the full moon. Restless, their nocturnal cycle disturbed by straining mechanical engines, monkeys scampered through the branches and along the vines, raining down pieces of fruit and sticks along with baretoothed challenges screamed into the night.

Geoffrey Masiga sat in the passenger seat in the second Land Rover in the caravan. He still wore the body paint, as did his warriors.

Men from the lead Land Rover were using chain saws to hack up a huge dead tree that had fallen sometime since the last arms shipment. The cacophony of steel teeth chewing through wood drowned out most of the other sounds.

Masiga laughed as some of his men tracked down his kills by flashlight, then held the bodies up in triumph.

Auta trotted up to Masiga's vehicle. "We're late." he said.

"Yes, but they will wait." Masiga got out of the Land Rover and walked toward the chain-saw operators. "Where else would they go with their cargo?"

"Nkimbo and Tumba have spotted movement around us," Auta said. He had to shout over the roar of the chain saws.

"Who?" Masiga demanded. He rested his hand on the .45 belted at his waist.

Auta shrugged. "They're not certain."

"Maybe they're seeing ghosts." Masiga spoke with certainty, because he believed in ghosts himself. But he'd never met one who wanted to harm him.

"We're vulnerable here," Auta said. "If the American soldiers—"

"The American soldiers are busy tucking their tails between their legs now," Masiga said.

"Perhaps someone else, then."

"No one would dare face us." Masiga gestured toward the line of military jeeps, Land Rovers and trucks. "And we're not vulnerable." He touched the pouch of diamonds tied to his loinwrap. "The cargo will be there waiting for us. We'll reach shore in only a few more minutes."

Auta nodded but didn't look happy about it.

Masiga had known the man since boyhood. Although brave and highly skilled, Auta had the habit of casting grave doubts on events when they didn't proceed exactly as he thought they should. Short-tempered, the Kawalusian king grabbed a nearby downed tree trunk almost six inches in girth and shouted for the chain-saw operators to move away from where they'd become mired by the huge tree.

Taking deep breaths, Masiga waded through the piles of sawdust, shoved the length of tree trunk he had in his hands under the area where the chain saws had been working, then started to lift. His muscles bunched and stood out in sharp relief under his skin. He knew the tree where he was attempting to leverage it weighed in excess of a ton. A group of his warriors came to stand around him, watching.

Snarling with the effort, unwilling to walk away from the offending tree, Masiga continued to lift. He was counting on the fact that with the trunk sawed almost in two, it wouldn't be able to support itself.

With a sudden, echoing crack, the tree gave way and broke into two pieces.

Masiga stepped back and ordered the lead Land Rover forward. The four-wheel-drive's front bumper touched the tree, then nosed into the eight-inch gap. Masiga commanded the driver to continue. At first the wheels spun, throwing loam over the jungle. Then the tires caught and the Land Rover shoved through, opening a gap big enough to allow the other vehicles to come after it.

A cheer went up from Masiga's warriors, but it was cut short by the chattering spit of autofire. Two men near Masiga were knocked to the ground by bullets.

Scrambling, the big man shouted orders to his warriors, gearing them into action. He ran back to his personal Land Rover as more bullets thudded into the vehicles from the jungle around them.

Several teams yanked tarps off the vehicles, revealing .50-caliber machine guns. They began firing at once, unleashing total destruction that lashed through the jungle.

Masiga took the Stoner 63 light machine gun from the rear of the Land Rover and added his fire to that of the others, while Auta led teams into the jungle. Taking cover behind the four-wheel-drive Masiga accepted the pouch of 30-round magazines his driver handed him.

A pair of men rushed him from the jungle. He brought the Stoner around in a tight arc, handling the weight of it easily on one arm. The swath of 5.56 mm rounds stitched the first man across the chest, turning his run into a stumbling fall that took him to the ground. The second man managed to heave a grenade in Masiga's direction before the machine gun fire jerked him to a stop, then slapped him down.

Recoiling from the danger zone, Masiga went to ground and covered his head just before the grenade exploded. Shrapnel imbedded in the side of his Land Rover, but he was untouched. He fed in another magazine and walked through the battleground, cutting down men with bursts from the Stoner. His warriors surged after him.

In minutes the battle was over and dead men lay across the jungle floor.

Masiga had lost only four men, while over twenty of the attackers had perished.

"Who are these people?" he demanded as the caravan sorted itself out. Three of the vehicles had flat tires that were in the process of being changed. Pausing beside a dead man, Masiga flipped over the corpse with his foot. Their markings identified them as part of the Kausa tribe, one of the smaller factions of Walukagi.

Auta marched up with a prisoner. The man was young and fierce. His hands were tied behind his back, and a thong was slipped around his neck. Auta kept a broad-bladed hunting knife against his jawline.

"They belong to Kwammanga," Auta stated.

Masiga turned to the prisoner. "There has been a truce between the people of Kawalusa and the people of Kausa."

"No more," the prisoner said defiantly. "You have broken the truce."

"Who are you?" Masiga demanded.

"Agbanli."

"Who sent you?"

"King Kwammanga."

"Why?"

"In the land beyond the water," Agbanli said, talking way beyond his knowledge of the world, "the whites you sell the treasures and diamonds and gold to attacked and killed some of the men my king owns."

"When?"

"Today."

"I didn't," Masiga said.

"Those men told my king's representatives that they came from you—that no more treasures or diamonds or gold were to be sold unless they came from you."

Masiga shook his head. "They lie. Go back. Tell Kwammanga that we must talk. Soon. Tell him that I did no such thing." He nodded at Auta.

Reluctantly the man slipped his knife over the prisoner's bonds, freeing him.

"Tell him that I forgive him his trespass against me," Masiga added. "And I send the men living back to him as a token of my good faith. Our war is with the whites. There is enough to go around for all of us."

The Kausan man nodded, then backed away into the shadows, calling to his comrades. When they deemed themselves safe, they broke and ran for the treeline.

Auta looked at Masiga. "Kwammanga would want no war with us at this point."

"I know."

"Yet, neither do I think that man was lying."

Masiga tossed the Stoner in the back of the Land Rover, ignoring the bodies he had to step over. "Neither do I. The munitions shipment tonight will see us armed strong enough to take Cape Anansi when the time comes. Once the Americans falter, we can step inside and seize the city and make it our own. Dealing with Kwammanga and Nanpetro can wait until then."

"Perhaps the attack came from Kame," Auta suggested. "He is a very greedy man."

"Perhaps," Masiga agreed. "I shall ask him."

"And if it was him?" Auta persisted.

"Then," Masiga said, "I will ask myself how much longer I need his assistance. There is going to be only one king of this country when I'm finished." He looked around at the dead men scattered in the jungle. "Nothing can stop us. An army met us tonight and we broke them. How can any one man hope to stand before us?"

Washington, D.C.
5:12 p.m.

"I'M SORRY, but Mr. Eliade isn't taking any visitors today. Working hours are posted, and it is after five."

Carl Lyons followed the young secretary's imperious finger to the neatly printed bronze placard on the wooden door leading to the suite of rooms that housed the WildStar Communications Washington lobbying group. The waiting room was tastefully done, but was about as original as a McDonald's restaurant along an interstate.

"He'll see me," Lyons said confidently.

Blancanales and Schwarz stood behind him, dressed in casual business attire and carrying expensive attaché cases.

"No," the secretary said, "he won't. And if you don't leave this minute, I'm calling building security."

Lyons glanced around the room again, spotting the small, slightly off-color rectangle in the wall montage of mirrors behind potted palms. He guessed it was a pane of one-way glass. "Call them," he suggested. "The more the merrier."

The secretary lifted the phone without hesitation. The building was located in Washington's downtown sector amid dozens of other businesses.

Abruptly the door behind her opened and a tall man with red hair stepped into the room. He wore sunglasses, a denim shirt and white tie and white jeans. He stood at least six feet four and was built like a linebacker. "Don't worry about it, Sheila," he told the secretary.

For a moment she appeared confused, then slowly cradled the phone. "Yes, Mr. Eliade."

"Why don't you go on home?" Eliade suggested. "Whatever filing you have left can surely wait until tomorrow."

"Yes, sir." She gathered her purse, a summer sweater and a few files, then left, giving Lyons a long look.

Looking completely comfortable, Eliade leaned against the door frame and crossed his arms over his chest. "How can I help you gentlemen?"

"You're Paul Eliade?" Lyons asked, reaching inside his jacket for the paperwork Price had readied.

"Yes."

"You're the business manager of WildStar Communications?"

"For the last five years, yes." Eliade grinned thinly. "Don't tell me we've made the Fortune 500."

"Hardly." Lyons didn't like the smug, easy manner of the man. As a political lobbying group from Germany, the company enjoyed a free hand around the city. "Where'd you lose the accent?"

"What accent?"

"WildStar's out of Germany, isn't it?" Schwarz asked.

"Yes," Eliade replied.

"Your papers say you're from Berlin."

The WildStar manager shrugged and grinned. "I didn't find an accent as profitable as Arnold Schwarzenegger."

Blancanales separated from the others, giving Eliade three fronts to consider. Eliade never shifted his attention from Lyons.

"You look like you've settled in here," the Politician commented.

Eliade grinned. "Is this going somewhere?"

"Do you know a man named Richard Carrey?" Lyons asked.

"Do I? You sound like a man with all the answers, and these are your questions."

"Guy thinks he's playing 'Jeopardy,'" Schwarz commented.

Eliade gave him a condescending smile.

Lyons got itchy between his shoulder blades. Price had said that WildStar Communications would have no reason to believe they'd been found out. Carrey was still in place, basically untouchable in Georgia. But money, once it started getting passed around, was damning. Anyone who worked with spreading it out as payoffs knew that. Eliade would know that he was living one step beyond the law and had to move fast to keep even that distance.

"We'll move on to final jeopardy," Lyons said. "Someone paid a half million dollars to a man named Richard Carrey because he's involved with a group known as the Brotherhood of Aryan Defense in Georgia. This group of white supremacists was responsible for the attack on Ambassador Henry Kalimuzo of Walukagi."

"I wasn't aware that Kalimuzo had received a recent political appointment."

Schwarz moved in to the secretary's desk. Lifting the phone, he punched in a long-distance number, then booted up the computer.

"Hey," Eliade said, "as amusing as this little confrontation has been, I think it's time to draw some lines."

Lyons unfurled the paperwork Price had generated, listing the physical environs of WildStar Communications as subject to search and seizure regarding incriminating evidence.

"What's the charge?" Eliade demanded, moving from the doorway and uncrossing his arms.

"Subversive activity against the United States government," Lyons stated.

"I think my lawyer should be here," Eliade said.

"Find another phone," Schwarz told him as he settled the handset onto a modem.

"I'll accompany you," Lyons said. He stepped toward the WildStar manager with a smile. Without warning, his vision started to blur and he felt dizzy. He looked at Blancanales and saw the Politician looking woozy and out of focus.

Eliade seemed unaffected.

"Gas," Lyons croaked, leaning back against the wall to make use of its solidity. He fumbled his .45 free of shoulder leather.

Eliade was already in motion, clamping a gas mask over his face. Reaching down, he yanked the computer cords out of the wall.

Lyons tried to make his voice work and couldn't. His eyelids felt incredibly heavy.

Surging up from the chair behind the desk, Schwarz dived for the fire-alarm pull mounted on the wall. His arm jerked. Then the clangor of warning bells shrilled through the room an instant before a whooshing noise almost overrode them.

"Breathe," Schwarz said. "Building's got an exhaust-fan system built in as part of the fire-prevention equipment. It's designed to suck out the air and smother flames. Whatever they fed into this room, it's going to blow clear."

His head already more together, Lyons made himself move forward. Eliade had vanished behind the door only seconds earlier. It was locked when he reached it. Lifting a big foot, he slammed it into the door beside the lock. Screws snapped audibly and the lock became a hunk of useless metal.

Lyons rammed through the door and found himself in a modular bullpen of tracked glass walls that sec-

tioned the huge room into a collection of smaller office
units. A shadow—distorted by the glass, the distance
and the lingering effects of the gas that had been used
against Able Team—rose up two office spaces away
with a gun in its hand.

Squeezing the .45's trigger three times, Lyons aimed
for the center of his target. Glass shards broke free and
went spinning, scattering across desk tops. The shadow
dropped.

Looking left, the big Able Team warrior spotted
Eliade amid a flurry of papers skating toward the ceiling. The exhaust fans hadn't just cleared the waiting
room, they'd been effective throughout the building.
Lyons found it getting difficult to breathe at all, but the
adrenaline rush was clearing the last of the narcotic fog
from his brain. He gave pursuit at once.

"Down, Ironman!" Blancanales roared from behind him.

Used to operating as a team for so long, Lyons went
to ground immediately. He heard the thundering crash
of a shotgun at his side as he skidded palms down along
the thin carpet. A gaping hole appeared in the wall on
the other side of him.

Eliade was less than twenty yards away, only now
disappearing into a cubicle at the end of the narrow
hallway.

Looking back toward the main entrance, Blancanales brought up a mini-Uzi that he carried inside his
briefcase. Brass spilled out of the ejector as he brought
it around in a sweeping arc. The 9 mm parabellum
rounds split the air less than two feet above Lyons.
Chunks of safety glass were knocked from the big windows.

"Go!" Blancanales ordered. Schwarz came through the door a heartbeat later, his machine pistol at the ready.

Lyons didn't hesitate, up and running like an Olympic sprinter. He covered the distance to the office Eliade had disappeared to, grabbed the door frame and swung himself around, the .45 up in his fist before him.

The three men in the room stood behind a mainframe computer, working hurriedly. Eliade had a 9 mm pistol in his fist, overseeing the other two.

"Stop!" Lyons ordered in his cop's voice.

The two men at the computer brought up pistols they'd been holding out of sight.

Lyons whipped back behind the door frame, leaving enough of himself exposed to focus with one eye and shoot. Knowing he was down to five rounds in the .45, he double tapped the two computer operators.

Bullets chipped at the door frame near his fingers. Eliade was still firing as he reached for the computer's keyboard.

Shifting the .45, Lyons fired his last round. The bullet caught Eliade in his right shoulder and spun him away from the computer. Shucking the empty magazine, Lyons fitted another into place as he invaded the room. He pulled the slide back and let it snap the first round into the firing chamber as he closed on Eliade.

The man stared at him dazedly, bleeding copiously from the shoulder wound.

"Ironman." It was Schwarz, just outside the office.

"Clear," Lyons responded. "Come ahead."

Schwarz swung around the corner, covering with the mini-Uzi.

"Check the computer," Lyons said. Shoving his pistol away from Eliade's easy reach, the Able Team warrior knelt and put pressure on the man's wound, stemming the blood flow.

Blancanales appeared in the doorway. "Everything's quiet out here. I counted three guys. Anybody get anything different than that?"

"No," Schwarz said, working the computer keyboard and staring intently at the monitor.

Lyons shook his head. "I need something I can make a compress out of. Guy's going to bleed to death if I don't do something here."

Schwarz went through the desk drawers and turned up a first-aid kit. He rifled the contents and passed Lyons the heaviest gauze bandages.

"Security's on its way," Blancanales said. "So's the fire department and an emergency medical team."

Examining Eliade, Lyons found that the man was already showing signs of traumatic shock, his skin tinged blue and his eyes rolling, unfocused, the pupils dilated. "Get the EMT guys on the radio. Let them know we got a gunshot guy here in bad shape."

Blancanales nodded and stepped out into the hall, where the reception was clearer.

"How's the computer?" Lyons asked.

Schwarz nodded. "The Bear's tapped in now. Whatever they knew, we'll know soon." He joined Lyons on the floor and worked to shut down the blood flow. "You should have just shot the gun out of his hand."

"Right," Lyons replied grimly. "When I learn that little trick, I'll do that very thing next time. Until then, keep that pressure on, Tonto."

CHAPTER NINE

Clad in a combat blacksuit, his features tiger-striped by camouflage cosmetics, gear strapped about his body and the military webbing he wore, Mack Bolan was the most dangerous predator in the jungle. He shuffled behind the cover he'd chosen, listening to the grinding transmissions of the approaching vehicles.

The Indian Ocean ran inland for almost a hundred yards from the coastline, then formed an arrowhead-shaped lake along the foothills of the Drakensberg Mountains. The jungle crowded in around the water, and in several spots the trees overhung the lake.

Despite the moonlight, most of the lake's surface was an unreflecting slate black. At first glance, the *Seahorse Moon* was invisible against the water and the night. Small enough to slip through the channel leading from the sea, the freighter still rode low in the water. From his earlier recon, the Executioner knew the lake bed was on average another thirty feet below the freighter's draw.

When the lights of the first vehicle came over the rise leading down to the lake, Bolan had been in place for almost two hours. After making the drop from the Grumman Goose and saying farewell to Jack Grimaldi, he had located the equipment Price had arranged to be dropped into the area and set up his attack perimeters. He'd finished less than twenty minutes earlier, forty-five minutes after the arrival of the *Seahorse Moon*.

Grimaldi had also brought in the Beretta 93-R pistol, sheathed in Bolan's shoulder leather, and the heavy Israeli Desert Eagle .44, now in a counterterrorist drop holster on his right thigh. He hunkered down behind the group of trees he'd chosen as his initial attack position. Taking his night glasses from the chest pouch, he focused on the line of vehicles managing the steep road, zigzagging down the broken terrain. The trees were less dense there, and he easily spotted the ranged markings he'd set up while planning the attack.

There were more jeeps and trucks than he'd guessed would be on hand. He assumed Geoffrey Masiga was making a show of force, perhaps in response to the attack on Ansell Dewbre and perhaps because of expected American retaliation in response to the murder of General McClendon. Bolan had listened to radio broadcasts off and on while setting up his strike.

Recalculating his estimates, he put Masiga's forces at somewhere near a hundred men in all. As they got out and walked down to the water's edge, the warrior was surprised to see many of them wearing what looked to be fresh white bandages.

Sweeping the night glasses to the deck of the freighter, he watched the loading crew come up from belowdecks and start lowering the pair of powerboats over the side in preparation for the transferral of the munitions.

The doomsday numbers sifted quietly in the Executioner's mind, beginning the deadly countdown. Reaching beside him, he caught the L-shaped handle of the Barrett M82A1 Light Fifty chambered in .50-caliber Browning rounds. The detachable magazine held eleven rounds, and Bolan had taped the mags together in pairs.

Setting up the massive weapon on its bipod, he got into a prone position behind the butt and brought the $10\times$ scope to his eye. The Star-Tron scope took away part of the shadows, but the thousand-yard distance made confirmation of an individual target difficult. The Executioner knew Masiga was on hand somewhere, though, and didn't give up the search. His primary objective was to remove the munitions from the play. Getting Masiga, if possible, would be a bonus.

He settled the cross hairs over the driver of the last vehicle in line. The man leaned against the hood of the Land Rover smoking a cigarette, his rifle slung over his shoulder.

The Executioner stroked the trigger, moving on to his next target before ascertaining the effect of the first round. He fired through the 11-round box in quick succession, hammering men and machines. Every other round was an incendiary, and he shot into gas tanks and exposed jerricans at every opportunity.

After he changed magazines, he took a quick look through the night glasses. Six dead men littered the battlezone, and two trucks were on fire while three jerricans exploded flames and fuel over the nearest Kawalusian tribesmen. The activity aboard the freighter had turned defensive. During his watch over the area, he'd seen the trio of 76 mm guns mounted on the deck.

Using the incendiary rounds had left him open to retaliation. Already heavy machine-gun fire was starting to find the range. Bullets chopped into trees and bushes less than twenty yards from his position. One of the freighter's gun crews fired his weapon and a 76 mm warhead screamed from the deck, arcing from the black velvet sky to smash against a tree trunk thirty feet away.

Bolan took momentary cover as the tree splintered and threw deadly shards of wood toward him. When he came up again, he saw a half dozen bristling wooden lengths shuddering and protruding from the tree he was behind. He pulled the Barrett to him and dropped the sights over the gun crew. There were no shields in place, so the three men working it were open to him.

He fired three times in quick succession, a rolling heartbeat of doom. All three men went down. The incendiary round that took the second gunman in the head flared briefly as it smashed through the man's skull. Then the Executioner went back to work on the rear vehicles of Masiga's caravan.

He was halfway through the fourth clip when he had to abandon the Barrett because his position was about to be overtaken. But he'd accomplished his first objective: any attempt Masiga's people made to evacuate the area in a hurry would be met with defeat. Disabled vehicles blocked the narrow path.

Staying under cover, aware that squads had already been sent into the jungle in search of him, Bolan crossed the broken terrain for a hundred yards to his next position. The cannonfire from the *Seahorse Moon* was falling faster now, tearing great pits in the ground and spraying dirt and foliage in all directions.

He ripped the camou tarp from the Mk 19 Model 3 automatic grenade launcher and checked the rectangular receiver. Beside the launcher, a box contained the 50-round link belt of 40 mm ammunition. Satisfied everything was ready, he glanced back at the freighter, then pulled the remote control from his combat harness.

As he'd expected and planned, the freighter's captain was pulling back from the action, readying for a run out to the open sea. His services had been bought and paid for, not his loyalty. Running afoul of an American blockade was the last thing he wanted to do.

After the freighter had arrived, Bolan had taken precious minutes to don scuba gear and attach explosives below the ship's waterline. He armed the remote control, then pressed the button.

Immediately a dozen concussive waves quivered through the freighter as her hull ripped out and she started taking on water. The gun crews quickly became aware of the situation and abandoned their posts. At the rate of speed the ship was going down, if they didn't get off soon the undertow would pull them down with it.

Finding his ranged markings, Bolan checked the grenade launcher's setting. Looking like a stubby machine gun on a tripod, the Mk 19 was capable of delivering its devastating carnage from 1750 yards out. Masiga's vehicles were hardly more than twelve hundred yards out.

He squeezed the trigger. Despite the sandbags he'd filled with mud from the lake banks and chained to the grenade launcher, the recoil was still tremendous. Five rounds out of six were armor piercing, followed by a CS combo smoker. The AP rounds wrecked havoc on the machines and men, and the smokers made it seem like the damage was even more extensive.

In seconds, even working on selective fire, the Mk 19's ammo box was empty.

Out on the lake, the freighter was listing badly, taking on water so fast there was no chance to save the munitions on board. The stern had already disappeared beneath the lake's surface.

Abandoning his second position, Bolan fell back farther, fading more deeply into the jungle. Explosions sounded behind him, letting him know the advancing wave of Masiga's army had reached the Claymore mines he'd planted. There weren't many, but they didn't know that and it slowed the pursuit.

He jogged, moving quickly. Masiga would set up a net in the area. The Executioner had left the man no choice. Even to retreat, Masiga had to protect his flank from further attacks.

The terrain turned steeper and he went into the high country. A backward glance showed him that eight vehicles were in motion, charging through the brush after him. One of them hit a mine, and the explosion ripped the front axle off, throwing the Land Rover into a tree. But seven made it through. Machine gun fire rattled off the branches over his head as spotlights blazed across him twice, trying to pin him in the light.

He lowered his head and sprinted for all he was worth, his legs pistoning him forward. Going into the play, he'd known escape was going to be chancy.

The lead vehicle was seventy yards out and closing when he reached the Enduro 350 motorcycle he'd hidden in a copse of trees. An M-249 Squad Automatic Weapon with a full C-MAG 100-round twin-drum unit rode in a boot across the handlebars.

Ripping three antipersonnel grenades from his combat harness in quick succession, Bolan threw them at the approaching Land Rovers and jeeps only forty yards away. The sudden eruptions at ground level in front of the vehicles panicked the drivers into thinking they'd hit another mine field. They slowed, giving the Executioner precious seconds to work with.

Getting the motorcycle up, he kicked it to life. The sudden blat of the two-stroke engine carried even over the roar of the Land Rovers and jeeps. Without warning, a jeep hurtled through the brush on his right. The driver fought the wheel, bringing it around to bathe him in the headlights.

The Executioner reacted instantly, grabbing the SAW from the handlebar boot and training it on the jeep as the machine gunner on the rear deck cut loose with his weapon. The 5.56 mm hardball rounds crashed across the headlights, extinguishing them, then shattered through the windshield and killed the driver. The machine gunner followed in short order.

Bolan shoved the SAW back into its boot, then dropped his foot on the gearshift lever. Releasing the clutch, he held on as the rear tire grabbed traction. He aimed his machine upward, dodging boulders, trees and brush while the jeeps crashed through the jungle after him. He ran with his light out, using the full moon and the glare of the headlights hot on his trail. Bullets whipped by him.

The probe had gone well: the munitions were no longer a problem unless Masiga had the time and the expertise to recover the weapons from the lake bed. And the warrior doubted that. The Kawalusian tribesmen didn't have much experience with diving or with modern weapons.

He crested the top of the steep rise with the motorcycle's engine whining. The sea was to his left, barely seen through the thick foliage, then wiped out by the sudden glare of headlights bursting through the branches and bushes.

Dropping his right foot, he managed a tight turn. The rear wheel spun out under him as bullets chopped a ragged line along the ground. Sparks flared from the front wheel and he knew at least a handful of spokes had been severed. To his right, a jeep roared by. Two men with assault rifles sat on the rear deck and tried to bring their weapons to bear while another man in the forward passenger seat struggled to get out of his harness and raise his rifle.

Bolan brought the motorcycle to a halt and grabbed the Desert Eagle. The pistol's butt connected smoothly with his palm and it came up effortlessly. He fired on the point, unleashing three 240-grain hollowpoints.

The bullets caught the jeep's driver in the side of the head as he brought the vehicle around. Out of control, the jeep raced for a tree and came to a sudden stop. Bolan reached for his harness as men stumbled from the wreckage. He yanked a grenade free, pulled the pin and heaved the bomb at the jeep. A short three-count later, the explosive went off, wreathing the machine and two of the men in flames.

He put his foot on the gearshift lever again and roared off as two more jeeps successfully made the sharp ascent. An open field, almost eighty yards across, separated him from an unbroken tree line where he was sure the jeeps couldn't follow. He twisted the accelerator more tightly.

Then the ground ahead of him erupted in a series of blinding explosions. His mind registered the fact that the detonations had to have come from mortars back down the hill. The guns aboard the freighter were out of the play.

He lost the motorcycle a heartbeat later, spilling across the handlebars still thirty yards from his goal. He tucked himself in a parachute roll, bruised his cheek on a rock and managed to push himself to his feet before he lost the impetus.

Working the combat harness by memory and touch, he freed two smoke grenades and pitched them ahead of him after pulling the pins, staggering one in front of the other at a forty-five-degree angle. Gunfire vectored in on him, chewing into the nearby landscape. The grenades went off with sharp pops, and dark clouds uncoiled around him like vicious genies.

Once he was inside the protective aura of the smoke, he changed directions almost ninety degrees, then cut back toward the tree line. The acrid smoke burned his lungs. Black spots danced in front of his eyes, and he worked to keep his breathing shallow.

He felt the brush under his hands before he saw it. Branches whipped at his face as he plunged into the trees. He abraded his arm even through the combat blacksuit when he collided with a rough trunk, but kept himself going forward.

Bullets chased into the trees after him, but they didn't find their target.

The Executioner noted the man ahead of him, taking advantage of the tree with a rifle cradled in his arms. His combat senses working overtime, the warrior threw himself at the other man as the gunner came around, lifting the weapon.

Bolan hit the man high, taking them both to the ground. He covered his adversary's lower face with one hand while his other dug for the Gerber boot knife. The steel slid free of the leather in an almost inaudible whisper.

On top of the man, Bolan looked down, his knife above the guy's Adam's apple. Even in the darkness he knew he was holding a guy with American military dress. Dog tags glinted at the soldier's neck.

"You're American?" Bolan asked, keeping the knife poised. He was acutely aware that Masiga's men were beginning a foot search for him. He had the window. To make good his escape, he had to keep moving.

"Yeah," the guy replied. "And you're Colonel Pollock?"

Pollock was an alias Bolan had used before, when operating in military functions under a weather-tight umbrella from Stony Man Farm. "Yes," he replied.

"They said you could identify yourself," the young American soldier said. "A code name."

"Striker," Bolan replied. It was the one the Farm used for him on most occasions.

"That's the one."

"What are you doing out here?" the warrior asked.

"Exfiltration."

"Me?"

"Yeah. Someone figured you might need some help." The young soldier got to his feet. "Personally I don't see that we were all that necessary, except that we have access to air deployment out of here. That was a hell of a run, sir."

"We?" Bolan asked, hustling the soldier deeper into the brush.

"Yes, sir. Force Recon Team Scorpion from Cape Anansi harbor."

The sounds of Masiga's men invading the jungle grew progressively louder as they got braver.

"You got a radio?" Bolan asked.

"Sure."

"Let's have it." Bolan took it, his mind factoring in the new variables at once. With an American team on hand and Masiga's troops spread out over the jungle, he didn't intend to let the opportunity to strike another blow pass by.

Cape Anansi Harbor, Walukagi
2:02 a.m.

"GREEN LIGHT!" Yakov Katzenelenbogen called out, seeing the signal for himself. His voice galvanized the rest of the team he'd assembled in the past fifteen minutes. Hurling himself forward, he leapt from the open door of the McDonnell Douglas C-17 and began the thirty-thousand-foot fall.

The rest of Phoenix Force followed him, trailed by twenty members of the 82nd Airborne.

Tracking through the cold wind, Katz barely made out the darkened harbor of Cape Anansi. Resistance to U.S. and UN military forces had increased since the death of General McClendon. As a result, two hours earlier the beachhead had been lost, along with twenty-seven men and a medical facility that had been plainly marked.

Price had arranged for the jump from Germany, then briefed the team on the mission they were assigned.

"Let's keep it together, mates," David McCarter called out over the headsets. "You're looking ragged up there." As ex-SAS, the Briton knew what he was talking about. "Manning, swing more to port. Now there's a good lad. Twelve, you're dropping too fast."

Katz turned his attention back to the harbor, his flight suit billowing around him. The altitude froze his oxygen mask to his face in spite of the tropical climate. He glanced at the altimeter on his wrist.

"Okay," McCarter said, "here's where we separate the men from the boys. Make the moves to your separate groups. Now!"

Since the withdrawal of American and UN troops, Masiga's men, and perhaps those of Kwammanga and Nanpetro, had set up fortifications to further resist the return of the forces with the morning. At least three Stinger bases had been set up on different buildings. An F-14 Tomcat had gone down forty minutes earlier while on an observation run. The pilot was thought to be held hostage because the chute had deployed.

Glancing up, Katz saw James and the other three men assigned to his team close ranks. Their target was the observation-and-communications tower that Masiga's troops had set up in the eleven-story hotel almost at the beachfront. The aircraft carrier, *Freedeburg,* had patched into the communications and triangulated it. Conversations over the channel had given them the locations of the three Stinger units that McCarter and the other teams would be taking out. The fifth unit was assigned to the beachfront to assist the arriving SEAL teams with their Omega boats. Once the beach was secured and booby traps—if any—were cleared, more troop deployment would begin via Sea Stallion helicopters and launches.

If everything went according to plan, the UN and U.S. forces would have a beachhead reestablished by morning.

Less than a mile before impact, Katz gave the signal for his team to hit the chutes. Black silk blossomed over his head and his descent slowed, though the ground still came up alarmingly fast. He found the hotel easily enough from the aerial pictures put together by the Intel teams aboard the aircraft carrier.

Features masked by combat cosmetics and wearing black uniforms, the guards atop the hotel didn't see them until it was too late.

Katz hit the roof and rolled. Managing to stay clear of the spilling chute, he unlimbered the H&K MP-5 SD-3 machine pistol from the sling on his shoulder. It came up and whispered death as he stitched two hardmen from shoulder to hip with a line of 9 mm parabellum rounds. One of them vanished over the side of the building, and a thin scream echoed up after him.

James covered the Phoenix Force leader's back as he raced for the access door to the top floor of the hotel. Intel suggested that the communications network was located there. When the three airborne commandos followed them, there was no one left living on the rooftop.

"The satellite dish," Katz instructed, waving off two of the team members.

They went at once, hands already busy taking the tools and explosives they needed to achieve the objective.

The access door opened in front of Katz. The hardman revealed in the rectangle of light was caught flatfooted. Katz's bullets punched the man back inside against the wall. The Israeli shook out the empty clip and inserted a fresh one as he strode over the corpse.

With the assassination of McClendon, the President and the UN Security Council were pulling off the kid gloves. It was going to be a whole new war by morning.

"One down," Manning called over the headset.

"Make it two," Encizo called a moment later.

Katz moved forward. The lights gathered strength, until he was blinking in the corridor. He stripped the oxygen mask from his face.

Four doors down, two hardmen ran out into the hallway, brandishing their AK-47s.

Katz unloaded, never giving them a chance, driving their bodies before him without mercy. He turned the corner, peering into the room as he leveled the H&K MP-5 SD-3.

Five men were still inside, working with the radio gear set up on a folding table. One of them spotted Katz.

The Phoenix Force leader squeezed the trigger, cutting the man down and sweeping the machine pistol across the room's occupants. "Grenade," he told James.

The ex-SEAL nodded and pitched an antipersonnel explosive into the center of the room. It went off a heartbeat later, scattering smoke, noise and bright lights.

When Katz looked back inside the room, no one was left alive. Two men from the rooftop came down and took up their assigned positions at the end of the hall. James and the third man held the opposite end of the corridor.

Keying his headset, Katz said, "The communications network just went down."

"Affirmative," McCarter replied, "and you can scratch the third Stinger site. We got a bonus, too. Bloke here turned all informative on us when we let him live. He knows where the flier is. Short trip from here, if you'll give us leave."

"Stand by," Katz directed, walking into the room filled with smoking ruin and corpses. He gazed out through a shattered window beside a wall studded with shrapnel. The *Freedeburg* was a dark shape way out on

the ocean, but he could barely make out the running
lights of helicopters already in the air waiting for the
strike to be called. "Come in, Four Leader."

"Four Leader here."

"Your situation?"

"Clear. Start the buses."

Katz glanced down at the beach and saw no telltale
muzzle-flashes. Team Four had obviously secured the
area in a hell of a hurry. "*Freedeburg,* do you copy?"

"*Freedeburg* copies." Admiral Myers's voice sounded
harsh and whiskey rough.

"Situation report."

"On your go."

"Go," Katz said softly. Out above the dark water, he
saw the Sea Stallions start their run toward the coastline. "David?"

"Aye, mate."

"You have your go on your rescue."

"Back soon." McCarter clicked out of the loop.

Katz took a final look around the harbor, then left
the room. Somewhere out in the night, he knew a specialty team was attempting to reach Bolan. Once the
Executioner was brought into the fold and given free
rein, the Israeli knew vengeance would descend on the
port city like nothing their enemies had ever seen before. And he was grimly pleased to be a significant part
of it.

Washington, D.C.
6:03 p.m.

"I'VE NEVER DEPOSED an ambassador before," Carl
Lyons said as he threaded his way through the club's
early-evening crowd.

"Deport," Blancanales said patiently. "It's deport. You depose a king. Guy's an ambassador."

"Might have been once," Lyons said agreeably. "But not today." A biker in leather and chains stood in front of him for just a moment, looking as if he might object to Lyons's passage, then reconsidered it and moved off.

"For an ambassador," Schwarz said sarcastically, "the guy shows real taste."

Looking around the downtown strip lounge, Lyons had to agree. Ambassador Linfred Mandan's secretary had reluctantly placed the man in the Tropical Heat club. Everyone else associated with the Walukagian embassy had already been given their walking papers by Able Team and the fleet of Justice marshals Brognola had appointed for the task.

Tropical Heat's theme seemed to be island girls and ranged from golden-haired Barbies with California accents to Polynesian beauties. Mirrors lined all four walls, and the accent was on mahogany and red leather. Clad in discreet casual wear, the security staff cruised through the guests effortlessly.

Lyons was aware of two men who'd picked up the three members of Able Team and were following at a distance. He knew Blancanales and Schwarz had noticed them as well.

Mandan, corpulent and fashionably attired, sat on one of the long red leather couches near the center stage. He was gray haired and fair skinned, and had a bikini-clad woman on either side of him. His arms were draped casually across their bare shoulders, and they acted as if they were hanging on his every word.

On the main stage in front of Mandan, a woman twirled around one of three poles that ran from floor to ceiling. She was dressed in a grass skirt and a lei that only occasionally covered her breasts. The reggae beat hammered out an insistent tune from the huge speakers overhead.

"He's not alone," Blancanales said.

Lyons glanced to his left and saw three men who were Mandan's bodyguards. The secretary had mentioned them earlier. After pulling their records and having Stony Man Farm run them, Lyons had found out all three were ex-East German Stasi who'd faded after the Berlin Wall had fallen. One of them was still wanted by German intelligence for the murder of a British courier.

"Got them," Lyons said. "Fan it out in case this doesn't go down easy."

Blancanales and Schwarz did as he'd said. One of the nightclub's security men went after them, leaving the other one facing Lyons.

"Can I help you?" the security man asked Lyons, meeting him at the three steps that led down into the more highly priced pit area, where the dancers' charms were more easily viewed.

Lyons flashed his Justice ID at the guy. "I'm here to pick someone up."

The guard gave him an easy smile. "Hey, there's only two ways out of here. Surely you can arrange this so there's no muss, no fuss."

"Can't wait," Lyons replied. "There's a plane waiting on the guy now."

"Cut me some slack here. The boss won't like this kind of shit."

Lyons gave the man a hard-edged cop stare. "If you want, I can arrange to take you and your boss out, too."

The guard held up his hands and stepped away. "I just don't want any trouble. We run a clean place here."

"Yeah," Lyons said dryly. "I could tell that from the way your flower girl has been passing out cocaine along with roses and teddy bears. Maybe I can arrange to call a friend at DCPD and get you a whole little raid going inside of five minutes. Of course, there's going to be a lot of pissed off Congressmen in the morning when they discover some of their aides have made splashes in the media."

"Right." The guard stepped back and gave his team a signal, drawing them away from Able Team.

His action instantly alerted Mandan's trio of watchdogs, who shrugged out of the attentions of the women they were with and stood.

Lyons continued down the steps, hit the red-carpeted floor and captured the wrist of the woman who coyly reached for him.

"Looking for a good time, handsome?" the scantily dressed woman asked.

"No, thanks," Lyons assured her. "I'm driving." He left her standing there looking confused.

Mandan looked up from the sunken couch. The tables ringing the area behind him held a dozen men who yelled at Lyons to get out of the way because he was blocking their view. Onstage, the grass skirt and lei had been discarded.

"Who are you?" Mandan asked.

"Justice marshal." Lyons gave the ID another workout.

"And you're looking for me?"

"Yep. You're being deported. Right now."

The watchdogs gathered closer, watching with bright interest.

"That's ridiculous," Mandan said. The two women on either side of him moved away, sensing the tension in the air.

"Why?" The speaker was Rudolpho Schierber, the man wanted by German military intelligence. He was tall and dark haired, his ice-blue eyes narrow and suspicious.

"The President has elected to no longer recognize Spraggue's government in Walukagi. Now the United States government views you and the people of your embassy as undesirables requiring immediate deportation."

"You can't do that," Mandan said.

"It's done, buddy. Now, are you walking out of here, or do you want me to roll you?"

"I demand to talk to the Secretary of State."

The front door of the club opened suddenly as federal marshals crowded through. As planned, select media cameramen came, too. When the cameras started shooting, the Tropical Heat clientele faded as fast as a pawnbroker's smile, and the dancers scrambled for what little clothing they'd been wearing.

"He sent you a goodbye note," Lyons said, handing over the official letter from the State Department.

Mandan took it slowly, read it, crumpled it, then dropped it to the floor. "I see." Without another word he gathered his coat and headed for the club's main entrance, covering his face with his hat so the photographers would have a harder time shooting him.

Schierber and his two men tried to follow.

"Not you, friend," Lyons said, stepping in front of the ex-Stasi agent. "You're under arrest."

"For what?"

"Extradition to Germany." Lyons knew that Brognola first intended to question the man at the Farm. As a hired gun, Schierber was too expensive and too savvy to hire on as an embassy guard for a failing African nation like Walukagi unless there was more being offered than what was on the surface. The head Fed intended to find out what it was.

Schierber shrugged as if to go along, then exploded into action. The big man threw himself at Lyons as he dragged a .45 from shoulder leather.

Expecting some type of physical response, Lyons was braced for the attack, but there'd been no way to prepare for the sheer ferocity the German exhibited. While grabbing the man's gun wrist, the Able Team leader also had to put a hand against the man's forehead and prevent the guy's teeth from burying in his neck.

They went down in a tangle of arms and legs. Lyons slammed Schierber's wrist against the edge of a low coffee table. The automatic slid out of the German's fingers and skidded across the floor toward two half-naked women fleeing from it.

Then Lyons felt the hot, numbing shock of Schierber's teeth digging into his trapezius muscle on his left side. Blood flowed under his shirt. Pulling away, he brought his other elbow up and across in a sharp blow, breaking Schierber's nose.

Stunned, the German released his hold.

With a roar of rage, Lyons surged to his feet, dragging Schierber with him. The German tried to fork him in the eyes with his fingers, but Lyons knocked the hand out of the way, turning the block into a lightning-quick jab that caught his opponent on his already-broken nose, and followed with a roundhouse that turned Schierber's head sideways.

Staggered, the German flailed in an attempt to defend himself. He landed two ineffectual blows to Lyons's upper body. Working methodically, the Able Team warrior chopped at the big man, unleashing crosses, uppercuts and jabs that drove his opponent back across the floor. A final uppercut knocked Schierber back against the wet bar servicing the pit area of the lounge.

While the man was off balance, Lyons seized the lapels of his jacket, yanked him off his feet and onto the bar top and dragged him along the smooth surface. Glasses and bottles tumbled to the floor. Planting himself, Lyons shoved Schierber the last few feet, slamming the man's head against the wall hard enough to knock the clock from above.

Unconscious, Schierber fell from the bar and thudded into the floor.

His breathing ragged from the effort of the fight, Lyons lifted his shirt and examined the bite wound. The teeth were clearly marked in the incisions, but everything seemed to be in place.

No one else in the Tropical Heat moved.

Blancanales came over with a pair of handcuffs and started to bind the German's wrists. "I guess we were both wrong," he said with a wry grin. "You weren't here to depose or deport. Man, I'd classify this as a case of *dispose.*"

"Yeah, well, let's get him out of here and checked over," Lyons said. "I want to know if I have to get rabies vaccinations." He and Blancanales grabbed Schierber's jacket and started to drag him out of the club.

CHAPTER TEN

Stony Man Farm, Virginia

"There's a new day dawning for the innocents in Walukagi."

In the computer lab at Stony Man Farm, Hal Brognola watched the special newscast with bright interest. Barbara Price was at his side, and Aaron Kurtzman had taken a breather at the horseshoe-shaped console.

The President looked grave as he stood in back of the microphone-festooned podium. The word the head Fed had received was that the room the broadcast was coming from had been cleared of reporters. The Man was there to make a statement only.

"As I am speaking to you," the President continued, "steps are being taken to reinforce American military intervention in Walukagi. We've all seen the tragic death of General McClendon. I know, as you do, that his murder was only the latest in a string of atrocities in that country."

To the left of the President, a window opened up and started showing silent footage of the attacks on American and UN soldiers since the beginning of the peace effort. The silence made the carnage even more appalling to Brognola. Soldiers died in machine-gun fire and explosions as the Walukagian refugees ran away in terror. When the smoke cleared, the grim spectacle of the recon team hanging from trees was played again. Even though Brognola knew the scenes had to be hard on the families, the nation needed to be reminded of what the stakes were.

"Only a few minutes ago," the President said, "Great Britain entered into an agreement with Henry Kalimuzo regarding the future of Walukagi. As the newly recognized ambassador of his country, Kalimuzo has been petitioning for Walukagi's return to Great Britain as a protectorate, as it was until 1980." Looking at the cameras, the Man paused. "Great Britain has accepted that petition and is fielding a military complement to help Kalimuzo take control of Walukagi. I have been asked by the British prime minister to intercede on Britain's behalf, adding to the help asked for by Ambassador Kalimuzo."

"He's not holding anything back," Price said.

"At this point," Brognola stated, "he can't afford to."

"Still," Kurtzman replied, "there's going to be a lot of angry people in Congress. It was one thing to be part of a peacekeeping mission in southern Africa, but another to go in as a deputized force. The lobbying groups representing German trade interests could go either way on this thing. They were developing some potential business relationships with Spraggue and his government."

"They were going to be dealing with ashes," Brognola said. "And they're fools if they thought there was any other way for this thing to end with Spraggue and his people in control. There's more going on in that country than a handful of warlords vying for control of the government. When we find who's behind Masiga, we'll know what the stakes really are."

The phone rang and Price answered it. When she was finished, she turned to Brognola. "Kalimuzo and Kissinger just made their flight out of Dulles."

Brognola nodded. It had been his decision to send the weaponsmith and a team of Stony Man blacksuits back to Walukagi. There was no way to restructure the political and military situation in the country without Kalimuzo at its head. And once the deal with Great Britain had been consummated, Kalimuzo had refused to stay any longer. Kissinger and the blacksuits had been sent as insurance on the Rockwell B-1 military flight capable of Mach 2 speeds. They'd be arriving at Walukagi in less than ten hours.

On-screen, the President continued. "It is my belief that the American people want to see justice served in that country, and that the sacrifices we've made over there will mean something. You have my word that that will be the case."

The screen cleared, returning the network back to the anchors.

"Okay," Brognola said. "The Man just went to the table and raised the ante. Now that the final dealing's going down, we'd better make good on that royal flush he just promised."

The Walukagian Coastline
2:07 a.m.

SPLITTING FORCE RECON Scorpion into two groups, Mack Bolan created a pincer trap. With the uncertainty of the darkness and the broken terrain, he led his group deeper into the jungle, pursued by at least thirty of Masiga's hardmen.

Already familiar with the topography of the surrounding coastal territory, the warrior chose a spot over the crest of the nearest mountain for the ambush. Force Recon Scorpion consisted of fifteen battle-hardened Marines. Taking four of them, he'd put up a brief gunfight, then broken and run, letting the hardmen know he was no longer alone, but that the added firepower obviously wasn't going to be enough to save them.

At first Masiga's men had milled in confusion, then, scenting blood, they came forward. Abandoned vehicles were parked behind them because they hadn't been able to get them through the tree line. Mortar fire still impacted against the ground ahead of Bolan and his group, but it was far enough away that it wasn't threatening. They were moving too close to the ragged line of hardmen for the gunners at the pickup point to fire indiscriminately.

Running at half speed, his combat senses at full alert, Bolan vaulted over a fallen tree and scrambled up the hillside. Taking cover behind a tree, he unlimbered the SAW and cut loose.

Two of the enemy gunners went down and he knew they wouldn't be getting back up. The rest went to ground and returned fire. Splinters flew from the tree trunk near Bolan's face. After making sure his group was still moving forward, he keyed the radio. "Striker to Scorpion Leader."

"Go, Striker. You have Scorpion Leader."

"Your location?"

"Solid. On your go."

Using hand signals, Bolan alerted the rest of his team. They fell into the positions where he waved them. The ragged line of hardmen was sixty yards away and closing. He reloaded the SAW with his last C-MAG 100-

round twin drum. Settling into his cover, the enemy now forty yards distant and slowed by the dense foliage, the Executioner keyed the radio and said, "Now."

Blistering fire opened up on both sides of the enemy and cut down the numbers immediately.

Working the SAW on 3-round burst, the Executioner picked his targets with extreme prejudice. Less than fifteen seconds later he called a halt to the gun play. As the smoke lifted, he was sure not one of the thirty hardmen was going to make it off the mountain alive.

There was no return fire.

Force Recon Scorpion appeared from out of the jungle and passed through the carnage they'd wrought.

Captain Vernon Hawkins, his face darkened by cosmetics and showing age beyond his years, jogged up to Bolan. "That's the lot of them."

"Our people?" Bolan asked.

"Two wounded, but they're still mobile on their own."

The warrior took his night glasses from his chest pouch and scanned through the trees. The bulk of Masiga's hardmen were still at the shoreline. A few of the men were attempting to venture into the lake.

"Only be a minute or so before they realize they can't raise anybody up here," Hawkins observed. "Then they'll start up with the mortars again."

"Yeah." Bolan put the night glasses away. "Is that helicopter you've got standing by armed?"

"Door gun, 20 mm cannon. Strictly a hit-and-git setup."

"What's his code name?" Bolan asked.

"Raven."

"Get him on-line for me."

"Done." Hawkins handed the radio to Bolan. "He has your code name. Says he knows you."

"Raven," Bolan said, "this is Striker."

"Good to hear from you, buddy," Jack Grimaldi replied. "Didn't expect it so soon."

Bolan grinned. "That makes two of us. What's your location?"

"Coming in on the rendezvous beacon Force Recon Scorpion has set off."

"Affirmative. I hear you have a 20 mm cannon aboard."

"Oh, yeah."

"Can you hit the broad side of a barn with it?" Bolan asked.

"Turn it edge-on," Grimaldi promised, "and I'll still nail it ten times out of ten."

"On your way over, drop Masiga a greeting."

"Roger."

Hawkins pointed as he and Bolan headed up the mountain. "There he is."

Peering intently, the warrior barely made out the running lights of the helicopter, recognizing it only a moment later as a CH-53E Super Sea Stallion as it sped in from the ocean. The mortar attack started again as the force reached the crest of the mountain. The explosions made a sporadic chain of destruction as they tracked through the jungle toward the Americans.

When the Sea Stallion opened up, it caught Masiga's men from their blind side. The concussive wave scattered vehicles and men. Before it could clear the target zone, tracers lit up the night with bright orange claws that faded without touching their prey.

The team's medic finished tending the wounded as the helicopter hovered briefly overhead, then dropped into the clearing at the top of the mountain. The rotor-wash slammed into Bolan as he jogged for the aircraft.

Around them, mortar fire started to rain from the sky, slowly at first, then gaining in intensity and accuracy. A tree was chopped in two by one mortar round, and thudded against the tail section of the Sea Stallion. Hawkins yelled at the line of men loading into the chopper, urging them to move faster. Once they were aboard, he climbed in after them.

Bolan swung into the copilot's seat across from Grimaldi. Before he had time to belt himself in, the Stony Man pilot kicked the rotor motors into high and it felt as if the helicopter jumped from the mountain-top.

Through the window, Bolan saw the tracers speed toward the helicopter, but they were either out of range or the gunners hadn't zeroed in on their target.

"I didn't expect you back so soon," Bolan said.

"Me neither," Grimaldi confided. The Indian Ocean was a hard, black slate surface beneath them. "Orders came through channels to field an exfiltration team for you and I cut myself in for the flying. Personally I didn't know if we were going to find you, or just a battleground where you'd been."

"Masiga and his people were late." Bolan glanced at his friend. "What orders?"

Grimaldi passed across a packet of papers. "Colonel Rance Pollock has been pulled back into active duty." He looked at Bolan and smiled. "You're being put in charge of the Walukagian theater, guy. How do you like being drafted?"

"I've always been a volunteer." Bolan split the seal and opened the classified documents. An overview of his mission was on the first page of the stack of papers. He scanned it quickly. "The British are involved?"

"Yeah." Grimaldi nodded. "The Prez came on the tube and said Great Britain is taking Walukagi back as a protectorate with Kalimuzo at its head. Whoever's hiding behind Masiga is going to have to come out of the woodwork soon."

Bolan started flipping through the documents, absorbing the tactical information with ease. Most of it was pretty much as he'd expected from what he'd managed to piece together.

Hawkins came forward and spoke to Grimaldi. "I got a guy back here who's going to need to see a doctor PDQ. Took a couple through the stomach and I don't want to chance gangrene. Instead of returning to the *Freedeburg,* the admiral says we should drop into Cape Anansi. The main medical team is already ashore setting up facilities." He glanced at Bolan. "If that's okay with you, sir."

"Yeah, it is," Bolan replied.

"I thought the medical teams were lifted earlier," Grimaldi said, "when Masiga's men put on the rout after McClendon was murdered."

"They were," Hawkins agreed. "Seems a special unit from Germany just put together a raid that reestablished the beachhead a few minutes ago."

"A German unit?" Bolan asked.

"No, sir." Hawkins shook his head. "They made the jump from Germany, but they're headed up by a guy named Katz. You know the guy?"

"Yeah."

Hawkins glanced at Grimaldi. "Interesting as hell, if you don't mind my saying so, sir. First off, the admiral gets a code red to pick you up and we just happen to have a pilot no one's heard of, who seems to know exactly where you are, and that the Pentagon tells us we have to use. Next, a special forces raid comes up on Cape Anansi when no one I know has even mentioned such a maneuver, and it's led by a guy who goes in and gets the job done, but I've never heard of him, either. But you know him."

"What's your point?" Bolan asked.

The captain grinned. "Just wanted to mention it so I wouldn't dwell on it. But it looks like this holding action we've been on since we've been here has just run its course."

"I'd say that's a fair assessment," the Executioner replied.

"Uh-huh. Well, it's good to know." Hawkins touched his fingers to his forehead in a brief salute and retreated to the back of the helicopter.

"Guy's going to talk when he gets back," Grimaldi warned.

"Let him," Bolan said, going through the latest aerial photographs using the penlight from his pocket. "It'll build some morale."

"Phoenix is here, too," Grimaldi said laconically. "Maybe we should just send a note to Masiga and whoever's backing him, let them know they might as well give up now."

"It should be that easy," Bolan said. "But whoever's pulling the strings on this operation has invested heavily. They're not going to go away without a fight. And that's exactly what they're going to get."

Cape Town, South Africa
2:27 a.m.

WILHELMUS KAMER sat on the plush couch facing the television in the den of his house. The blinds were pulled over the bulletproof glass, shutting out the night. He worked the remote control, channel surfing through the news stations. The U.S. President's message was being replayed during every news break.

Feeling the anger and tension welling up inside him, Kamer turned to Sonnet Quaid, who was seated behind him at her desk. "The fucking British," he said in disbelief.

"Yes," the woman replied.

Jakob Vanscoyoc stood in front of the bookcase, a collected works of William Shakespeare in his hand. He looked as imperturbable as ever.

"Why?" Kamer demanded. "The cost to the British is going to be expensive."

"Only if the engagement is a prolonged one," Quaid replied, punching the keys." If they stay in-country less than a month, according to the agreement Kalimuzo made with the British prime minister, Great Britain will actually realize money on the arrangement."

"How?"

"Long-standing trade agreements after the fact," Quaid answered. "I hacked my way into the English international computer system, cross-referencing with files I can get from MI-6, and verified that."

"But that's based on Great Britain's ability not only to acquire a provisional government in Walukagi, but to hold on to it, as well. How the hell could the prime minister package that to the House of Commons?"

Quaid looked at him. "Because, as I just discovered while thumbing through the national secrets of the U.S.A., the President gave the British a blank check and agreed to cover any shortfall they might have on the recovery of the debt.''

''The American Congress agreed?''

''Apparently.''

Kamer looked at the replay of the President's speech. ''By agreeing to help the British, the Americans have removed themselves from the possible accusation of self-serving interests. And maybe from a lot of profits, as well.''

''Walukagi's still going to need an enormous amount of development capital,'' Quaid said. ''America has the deepest moneybags. They'll still buy into businesses and government in Walukagi. And they'll have British cooperation even if they don't have their blessings.''

''Congress agreed to underwrite British involvement?'' Kamer asked.

''By almost ninety percent,'' Quaid replied.

''Their confidence is astounding,'' Kamer said.

Vanscoyoc looked up from his book and grinned without humor. ''At the moment, the Americans do have the winningest military around. There is a certain amount of bankable collateral inherent in that.''

Kamer watched the television with interest. ''Then let's see how bankable they think it is. All they've managed to do with this strategy is delay defeat. With the British so deeply involved, the virus can run rampant through most of Europe, as well.'' His mind was working now, seeing the path to victory despite the unexpected turn. Crossing the room, he stopped at the glass-covered topographical map of Walukagi. It had been rendered in sepia overtones, playing out the imperial designs he had. The Mpunga River crawled like a caterpillar through the jungle, then spilled out into the Indian Ocean at the heart of Cape Anansi.

"The Walukagian embassy has been emptied, too," Quaid said.

"By whose order?" Kamer was only mildly interested.

"The President."

"I'd say he's pulling out all the stops," Vanscoyoc commented.

"How the hell is he going to stop a plague?" Kamer asked. "For all the United States' military might, how are they going to defend against something that can eat them from the inside out?"

"You're going ahead with the virus?" Quaid asked.

Kamer looked at her, noticing that her features seemed tighter. "Yes. They've given me no choice."

"I don't think you wanted one."

"No, not really. Sooner or later, the U.S. would have been a problem. I'm glad to deal with them early on. The earlier they are brought to their knees, the earlier I can get on with my plans for that country."

"Then I want to be the first on the list of inoculations."

"I'll hold your hand," Vanscoyoc said, "because I'm next."

Kamer smiled thinly, then looked at Quaid. "There's a gathering of American blacks in Washington, D.C., scheduled for first thing in the morning. Do you know where they'll be headquartered?"

Quaid used the trackball on the laptop computer to click hurriedly through the menus. "The Samuelson Hotel. It's in Georgetown."

"And most of them will be there by tonight?"

"Yes. I tracked them down through the FBI. With everything that's been going on concerning Walukagi, FBI orders were cut to watch black organizations for possible trouble—both aimed at those groups as well as coming out of them." Quaid smiled. "I also got access to the travel agent who's been booking the flights and motel rooms for the group. From the list, there's going to be a cornucopia of writers, businessmen, actors and singers on hand."

"What are they going to be there for?" Vanscoyoc asked.

"To show support for the President's decision to aid the British," Kamer answered. "Get in touch with Pearrow in Norfolk and have him activate that chapter of Satan's Blitz that we've subsidized. Arrange a little greeting for them. We'll see how much support they want to show after they've been shot at."

"Bikers?" Vanscoyoc asked.

Kamer nodded. "They're more organized for violence than that Aryan group. Most of them even have German blood."

"Pedigreed," the Dutchman said.

Kamer eyed the man, knowing Vanscoyoc's very nature sometimes pushed him to the edge of insubordination. "If you like."

"You're thinking of invading the hotel?" Quaid asked.

"Yes."

A small smile twisted her beautiful lips, and Kamer knew her bloodthirsty nature was riding high in her. "At ten o'clock," she said, "these people are meeting in a jazz club near the hotel called the Bayou Blossom."

"All of them will be there?" Kamer asked.

"The main dining room has been reserved. It seats almost a hundred people. The press will be alerted."

Kamer thought that over. The Satan's Blitz bikers weren't afraid of notoriety. To get within the inner circle, a chapter member had to kill a member of a cop's family. "Then that's what we'll do. Will Kalimuzo be with them?"

"No. According to my Intel, Kalimuzo left Washington within the last hour."

"He's coming back to Walukagi?"

She nodded.

Kamer smiled and shook his head. "The fool. What can he possibly hope to do here?"

"It would make a nice execution," Vanscoyoc noted.

"Yes," Kamer agreed. "When is the esteemed ambassador due back?"

"ETA is twelve noon," Quaid answered. "Our time."

"I'll arrange a meeting," the Dutchman said.

"Fine," Kamer stated. "But you'll do that after you've visited the Cape Anansi water supply stations."

"How portable is this virus?" Vanscoyoc asked, putting the book away.

"The amount you'll be putting in the two supply stations is in powder form. Two ten-pound bags. Enough to contaminate the water supply on hand." Kamer shrugged. "If necessary, we'll find another way to get the virus into the water systems. But I don't think it'll be necessary."

"It's inert in powder form?"

"Yes."

"There's still a lot of people in Cape Anansi who're using the river for their water."

"Doesn't matter," Kamer stated. "The American medical teams are using the water lines for their needs. The sterilizing agents they use won't touch Maaloe's virus." He looked back at the map. "Once we get it into the water system, that whole city will be contaminated in hours at its present usage level. Now or later, those soldiers will fall. And only I can save them." He paused. "If the price is right."

Cape Anansi, Walukagi
3:11 a.m.

EMERGING FROM THE SHADOWS before the sentry could move, David McCarter thrust the barrel of his Browning under the man's chin, and said, "Don't lose your head, mate."

"No," the man agreed, raising his arms.

With deft movements, McCarter quickly frisked his man, removing the AK-47 assault rifle, a Smith & Wesson 9 mm pistol, and two knives. He found a plastic bag of human ears in the man's shirt pocket.

Hardened by his years with the SAS and the atrocities he'd seen during service, followed by his years with Phoenix Force, McCarter maintained his calm. He tossed the bag deeper into the alley. "Hands down," he ordered his prisoner. "Act naturally."

Considering the man had a gun shoved into the back of his neck, the Briton figured the guy was doing a fair facsimile of natural. He tapped the transmit button on his headset. "Phoenix Two to Phoenix One."

"Go," Katz radioed back.

"I've got my bird in the bag."

"Affirmative."

McCarter glanced at his watch. Around him, Cape Anansi was still reeling from its latest invasion. There were scattered fires around the city, set by Masiga's retreating forces to thin the American and UN troops moving into the downtown sector again. Military resistance had been short-lived and shallow once the Stinger bases were knocked out.

"Phoenix Three," Manning said, coming onto the com-loop. "We're clear here."

"Acknowledged, Three," Katz replied. "Five?"

"Five has the high ground," Calvin James said. "Two, you're covered."

"Acknowledged," McCarter said. Unable to resist looking, he scanned the two-story structure at the end of the alley. James was on top of it, peering through the night scope of a Beretta M-21 sniping rifle, but the Briton couldn't spot him.

"One, this is Four," Rafael Encizo said quietly. "We're up."

"Two copies," McCarter said. He moved his prisoner forward slightly, taking up a new position in front of the broken plate-glass windows of a farm-tool company.

The man was stiff as he stared out at a Land Rover making its way up the deserted street. The U.S. and UN forces had set up roadblocks across the main thoroughfares, cutting down on traffic.

"Wave to them," McCarter urged his captive. "Make nice. After all, they're bringing money."

The man waved woodenly.

"Put some enthusiasm in it," McCarter growled, "or I'll shoot you and wave your bloody arm myself."

Inspired, the man waved.

The Land Rover's headlights played across him for an instant as it slowed and pulled in to the curb. Four black men were inside, all wearing hard looks that had been stamped onto them through a life of violence.

McCarter pushed his prisoner forward, dropping the Browning so it was out of sight.

"Stay left, Two," James said softly over the radio. "Don't foul my shot."

Making no reply, McCarter stopped his man just a few feet from the side of the Land Rover.

"Who is this man?" the guy on the passenger side demanded.

"Guy in the back has a sawed-off shotgun, Two," Manning said in his ear. He was set up across the street.

"I'm helping with the collection," McCarter stated affably.

"Who is he?" the man in the passenger seat demanded again. A briefcase sat in his lap across his knees. The driver kept watch on the street.

Katz had paid attention to some of the Intel that had been gathered in the past half hour, choosing to make two strikes immediately. This one was against Masiga's money people, who were managing a drop back inside the country.

McCarter's prisoner shrugged helplessly, and said, "I don't know."

Instantly the man in the rear seat brought up the sawed-off shotgun and pointed it at McCarter. Tires screeched out on the street, but the Briton knew it wasn't from the Land Rover.

Going to ground, McCarter heard the load of buckshot split the air over his head. His prisoner caught some of it and went spinning into the garbage-strewn gutter.

Scrambling on knees and elbows, McCarter raised the Browning as the man in the rear seat pumped his weapon and aimed again. Then a crimson dot dropped over his left cheek a heartbeat before his head was slammed backward. The shotgun dropped from nerveless fingers. An instant later the sound of James's shot reached McCarter's ears.

The Briton threw himself into a roll as bullets smacked into the pavement where he'd been. He came up on his knees as the Land Rover sped away from the curb. Throwing his arm out in front of him, McCarter fired the Browning rapidly.

The 9 mm rounds took out the back tires, then the heavy pickup truck Encizo had liberated for the occasion swerved into a collision course with the Land Rover from the side.

The immense weight of the pickup, already moving at a considerable rate of speed, knocked the Land Rover sideways, pinning it up against a lamp post. Katz spilled out of the passenger door, an Uzi in his fist. When a gunman shoved himself out of the rear seat holding an assault rifle, the Israeli burned him down with a short burst.

McCarter sprinted forward, caught the passenger-side door and showed the guy the Browning. "I wouldn't," he advised as the man reached for a weapon sheathed in shoulder leather. "You're a day late and a pound note short."

"Who are you with?" the man demanded. "Kwammanga? Nanpetro?"

"Give me the briefcase or die," McCarter replied.

Katz took up position on the driver's side of the Land Rover, and the pickup pulled away from the wrecked vehicle.

"You're a dead man," the guy in the passenger seat promised. "When King Masiga finds out about this, he will show you no mercy."

"You tell your King Masiga that no mercy's going to be shown toward him," McCarter said as he took the briefcase. Carrying it to the front of the Land Rover, he opened the locks with a pick and checked the contents. Stacks of money rested neatly inside. As he closed it, he looked at Katz. "It's all here."

"Let's go," the Israeli said gruffly.

McCarter clambered into the rear of the pickup, his Browning never wavering from the two survivors in the Land Rover.

"Okay, Three and Five," Katz transmitted, "get clear."

Both the remaining Phoenix Force members cleared the channel. Five minutes later Encizo pulled the pickup in beside a low-slung French sedan and the team made the transfer, only waiting two more minutes for Encizo and James to join them.

"Think they bought us as a rival interest?" the lanky ex-SEAL asked as he settled in the rear seat.

Katz nodded. "By morning, Masiga should know what happened. When we make the next hit against Nanpetro, incriminating Kwammanga's people, all three warlords will be confused. Since the arrival of the U.S. and UN forces, they've had the luxury of a common enemy. Tonight we're going to take that away."

McCarter silently agreed as he looked out over the war-torn and darkened city. Divide and conquer was one of the oldest strategies in the book. "The idea of three bandit armies lying fallow when they could be attacking one another just didn't sit well at all," he said with a cocky grin. "But this—this is what I call being productive."

CHAPTER ELEVEN

Cape Anansi Port, Walukagi
4:23 a.m.

Admiral Nathan Myers was a rugged man in his late fifties. Stocky and short-legged, with gray hair and enough charismatic presence to fill a room, he ran his ship with an unflinching grip. He smoked his pipe in tight-lipped silence as he watched the Stony Man warriors put the operation together in the Combat Information Center in the bowels of the aircraft carrier.

Mack Bolan had taken an instant liking to the grizzled naval officer. After providing them room and equipment, the admiral had made himself scarce until he was needed.

The CIC was filled with computers, sensors, radar and sonar displays and fire-control boards. Maps were spread across the huge conference table in the center of the room, and two plastic dry-erase boards stood nearby.

Bolan surveyed the maps, going over the mental list he'd prepared. The aircraft carrier was only ten kilometers from the coast of Cape Anansi, supported by ten escort ships. A complement of attack helicopters and aircraft stood by, only minutes from any skirmish that might break out. Four of them were V-22 Ospreys equipped for antisubmarine warfare, although there was little chance that Masiga or one of the other warlords had the ability to strike from underwater.

"This ship," the admiral said, "is a floating fortress. Nothing is going to touch us if I don't want us touched."

Bolan nodded as he surveyed the half dozen monitors hooked up by satellite link to video feeds around Cape Anansi. "I'm going to hold you to that, sir."

"You do that, son." Myers struck a match and relit his pipe. "You've got your beachhead reestablished and medical services up and running. Our patrol boats, and UN boats working under our aegis, control the harbor. You've got a full company of MAF over there. I'd say our presence is pretty well felt right now."

"I know," Bolan replied. "But it takes more than a heavy hand to win over a country." The warrior had learned that back in Vietnam. "Masiga, Kwammanga and Nampetro have to be nullified before we can attempt any kind of reconstruction in Walukagi." He glanced at his watch. "Kalimuzo will be here in less than eight hours."

"We'll get it done, Colonel," the admiral said.

"Still," the Executioner said, "that's a lot of jungle out there." He studied the view provided by the bank of cameras along the western edge of the city. In the moonlight, the jungle looked impenetrable and unforgiving. He knew it could be both. "Any of those groups could hole up out there for years."

"The first of the tanks are reaching shore," Gary Manning said.

Bolan checked the monitors set up over the port and watched as the LCU, the Landing Craft Utility, powered up to within twenty feet of the beachhead. Four M-60 A-3 battle tanks jerked forward, rolling down the open gate into the ocean. The waterline crested just below the top of the treads and they drove into the port easily. Beyond them, a helicopter was taking off from the repaired landing field. Although still not set up for any aircraft other than helicopters or planes with vertical takeoff and landing capabilities, cargo was being unshipped regularly.

"Where are the other four tanks?" Bolan asked.

"Right behind them," Manning said. He wore a radio headset and scanned the yellow legal pad he held. "The six M-2 Bradleys are on their way, too. We're about twelve minutes ahead of schedule."

With Grimaldi overseeing the flybys from the aircraft carrier and from the landing field inside Cape Anansi, the U.S. forces controlled the land, sea and air.

"Got another report here from one of the recon groups inside the city," Calvin James said. "Apparently there was another dustup between Masiga's men and one of Nanpetro's groups."

"Casualties?" Yakov Katzenelenbogen asked from the other side of the conference table. Before him, on specially sectioned squares of Cape Anansi topography, were red *X*'s denoting sniper activity that still plagued the U.S. troops. As near as he and Bolan could figure, the attacks were from floating groups of Masiga's men.

"No civilians," James answered, "but we had two soldiers wounded who tried to contain the situation. Fourteen prisoners were taken."

"If this keeps up," the admiral said, "we're going to have to assign a work group to build a brig to handle the overflow we can't hold in the buildings we've commandeered."

"Striker," David McCarter called, "you and Katz have an incoming message."

Bolan left the table and crossed the CIC to the small ready room off to the side. Katz joined him, then pulled the door shut. Seated in front of the computer system that handled the scrambled messages coming in from Stony Man Farm, the Executioner entered his private code.

The monitor cleared instantly, revealing the faces of Brognola, Price and Kurtzman.

"How are things there?" the big Fed asked.

"We're holding our own," Bolan replied. "But that's not the objective we want to be working on here."

"I know," Brognola said. "So far we haven't been able to penetrate the jungle to find Masiga's strongbase. But Barb's come up with something that might work."

Price looked into the camera. "We've got a satellite with Global Positioning capabilities that will be able to monitor your area within the next three hours. When Kissinger arrives with Kalimuzo, he's carrying four microprocessors that Aaron's designed. These microprocessors are very small, with self-contained batteries that will last seventy-two hours. After that it goes inert. You know who Masiga's people are among your prisoners?"

"Yes," Katz replied.

"These microprocessors are small enough to be inserted into the human body with a large needle," Price continued. "The target areas should be a large muscle group, preferably the thigh or hip, and entry should be through an existing wound so your prisoners won't get suspicious, and so the microprocessor can't be felt through the skin. Once they're in and activated, stage a jailbreak and see that these people are released. Some of them should head back to Masiga's village. You've got access to three AWACS aircraft that shouldn't have trouble tracking the signal put out by the microprocessors."

Bolan looked up at Katz. "It'll play."

The Israeli nodded. "It's worth the effort."

"We'll set it up," Bolan said.

"The hardest part," Price said, "will be finding someone wounded like that who can still navigate."

Suddenly the bottom of the monitor flared an angry red. "Hold on," Bolan said, leaning forward and moving the trackball, maneuvering the arrow cursor for the icon that opened the line to the CIC.

The transmission from Stony Man was reduced to a small window in the lower right corner. The main screen was filled with a street scene from Cape Anansi's downtown area. Two U.S. Marines were on the sidewalk, pools of blood around their bodies.

Slipping the headset on, Bolan said, "What am I looking at?"

"The latest pair of victims from the bloody sniper teams spread throughout the city," McCarter growled.

Three men in fatigues rushed out of cover and grabbed the wounded Marines by their clothing, then started to drag them to safety. Bullets pocked the sidewalks, and one of the wounded men was hit once more in the leg.

"We need to shift focus," McCarter said. "Move from the aggressive-defensive mode we've been in since retaking the city and move into an aggressive-offensive one."

"Agreed," Bolan said. "What would you suggest?"

On-screen a military Hummer screeched to a stop beside the attack zone and two men got out, scrambling for position.

"With all the automation you have aboard this ship," the Briton said, "I was thinking Manning, James and myself were free enough to see if that pattern Katz has turned up for the sniper vantage points is going to pan out."

"Get it done," Bolan said. "But stay active on our special frequency. If there's anything we can do from here, let us know." Although he knew strategy was everything in a battle, and the work aboard the *Freedeburg* had to be done, the warrior was ready for action himself.

McCarter cleared the channel.

Bolan shifted the focus on the monitor back to Stony Man Farm.

"What about the money that was recovered from Masiga's people?" Katz asked.

"We haven't found the handle yet," Brognola said. "But we're working on it."

"The money's important," Katz said. "Masiga's not the type to shovel it into mason jars in the backyard. And from what we've discovered, the amount is considerable. It's got to be going somewhere."

"Even the action between Masiga and Dewbre required more pull than Masiga would normally be able to leverage," Bolan said. "Somewhere in here, there's a silent partner."

"It's the same guy who hired the Brotherhood of Aryan Defense to make the strike against Kalimuzo," Price told them. "We're working it. The computer systems Able Team raided turned up other names we're checking into."

"One of them paid off," Kurtzman said. "Nolan Pearrow is an international broker who handles overseas accounts. Primarily closing them out. He's done some work for various agencies over the years, but still operates strictly free-lance with no national loyalties. We intercepted a phone call over a wiretap in the last hour that indicates he's been assigned to stage an attack against someone in the D.C. area."

"Do you know who?" Bolan asked.

"Not yet. But we're working on it."

"Able Team is standing by," Brognola stated.

Bolan turned the information around in his head, trying to make sense of it. "That doesn't scan," he said. "If the battle is here, and Kalimuzo is en route, why strike at anyone in the U.S.?"

No one had an answer.

"When we find out where Masiga's money is," Katz said, "and know who his partner is, maybe we'll know then."

"We'll also know when we find out the identity of the intended victim or victims," Bolan added.

"We'll keep you posted," Brognola said.

Bolan nodded and cut the transmission.

Cape Anansi Water Supply Station #2— Walukagi
5:09 a.m.

JAKOB VANSCOYOC LED his team into the heart of the water supply station, winding through the narrow corridors by memory. Sonnet Quaid had provided maps of the station and the surrounding area. U.S. forces had been diverted from the station by a mortar attack several blocks away. Over the dulled thumping of the huge water pumps and filtering machines, the sounds of mortars going off could still be heard.

He was dressed for the night, all in black, and wore a black ski mask over his cosmetically darkened features. Halfway to his target destination, he and his team turned the corner and came within an arm's reach of a maintenance person.

The guy wore coveralls, then a panicked look as he went for the pistol holstered at his side.

Without hesitation, the Dutchman lifted his silenced pistol and pumped two .45-caliber rounds through the man's head. He caught the corpse, then eased it to the floor.

Five minutes and two deaths later, he broke into the last door to the main filters. Light filled the room, and the walls trapped the deafening noise. Without earplugs, he was hammered by the sound. He opened the access panel Quaid had researched and found to be the one they needed, then held an oxygen mask over his mouth and nose while the virus-contaminated powder was added to the mix already flowing through the system. From this point on, the water-cleansing process wouldn't be harmful to the virus.

Once more out in the main corridor, Vanscoyoc waved his unit into action. As a cover-up, he'd decided to make it look like a hostile unit had broken into the water supply station with the intention of shutting it down. Plastic explosive was planted in five separate places, close enough to main pumps and valves that it would appear to be a sloppy or misinformed attempt.

Another maintenance man walked in on him as he set the timer.

"Hey, who're—"

Before the man could utter another word, Vanscoyoc fired his pistol twice, driving the man backward against the wall. One of the bullets went through the body and scored the cinderblock surface behind him.

The Dutchman started the timer and ordered his men out of the building. In the distance, the mortar attack had been silenced. He'd lost no men. Three minutes after they quit the building, the first of the explosions went off, starting a fire along the roofline. The fire-suppression system was connected to the pump-house main, so the drain to fight the fire would cycle the virus through the pumps and into the city faster.

They loaded into the vehicles they had waiting and made the loop around the outer perimeter of the city, avoiding the U.S. and UN checkpoints that Quaid had identified. Vanscoyoc figured the remaining water supply station would be as easy to penetrate. The only thing that left him with a feeling of anxiety in the pit of his stomach was whether Kamer could really control the virus as well as he said he could.

But he'd been inoculated against it, so the Dutchman figured he had nothing to lose and everything to gain.

Washington, D.C.
10:13 p.m.

"YOU SURE THIS IS GOING to go down?"

Occupying the passenger seat of the unmarked car, Carl Lyons looked at Rollie Maurloe and said, "No. But I got people behind me who believe it will."

They were seated across the street from the Bayou Blossom in Georgetown. It was Sunday evening and most of the shops were closed, but the restaurants and bars were still doing business. Georgetown Park Mall was south of them, on the same side of the street as the nightclub they'd staked out.

Maurloe was a detective sergeant with the Washington, D.C., police department. Tall, broad and black, Maurloe wore his light trench coat and creased fedora with the easy aplomb of a tough guy in a Jimmy Cagney movie. He carried a Delta Elite in a shoulder holster, and kept a beefy hand on the Remington Model 870 pumpgun canted forward toward the dash.

"One of these days, son," Maurloe said, "we're going to have a talk about these friends of yours."

Lyons had worked with Maurloe before, coordinating other efforts and cleaning up after still others. The big cop was a true trooper who still believed in the job even after years of serving in a corrupt city where executive privilege swept a lot of dirt under the carpet.

Rather than deal with the false identities Stony Man created for him to work under, Lyons had told Maurloe his name was Carl and let it go at that. Brognola's SOG contacts pulled plenty of weight to keep anyone away from Lyons's cover. If Maurloe had ever figured out who Lyons really was, he'd never let on.

"Still," Maurloe said, "it won't be a total bust if I get to slip inside and get a few autographs. My wife's into all that big-star shit. She was pissed as hell that I wasn't home tonight because she'd made a special dinner. Maybe even laid out that nightgown I like to see her in so much. I get an autograph from that 'Saturday Night Live' guy or Gumble or Whoopi, maybe dinner tomorrow night can be just as special. Otherwise it'll be like the coming of the second ice age around my house for a few days."

"Sorry," Lyons said, and meant it. For a time during his LAPD days he'd been married, too. But the job had kept getting in the way of the marriage, and he hadn't been able to walk away from the belief that what he was doing out on the streets really mattered. He tapped the button on his headset. "Gadgets. Pol."

"Here, amigo," Blancanales radioed back.

"Any word from the Farm?"

"Just to hold tight. They're convinced it's going to happen." The other two members of Able Team were sheltered in a parking garage with part of the tactical force Maurloe had rounded up at the request of the Justice Department.

"Well, looky there," Maurloe said, reaching for his radio handset.

Glancing down the street, Lyons saw the trickle of traffic going by, most of it moving around the Georgetown trolley coming up the street. "What is it?" the Able Team leader asked.

"You know about that trolley?" Maurloe asked.

"Yeah. The Intel package I got on the area says it's a free mass-transit line that runs up this street."

"True," Maurloe said, "but it almost never runs after 3:30 p.m., and for sure never on Sundays or Mondays. This is a Sunday, and that's a goddamned Trojan horse."

Maurloe raised the handset to his mouth. "Blue Angel Units, this is Blue Angel Poppa. The ball is in play."

The units quickly radioed in and Maurloe gave them their orders. Besides the patrol cruisers, he'd even managed a helicopter.

"Pol," Lyons radioed.

"Go."

"Can you get a fix on the trolley?" Stony Man Farm was providing satellite linkage, complete with infrared and thermal imaging.

"Yeah," Blancanales said.

As Lyons watched, the trolley neared to within a hundred yards of the nightclub.

"Ironman," Blancanales said, "according to this readout, there are forty, maybe fifty people aboard that trolley."

"Got a news flash for you, ace," Lyons said. "That trolley's not even supposed to be running right now. Broaden out your search and let's see what else we can find that doesn't go with this picture."

The trolley reminded Lyons of the ones he'd seen in San Francisco, except this one ran on rubber tires and under its own power. The windows were dark, and not even the glow from the instrument panel revealed anything about the driver.

"All of a sudden," Maurloe said, "I've got the feeling we're going to regret not simply calling in a bomb scare to that nightclub a half hour ago and getting those people out of there."

"That would have put them back in the hotel," Lyons replied. "Too many points to cover to take care of everybody. This way we've only got the front door and the back. We shut them in, the bikers have to go through us."

"You feel lucky?" Maurloe asked.

"What do you mean?"

"We got to stop that trolley somehow," the cop replied, opening his door. "Figure the direct approach will clear the air damn quick."

"I read you," Lyons said. "You take out the tires and I'm on the driver."

Maurloe nodded and started to walk toward the trolley on an interception course. The shotgun was hidden by the flowing folds of his trench coat.

Getting out of the car, Lyons concealed his Calico machine pistol under the long navy duster he wore. The helical drum atop the vicious little assault pistol held one hundred 9 mm parabellum rounds. He carried his .45 Colt Government Model in shoulder rigging and his .357 Magnum Python on his hip. Point Blank body armor covered his torso.

"Hey, Ironman," Schwarz called out, "this isn't the OK Corral. You guys are going to get your asses shot off."

"Not if you provide covering fire at the right time," Lyons replied. "If they see a lot of activity on the street all of a sudden, they could scatter. Maybe this way we can disorient them, give us an edge for just long enough."

Lyons and Maurloe intercepted the trolley fifty yards from the nightclub. The Able Team leader's finger rested easily on the Calico's trigger as Maurloe threw out a big hand and acted as if he was flagging down the trolley.

The driver merely honked the horn and didn't slow.

Through the darkened window obscured by flashes from the passing streetlights, Lyons saw the barrel-chested driver riding high behind the steering wheel. The guy wore a leather jacket and a short-brimmed hat, with light reflected from chains crisscrossing it all.

"They're not going to stop," Lyons said as the trolley neared to within twenty feet. "Do it."

Maurloe fired the scattergun from hip level, aiming at the street in front of the right front tire. The double-aught pellets sparked against the pavement, then ricocheted through the steel-belted rubber, deflating it instantly. The trolley dropped several inches and began to list toward the curb.

The windshield on the other side of the driver suddenly erupted into fragments as gunfire crashed through it.

Lyons brought up the Calico and braced it over his free arm. Squeezing the trigger, he tracked a line of bullets across the front of the trolley from right to left. His initial burst slammed into the driver and tore him from the wheel.

The trolley was almost on top of them when Maurloe took out the other tire. They both went right, away from the staggering vehicle as it charged into a light pole and took it down in a blaze of electricity.

An instant later, Washington, D.C., police cruisers flooded into the immediate vicinity, blocking any chance of retreat or advance by the trolley. Men dressed in black leather broke from the doors of the vehicle in three directions, weapons already out and firing.

Bullets tore through Lyons's duster, two of them slamming into the Point Blank armor. He went to ground in a diving roll that brought him up beside the trolley. Across the back of his duster were yellow luminescent letters that identified him as part of the DCPD task force.

Four men at the end of the trolley turned and fired at him. The big Able Team warrior cut them down without mercy. Price and Kurtzman had researched the biker gang thoroughly, and the Intel they passed on to Lyons had suggested nothing remotely human about them. They dealt in pain and death, and bought stock in misery.

Schwarz braked the van he was driving to a shrieking halt behind a police car. He and Blancanales leaped out, brandishing weapons.

A length of pipe shoved its way out of a window above Lyons's head and he recognized it a heartbeat later. "Rocket!" he yelled, swinging the Calico around.

Then the tube belched flame and the warhead streaked for the line of police cars. The explosion lifted the first car from the ground and flipped it onto the vehicle behind it.

Knowing they were trapped if they didn't fight, the bikers formed a flying wedge and shoved through the broken line of police cruisers. Most of the Satan's Blitz members carried high-capacity 9 mm pistols, but the ones with assault rifles chewed through the uniformed cops with sheer savagery.

"Dammit!" Maurloe yelled beside Lyons. "We're not going to be able to hold them."

"We've got to," the Able Team leader replied.

"Ironman," Schwarz called over the headset. "Satellite recon just tweaked on reinforcement coming out of the alleys behind us. They had the deck stacked."

"Damn," Lyons said, spinning to face the other direction. He paused, halfway out into the street, a biker in his sights. He squeezed the trigger and put the guy down.

"What?" Maurloe asked.

Before Lyons could reply, the answer was made clear.

More than twenty motorcycles roared onto the street and charged the line of cops. Maurloe's shotgun boomed, and one driver was blasted from his seat. The bike fell over, then skidded into Able Team's van.

His senses on overdrive, Lyons was grimly aware that civilians had ventured out onto the sidewalks from the restaurants and bars. It didn't take them long to decide they weren't where they needed to be.

Lyons held his ground and unleashed the Calico on full-auto. Several of the cops carrying CAR-15s did the same. The Calico clicked empty as a biker veered his motorcycle toward Lyons, a man on the back intending to take him out with a revolver shot.

Letting the machine pistol hang from the strap around his shoulder under the duster, Lyons put his hands out and caught the motorcycle's handlebars. A bullet whipped by his cheek as he planted his feet and yanked to one side. The forward momentum of the bike knocked Lyons backward, but he'd knocked it off course.

Out of control, the motorcycle spilled both riders and slid across the street, smashing into a trio of newspaper stands chained in place. Both men scrambled to their feet, bringing weapons up.

Lyons drew his Colt Python .357 Magnum and fired instinctively, using the double action. The hollowpoints caught the Satan's Blitz members and spun them away. Beside him, Maurloe's shotgun boomed again and put down another biker.

A smoky haze filled the street from canisters the bikers had thrown, blurring images.

Lyons filled his weapon's cylinder with a speedloader, then grabbed the .45. There was no time to fit another magazine onto the Calico. Everything around him was confused. But he had the impression that the Washington cops were turning the tide.

"Ironman," Blancanales called over the headset.

"Go." Lyons didn't try to find his teammate, and kept firing his guns at the targets he found open to him.

"In the back, behind the trolley."

Lyons looked and barely made out the motorcycle hiding there, until it came speeding out, carrying two riders. He tried to get target acquisition, but the uniforms were too mixed in with the bikers to get a clear shot. The motorcycle sped around the police car at the end of the line, then made the jump up over the curb, turning toward the nightclub. "What about it?"

"The rear rider's carrying a satchel," Blancanales said. "If it's filled with explosives the way I think it is, and they get it inside the nightclub, they can still do a lot of damage."

Spotting Blancanales now, Lyons saw that the man was too far away from the speeding motorcycle to reach it. The bike was slowed by the cars. The man on the rear was finishing working on the satchel's straps. None of the cops were on the Able Team frequency and didn't recognize the potential danger.

Lyons began pursuit at once, breaking into a full run through the police cars that had blocked the trolley's passage. On the other side of the blockade, he pistoned his legs, shrugging out of the duster and the Calico's sling.

Ahead of him, the motorcycle cut across the street, aiming for the front of the Bayou Blossom. A Camaro, parked against the curb facing Lyons, separated them. Putting everything he had into the effort, the Able Team warrior vaulted up onto the hood of the sports car, planted a foot on the rooftop and used it as a platform for a full-body tackle.

The impact drove the air from his lungs, and for a minute he wondered if he'd hit the motorcycle too high. He rolled painfully across the sidewalk, his lungs screaming for air as his body tried to assess the damage he'd sustained.

Both bikers were down. One was trapped under the bike, the other sprawled at the base of the phone booth at the corner of the nightclub.

The satchel was only a few feet away.

The guy under the bike came around first, his Smith & Wesson up and tracking.

Lyons let loose a trio of rounds, all three drilling through the guy's bubble goggles and slamming him to the ground. Gasping as his breath returned to him, the Able Team leader shoved himself to his feet and staggered toward the remaining biker.

The guy pointed a Beretta at him, but the barrel shook. The eyes over the sights were bloodshot and frightened.

"Your choice, pal," Lyons said coldly. "Makes no difference to me if you walk out of here or if they carry you out in a body bag."

For a moment the tension held. Light from the whirling cherries atop the police cruisers flickered across the biker's bearded face. Then he threw the gun away and rolled facedown on the sidewalk, hands behind his head.

Lyons cuffed the man, then went to see about the satchel. He barely had it in his hand when Blancanales and Maurloe jogged up to join him, bloody and worn from the battle. Out on the street there was no more gunplay. Satan's Blitz, what remained of it, had opted for surrender. The helicopter Maurloe had requisitioned hovered overhead, streaking light over the immediate vicinity.

Just as Lyons was about to open the satchel, a single gunshot rang out, flat and harsh. When he looked up, he saw Schwarz with a Beretta in his fist, pointing it at the man Lyons had handcuffed.

The biker had a neat round bullet hole between his eyes.

Without a word, Schwarz crossed the sidewalk to the dead man and knelt. Turning, he tossed a square-shaped object at Lyons, who caught it automatically.

"Remote control for the satchel explosive," Schwarz explained. "He had you guys cold."

"Not quite," Lyons replied. He dropped the remote control and cracked it underfoot. "You were here."

"There's that," Schwarz agreed with a grim smile.

Cape Anansi, Walukagi
6:21 a.m.

DAWN STREAKED pale golds and pinks to the east, reaching through the clouds to touch the emerald waters spreading out from the fortified coastline. And it sparked off the assassin's rifle barrel as it was thrust through the open window above one of the supply-route streets U.S. forces were maintaining.

David McCarter peered through the scope mounted on his sniper rifle. He was two buildings down, a story below, and across the street from the assassin, one of Masiga's men. The angle was all wrong, but he was determined to make the shot.

"You verify him?" the Briton asked.

Manning sat beside him, a pair of binoculars to his eyes. "Oh, yeah. The uniform. The tribal scars. He's one of the bad guys. Can you take him?"

"I think so." McCarter took up trigger slack and leaned into the rifle's buttstock.

They were in a small room that had been used for storage. A layer of dust covered the piles of furniture and boxes behind them and filled the air with the scent of trapped must.

"I'm on my way," Manning said. "In case you don't."

McCarter nodded. No matter what, they couldn't afford to let the guy get a kill. Manning drew his side arm and moved out of the room with a speed and grace that belied his size.

According to the logistics Katz had worked out, there were anywhere from three to six sniper teams working for Masiga throughout the city. The assassinations and attempted assassinations had continued during the night. So far, four American soldiers and nine civilians had been added to the casualty list. For the past hour and seventeen minutes, though, things had been quiet. Until the Phoenix Force team tracked onto the killers in the other building.

Unable to lock onto the assassin, McCarter put the cross hairs over the rifle barrel and held steady. The assassin's weapon roved restlessly, moving so slowly it was almost hypnotic.

There was no way to know how deeply Masiga had cut into their intelligence lines. Duplicity on behalf of the Cape Aransi citizens was a way of life. But when McCarter saw the jeep approaching, he dropped the scope over the passengers and saw Captain Vinnie Madden, who was a linchpin for the command and control efforts in the city, riding in the passenger seat.

"Gary," McCarter said over the headset. "Go."

"I've got to take the shot, mate. Got no choice." The Briton focused on the barrel, intending to damage it or possibly knock it out of the man's hands. "But I can't confirm the kill."

"I'm at the back door. Go for it."

The rifle barrel moved, and from its angle, McCarter knew his prey had to be up against the wall. He switched his target, bracketing the brick masonry where he knew the sniper had to be hiding. The sniper rifle was loaded with armor-piercing rounds. Knowing the large .50-caliber bullets had been designed with tanks in mind, he figured they'd easily blow through the brick.

He fired through the 11-round clip as fast as he could squeeze the trigger. Thunder erupted out onto the street where dawn had drawn long shadows from the buildings. The jeep bearing Captain Madden pulled into an alley off the main thoroughfare, while pedestrians and motorists in other cars faded into the nearest hiding places.

A large crater opened up in the wall.

Dropping the sniper rifle, McCarter ran from the room and sprinted across the street with the Browning in his hand as American soldiers gathered. He rushed up the stairs, breathing hard.

When he reached the fourth floor, he found Manning inside, holding his Beretta on a young Masiga hardman who stood stiffly erect, his hands clasped on top of his head.

At his feet, covered by part of the rubble from the broken wall, was another gunner. A Lee-Enfield rifle lay nearby. At least one of the Barrett's rounds had mushroomed and hit the assassin in the head.

"Do you speak English?" McCarter demanded of the young tribesman.

He didn't answer.

McCarter raised his Browning and pointed it at the man's head. "If you don't speak English, you're of no use to me."

"I speak English."

"Then you deliver a message for me when you get back to your tribe," McCarter said. "You tell them whoever they send into this city to assassinate United States and United Nations soldiers is going to have me to answer to. Do you understand?"

"Yes."

"I'm going to make it my life's work for a while to hunt down every sniper Masiga puts into Cape Anansi." McCarter reached into a shirt pocket and pulled out a coin. "You show them this when you get there." He tossed the coin across.

The hardman caught it, gazing at the bullet hole that had ripped through the center of the nickel.

McCarter had made five of them so far, using an M-16. "You tell them that's all they're going to receive for their foolishness. One plugged nickel for each team I find."

The man nodded and closed his hand over the coin.

"You're the only man who gets to live," McCarter said. "Everyone else, I execute. Now get out of here."

Slowly at first, the man walked toward the door. Once he reached it, however, he dropped his hands and ran.

McCarter stepped to the window beside the exploded wall and called down to the soldiers gathered below, letting them know the threat had passed. A large crowd of citizens had gathered behind them.

Turning back to the corpse, McCarter grabbed its bloodstained shirt lapels, pulled it to the window and shoved it out.

Arms and legs flailed as the body turned in the air, then the corpse dropped into a broken heap on the sidewalk.

McCarter leaned out the window. "Killers will be killed," he promised, "and anyone who peddles information to Masiga's people will be dealt with harshly, as well." The crowd reacted instantly, talking among themselves.

"Your bit for PR?" Manning asked.

"My bit for putting bloody stool pigeons on notice," the Briton replied. He glanced at the wreckage in the wall and felt partially satisfied. It was a start, and it had been done publicly enough to draw attention. He hoped Masiga got the message.

"Let's drift, mate," McCarter said, lighting up a cigarette. "We've only got about five hours before Kalimuzo returns to the city. He's going to be a prime target. Maybe we'll get lucky and thin out some more of the gunners before then."

CHAPTER TWELVE

Cape Anansi Coastline, Walukagi
11:49 a.m.

"There they are," Katz said.

Bolan followed the Israeli's direction, looking up into the bright blue sky. White parachutes mushroomed into being, hundreds of feet up, as the huge jet streaked overhead. The Executioner counted twenty of them.

The LVTP-7 armored personnel carrier bobbed gently on the surface of the Indian Ocean. Bolan had requisitioned it from the USMC amphibious forces. Five miles out to sea from the Cape Anansi coastline, he felt relatively secure from Masiga's men. They were still well within the protective shadow cast by the USS *Freedeburg*.

Although only armed with a .50-caliber machine gun, the LVTP-7 was capable of doing fourteen knots in the water and sixty miles per hour on land. Bolan had chosen it to pick up Henry Kalimuzo, Cowboy John Kissinger and the blacksuit team, arriving from Stony Man Farm. With the APC, they could make the shoreline and continue on without making a transfer that would expose the country's new political head to assassins' guns.

Bolan changed frequencies on the headset and tapped the transmit button. "Stony One to Sureshot."

"You've got Sureshot, Stony One," Kissinger replied. Despite the factors of the plummeting altitude and the other frequencies in the area, the communications loop was clear as a bell. Kurtzman was providing enhancement from the global positioning satellite locked into geosynchronous orbit twenty-three thousand miles out.

"We're going to pop smoke," Bolan said. "You can home in on that."

"Roger."

Katz pulled the pin in a signal smoker and tossed it into the green water. The grenade exploded, then shot a column of crimson smoke straight out for almost ten feet.

"We read you five-by," Kissinger said.

"See you when we see you," Bolan said. He resumed examining the black-and-white and color photographs in his hand. They'd been taken at both water supply stations serving Cape Anansi's needs.

"It reads like a botched pair of guerrilla attacks," Katz said. "But it doesn't feel that way."

Bolan went through the two dozen pictures again as the parachutists overhead continued to fall toward them. He'd almost memorized them. Bodies were strewn around the processing plants, indicating the attack had come from outside, and damage had been done.

But there hadn't been enough damage. His combat senses had been tingling a warning ever since he'd first seen the sites. Hearing about them over the radio, they had sounded like failed attempts at shutting down the city's water supply. With the river nearby, though, it would have been only a couple of hours before allied forces were up and running again. He could see nothing that could have been gained even if the teams had been successful.

Judging from the shrapnel scoring and the soot collected on the walls, enough explosive had been used to destroy the pumps. Except that it had been improperly placed.

"This isn't what it looks like," Bolan agreed. He tapped the photographs for illustration. "Eleven men were killed in all. Only two of them died as a result of the explosions. The rest were shot."

"With two rounds apiece," Katz said. "Yes, I'd noticed that."

Bolan figured the Phoenix Force leader had. Mossad agents were trained on .22LR pistols and taught to double-tap a target. Other special forces around the world were trained similarly.

"If they're trained so well," the Executioner went on, "and didn't lose anyone themselves, how is it that they failed to complete their objective? They had to have had a munitions guy."

"I agree."

Flipping back to the reports filed by the Marine recon officers covering the sites, Bolan said, "Look at the time. Twenty-seven minutes apart, with engagements with Masiga's men only a few blocks away each time."

"They were providing cover for the covert activity."

"Yeah, but with the time lag, that suggests only one small team."

"And you have to ask yourself how a team highly skilled enough to penetrate both water supply stations without losing anyone could miss both targets so badly."

Bolan was silent for a moment. "They didn't miss, Yakov. Whatever they were supposed to do, they did."

He looked up at the parachutes. "Dammit, I wish we had been able to move on this sooner."

The recon officer's report hadn't hit his desk until twenty minutes earlier.

"It looked like a pair of failed raiding missions," Katz said. "The recon soldiers reported it according to SOP."

"I know." Bolan saw Kalimuzo disengage from his parachute and drop into the water less than thirty yards away. "The thing that bothers me is the idea that someone was betting on that."

"You've got the *Freedeburg*'s medical team investigating the water supply now," Katz said. "You're doing all you can."

The warrior nodded grimly. "As a tactician, I'd have known how much the enemy could do in response, too. Somewhere in here, we're behind an eight ball we don't even know exists yet, operating on someone else's timetable. And with the city water involved, we may not have a hope in hell of containing it before it's too late."

"Not at first," Katz said. "But whatever it is, we'll find it. Then we'll know what needs to be done."

The Stony Man blacksuits swam to the floating APC and pulled themselves up, maintaining a protective ring around Kalimuzo.

Walukagi's new prime minister was soaking wet and bedraggled looking, dressed in slacks and a short-sleeved turtleneck. He extended his hand to Bolan. "You're Colonel Pollock."

"Yes." Bolan took the hand and felt the strength of it. He introduced Katz, who shook hands, as well. "And you're the new prime minister."

"I've never been prime minister before," Kalimuzo said with a wry grin. "This will take some getting used to. Despite my political moves leading to this moment, I never really thought it would come this far.''

"Hell," Kissinger said, clapping the man on the shoulder, "until a few minutes ago, you'd never made a parachute jump. I can see this is going to be a red-letter day for you."

Bolan looked at the man. "Are you prepared to go ashore now, or do you want to take some time aboard the *Freedeburg?*"

Face grim and exhaustion filling his eyes, Kalimuzo walked to the end of the LVTP-7 that faced Cape Anansi. "That's my country out there, Colonel. Over the years I've been branded outlaw and traitor and self-serving idealist by the whites in charge, and by some of the blacks. Maybe I've earned all those names at one time or another. I've lied and cheated, and even killed for my people, and earned the enmity of a great number of people. Even the people I helped, the parents and politicians connected to hostages Masiga and his men have kidnapped over the years, are convinced I aided them only to further my own ambitions."

Bolan heard the crack in the man's voice and knew that powerful emotions drove Kalimuzo.

"But today," the man said in a lower voice, "today, I'm wearing the mantle of a patriot. I don't want to delay going into that city. When the people see me, maybe there'll be some hope where there was none before. If I can give them nothing else, I want to give them that."

"Couldn't think of a better reason," Bolan said. He opened the APC's hatch and ushered the man inside.

Outside Cape Anansi, Walukagi
1:09 p.m.

PERCHED ON AN OUTCROP covered by the relative security of trees and brush, Rafael Encizo stared through binoculars at the thin ribbon of highway leading back into the port city. Perspiration darkened his jungle fatigues and beaded along the camou scarf he wore as a headband. At his side was an Austrian Steyr SSG 69 sniping rifle chambered in 7.62 mm.

The headset crackled in his ear. "Phoenix Four, this is Five."

"Go, Five."

"We just passed the outer marker."

"Affirmative, Five. I'll be looking for you." Encizo looked over his shoulder and spotted the two force recon Marines tucked away in their positions. Each man nodded, letting him know they'd heard the transmission.

The operation was tricky. With Calvin James aboard the approaching medical ten-wheeler as driver, and three other soldiers as guards, managing the "jailbreak" for Masiga's hardmen in the back was going to require split-second timing to make it seem real. Through channels they'd uncovered during the early morning hours, they'd leaked information back to Masiga's people that the medical van would be in the area restocking recon teams while en route with prisoners from the base hospital that U.S. forces had established in the port city.

"I've got you," Encizo said over the headset. He reached for the Steyr SSG 69 and pulled it to his shoulder. "What's your speed?"

The medical ten-wheeler was clearly marked with red crosses on both sides and on top of the truck's body. It made the curve that disappeared into the tree line, coming straight toward Encizo's position a hundred feet below.

"Forty miles an hour."

"You can handle it?"

"We're going to find out," James replied. "Get it done."

Peering through the telescopic sight, Encizo put the cross hairs over the driver's-side tire, then squeezed the trigger. The bullet flew true, drilling into the tire and deflating it immediately.

The ten-wheeler shivered and the brakes locked up, throwing it sideways.

Encizo worked the bolt action, then blasted the other tire.

Out of control, the medical truck flipped over on its side and screeched across the road. It came to a stop just off the roadside, against the trunk of a large tree. Long scars marred the pavement behind it.

As arranged, the back door on the truck sprang open. It didn't take the prisoners long to get the idea they were free men again, and they poured out of the back speedily. Of the sixteen, four had the microprocessor transmitter implants designed by Kurtzman.

James crawled out of the cab and started shouting at the fleeing prisoners, waving his pistol around meaningfully.

"Shoot him," Encizo said to the recon soldiers.

They both fired without comment.

Still gazing through the scope, Encizo saw his teammate take the impacts and roll from the truck, crimson staining his shirt.

Two of the guards were working to get the third one free of the cab when gunfire broke out below Encizo's position. Through the trees, he spotted the band of hardmen almost two hundred yards away. Without hesitation, they started to advance toward the overturned truck.

"Reload," Encizo directed the two Marines. "Pick your targets and fire at will." The confusion of the jungle and the sound of gunfire would hopefully conceal their position. He picked off one of the gunners with a shot through the heart, the 7.62 mm round picking the man off his feet and throwing him backward.

The Marine guards took cover behind the medical truck and tried to return fire.

"Guardian," Encizo called over the headset, "this is Phoenix Four." He kept working the bolt action, putting down a second gunner.

"Go, Phoenix Four."

"Bring it in. We're cutting it thin here."

"Affirmative."

Encizo rode out the recoil of the sniper weapon and chambered another round from the 10-round box. Before he had time to work the bolt again, a tank roared into view, flanked by two Hummers and a two-and-a-half-ton truck.

Masiga's men broke and ran deeper into the jungle, taking the "escaped" prisoners with them.

Encizo let out a tense breath. If everything had worked properly, the enemy would never know that the shots that had taken out the truck tires had been his. The Marine crew in the Hummers only gave a show of pursuit and fired their machine guns over the heads of the fleeing hardmen.

Tapping the headset, Encizo said, "Phoenix Five."

"Here," James replied. Down on the highway, the ex-SEAL roused himself and stood. "Dammit, those rubber bullets hurt even through the damn Kevlar. Next time, you get to be the guy getting shot."

Encizo grinned, then jogged down the steep incline through the trees and brush to make the jump back into Cape Anansi. The banded quail had been flushed. Now it remained to be seen if they would give away Masiga's hidden base.

Presidential Palace, Cape Anansi
Walukagi 1:17 p.m.

THE ATTACK BEGAN blocks from the presidential palace.

Mack Bolan rode in the passenger seat of a covered Hummer, riding point on the entourage going downtown. There was no warning.

An explosion ripped a pothole in the street, adding one more to the many already in existence. From the angle, the warrior guessed that it was coming from a rooftop.

Katz had remained aboard the LVTP-7 with Henry Kalimuzo. The APC could carry twenty-eight passengers plus its three-man crew, but had no gun ports to return fire. The driver immediately took evasive action.

Bolan reached for the handset. "Keep moving," he growled. "Once we get to the palace, we can fall back and draw defensive lines."

"Agreed," Katz radioed back.

Another warhead found the range and the accuracy, and slammed into the side of the APC, dripping fire and spewing smoke. The heavy unit shivered visibly on its tracks.

"G-Force," Bolan said, shifting to another band. He scanned the nearby buildings and spotted the gun crew on a three-story structure just as gunfire sprayed across the front of the Hummer and took out the windshield. Bullets ripped through the vinyl of his seat, and at least one of them hit his driver.

The Hummer pulled drastically to the left, then the driver recovered enough to bring the vehicle to a stop.

"Yeah, Striker?" Grimaldi called back.

"We're under fire here," Bolan said, opening his driver's shirt and finding a bullet wound high up on the man's shoulder. There was no immediate danger, except the bleeding. He reached into the med kit under the seat, took out a compress and pushed it against the wound. "Hold that."

The soldier nodded and put his hand over the field dressing.

"We're on our way," Grimaldi said.

More gunfire had joined the rocket attack.

Bolan lifted his Galil AR assault rifle/M-203 grenade launcher combo and broke into a run, trailed by the two Marines who'd been in the Hummer.

He rounded a pickup sitting on blocks, its wheels long-since stripped, and brought up the Galil. He looked through the open sights under the scope, then picked up his targets. A man on top of the building was staring down the length of his rocket launcher, aiming it at Bolan, when the Executioner squeezed the trigger.

Bolan felt the recoil of the Galil, then the larger impact of the warhead detonating against the pickup's side. He put a hand out and shoved himself away as the vehicle came off the blocks. Across the street, the RPG gunner fell from the building in a swan dive.

The pickup smashed through the boarded-over front of a dentist's office and stopped halfway inside, bumper resting against the white dentist's chair.

Seeing at least one more rocket person atop the building, Bolan aimed the rifle again and triggered the M-203. The grenade launcher kicked the 40 mm grenade toward its target in an arcing trajectory. An instant later it exploded, blowing two more men from the rooftop.

The LVTP-7 was ahead of the warrior now, lumbering toward its destination, fire from incendiary rounds clinging to its steel sides. The track on one side had been damaged badly enough that it flapped, making a shrieking and beating noise against the ground and the vehicle.

The two Hummers behind it had closed up ranks, running almost bumper to bumper with the Marine amphibian.

Bolan ran, seeing the design of the trap in his mind. Rocket launchers had been placed behind them, driving them forward, like beaters chasing tigers through the jungle. He'd taken out one of the launcher teams, and the Marines in the Hummers had used their .50-caliber machine guns to drive the other team to cover. They were concentrating on what was behind them, not what was coming up.

He tapped the transmitter button on the headset, winded from the exertion of running flat out. "Yakov."

"Go."

"It's a trap."

Whatever reply the Israeli might have made was suddenly lost in the thunder and clangor of the eighteen-wheeler that appeared in the middle of the intersec-

Now the knowledge served him another way. Reaching forward, the Executioner slipped his finger onto the M-203's trigger, aimed and squeezed.

The 40 mm warhead exploded against the street beside the minivan's back tire a heartbeat before the TOW fired. A hole opened up in the street and devoured the back half of the vehicle. Suddenly tilted off balance, the TOW crew lost control of their wire guidance systems. The deadly missile shot past the APC and slammed into a building, crumpling one of its corners and spilling half the structure into the street.

Katz trained the .50-caliber machine gun on the exposed underside of the minivan and loosed a steady burst that contained incendiary rounds. The gasoline tank exploded, then engulfed the vehicle in flames. Leaping from the tilted top of the minivan, the TOW crew abandoned the weapons system.

Bolan rolled around the corner of the building and fired deliberately, putting all three men down and making the retaliatory statement. He caught a brief glimpse of the copper-haired man driving swiftly away.

At the other end of the street, the eighteen-wheeler was readying itself for another pass. Already moving at speed, it screamed at the APC like a runaway locomotive. When it was seventy yards from the LVTP-7, the imposing bulk of a Sea Stallion filled the air. The rotors shrieked as it flew on an interception course between the buildings. Then it opened up with the Hellfire missile pod mounted under the stubby left wing.

All four missiles struck the vehicle and reduced it to an avalanche of flaming debris that rolled to a stop thirty yards from the LVTP-7. As the Sea Stallion flashed by, it was flanked by two Sikorsky H-76 Eagle-armed utility helicopters that swept over the enemy troops. Twenty-millimeter rockets flared from the cannons mounted on the stubby wings. The street broke and crumbled, and the hole the minivan sat in widened until it completely swallowed the vehicle.

Bolan tapped the headset. "G-Force."

"Go, Striker."

"There was a blue Toyota pickup involved in the attack. Can you spot it?"

"I'm looking, buddy."

Bolan sprinted across the street and joined Katz on the APC. The amphibian started, then limped off toward the presidential palace again, the two H-76s floating into protective positions overhead. The Executioner watched the Sea Stallion make a couple of circles over a four-block sector, hovering just above the buildings. Then it came to a stationary position, the nose canted slightly downward.

"I found it, Striker," Grimaldi radioed, "but nobody's home."

"Affirmative," Bolan replied. He cleared the channel, then got on the frequency used by the majority of the U.S. and UN teams working the beachhead. In terse sentences, he gave the man's description, adding that he thought the man was in a supervisory role during the attack.

"If he was," Katz said, "he's the first white man we've seen inside Masiga's organization."

Bolan nodded as he surveyed the presidential palace.

Constructed in boxy Mediterranean architecture, the three-story palace dated back to the late eighteenth century. Wrought-iron fences ten feet tall enclosed the outer courtyards. Painted white, with a deep red tiled roof, the palace had a widow's walk on the third floor that overlooked an inner courtyard on the other side of a drive-through gate under a massive canopy.

Government security people still supporting Pernell Spraggue's bid for leadership in Walukagi maintained the perimeter, but gave way quickly to the APC and the two menacing H-76s.

Spraggue met them under the canopy. He was a lean, pale man with a six-inch goatee and silver hair severely pulled back. The military uniform he wore was rich in detail, a designer's dream of self-importance done in cream and crimson. A gold sash around his waist held up a ceremonial German saber.

Accessing the headset frequency used by U.S. forces, Bolan said, "Bring in the equipment for Ambassador Kalimuzo and the new perimeter defense systems." As the APC rolled to a halt near Spraggue, the Executioner vaulted onto the ground.

A look of hope entered Spraggue's eyes, then was quickly dashed when he saw Kalimuzo pushing up out of the LVTP-7. "I take it this isn't exactly a social call," he said weakly.

Bolan glanced over at the satellite receiver in the courtyard and knew the man had access to the latest news. "No," he stated.

"I'm not giving up my position here," Spraggue promised. "I've been here for twelve years, been through every kind of hell imaginable during that time. You can't make me leave."

Kalimuzo strode forward, his face filled with anger. "You're partly to blame for the shape this country's in now," he accused in a harsh voice. "You cut deals with your business associates in South Africa and sold out the real people of this country. You were stripping Walukagi of everything that had any kind of intrinsic value, and at the same time leaving the situation open to other predators like Masiga, Kwammanga and Nanpetro."

"Lies!" Spraggue shouted. "I did everything I could for these people! Their own greed is consuming them!"

Bolan scanned the crowd gathering along the outer fence. Men, women and their children, all citizens of Cape Anansi, were pressed to the bars with interest. English was the official second language of the country, so the warrior knew most of them understood what was being said. With their voices amplified by standing under the canopy, there was no way they could miss the argument.

Kalimuzo paused for a moment, looking deeply into his opponent's eyes. "When you destroy dreams," he said forcefully, "when you cause hope to wither and die, only the basest of emotions will live. You and your business associates have tried to take away the future of this country, have tried to murder it and rape it and degrade it out of existence. But as long as one child of this country lives, there'll be dreams and hopes. You can't smother them all. And out of all the evil you have loosed on Walukagi, none of it will last. Because when those dreams and hopes take root again, people will rise up to fight predators like you."

When Kalimuzo finished, there was a brief silence. Then, slowly at first, the sound of clapping started to echo from the fence.

"Striker."

"Go," Bolan said into the headset's mouthpiece.

"This is Foxbat Leader."

"I read you, Foxbat Leader." Bolan didn't recognize the voice, but he knew from the Intel reports that the code name belonged to Colonel Lamont Harrison of the British SAS.

"Heard you lads had a bit of a dustup," Harrison said.

"Yeah, but we seem to have that under control at the moment."

"Affirmative. We're above you, getting ready to deploy into the harbor."

Bolan looked at the gathering crowd thronging outside the perimeter gates. "How would you like to make a hell of an entrance, Colonel?"

"Chap, everywhere I go, I'm always at my dashing best."

"Yeah, well, I'm thinking of something along the morale-boosting lines here."

"What do you have in mind?"

"Do you have a flag?" Bolan asked.

Across from him, Katz smiled and nodded. There were a lot of people in Walukagi who wouldn't know how to take British involvement in their politics. With Kalimuzo taking over the presidential palace, a statement needed to be made.

"That's affirmative," Harrison said.

Bolan outlined what he had in mind.

"Your time here is done," Kalimuzo told Spraggue. Then he took a step forward, invading the man's personal space. "You can walk out, or I'll drag you out if I have to."

"You wouldn't dare," Spraggue said, his hand dropping to the saber hilt.

Kalimuzo reached out and placed his hand over Spraggue's. "Draw that piece of steel and I'll bury it in you."

A chant started at the fence. Slowly at first, then with gathering intensity, the Walukagians began calling out Kalimuzo's name.

"I'd go," Bolan said softly. "While you still have the option of walking. He can become a hero right here and now by knocking you on your butt. And I'm betting he can do it."

"I'll need my things," Spraggue said.

"They'll be taken to you at the port," Bolan told him.

"My car is in the garage."

"You'll take one of ours." Bolan waved to a pair of Marines, who escorted Spraggue off the grounds to a waiting Hummer.

Wild cheering broke out around the presidential palace, then started to quiet as the crowd looked skyward.

"They see them," Katz said, looking up.

Bolan followed his gaze, spotting the cluster of parachutes dropping earthward. In minutes, the first of the SAS warriors touched down. They smartly gathered up their shrouds and collapsed their parachutes, all of them making standing landings.

One of them, managing with a skill Bolan deeply respected, came down with a British flag attached to a slender pole. When he touched down, he planted the flag into the ground with a quick thrust. Although the pole was thin, it supported the flag gallantly.

A lean man with neatly clipped sandy hair stepped forward and came to a halt in front of Kalimuzo. He saluted sharply. "Prime Minister Kalimuzo, I'm Colonel Lamont Harrison of the United Kingdom's Special Air Service. On behalf of the British government, I want you to know we're here to help."

"Thank you, Colonel," Kalimuzo said, but his response was almost lost amid the riotous cheering of the people filling the streets.

Bolan faded from the immediacy of the moment. Katz followed.

"Pomp and polish," the Israeli said. "The British have always had a flair for it."

"True," the warrior replied as he surveyed the wreckage in the street. "But this war isn't over by half." The headset beeped, letting him know there was an incoming message from Stony Man Farm.

He switched over to the frequency. "Stony One."

"Stony Base," Brognola said. "How tied up are you there, Stony One?"

"We've just experienced a British invasion," Bolan replied. "And Kalimuzo has been officially recognized as the new prime minister of Walukagi."

"You're ready to hand off the bulk of the perimeter maintenance to the Britons?"

"Affirmative. With Admiral Myers and the *Freedeburg* acting as home base here, there should be no problems with communications. Activity in the street is another matter."

"Understood," the head Fed said. "We caught most of the ambush on CNN and from the satellite."

"There was a redheaded man involved in the ambush," Katz said.

"We know. The Bear's lifted photos from the BBC footage, since they were in a position to catch the guy head-on and in profile. We're working it now." Brognola paused. "But you need to stand ready there. When we took Pearrow into custody after the action Able Team put down, we turned up some Intel in his files that's helping us track the people working with Masiga.

Turns out Pearrow was also fencing some of the better pieces of artwork to collectors here in the States. Able Team's working that angle out now, and we should know something soon. Some of Pearrow's money came out of South Africa.''

''That's no surprise,'' Bolan said. ''Dewbre was fencing weapons from South Africa. That connection was to be expected.''

''Right. We're going to flush these people out of the woodwork,'' Brognola promised, ''but you and Phoenix are going to have to be ready to respond.''

''We will be,'' Bolan said. ''Has there been any news of the men who had the microprocessors implanted?''

''They're moving away from Cape Anansi at the moment,'' Brognola said. ''They've split up, however. Three are going more southerly and the other is headed almost due north.''

''If there'd been a way to encode each microprocessor to give a unique signature,'' Katz said, ''it would have helped. Or if we'd been able to determine what tribes these people came from.''

''Agreed. But for now we have this. The AWACS are picking the signals up perfectly, so hopefully something will break in the next few hours.''

''Keep us posted,'' Bolan said.

Brognola said he would, then broke the communication.

Looking out over the death and carnage in the street near the presidential palace, Bolan saw the first of the cargo trucks coming toward them. There was enough equipment loaded onto the vehicles to fortify the palace to withstand and repel most ground-based attacks. Soldiers got out of the back and started stringing barbed wire around the outer perimeter.

The headset beeped again.

Bolan answered it. "Striker."

"Striker, this is Dr. Beecham. I need to talk to you about those samples we took."

The Executioner looked at Katz. Once they'd found out about the near misses on the water supply stations, they'd agreed to have the water tested. A cold feeling of dread ran down Bolan's spine. "I'll be right there." Then he radioed for Grimaldi for a ride back to the *Freedeburg*.

CHAPTER THIRTEEN

Bethlehem, Pennsylvania
7:36 a.m.

Carl Lyons stood on the massive front porch of the elegant Victorian mansion and pressed the doorbell. Fall had already touched the dense forest around the estate, spilling multicolored leaves to the ground. He saw them through the bars of the perimeter fence, but found only a handful blowing across the landscaped grounds.

Beyond the front security gate, where two uniformed guards watched everything with hawk-eyed efficiency, Blancanales and Schwarz were running backup on the play in a full-size Chevy Blazer that bore federal government plates.

Lyons wore a well-cut three-piece suit that had come off the rack, and kept the jacket unbuttoned so the Colt Government Model .45 in the paddle holster at his back waistband wouldn't be so noticeable. He also carried a leather briefcase to complete the look.

Just as the last bonging echoes of the doorbell faded, the door was opened. A young, dark-haired and dark-eyed houseman with the build of a weightlifter looked at Lyons. "Mr. Lundquist?"

"Yes," Lyons said. He showed the man the necessary documentation that proved he was Carson Lundquist, an agent of the Internal Revenue Service.

The houseman stepped back into the mansion. "This way, please. Mr. Cronley is waiting for you in the drawing room."

Lyons fell into step behind the man, following him through a foyer decorated with pressed wildflowers and antique decorative glassware.

The drawing room was behind two massive doors. The houseman opened them both and stood to one side, presenting Tyson Cronley with a flourish.

He stood beside the huge fireplace with a golf putter in his hand, eyeing a ball. He'd made his fortune in the oil business, first as a driller, then as something of an inventor when he'd designed two valves and a collar attachment that had made some drastic changes in the industry. Even with the depressed domestic oil market for new drilling, he still managed sales inside the U.S., and had opened up trade with European, Russian and Arabic oil companies. His annual tax was in the high seven figures, and his income exceeded that.

Cronley tapped the ball and sent it speeding across the green that covered a third of the huge room. Obediently it dropped into the cup, where a spring mechanism immediately sent it spinning back out. He stopped it with the putter and set himself for another shot.

"That will be all, Wentworth."

"Yes, sir," the houseman responded. He took a last look at Lyons, then exited and closed the double doors.

"Mr. Lundquist," Cronley said in a deep baritone, eyeing the golf ball again. He was in his early sixties, slightly heavy for his six-foot frame, with dark hair turning fashionably silver, and a darkly tanned face.

"Right," Lyons said.

"Of the I-R-S." Cronley said each letter with impact, then swung the putter, sinking the ball again. The cup sent it whizzing back, to be stopped by the putter once more.

"Right."

"I pay an exorbitant amount of tax annually," Cronley said. He whacked the golf ball again, effortlessly placing it where he wanted.

"Yes, sir. I've looked over your tax returns."

"Then what are you doing here?"

"Some information came into our hands concerning tax evasion."

"On my behalf?"

"Yes, sir." Lyons waited to see what would happen once he'd dropped the bomb.

"Perhaps you people should check your figures again. I hire a fleet of income-tax experts to take care of my business accounts."

"This didn't come from your business accounts," Lyons said. He placed the briefcase on the desk and opened it, taking out a fistful of photos. "It concerns these." He fanned them out like a winning poker hand.

"And what, pray tell, are those?"

"African artifacts that aren't supposed to be out of their native countries but have ended up for sale to certain extremely interested investors." Lyons paused. "Like yourself, of course."

"You flatter me," Cronley said with a disarming smile. "You're talking more culture than this old country boy could ever hope to achieve. Even cow-pasture pool is a stretch for me."

"No, sir." Lyons easily remembered the guy's background from the dossier provided by Price and Kurtzman. "Since earning your fortune, you've also received a doctorate in archaeology from London University."

"Most people tend to forget that." Cronley lined up the golf ball again.

"We found it."

"I'm of English stock, you know."

Lyons didn't say anything. He'd learned as a cop how to use silence as an implied threat.

"Wealth is a funny thing," Cronley said as he hit the ball and saw it go bouncing from the lip of the cup. He looked irritated for a moment, then crossed to the corner of the room, where a coffee service was waiting. "When you think you have more money than you could ever possibly use, you start finding new uses for it. Acquisition becomes important." He waved a hand at the house. "I can show you rooms of things I'd at one time have never known existed, much less cared about. Now I possess them." He smiled. "And found that I delight in doing so."

Lyons nodded, sensing that Cronley was getting ready to deal.

"At first it was things from the West." Cronley gestured toward the leather-bound Louis L'Amour books that filled several shelves. "I read every word that man wrote, then spent time in some of the places he wrote about. I brought back items I treasure a great deal. Some I found on my own, and others I bought. Then I went through what I call my European phase."

"Progressing to Africa," Lyons said, wanting to move the talk back to the chosen topic.

"Yes. There are artifacts from those countries that reflect widely different cultures. Besides the indigenous peoples, there are also influences left by the British, Portuguese, Italian, Spanish, French and so on. A veritable smorgasbord of the ancient and imperialist periods of the world."

"And you had the chance to acquire some of the artifacts from Walukagi?"

"Yes." Cronley poured two cups of coffee and gave one to Lyons. "I have a British officer's uniform dating back to the 1760s, an astrolabe from the early nineteenth century and a pair of dueling pistols supposedly taken from the *One-Eyed Jack,* a pirate ship that belonged to Bartholomew Roberts in 1721, a year before his death at the hands of Captain Chaloner Ogle of the HMS *Swallow*. Of course, they didn't start out as Roberts's dueling pistols. I'm having them authenticated now, but I believe they belonged to a Charles Clayton, also known as Lord Greystoke of the House of Lords."

"You got them from a man named Pearrow."

"Now we're down to the nut-cutting," Cronley observed, "as my father would have put it."

"Yeah. And yours are the ones on the table."

Cronley sipped his coffee. "You're here to deal, Mr. Lundquist. That's why it's only you and me this morning, and not an army of lawyers besides. I knew that as soon as I talked to the young lady earlier this morning. The IRS doesn't normally make it a practice to call taxpayers at such inconvenient hours about a discrepancy."

"Not reporting business transactions worth millions is a felony," Lyons said. "And I'm sure the customs offices would take a certain amount of offense at your collections."

"What's the bottom line here?" Cronley asked.

"We could make a hell of a lot of trouble for you."

"But you won't."

Lyons didn't reply.

"In exchange for what?" Cronley pressed. He didn't appear stressed at all.

Lyons knew the man had enough money to hold out for years, then probably walk away from the whole situation. But there was also the man's public image to consider. A smear campaign by the IRS could cost millions. "For the names of the people who sold you the artifacts from Walukagi."

Cronley chuckled. "You already have Pearrow. What more do you want?"

"The people behind him."

"Then you should ask him."

"We did," Lyons said. "He said he didn't know."

"And you, of course, believe him?"

"He makes a very convincing argument." Price and Brognola had both agreed that they believed Pearrow was telling the truth.

"Of course. And what makes you think I might know?"

"Because you're a savvy kind of guy," Lyons said. "You made your fortune the hard way, you earned it. You wouldn't let anyone burn you. I think you have your own resources for checking back on the things you buy."

Cronley considered that, then smiled. "You're right. This collecting business can be quite expensive. It's all done for ego. You'd be surprised at how many dealers out there can knock off an almost perfect replica of a genuine antique."

"Who was behind Pearrow?" Lyons asked. He masked his impatience and took another sip of the coffee, hardly tasting it. With the situation in Walukagi, with Striker and Phoenix caught up in God knew what kind of spiderweb of conspiracy and counterconspiracy, the Stony Man teams needed information in the worst way.

"What do I get out of this?" Cronley asked.

"Your collection. Intact."

"By the time you get a court order, it might not be here anymore."

Lyons reached inside the briefcase and took out the federal documents. "I already have it. And I've got a team waiting outside your gate." He showed the man the walkie-talkie on his belt. "We can take possession of this house immediately."

Cronley put his cup down.

"So what's it going to be?" Lyons pressed.

"I don't think you're exactly the IRS type," Cronley said. "I've dealt with them before. You're a hard guy."

"Only if I have to be."

"I get the feeling I'm in deeper than I'd thought."

"You can get out of it real easy," Lyons said.

Cronley nodded, more sober and less in control than he'd been. "You're right. I did have the people behind Pearrow checked out, and I don't think he's aware of who they are, either. But I found out."

"Give me a name," Lyons said, "and I close that briefcase, leave the papers unfiled and walk right out of this room."

"White Tiger Investments," Cronley answered. "It's owned by a man named Wilhelmus Kamer."

Lyons nodded and closed the briefcase. "Thanks for the coffee." Halfway across the room, Cronley's voice stopped him.

"This man, Kamer. The word I got was that he's a very dangerous man."

"Yeah. We were kind of expecting that." Lyons let himself out.

Stony Man Farm, Virginia
9:01 a.m.

HAL BROGNOLA STARED at the face on the wall screen at the other end of the computer lab. Price was beside him, and Kurtzman manned the computer keyboard controlling the dissemination of information.

On-screen, Wilhelmus Kamer was frozen in front of a tall building in downtown Cape Town, a black-and-gold leopard at his side. A group of people were talking to him.

"This is the guy we're looking for?" the head Fed asked.

"He's the man behind White Tiger Investments," Price said. "We're running background checks on him now."

"Show me what you've got." Brognola rubbed his eyes tiredly. The long hours were taking their toll, and many of them had been spent on the phone coordinating different operations to supply and support the Stony Man teams in Walukagi.

"Kamer's been around South Africa since he was born," the mission controller said, staring at the man. On-screen, a montage of pictures started sifting like playing cards, underscoring her words. "White Tiger Investments has been in the South African papers for one reason or another for years. A lot of research has gone into how Kamer was able to amass his fortune."

The scene shifted, showing a much younger Kamer dressed in battle fatigues. He was shown leaping over an overturned jeep, an explosion going off behind him as he shielded his dirt-streaked face with his arm. He carried an assault rifle in the other hand. A bandolier of bullets crossed his chest. The tag line for the picture gave credit to the *National Geographic*.

"He started out in the Rhodesian War," Price continued, "and ended up on the losing side. Black independence was granted in 1980."

This time the screen showed footage from a CBS news broadcast, regarding the former Rhodesia. A group of white soldiers marched in ragtag fashion through a jungle while a Huey UH-1D hovered overhead, a door gunner training a .50-caliber machine gun over them. A red circle appeared on the screen, highlighting Kamer.

"After the war," Price said, "Kamer started his own mercenary teams, working for whoever had the money, and sometimes hiring out to both sides. The CIA worked with him for a time, which is probably where he got his connection to Pearrow, but booted him out of the free-lance roster when they caught him selling them out."

Another picture settled onto the screen, this one of Kamer dressed in combat black for a night mission. The background was obviously the cargo area of a plane. Other men stood waiting, parachute packs on their backs.

"He spent six years doing that, then branched out into robbery and murder for profit. He worked with men he'd met during his mercenary days. His partners often didn't fare very well, but his fortune grew."

A newspaper article with a black-and-white picture of Kamer was next. The man wore a black tux and held a brandy snifter in one hand as easily as he'd wielded the assault rifle. The scene was a festive party, and his audience consisted of two beautiful women in evening gowns. All three were laughing. The headline read: Cape Town Benefit for Save the Children a Gala and Successful Affair.

"His targets were small villages and other bandits," Price continued. "Not many were left to testify against him. He took ivory, diamonds and gold."

"And national treasures," Brognola added.

Price nodded. "Once he started traveling in the wealthier circles, he acquired a knowledge of culture."

"Like where to put the price tag and how much," Kurtzman growled in stern disapproval. He worked the trackball mechanically, watching the three monitors before him.

"Oh, yes," Price said. "And he used his newfound fame to win even more friends."

The parade of faces that followed were only partially recognizable to Brognola. The ones he did know were connected with emerging German interests after the Berlin Wall fell. "German money."

"Yes."

The succession of shots broadened to show Kamer acting the part of the big-game hunter with his new friends. There was a photograph of him with his foot on a lion's chest, his arm wrapped around the shoulders of a skinny man in pith helmet and khakis. Other photos followed, continuing the theme.

"In 1990 he opened White Tiger Investments and sunk most of his capital into South African real estate and businesses."

Real estate contracts, business licenses, tax forms and several prospectuses for different companies showed on the screen. Brognola didn't try to memorize any of it. Price would boil it down and generate hard copy.

The screen changed once more, coming to a rest on Kamer as the big-game hunter once more, wearing an Australian hat with the brim pinned up on one side. His weapon was a Nitro Express rifle, and he had the sole of an alligator boot resting against the horn of a dead rhinoceros. His grin was cocky and sure.

"What's his interest in Walukagi?" Brognola asked. "Aside from the obvious national treasures he's been taking out of the country."

"He links up with Masiga," Kurtzman said. He tapped the keyboard, bringing up different accounts. "A number of banks have accounts that trace back to Kamer and to Masiga."

"So they do business with each other," the head Fed said irritably. "That doesn't put Kamer on the scene at Walukagi as part of the effort to control the country."

"The holdings of White Tiger Investments in South Africa are shaky," Price explained. "With the ascent to power by the ANC, Kamer could see everything he's worked for and killed for go straight down the drain. Even though he's got an army at his beck and call, and I can show you the payroll sheets to prove it, there's no way he could take a stand in South Africa." She paused. "But he could in Walukagi."

Brognola turned it over in his mind.

"Another thing is the money for the attacks against Kalimuzo and the people at the Bayou Blossom last night," Kurtzman added. "That didn't come out of any accounts Masiga has anything to do with. Those were purely from the coffers of White Tiger Investments once you got past the smoke screens. Kamer has been working his own agenda here, in spite of Masiga."

"There's a wealth of resources in Walukagi," Brognola said. "We all know that. And if Masiga was in Kamer's pocket, it would give him somewhere to run if the political climate in South Africa turned nasty. But he's always cut himself in for something bigger than the surface value of things. At least, judging by his later career." He glanced at the monitor to Kurtzman's right, which showed current news footage of British soldiers making their presence known on the streets of Cape Anansi.

"The only way to know that," Price said, "is to ask him when we find him. We've already got enough on him for several international indictments."

Brognola shook out two antacid tablets for his stomach. His cop's instinct was sending out warning signals that he couldn't ignore. "We're missing something here," he said, staring at the PR picture of Kamer advertising White Tiger Investments.

"Those pieces will drop in," Price said. "At least now we have the border. We know what to look for even if we aren't sure what it is."

"Hal."

All three of them looked up at Carmen Delahunt. "Striker's on line one."

"I've got it," Kurtzman said. "He's coming in by satellite from the *Freedeburg*." He punched keys on the computer. The middle monitor on his desk flickered, then showed Mack Bolan and Yakov Katzenelenbogen standing in the office off the CIC.

"We've got a problem," the big warrior said without preamble. "Early this morning someone hit the water supply stations in Cape Anansi. On the surface it looked like failed attempts to destroy the water supply."

Brognola felt his stomach tighten as he realized the other shoe was about to drop sooner than he'd expected.

"As a precaution, Yakov and I asked the medical teams aboard the *Freedeburg* to analyze water samples cycling through the systems now, comparing them against water supplies that had been taken earlier. According to the findings, a virus has been introduced into the water."

"What kind of virus?" Brognola asked.

"Dr. Beecham's not certain yet," Bolan answered, "but he believes it's an animal virus."

"With humans as the animal targets," Brognola said. They were all silent for a time.

Then Katz said, "Whatever it ultimately is, it's been in the water system long enough to get to most every man, woman and child in the city. With the action taking place this afternoon, if it is contagious now, there's no telling how far it could spread."

"What about the *Freedeburg?*" Price asked. "Can the carrier's integrity be maintained?"

"I don't know," Bolan said. "If we start the clock at the time the water supply plants were hit, we've still had shifts of people come and go aboard the *Freedeburg.* Depending on how contagious this virus is, everyone could be infected."

Brognola knew Bolan was talking about the Stony Man teams, as well.

"Dr. Beecham thinks that anyone who hasn't drunk the water or been exposed to blood from a potential victim might be risk free," Katz said. "With that in mind, we quarantined the ship and put questionable people ashore."

"Does anyone know why?" Brognola asked.

"Not yet," Bolan replied. "Not for sure. But people will talk."

"Yeah, I know," the head Fed said. "And there's plenty of reporters to pick up on the gossip."

"Striker," Price interjected, "I'm having Aaron patch a satellite channel through to Walter Reed and the

Center for Disease Control in Atlanta. They can work with Beecham and maybe figure out what this is and combat it."

Bolan nodded. "What about Masiga's men?"

"Still moving," Brognola answered, "but if we have to, we can make a creative leap at this point and get close to Masiga's stronghold. Once we get a time frame, if we don't know anything more definite, we'll act on that. It won't be the surgical strike we want, but we can make a stand."

The two Stony warriors agreed.

"We've got some new Intel downloading to you as we speak," Brognola said. "It appears Able Team has turned up Masiga's silent partner. A man named Wilhelmus Kamer."

"Where can we find him?" the Executioner asked.

Cape Town, South Africa
5:20 p.m.

"THEY KNOW who you are."

Wilhelmus Kamer stared hard at Sonnet Quaid. "How?"

The woman sat at her desk in front of her computer. She tapped the keyboard as she worked. "It has something to do with a man named Tyson Cronley. Do you know him?"

Kamer nodded tightly. The American oilman had paid an outrageous amount for a pair of dueling pistols Masiga's men had taken from a Kausan man in the jungle. "But how did he know about me?"

"I don't know." Quaid shrugged. "My ability to peer into the covert team's activity is extremely limited. I picked up Cronley's name only a few hours before your files were suddenly pulled worldwide. They even accessed newspapers from all over South Africa."

"They know I'm here." Kamer started pacing.

"I'd say that's a good bet. And there's something else." Quaid tapped the keyboard again.

Peering over her shoulder, Kamer watched as the color monitor rolled news footage of the aircraft carrier sitting out in the Indian Ocean. A steady convoy of landing craft and cargo boats streamed from the ship, carrying supplies and men.

Quaid adjusted the volume, and a man's voice could be heard. "—knows exactly what the activity aboard the American flagship means, but hands seem to be determined to work around the clock. Elsewhere, in the presidential palace, behind the new security systems set up by the United States Marines and protected by members of the British SAS, Prime Minister Henry Kalimuzo goes about putting his country back in working order." The scene shifted to shots of the British military performing high profile patrolling of the Cape Anansi streets. "No one knows for sure how many—"

Quaid shut off the link. "I'm willing to bet they found out about the virus, too. Vanscoyoc was sloppy with the attacks on the water supply stations."

Kamer looked around the big house, realizing for the first time that he didn't relish the idea of leaving it. The house had been his home for a number of years. "Vanscoyoc performed adequately. Those people are overly suspicious. The only way they could have found the virus is to have centrifuged the water and used an electron microscope."

"They're quarantining the area, goddammit," Quaid said. "Can't you see that? That's why they're leaving the ship. They're cutting their losses, drawing a line at whatever attrition they expect."

"They don't know anything about the Apocalypse Virus," Kamer said. "They can't know what to expect."

"Maybe not, but they're preparing for it."

"Let them." Kamer stared at her. "The more they try to prepare for the unknown, the more noticeable their actions are going to be to the media. By the time they release the truth, that country's going to be ready for mass hysteria."

Quaid sank into quiet, reflective thought. "Maybe you're right."

"Of course I'm right. All they've managed to do is move up the timetable."

"You said the virus wouldn't start showing effects for at least two months."

"As far as driving the host body insane, it won't. But in forty-eight hours the changes in the host become irreversible. They'll lose the soldiers they have in Walukagi, and most of the people in Cape Anansi, as well."

"But that won't get the virus to the United States," Quaid protested.

"No." Kamer looked at her. "You really hate the Americans, don't you?"

She arched her brows and met his gaze. "Only their pompousness."

"You've never said why. When I found you in Berlin, after the wall fell, you exhibited the expertise I've always found so useful, but you've never said why you hate them."

"No. I never have. It's a closed and boring subject."

Kamer was intrigued, but shelved his questions. "Even if the Apocalypse Virus isn't introduced into the United States as I'd anticipated through this action, it still can be. As you know, Maaloe's laboratory is based in Minnesota. There is time to strike again."

"I'll make you a deal," Quaid said, getting out of her chair. "If you can introduce the virus into the U.S. at this point, as you'd first planned—" she put her hands behind her back and untied the bra top of her mustard yellow bikini, which dropped to her bare feet "—then you can have me any way you want me for a whole night." The bikini bottoms slithered down her legs to the floor.

Kamer smiled at her.

"That's a generous offer," she said coyly. "The girl, the gold watch and a head start on your own country."

"What's to stop me from taking you right here and now?" Kamer felt his body responding to her allure.

"Me," Quaid replied. "I can promise you that one of us would die in the attempt." She smiled without warmth. "Besides, I assure you, you'd rather have me as a willing partner." Without another word, she strode naked from the room and up the staircase

Silently Kamer watched her go. Then he broke himself out of his trance and started making the preparations necessary to evacuate his holdings in South Africa. At the present, he had nowhere else to go but to link up with Masiga in Walukagi. He hated the idea of staying with the man, even though they were supposed to be partners.

But that, he reminded himself, wasn't a situation that would last much longer than he needed Masiga or the army he controlled.

Aboard the USS Freedeburg,
6:37 p.m.

"BESIDES KAMER AND Masiga, there are a couple other people you need to know about." Mack Bolan passed the two dossiers around the conference table to the men of Phoenix Force, Jack Grimaldi and John Kissinger. They sat alone in the carrier's CIC. The big warrior's voice echoed off the steel bulkheads. "First up is Jakob Vanscoyoc, called the Dutchman. A number of other aliases are listed there."

"Seems like a well-rounded guy," Calvin James said, scanning the sheets. "Murder, mayhem and malevolence. He's got the three M's covered."

"Make no mistakes," Yakov Katzenelenbogen said, "this is a very dangerous man. Video footage from the attack on Kalimuzo earlier leads us to believe he organized it."

"Also," Bolan added, "with Vanscoyoc in the area, that puts him up for the water-supply-station explosions and the introduction of the virus."

"What do we do with him if we find him?" David McCarter asked.

"Take him alive if you can," Katz said. "But if you can't, put him down. He figures to be a major player, and maybe a lead to the nature of the virus, but there are other possibilities open to us. I don't want him to have a chance to slip behind us."

Bolan surveyed the men in the room. With the specter of the virus hanging over them, their futures uncertain because some of them had undoubtedly been exposed to it, they were all still willing to play the hand they'd been dealt to the last card. There was no one he'd rather lead into battle against long odds.

"The other person," the Executioner went on, glancing at the pretty face in the next photo, "goes by the name Sonnet Quaid. As you can see from her dossier, we have little information on her. But we know she provides much of the intelligence Kamer's been working from."

"Pretty little thing, isn't she?" Jack Grimaldi commented.

"You'll notice," Bolan said, "in the small amount we do have for her, that she knifed a couple men in a bar who became rather aggressive in their demands. Kamer used his influence to have the second-degree-murder charges dropped. From witness reports, the two men had given up when she killed them."

"Where's Kamer now?" Rafael Encizo asked.

"Our best guess," Bolan admitted, "is that he's on his way to join Masiga. Hal called in a few favors from the CIA and had the offices of White Tiger Investments searched, as well as Kamer's home. No one was there."

"But we have Masiga targeted?" Gary Manning asked.

"Yes." Bolan unfurled a topographical map of Walukagi and spread it across the conference table. "Kurtzman's microprocessors worked." He tapped the map. "Masiga's stronghold was triangulated—here—by the AWACS."

"However," Katz said, "we weren't able to get any satellite pictures because the jungle is too dense there. We sent a couple planes over, but they weren't able to improve any on what we had."

Bolan studied the map. "According to reports we've been able to get from people who've lived in the area, that part of the jungle is treacherous. Built on the side of the Drakensberg Mountains, the stronghold is all broken terrain near the Mpunga River."

"What kind of armament can we expect?" John Kissinger asked.

"Primarily artillery," Bolan replied. "But that's a guess. They'll be heavily fortified and dug in."

"And hopefully not expecting us," Katz said.

"Who's going in?" McCarter asked.

"We are," the Executioner answered. "Us, and the twenty blacksuits that shipped with Cowboy from the Farm."

"How?" Grimaldi asked.

"Without wings," the hellfire warrior replied. "There's a train line that'll take us within eight klicks of Masiga's base."

"They'll hear us coming," Kissinger stated.

"No," Katz said. "We'll take the train from outside the city. It's been stopped out there for days, anyway, unable to travel into the downtown area. No one should know we're using it."

"Even if they do," Bolan said, "this is going to be a hit-and-git strike. We should be on them before they know it." He looked around the room. "Any questions?"

There weren't.

"All right, grab your gear and get it together. The train pulls out at 8:15, which should be about dusk." Bolan folded the maps and put them away, thinking about the mission. Masiga's troop strength was estimated at somewhere near four hundred. Twenty-eight men going up against them didn't sound like much. But as he and Katz had agreed, it wasn't just any twenty-eight men.

Outside Cape Town, South Africa
6:41 p.m.

WHILE WILHELMUS KAMER was giving orders to the crew loading the De Havilland airplane inside the hangar, Sonnet Quaid picked up the slim valise she'd packed with money and slipped into the shadows.

Her job with the South African was done. She'd used his network for all she was able, found out new information about the hidden counterstrike base in America and helped escalate events to a head.

Dressed in black jeans, a black turtleneck and black boots, she melted into the night. On a hill almost three-quarters of a mile away, she stopped to rest and to watch the plane take off.

Minutes passed while she gazed up at the stars. Then she heard the roar of engines and saw the De Havilland go screaming into the air, heeling over to head in the direction of Walukagi. She hoped Kamer's parachute opened when he reached Masiga's stronghold.

Then she reached into the case at her hip and took out the cellular phone. She punched in a series of numbers to first access the special satellite overhead, then added the phone number she wanted to call.

"QuesTech," a man answered in a smooth voice.

"Mr. Wysiek, this is Sonnet Quaid. I've pulled out of the operation."

"Then I'll see you back here soon?"

"Yes, sir."

"What about Mr. Kamer?" Wysiek asked.

"On a collision course with Brognola's people."

"Excellent, Sonnet. He's going to use the Apocalypse Virus?"

"Yes."

"And the antidote?"

"I was inoculated before I left."

"Excellent. We can get the necessary antibodies from you. I wish Mr. Kamer every success with his endeavor, then."

"Frankly," Quaid said, "I don't see how they can stop him."

CHAPTER FOURTEEN

Thirteen Miles East of Cape Anansi
Walukagi—8:13 p.m.

Sunset faded fast from the sky, leaving a bloody bruise for only a few minutes.

Mack Bolan stood beside the ancient, steam-powered locomotive, listening to the hiss of heated air and watching the British soldiers patrolling the perimeter of the city. Like the rest of the Stony Man warriors, he was outfitted in black. The Beretta 93-R was in shoulder leather and the Desert Eagle rode his hip. A Franchi SPAS 15 combat 12-gauge shotgun was slung over his shoulder. His face was tiger-striped with combat cosmetics. On the ground beside him was his combat harness, loaded heavily with gear he anticipated needing for the strike.

"If something doesn't break by morning," Kissinger said as they watched the roving guards, "there's going to be a whole town of pissed-off citizens ready to lynch the people they thought came to save them."

Bolan nodded. The media was already starting to take issue with the fact that the British, U.S. and UN forces were limiting the Walukagians' ability to travel out of the city. But not knowing what the virus was, or what it might do, the military brass had opted to close down the city. Morning would prove whether the citizens still had their rights or martial law was going to be instituted.

The last time Bolan had seen the new prime minister, the man was sitting in the presidential palace with his cabinet members and representatives of the United Kingdom. He'd been told about the virus.

"Let's get it done," Bolan said, grabbing his combat harness. He waved the Stony Man warriors onto the train. He climbed up into the engine with Katz and stood behind a Kausan engineer they'd borrowed for the operation. Other members of the Stony Man teams could operate the engine, but the engineer knew where all the dangerous spots were.

The train took off with a jerk. Besides the engine, there was a coal car and one passenger car. The rest of the team and its gear was crammed into the passenger car.

As the engine gained speed, Bolan took out his map case and unfolded the map of the train line leading to their drop-off point. He used a penlight to trace the route. "Only one place worries me," he said to Katz.

The Israeli nodded. "The bridge over the Mpunga River."

"Yeah. We're going to be vulnerable there."

"Gary can check for mines," Katz said.

"There's still missile attack."

"It's only a quarter mile across," Katz said. "If it's not mined, I don't think they could take it out with rockets before we could cross. If they do, we're on foot, anyway. All we've lost is the element of surprise, and they don't have a railroad to get back into Cape Anansi easily."

"Unless they get us as we're crossing," Bolan replied.

"That," Katz said with feeling, "is something I don't like to think about."

Stony Man Farm, Virginia
12:19 p.m.

"WHAT AM I LOOKING AT?" Aaron Kurtzman asked. He gazed at his left monitor, the one Huntington Wethers had accessed to show the results of the tissue culture Dr. Beecham had come up with aboard the USS *Freedeburg* after working with Walter Reed and the Center for Disease Control. Price and Brognola stood at his side, with Able Team spread out around him.

"Cells taken from a chicken embryo from Cape Anansi," Wethers said. He tapped his keyboard and caused the image to magnify on Kurtzman's monitor. "Dr. Beecham set it up almost immediately after talking to Striker."

The mass of pinkish gray tissue at the bottom of the glass dish didn't look healthy at all. Kurtzman felt his stomach lurch in silent protest.

"With the chicken embryo," Wethers went on, "Dr. Beecham set up the perfect environment for the virus. No antibodies. Nothing that would challenge it or keep it from growing."

"How long would this take to develop in the human body?" Brognola asked.

"The best guess the top guns can offer is somewhere between a month and two months in the average adult, depending on the individual's resistance to infection. And they're still not sure what it does."

"But the people who've been affected have time before it activates?" Price asked.

"They think so. But again, they aren't sure. They've never run into anything like this before. Until they get a chance to break down the RNA or DNA, they're going to have no way of telling."

"Or until it starts showing up in the affected people," Rosario Blancanales offered.

"Right. The only thing they've been able to confirm so far is that there is a very real threat in Walukagi."

"Aaron," Akira Tokaido called from the front of the lab.

Kurtzman looked up at him.

"Just clued into a CNN broadcast," Tokaido said. "Wilhelmus Kamer's center stage." In front of the young computer hacker, the wall screen rainbowed, then settled down into the features all the Stony Man personnel were familiar with.

"—won't tolerate American and European interference in the affairs of African nations," Kamer was saying.

"Where's this coming from?" Brognola demanded.

"A patch-through on the CNN satellite," Tokaido answered. "I'm trying to triangulate the source, but the best I can come up with is Walukagi or South Africa."

"—suffered enough losses while the rest of the world has looked on," Kamer continued. "You people abhorred the apartheid in my country, while in your own you still practiced racial prejudice on a daily basis. We don't need that damn knee-jerk radicalism here. There are many of us who've worked to build our lives down here, in an economic system that was a good environment for us. We stand to lose everything, yet none of you seem to be aware of it."

Kurtzman glanced back at the tissue culture on his monitor. He couldn't find any sympathy for Kamer.

"This time, though, you're not going to be able to back away so easily," Kamer promised. "The Americans are so used to their ability to race into a situation and start throwing their weight around. But you're going to lose people in Walukagi by the dozens, and if you attempt to bring them home, you're going to lose even more."

Checking the other two monitors, Kurtzman saw the background investigations he was doing on White Tiger Investments were narrowing down the field. He'd altered the program to chase down only leads that led to investments in pharmaceuticals and research-and-development companies. The virus had to have been created somewhere within Kamer's holdings. As he watched, a name popped up. He tapped the keyboard.

"I've introduced a killing virus into Walukagi, one that affects the brain and transforms the person afflicted into a psychopathic killer. That virus has infected every soldier, every person over there," Kamer said.

"He's a lying son of a bitch," Lyons growled.

"Yeah," Brognola replied, taking a fresh cigar from his jacket pocket and clamping it between his teeth. "But that's not how the public is going to remember it."

"I also have the antidote to the virus," Kamer said. "In exchange for that, I want U.S., UN and British forces out of the country by morning. There's a forty-eight-hour incubation period for the virus. Once that time is passed, not even the antidote I have will do any good."

"Is that possible?" Price asked Wethers.

Wethers nodded. "A virus gets into a cell and changes it. A lot of cancers are thought to be viruses. The virus cells could reproduce for weeks before showing any physical signs in the host.''

Kurtzman prodded the computer, searching for more information from the data bases he was hooked into. He pulled tax reports, international newspapers, scientific journals in a half dozen different languages and various espionage agency files he had access to.

''If you don't accept my offer,'' Kamer said, ''there won't be anything left of Walukagi to save. And if you attempt to double-cross me, you won't even be able to save yourselves.'' The transmission abruptly ended, leaving blank space until the producers realized there wasn't going to be anything else and switched back to the anchors.

Kurtzman killed the transmission. ''I've got something.''

''What?'' Brognola asked.

''A possible name,'' Kurtzman replied, warming to his subject. He punched the keys, bringing up a picture of a man in his late fifties, with narrow eyes that looked magnified by the black-rimmed glasses he wore.

''Who's that?'' Hermann Schwarz asked.

''Dr. Linus Maaloe,'' Kurtzman said, pulling up the man's stats. ''Born in Stockholm. Education completed in Antwerp. Specialized in germ warfare, particularly viruses.''

''He connects to Kamer?'' Brognola asked.

''Maaloe connects to Flair Subsidiaries, which—through three holding companies that were a bitch to get through—connect to White Tiger Investments, then to Wilhelmus Kamer.''

''What makes you think Maaloe designed the virus?'' Price asked.

"The way Kamer described it," Kurtzman replied, "puts me in mind of some things DARPA was working on back when I drew a check from them. There was a virus that came up in one of the think-tank discussions among the upper brass, which I happened to be a member of at the time, that had to do with attacking the brain and causing disassociation, paranoia and an almost direct adrenaline overload to the flight-or-fight instinct."

DARPA was an acronym for the Defense Advanced Research Projects Agency. During his short tenure there, Kurtzman had seen all sorts of nasty creations and proposed creations.

"I placed a keyhole in the computer programming before I left," Kurtzman said, "so I could tap in occasionally and take a look at what they were developing. Anyway, I used that access to check through their closed files. The guy who came up with this radical virus didn't get funded because there was no way to justify the end result. It was way the hell too far out from Geneva conventions. And a lot of research was being put into the SDI systems at the time."

"The scientist who was turned down was Maaloe?" Lyons asked.

"Bingo," Kurtzman replied. "He's been around the world a few times since, working for various pharmaceutical companies in R & D. He's never held a job for long."

"Until he got one with Kamer by way of White Tiger Investments," Brognola said.

"Regular Cinderella story," Schwarz commented.

"Where can we find him?" Brognola asked.

Kurtzman brought up a map of Minnesota, then magnified the area he was searching for. "Here," he said. The name of the town was highlighted. "Near Park Rapids and Lake Itasca. I don't have any pictures of the place. Yet."

"Are you sure he's there?" Lyons asked.

"No. But it's a starting point."

Price studied the map. "If I was Kamer and I was relatively sure no one knew about Maaloe, I'd want him kept in an out-of-the-way place where I could get my hands on him quick if I needed to."

"That," Kurtzman said, "sounds like Minnesota. But there's something else to consider. Lake Itasca is the starting point of the Mississippi River." He tapped the keyboard and enlarged the map to show the continental United States. The Mississippi River snaked through the heart of the country, reaching down to the Gulf of Mexico. "With the viral spread in Walukagi, we know it can be carried through the water."

"My God," Brognola said hoarsely. "If Maaloe's still up there and Kamer decided to dump the virus into the lake water, that viral infection could spread across the country in weeks."

"Provided he could manufacture a sufficient quantity," Kurtzman said. "Yeah, I'd say that's possible."

"And that's assuming it hasn't already been done," Price pointed out.

The thought settled heavily over the room, interrupted only by the ringing telephone. Brognola answered it, then moved into Price's office to complete the conversation. Kurtzman knew from the caller ID that the call had come from the White House.

Moving on, his mind working furiously, the cybernetics expert accessed dozens of BBS's he was familiar with, matching the names he found there against the employment records he got on Flair Subsidiaries from the IRS and Immigration. Since Maaloe was an alien, he had to be registered with the INS. Working with the knowledge that scientists and specialists were often locked away from the rest of the world for days, weeks and months at a time, and missed the ability to communicate with others, he figured that he'd find Maaloe on one of the international BBS's.

Eighteen minutes later he found Maaloe had been logging on with a BBS in New York that catered to scientific circles specializing in chemistry and biology. He looked over the entries as he checked the e-mail. Besides using his own name, Maaloe had been in regular correspondence with four people on the BBS. Kurtzman automatically punched in requests for background checks on the other names he found. But the main thing he discovered was that the last entry made by Maaloe had been from Flair at 8:47 that morning.

"He was there this morning," he told Able Team and Price. "So there's no reason to think he's not there now."

Lyons looked at Price. "We get a plane, and we can be there and set up inside of five hours. Striker and Phoenix may have the jump on us, but we can catch up."

The mission controller nodded, then got out her cellular phone and started making the calls to put the mission in motion.

The first thing Kurtzman noticed when Brognola returned from Price's office a few minutes later was the dark scowl the big Fed was wearing.

"We're go on the attempt on Flair Subsidiaries," Brognola said, "but the Man's going to order the military to enforce the quarantine in Walukagi till we know more about what we're up against. He and the other nations' heads have decided not to risk spreading the virus any further than it may have already gone. Not a plane, boat, Hummer or man is supposed to move out of that area from this point on.'' He looked at the map of Walukagi and let out a deep breath. ''Wherever Striker and Phoenix are out in that jungle, they're on their own.''

Mpunga River Bridge, Walukagi
9:43 p.m.

CLINGING TO THE OUTSIDE of the locomotive as it started out onto the bridge, Mack Bolan scanned the surrounding jungle. The river was dark and swift seventy feet below, white water showing in the pale moonlight. The wind carried a biting chill that penetrated the warrior's combat blacksuit.

Gary Manning had pronounced the bridge safe and secure less than ten minutes earlier after spending twenty minutes crawling through the support beams and checking out the other side of the divide.

Holding on to the side of the locomotive with one hand, the Executioner used night glasses to survey the jungle below. Calvin James was using a thermal imager. So far, neither man had spotted anything. Aboard the train, they weren't able to set up the miniature satellite dish and take advantage of the Stony Man Farm uplink.

Approaching the midway point, Grimaldi accessed the headset frequency. ''I hear a plane,'' the pilot insisted.

Bolan listened intently, but couldn't hear anything. Still, he trusted the pilot, and Grimaldi knew everything there was to know about anything that flew.

"He's right, mate," McCarter said. "Coming from the right."

Bolan slipped through the engine compartment and spotted Katz at the window, staring out into the night sky.

"There," the Israeli said, pointing. "Flying barely above treetop level."

Already on the move, Bolan made out the plane shape as he grabbed the H&K 11E machine gun from the rear of the engine. A 50-round drum of 7.62 mm rounds was in place. Scrambling, he shoved his way up onto the top of the engine, followed by Katz. The wind cut into his face as he climbed on top of the flat surface. The train rattled and rolled beneath him, but he still heard Katz urging the engineer to greater speed.

"It's not one of ours," Grimaldi said. "That's a Russian Su-25 Frogfoot."

Bolan lay prone across the top of the racing locomotive and shouldered the H&K 11E. He knew the Frogfoot's designation even if he hadn't readily recognized it against the night. He put the machine gun's sights over the wide-winged plane and steadied himself. The Frogfoot was almost a thousand yards out and closing fast. The plane was a combat support aircraft much like the A-10 Thunderbolt, with air-to-surface strike capabilities with passive missiles and bombs.

"Take it down," the warrior ordered over the headset. Then he squeezed the H&K 11E's trigger in short bursts. The tracer rounds sizzled through the sky as they streaked for the attacking fighter plane. Gunfire from the passenger car joined his.

He locked onto the Frogfoot and blasted through the remainder of the ammo drum. Smoke wisped out behind the plane's cowling as it came within two hundred yards of the train. Twin air-to-surface missiles leapt free of the wings, dipped for an instant, then cut the air like dolphins entering the water.

"Striker!" Katz called.

Bolan caught the fresh ammo drum the Phoenix Force commander slid across the top of the train just as the missiles struck the bridge ahead of the train. The superstructure shivered but held, flames wreathing the truss suspension.

With the drum locked into place, Bolan laid his sights over the Russian fighter again, then pulled the trigger.

The Frogfoot was less than a hundred yards away, looking like an attacking falcon with a full wingspread. Machine guns flared on both sides of the aircraft's body, then bombs spilled out, dropping in a line toward the bridge and the train.

Less than fifty yards in front of the locomotive, with less than two hundred yards to go to the other side of the chasm, the bombs struck the bridge and destroyed it. Sheared almost in two, it broke.

Bolan had a momentary sensation of free-fall, then felt the train drop beneath him. He spun in the air, then kicked out away from the engine. The Mpunga River was below, wide enough and deep enough to allow him to survive the impact.

If he could escape the steel corpse of the train that threatened to drop on top of him.

Stony Man Farm, Virginia
1:46 p.m.

INSIDE THE COMPUTER LAB, Hal Brognola watched the destruction of the Walukagian train in grim silence. The wall screen, plugged into the satellite over the country, captured it all. He saw the fat bodies of the bombs slam into the bridge, rending steel like paper. A moment later the attacking Russian fighter blew up and rained flaming shrapnel across the water and jungle below. The silence made it all surreal. Except that the men who might be dying were his friends and possibly the last hope of a country.

With the bridge blown to pieces, the locomotive, coal car and passenger car tumbled free of the tracks. From the satellite's perspective, they looked like a child's toys thrown toward the river below.

"Can you track them?" he asked.

Kurtzman shook his head. "The satellite's maxed out now. With everything we're running through it, I'm surprised it's stayed viable. The Intel swaps between Walter Reed, the Center for Disease Control and the *Freedeburg* are taking a lot, as well as regular communications."

Brognola shook out two antacid tablets and chewed them.

"If Striker and Phoenix are out of it," Price said, "there's no one to stop Kamer and Masiga from spreading that virus even further."

"Going by Striker's timetable, and the information Kamer gave us," Brognola said, "we've still got about twenty hours to operate in. I'm going to talk to the President, see if I can persuade him to send in a covert unit from SEAL Team Six or the SAS." He gazed at the flames still clinging to the bridge above the Mpunga River. "It's either that or give up now."

Price nodded. "Do that. But I'm not counting those people out yet. They may be alone and in hostile territory, and their operation ripped all to hell, but they won't quit unless they're dead."

"I know," Brognola said. "But I've got to prepare for that, too." He turned away. "Let me know if you find out anything."

Mpunga River, Walukagi
9:48 p.m.

NIGHT GLASSES HELD TIGHT to his eyes, Wilhelmus Kamer cursed the distance that separated him from the battle site. The bridge over the Mpunga River ended in a mangled curve halfway out. The river was a twisting piece of black licorice that disappeared into foliage in the distance.

He stood as close to the edge of the outcrop as he dared. A 125-foot plunge awaited him if he made a single misstep.

"They're dead," Masiga said from behind him.

Kamer turned on the man angrily. "We don't know that. Those men have been extremely dangerous to us."

Masiga looked like an ebony giant, glazed in reds, blues and greens, wearing a loincloth and a necklace made up of the teeth of big cats. More than a hundred warriors stood behind him, all painted like their king.

For an instant Kamer felt as if he were walking barefoot on the edge of a very sharp knife. Out on the outcrop, there was no place for him to go. But he knew he wasn't going to back down. His hand grazed the holstered pistol at his side.

Maybe Masiga saw the movement and read the determination in his eyes, or maybe the big man realized how much he still needed his white partner. Kamer wasn't sure. But Masiga took a step back, turning to face his warriors. "I'll send men into the bush to bring you their bodies. If any live, they'll bring you those bodies, as well." Then he melted into the darkness, taking his men with him.

"Kind of tense there," the Dutchman said laconically. He shoved his pistol back into the paddle holster behind his back.

"The man's a fool," Kamer snarled. "Those men are highly trained and very competent."

Vanscoyoc nodded. "I'd have to agree with you. They took that plane down even with the bridge and the train being shot away beneath them. I don't know many who would have had the courage or skill to do that."

"They did," Kamer said. "And I'm not going to feel at peace until I see their corpses at my feet." He turned and walked down the incline to his Land Rover. Sharde sat in the back, her attention never wavering.

"I think," Vanscoyoc said as he swung into the passenger seat, "that Masiga's going to get damn tired of working with us in the next couple days."

"It won't matter," Kamer said with a grin. "I control the antidote. The inoculations Masiga and his tribe got were all placebos."

"They've been exposed to the virus, too," the Dutchman said.

"Yes, and they're going to die. When I cut my deal with the Germans, I'll have an army ready, willing and able to take control of this country."

"Do you really think the U.S. is going to back off?"

Kamer nodded, thinking of the industrial complex near Lake Itasca in Minnesota. "They'll be having problems of their own in a short time."

The Mpunga River, Walukagi
9:49 p.m.

THE SHOCK AND THE FORCE of hitting the cold water had almost rendered Mack Bolan unconscious. But he'd dived deep, knowing the train was falling almost on top of him.

The river was nearly thirty feet deep under the bridge. He made contact with the muddy river bottom, then straightened out just as the locomotive smashed into the water above and behind him, creating a false wave. Riding the wave, he stroked for the top, his lungs almost bursting from the effort.

He surfaced near the riverbank in water shallow enough to stand in, yet in a place where the foliage hid him. He checked himself with his hands as he saw other figures rising from the river, as well. Other than a scattering of bumps and bruises, everything seemed to be intact.

Sliding the Franchi SPAS 15 forward, he flicked off the safety and let the water drain out of the barrel. The mouthpiece to his ear-throat headset was bent, but after he pulled it back in place and tapped the transmit button, he discovered it was still working.

"Me," the figure in front of him said, stepping into a brief span of moonlight. Gary Manning's right eye was swollen, and the flesh around it was already showing signs of purpling.

"Are you okay?" Bolan asked.

"Found a rock," the Canadian admitted ruefully, "after it found me."

Katz appeared out of the darkness behind the Executioner, panther quiet in the gloom and wholly intact.

His Uzi was held at the ready. "I take it we lost the element of surprise," he said.

"In a big way," Bolan responded.

"They'll be sending someone to see about us," Katz said. "We know they weren't anywhere close by, so we have some time."

Bolan looked out at the water. The bridge was still in flames overhead, and the locomotive resembled a blunt spear that had been thrown into the river. "Not much. And this place isn't even good enough for a holding position."

"Agreed."

Quickly Bolan gave orders over the headset, getting the survivors together and counting of personnel. In less than two minutes he knew that three of the blacksuits were MIA, as well as the Kausan fireman, and that Masiga's hardmen were closing the net. Engines strained in the distance.

"They're going to be looking for us downriver," McCarter said. "They'll figure the current took us all down."

Bolan nodded. They were hunkered under a clearing a hundred yards from the river. The Kausan engineer stood with them. "If we can break through the perimeter without alerting them," the Executioner said, "we can gain a lot of ground by heading upriver before they figure out what happened." Nothing was said of the equipment they'd lost. What wasn't destroyed had been lost in the river. All they had was what each man carried as personal gear.

"Once we find a place to hole up," Katz said, "we should be able to contact the Farm and see about an airlift for more supplies. One way or another, Kamer's got to be put down.''

Bolan agreed. It wasn't much of a plan, but under the circumstances it was all the Stony Man warriors had open to them. He assigned McCarter as point, with Manning and James as wings. Encizo carried the pack containing the LST-5C satellite radio they'd use when they had time. From the cursory examination he'd been able to give it, the Cuban had deemed the radio still functional.

The sound of engines was almost on top of them when they started to move out, keeping low in the tall grass and using the boulders as cover whenever possible. Voices, speaking the Kawalusian dialect, sounded increasingly frantic.

"Down," McCarter whispered suddenly over the headset.

The blacksuits and the Phoenix Force members went down automatically. So did Grimaldi. Kissinger took the engineer down with him, clapping a big hand over the man's mouth.

"What is it?" Bolan asked, peering through the long grass. Most of the enemy was seventy yards and more away.

"Roving team," the Briton answered. "Three men."

"We're going to take them quiet," Bolan said. "Calvin, you're with me."

James radioed an affirmative. In seconds he met Bolan at McCarter's position. With no words between them, the three Stony Man warriors advanced on the hardmen, who went through the tall grass haphazardly with bayonets affixed to their AK-47s.

Bolan targeted the man on the left, exploding from hiding with a Cold Steel Tanto combat knife in his hand. James and McCarter could have been his shadows. He caught the man from behind before he knew death was a whisper away. Holding the man's head back, the Executioner drew his knife across his adversary's exposed throat, then held him until he stopped kicking.

Fisting the corpse's shirt, he pulled the dead man into the grass and left him where he wouldn't be easily found. The two Phoenix Force warriors did the same.

Bolan tapped the transmit button. "Move out."

By the time they reached the ragged terrain of the Drakensberg Mountains, more than a hundred men were sweeping the river. Sheltered by the rock, Bolan and Katz studied the maps, trying to decide their next move. Bolan knew that any quick attempt to get back across the Mpunga River would probably meet with defeat.

"Our best choice," Katz said, "is to remain with the infiltration and hope to make contact with the airfield soon. Maybe in addition to more equipment, we can form other attack groups."

"And go head-to-head with Kamer and Masiga?" Bolan asked.

"Or retreat," Katz replied. "But I didn't come here to retreat."

"Neither did I." Bolan looked over his men. Guards had been assigned while they took a breather, and he'd ordered them to eat some of their rations. When a soldier was hiding and running for his life, a luxury like eating reminded him that he had some control over his existence.

All of the men in his group were seasoned fighters who'd warred around the globe. None of them would be thinking of giving up.

"And neither did they," Katz said.

"Our best chance is to stay with the mountains," Bolan told him. "We can fight a holding position if we have to, and wait on reinforcements and more equipment. At this point, we're not totally cut off from our options."

Katz nodded.

A pained look on his face, Grimaldi joined the two men. A pair of night glasses hung around his neck. "They found one of the missing guys downriver. He's dead. But they're obviously getting antsy that they haven't found any more bodies. Masiga's beginning to pull his people in tighter."

"Any sign of Kamer?" Bolan asked.

"Once. So we know for sure the bastard's there."

Bolan borrowed the night glasses and climbed out on the rock face where they'd taken shelter. He scanned the riverbanks below them. The enemy force ran in ragged lines on both sides of the water, flashlights playing out ahead of them. There were so many of them they looked like a collection of fireflies.

"They'll spread out the net now," Katz said at his side. "There won't be much doubt that most of us have escaped."

"I know." Bolan looked farther down the rock face to where Encizo was working on the radio. So far they hadn't been able to make the Stony Man uplink even though the unit had power. "How's it coming, Rafe?"

The Cuban shrugged. "Given more time, more light, I think I can fix it."

"I'm going to hold you to that." Bolan scanned the ridges in both directions. Instinct told him to keep heading upriver. Masiga's hardsite lay in that direction, but they weren't expecting the Stony Man warriors to come that way. More than anything, the covert force needed breathing space.

"Striker. Yakov."

Bolan turned to see Kissinger walking toward them with the engineer limping at his side. The man's leg had been badly bruised and possibly fractured. His face was gray with the pain.

"I've been talking to Brahim," Kissinger said, "and he tells me he knows a spot where we might be able to hide out till we figure out our next step." A wry grin twisted the armorer's face. "You're going to love this."

"In which direction?" Bolan asked.

"Upriver," Kissinger replied. Then he told them where.

CHAPTER FIFTEEN

Scorpion Falls, Walukagi
11:03 p.m.

The roar of the falls drowned out all other sounds in the surrounding jungle. Bolan had to yell to hear himself above it. The falls sluiced through one of the lower levels of the mountains, then came tumbling down forty feet to plunge into the Mpunga River. Almost thirty-five feet across, the falls presented an avalanche of water.

Kissinger crept back along the rock face almost twenty feet up, emerging from under the falls. His face was wet from the spray, and his blacksuit gleamed.

"There's a cave back in there," Kissinger yelled over the headset.

"Can we make it in?" Bolan asked. He had the team spread out, standing guard. So far there were no signs of pursuit from Kamer or Masiga. Almost two miles back, he'd checked the coordinates of Masiga's stronghold against the coordinates that the GPS had given for the microprocessors. Kurtzman's tracking devices had been on the money.

"I've driven pitons in along the way, and I've got it roped off. Everyone we've got can make it." Kissinger continued coming, making his way deftly. "If it wasn't the rainy season, we'd probably be able to get in from below a lot easier. There's another, larger opening below. This one, it's more like a door than anything else.

There's even some steps carved into the stone. I used a penlight a little. Did you see it?''

"No," Katz replied.

"I thought maybe you wouldn't. There's a tunnel that leads down to the main cave, but I didn't go in. Though, at a guess, I'd be willing to bet it's just like Brahim said and there's plenty of room for us to hide out." Kissinger made the final leap onto the soft ground.

Bolan turned to James. "Calvin, pick three men and you're our outer-perimeter security."

James tossed him a wave, then chose his team out of the blacksuits.

"There's a back way out, too?" the warrior asked Brahim.

The man nodded. "My grandfather told me about this place. Once, pirates lived here. They raided along the coast, even down into Cape Town and Cape Horn. Then they would come here and hide while the British ships hunted for them. They had ways in and ways out because they didn't want to get trapped. Sometimes they would spend months here, plundering wherever they chose, then returning. The last pirate to use this cave was a man named Bartholomew Roberts."

"No one else knows about this place?" Katz asked.

"Many people are aware of it, but no one goes here anymore. This is a place of the dead. Sometimes fortune hunters venture inside, but everything of any worth has already been taken, although my cousin saw a man walk out of there a few years ago with a set of dueling pistols that had been hidden away inside." He looked up at the falls. "Before this was Scorpion Falls, it carried another name. A Kausan name. But that has been stripped from us as surely as the treasure the pirates left."

"Does Masiga know about this cave?" Bolan asked.

"Yes. But I don't believe he will think of it. As I said, no one comes here anymore. And the rainy season makes it especially hard to get to."

Bolan looked at Katz. "If we go in there, we could get trapped."

"If we stay out in the open, we could get spotted," the Israeli said, playing devil's advocate. "Inside we can get situated, get some of our equipment checked and maybe set up a drop from Cape Anansi."

"Then let's take a look inside and see what we have to work with." Bolan let Kissinger take the lead, then followed. Katz came next, trailed by Grimaldi and the rest of Phoenix Force, then the blacksuits and Brahim.

Water from the falls sprayed over Bolan as he made the climb, soaking the combat blacksuit, which had almost dried during the forced march from the bridge. His fingers and boots found precarious holds on the rocks, aided by the rope Kissinger had stretched taut through the pitons.

The hole leading into the side of the smooth rock under the falls was barely five feet high and three feet wide. The entry ran for six or seven feet, and the Executioner had a hard time getting through.

"Step at the bottom," Kissinger warned.

Bolan found it and went on. Then the armorer switched on his penlight, illuminating the short, narrow tunnel they were in.

"I figure the pirates must have been pretty short," Kissinger said. "Haven't found anything man-sized in here. Yet."

Bolan walked down the steep descent with his combat senses taking in information. The air was drastically cooler here, moist and heavy. Names had been carved into the walls with sharp blades. Some of them had dates that went back more than two hundred years. He felt some of the history that surrounded him.

"Brahim," he called.

"Yes?"

"Is this place fed by an underground spring?"

"Yes. That's why it's so cold here."

"It's just above forty degrees Fahrenheit," Katz said. "It would have been a good spot for any perishables the pirates might have had."

"Or a wine cellar," Grimaldi added.

Almost two hundred feet farther on, Kissinger came to an abrupt stop. "Son of a bitch," he said in a low voice. Then he made adjustments to the penlight, widening the beam.

Bolan stepped around the armorer, reaching for his own penflash and adding the light to Kissinger's. There, trapped in the glare of the two beams, was an underwater lake almost eighty yards across and more than a hundred yards long. Light glimmered from the gentle ripples. Inside the cavern, the sound of the falls was muted, distant.

Stalactites dripped from the uneven cave ceiling forty yards overhead, and limestone drapery lined the walls, giving the environment a delicate appearance. The shoals of the underground lake were wide and generous. It was easy to imagine pirates sitting around camp fires on rum barrels, talking about their latest conquest.

Especially with the sixty-foot sailboat dry-docked on tree trunks that had grayed with the passage of centuries. She was proud and tall, her rapier bowsprit as long as her hull. The single mast stabbed toward the cave ceiling, stopping little more than ten yards short of touching. The rigging was naked, the sailcloth missing.

"Good Lord," one of the blacksuits said. "That's an English sloop. Eighteenth century from the cut of her."

Bolan looked at the man. "What's your name?"

"Dana Henry, sir," the man responded.

"Navy?"

"SEALs, sir."

"You know about ships like that one?"

"I sure do." Then he added, "Sir."

"Join me."

"Yes, sir."

Bolan led the way down, followed by Katz. The way was slippery, but the stone stairway continued. The Executioner drew the Beretta 93-R and flicked off the safety. Even though he'd been told the cave would be vacated, he didn't want to take any chances.

He hit the transmitter. "McCarter."

"Yeah."

"Get Brahim and find the back door to this place."

"You got it, mate."

"Rafe," Bolan said.

"Yes."

"Let me know as soon as you get that radio up and operational."

"Right."

When they reached the sloop, Bolan examined it carefully. The wood showed some age and some wear and tear, but looked intact. Evidently her hull had been scraped clean before she'd been stored.

"God, but she looks to be in good shape," Henry said, touching the wood with a gentle hand.

Bolan played his beam over the sloop as he made his way around her. On the other side, he found a rope ladder. He went up carefully, the Beretta clenched in his fist. Katz completed the walk-through on the ground.

When Bolan stamped his foot against the wooden planking, it sounded strong, resilient. Even the small lifeboat in the bow looked in mint condition. He figured that the coolness of the cave had helped contribute to preserving the wood.

He played his light over the rest of the deck as he walked it, finding the rough places where the cannon had been moored.

"They took the cannon," Henry said, swinging up over the side. "Collectors would have paid a fortune for it."

"Go belowdecks," Bolan said. "Find out if she's as together inside as she appears to be outside."

"You got it, skipper." With a happy, boyish grin on his face, Henry disappeared into the hold.

"Striker," Katz called over the headset, "I'm at the stern."

Bolan crossed the deck, then peered over the sloop's railing. There, at the edge of the cave lake, stood the Israeli playing his flashlight over two skeletons in the water that had been bleached white.

"These," Katz said, "aren't a holdover from the pirate days."

Scorpion Falls, Walukagi
11:29 p.m.

"I FOUND A COMPLETE SET of sails in the hold."

Bolan looked up at Dana Henry, closing his war book, where he was sketching in what he remembered of Masiga's stronghold. Across from him, Katz was working on similar drawings so they could compare notes. "What kind of shape are they in?"

"Fair to good," Henry replied. "Yellow with age, creased, but that wouldn't matter in the wind. No bugs, no rot, no mold. I'd say they were bought to reoutfit her but they'd never gotten around to it. If we needed to, I believe we can use them." He shrugged. "Of course, I'd like to limber them up some first. Work a little oil into the cloth to soften it and make it water resistant."

Bolan considered that. The sloop didn't figure into anything he had planned, except as an outside shot as transportation to an LZ now that he knew it would float. But giving the men work would keep morale up. "Pick a team," he told the SEAL, "and get it done."

Henry saluted and moved off.

Bolan returned to his work in the war book. James was still maintaining perimeter guard without incident. Masiga's men had never even come close to the cave.

The sloop ended up life as the *One-Eyed Jack,* according to a few pages of the captain's log that Henry had found behind a false wall in the main cabin. She'd been a second ship in Captain Bartholomew Roberts's pirate navy. During her brief career with Roberts, the ship had taken eight prizes. The two skeletons at the stern had turned out to belong to archaeologists, according to Brahim, two men who'd been killed more than thirty years ago by looters.

Bolan and Katz compared their drawings. They both agreed on the general configuration of the hardsite. Partially built into a cave system, Masiga's chosen location for a fortress took advantage of a lot of local cover. A wooden palisade fence, between ten and twelve feet tall around the outer perimeter, completed the defenses.

"Looks like we pretty much agree on the basics," Bolan told the Israeli, "but before we go in there, we need to know where the main guns are."

"Agreed," Katz said. "If we can knock them out quickly, our raid will be far less costly. So we'll have to do a little more recon before we contact the *Freede-burg*.''

"Yeah. I figure you and I can handle that ourselves. McCarter can be in charge here.''

"When?"

"It's not getting any earlier," Bolan said, "and a strike at dawn would give us the greatest window of opportunity.''

Katz nodded and put his papers away.

Bolan closed the war book and looked at the sloop as Henry and his crew started to spread the canvas sail. Despite their situation, the virus spreading in Cape Anansi and the busted raid, his mind cycled around the *One-Eyed Jack,* imagining all the battles she'd probably been through.

"Yakov, Striker," Encizo called over the headset. "I've got Stony Base on-line.''

Gathering their gear, the two Stony Man warriors double-timed it around the sloop and back up the stone stairs, taking the branch leading to the back way out, which McCarter had found and cleared in case it was needed.

Encizo had set up the radio on top of the mountain that helped form part of Scorpion Falls. Over the rise, much of the noise of the falls was dampened.

Bolan took the handset. "Stony One to Stony Base.''

"Go, Stony One. You have Stony Base.'' Brognola's voice sounded tired but hopeful.

In quick, terse sentences, the Executioner explained the operation as he'd refigured it with Katz. When he mentioned getting supplies by way of Cape Anansi, the head Fed interrupted him.

"Cape Anansi's been quarantined," Brognola said. "The President's orders, as well as the general consensus of every government leader who has military over there. At this point, I can't even stir up the dust in that city."

"A quarantine isn't going to stop Kamer or Masiga," Bolan said.

"I know. But our hands are tied as far as Walukagian involvement goes."

Bolan looked out at the distance separating Scorpion Falls from Masiga and Kamer. There was no way he could sit idly by while they blackmailed the world. Even if Able Team succeeded in its assault on Flair Subsidiaries in Minnesota, Kamer couldn't be left to roam free. "Mine aren't," the big warrior said. "I'll get back to you." He broke the connection and looked up at Katz. "We're on our own."

"So I heard. What do you propose to do?"

"First," Bolan said, getting up and walking back inside the cavern, "we're going to lean on Chief Henry and make sure that sloop's ready to sail by dawn. On a good day, with the wind to her back, he says that sloop will do eleven knots. That puts us fifteen to twenty minutes from Masiga's stronghold."

"Even so," Katz said, "that leaves us without any weapons but the small arms we managed to escape the train with."

Bolan glanced at the Phoenix Force leader. "Yeah, but I know where we can find some more."

The Mpunga River, Walukagi
12:13 a.m.

RECON WORK WAS nothing new to David McCarter, and he surveyed the fort straddling the tributary of the Mpunga River with grave interest. Bolan had outlined his plans for the attack, and they were as daring as any the ex-SAS commando had ever heard.

And much of it hinged on the work he was doing now.

Manning and two of the blacksuits were working backup on the probe, but the big Canadian was deeply involved in computations and a deadly geography of his own.

Moonlight kissed the steel of another piece of artillery mounted along the palisade wall. He diligently wrote it down and marked its space on the map he'd drawn close to scale. So far, there were seven of them. Eight, he figured, was a more round and logical number. While Manning and his team crept forward with the logs of C-4 they'd scrounged from the rest of the strike force, he kept looking for the missing gun.

Dawn was going to break all too soon, and with the all-or-nothing strike they had planned, there wasn't a moment to lose.

The Walukagian Coastline
12:52 a.m.

MACK BOLAN LOOKED at the placid water, then at the shoreline, which still showed signs of the attack that he'd directed against Masiga twenty-three hours earlier to prevent the delivery of Ansell Dewbre's munitions. It didn't seem possible that so much had happened in such a short time.

"Where did the *Seahorse Moon* go down?" Calvin James asked.

They were standing beside the canvas-covered flatbed truck Brahim had helped them get from a nearby village. The engineer had taken care of the arrangements while the Stony Man warriors remained out of sight in the bush.

Bolan pointed. "There. I planted explosives below her waterline. Not enough to totally destroy her, but enough to put the freighter down."

James was skinned down to his skivvies, and a blacksuit with SEAL training was helping him into one of the three air tanks Brahim had purchased from some of the young men in the Kausan town. The air tanks, it turned out, had been some of the extra benefits the Kausan men had taken from Cape Anansi's first wave of UN peacekeepers and a boatload of South African mercenaries who'd been diamond hunting and gold prospecting off the coast. There was also a diesel-powered air compressor if they needed to recharge the tanks.

"Should be a piece of cake," James said, cinching the belts. "Working in two-man teams, we can get a lot done in a short amount of time."

"We're going to have to," Bolan said. He'd set aside almost two hours for the recovery operations, forty-five minutes for transportation and two hours and twenty minutes for the installation of the guns. The sun was supposed to rise at 7:17 a.m., and there would be prevailing winds from the north-northwest, with a chance for rain from a tropical storm farther up the coast.

"The hardest part is going to be working in the dark." James switched on the big waterproof lantern one of the blacksuits had given him. "But once we find the freighter, that'll get easier, too."

"Watch yourself down there," Bolan cautioned.

James nodded and waded into the water, slipping his mask and mouthpiece into place. One of the SEAL-trained blacksuits followed him.

Katz was helping set up the primitive block-and-tackle arrangement they'd designed using trees and lengths of rope.

"We'll be done before Calvin needs us," Katz said. "The heaviest thing is going to be the 76 mm guns."

"I know, but if they're salvageable, we need them. Without them, that sloop will become kindling in a heartbeat when we go up against Masiga." Bolan checked his watch. Time was slipping away from them. He went to the truck, slipped behind the wheel and moved the vehicle toward the shoreline, staying on top of the driftwood to keep from sinking into the mud. The other blacksuits had gathered the wood for that purpose.

By the time he got back to Katz, the block-and-tackle assemblies were finished.

"Crude," the Phoenix Force commander commented, pulling on the ropes, "but effective."

"Yeah." Bolan stared down at the dark water, then saw the flare of the underwater torch James had taken down with him. "Calvin's found the first of them." He watched and waited, feeling the numbers whisper through his mind, drawing them closer to the center of the web of violence that had spun out to cover Walukagi, to the moment of survival or death.

Stony Man Farm, Virginia
11:41 p.m.

HAL BROGNOLA STOOD behind Aaron Kurtzman's big desk and stared at the wall screen at the far end of the room. It was split, showing the scenes at Minnesota and Walukagi. On the left was Flair Subsidiaries, looking bleak and harsh from the northern winter already settling over the land. The industrial complex was shaped like a giant *O*, leaving space in the center for an employee parking lot, as well as tighter security. Dr. Linus Maaloe wasn't at home. Able Team had already checked on that. But activity at the plant was up, according to one of the local deputies Lyons had spoken to. For the moment, Able Team and a group of Justice marshals were on either end of the state highway that ran past the complex, waiting to go into action. There was no other way in or out of the complex unless someone went on foot through the woods.

On the right side of the screen was the Mpunga River and Scorpion Falls. The picture was soft and hazy, tinted by a dawn that wasn't quite going to make it through the rain clouds. It had started raining there an hour earlier. If he looked hard, he could barely make out the canvas-covered flatbed Bolan and Phoenix Force had used to haul the recovered guns back to the cave. The big Fed still marveled at what the team had been able to put together.

"Where'd they get the hardware to bolt the guns to the deck?" Kurtzman asked.

"Manning and his team ransacked a toolshed at Masiga's stronghold while they were setting charges," Price answered. "What didn't work outright, they managed with shims and auxiliary support struts. None of it's permanent, but maybe it's enough."

Brognola glanced at the clock and saw the sweeping second hand wiping away the time they had remaining.

Then the phone rang.

The big Fed scooped it up and identified himself.

"Are they ready in Walukagi?" the President asked.

"Yes." Brognola had talked to Katz fifteen minutes earlier, and the Israeli was expecting to be finished on time.

The President let out a long breath. "I don't know, Hal. If they were properly equipped, if Masiga and Kamer weren't on them, maybe I'd feel more sure about this. We have no options about the operation in Min-

nesota. I can't allow that threat to exist. But in Walukagi—there could be a lot of people lost.''

"Sir," Brognola said in a hard voice, "those people
are already lost. Striker and his team are trying to save
them. And they're prepared to give their lives doing
that. If Kamer follows through on his promise to pro-
duce the antidote for those people, which I quite frankly
doubt, he's still going to be in place there.''

"I know.''

"He and Masiga are tumors," Brognola said. "The
only way to prevent them from harming anyone further is to excise them. And right now we've got people
poised over there who can do that.''

There was only a brief hesitation. "Get it done, Hal.
Call me if there's anything we can do.''

"Just be ready with that air support when the time
comes.''

"The pilots aboard the *Freedeburg* are standing by to
scramble.''

"Good enough." Brognola broke the connection and
looked up at Price and Kurtzman. "We're on.''

Kurtzman quickly booted up communications links
with both teams.

Price took the handset. "Stony Base to Stony teams.''

"Go, Stony Base," Bolan answered. "You have
Stony One.''

"You have Able One," Lyons echoed.

Price said, "You have your green light. Good hunting.''

"Fifteen minutes," Bolan said, "then Able can begin its end of the operation.''

"Affirmative," Lyons replied. "From now.''

The com-loop cleared.

Brognola shook out a couple of antacid tablets and
washed them down with cold coffee from the cup at his

side. The stakes were on the table, and it was time for the final roll of the dice, winner take all.

Scorpion Falls, Walukagi
6:43 a.m.

"PULL!" MACK BOLAN YELLED over the muted thunder of the falls. He took a firm grip on the oar and began to pull, straining his back and shoulders. Around him, the rest of the team pulled, as well. Chief Henry stood behind the wheel, then began calling out the strokes.

Slowly the *One-Eyed Jack* began to move, edging toward the mouth of the cave under the roaring falls. Her hull was watertight, but drew eight feet of water, leaving her less than a yard from bottom in the cavern. Her sails were furled, and her mast and bowsprit stood out naked and hard and lean.

The men pulled the oars in unison, gaining speed as they cut across the underground lake toward the falls. Getting through the plunging water was the hardest part of getting out onto the open river. Enough water was coming down to possibly sink the sloop. Bolan and Katz had figured that two hundred years ago the river hadn't been as full, and that possibly other tributaries had changed course over the years, adding to the flow.

Manning had come up with the solution. With two of the SEAL-trained blacksuits, he'd planted charges along the riverbed above the cave, farther up the mountains. When detonated, they were supposed to form a concussive wave that would greatly slow the river flow for a few seconds, allowing the *One-Eyed Jack* time to slide through the cave mouth.

Bolan and Katz had given the operation their approval. Otherwise they'd have had to chance sinking the ship.

Manning stood in the stern, his remote-control detonator in his hands. "Ready!" he shouted.

The sloop cruised on, dropping to within ten feet of the water.

"Now!" the Canadian yelled.

Bolan pulled on the oar harder, knowing the other men were redoubling their efforts, as well. The muffled boom of explosions echoed inside the cavern. A few stalactites fell from their moorings and knifed into the water.

The falls hit the bow of the sloop and pulled her down, beating incessantly against the hull and splashing over her crew. Then the deluge slowed, and the water ran from her deck.

Bolan kept pulling the oar, feeling sweat coat his limbs from the effort. In a heartbeat they were through the cave mouth, the mast almost scraping the ledge overhead. When the water started back, it only caught the last few feet of the sloop.

For a moment the ship spun crazily, trapped between the opposing forces of falling water.

"Pull!" Henry yelled. "We aren't out of it yet!"

The Stony Man team bent to the task with a vengeance. Then the *One-Eyed Jack* seemed to become a living thing, dominating the water with a wild power and cleaving her course. The falling rain was gentle by comparison.

"By God," Henry whooped, "you did it. Now get up there and get me some sailcloth and I'll show you what this rig can really do."

Shipping their oars, Bolan watched as the hands scattered across the sloop and started raising the sails.

In minutes she was fully rigged, and the wind whipped the canvas out with stiff cracks. The Executioner felt the pull of the sloop immediately and knew she was running with the wind now and not the water. She creaked, but she held and ran magnificently.

The two 76 mm guns mounted in the bow of the vessel on either side of the bowsprit gleamed. The bolts holding them in had been the best they could manage, and the Executioner felt they would serve. Four machine guns—two .50-calibers and two chambered in 7.62 mm—were mounted in front and on both sides. No guns were mounted in the stern. Once they reached the stronghold, their enemy would only be before them.

"Run up our colors," Henry bellowed.

Jack Grimaldi produced a flag, which he attached to the mast. He ran it up and the wind instantly unfurled it. The red, white and blue looked strong against the dark sky.

"Never thought I'd ever be a pirate," the pilot confided when he returned to the railing where Bolan and Katz stood.

"Well, mate," McCarter said good-naturedly, "I have to tell you. If you break out in sea shanties any time soon, we're going to use you as the anchor."

Bolan went forward to stand in the bow. He gripped the railing as he stared out over the broken terrain of the Drakensberg Mountains. They were racing the dawn, but with the spotty cloud cover holding, he knew it improved their chances. Kamer and Masiga wouldn't be expecting an attack, but they'd have guards posted along the way. They'd know before the *One-Eyed Jack* reached small arms distance of the palisade gates.

And by that time, Bolan hoped the doomsday numbers were against their enemy and not the crew of the pirate ship.

CHAPTER SIXTEEN

Near Park Rapids, Minnesota
11:13 p.m.

Carl Lyons had always been a man of action, and the more direct, the better he liked it. The Justice marshals were in the process of finding that out.

Behind the wheel of the black Oldsmobile Bravada sports utility vehicle, the Ironman led the way onto Flair Subsidiaries grounds. He ignored the security gatehouse and crashed through the red-and-white-striped bar.

"We could have stopped," Marshal Martin Breckenridge commented quietly from the passenger seat. "We do have federal warrants that allow us search and seizure rights."

"Sure," Lyons said agreeably. "And while we're pushing paper at them, they could be dumping that virus into Lake Itasca."

"The lake's more than a mile from here," Breckenridge replied. "We've got the area surrounded."

"Look," Lyons said, "this isn't a police action. That isn't a perp in that building. That's an enemy. If he wants to give up, fine. But I'm not going in shooting high." He glanced in his rearview mirrors, seeing the line of cars following him. All of them were unmarked but had magnetic cherries flashing on the rooftops.

Two security cars marked with Flair Subsidiaries ID approached them on an interception course. Lyons was able to discern at least two men in each vehicle.

Without warning, autofire sparked from the rear seat of the nearest security vehicle and chopped holes in the Bravada's windshield.

"Shit!" Breckenridge said, clamping his hand on his cowboy hat and slouching in his seat.

"You want to fire a warning shot?" Lyons asked, taking evasive action. The security car locked onto him, driving at his side as he streaked for the main entrance.

"Hell, no," Breckenridge said. He unlimbered his 10 mm Delta Elite and fired through the side window. His bullets took out the driver's-side window and ran in a line back toward the passenger window in the rear.

The security car went out of control and slammed up against the Bravada, locking momentarily. Lyons yanked hard and freed the big 4 × 4 with a rending screech. An explosion sounded behind him. When he looked, he saw one of the marshals' vehicles go spinning away like an overturned turtle.

"Ironman," Blancanales called over the headset.

"Go."

"They've got a gunner on the roof armed with an M-203."

Lyons glanced up at the roof and saw the man draped in shadows. There was a spark of flame. Pulling hard right, the Able Team leader barely avoided the 40 mm warhead that impacted just ahead of his previous course.

"Oh, yeah," he said sarcastically, "I can really see these guys going for a federal writ about now." He stepped hard on the brake, aware that other Flair gunners had taken up the battle, as well. Bringing the Bravada around sideways so his side faced the industrial

complex, Lyons grabbed the sniper rifle and flicked off
the safety. He raised the rifle to shoulder level as the guy
on top of the building readied the grenade launcher to
fire again.

The cross hairs settled over the man from thirty yards
out. Lyons stroked the trigger, then watched through
the scope as the man's head jerked backward beside the
butt of his weapon. The corpse dropped.

Getting back behind the wheel, Lyons spotted a delivery ramp at the side of the industrial complex. He
threw the vehicle in gear and sped toward the ramp.

He double-clutched, threw the 4 × 4 into a controlled
sideways skid and lined himself up with the ramp. In
front of the building, the Flair security forces were laying down a withering line of fire, using heavy machine
guns that had been brought from inside the building.
Evidently they'd been in a state of readiness for some
time. If the Flair security teams' solidarity wasn't broken, Lyons knew the other marshals would be taking
some significant losses.

He pinned the accelerator to the floor, felt the tires
slip traction for just an instant, then find it. He shifted
into third just as he hit the ramp.

The Bravada's engine whined in protest as the tires
left the ground and it became airborne for almost sixty
feet. It hit the glass wall of the building with the nose
still climbing for the sky.

For Lyons, the world suddenly seemed to be made of
glass. Then it shattered, coming apart in shiny jagged
edges. Metal support struts ripped loose and battered
the 4 × 4.

The Bravada landed like an ungainly cat, managing
to come down on all fours, but not in a stylish manner.
Making himself move, Lyons freed the seat belt and
grabbed the Calico machine pistol from under the seat.

Breckenridge was a half step behind him, carrying an H&K MP-5.

The 4 × 4 had landed just past the center point of the huge hallway that stretched in both directions. Security lamps illuminated the scene in a ghostly half-light.

A pair of security guards confronted Lyons as he streaked toward the front of the building. He cut them down in a blazing figure eight without breaking stride. Turning the corner, he spotted another guard just as the man fired.

The high-caliber rounds lifted Lyons from his feet and threw him backward. His breath was knocked out of him, but the Point Blank modular armor he wore stopped the bullets. He swept the Calico across the gunner and put him down.

Shoving himself to his feet and forcing his stunned lungs to work, he pressed on. Passing another corner, he found himself at the front of the industrial complex. Gunners were gathered in the lobby at the floor-to-ceiling windows, assault rifles spitting out a deadly barrage.

Lyons ripped two grenades from his vest, pulled the pins and lobbed the bombs toward the line of gunners. They bounced across the floor for a moment, attracting the attention of one man who tried to yell a warning and stand up at the same time. The first grenade blew him through the shattered window he stood in front of. When the second one went off, Lyons stepped around the corner.

The destruction had been almost complete, leaving seven dead men in its wake. With select bursts from the Calico, Lyons added three more to the list.

He tagged the headset's transmit button. "Pol. Gadgets."

"Go."

"Go."

"Front door's open."

"Thought that looked like your handiwork," Schwarz said.

Lyons grinned and headed back down the hallway he'd come through. "Didn't want you to miss the party."

The hallway had nearly a dozen doors, and Lyons went through them systematically. When he tried a knob and found it locked, he lifted a boot and smashed his way through. Most of the rooms were offices. All of them were empty.

By the time he was on the last one, Blancanales and Schwarz had caught up to him. They had a prisoner between them, the guy's hands cuffed behind his back.

"There's a lower floor," Blancanales said. "Our new friend is going to show us the way."

"He said Maaloe's below," Schwarz added. He shoved the prisoner ahead of them, letting him feel the barrel of the Beretta 92-F behind his ear.

They moved at a trot. Lyons brought up the rear, listening to the channel used by the federal marshals as they closed down the ground level. Resistance on the part of the Flair security people was dying away.

An office around the next corner had a false door. A hidden switch slid it out of the way and revealed a set of stairs. Blancanales took point, disappearing around a sharp corner. A dim yellow bulb provided the only light.

"What's down here?" Lyons asked the prisoner.

"Don't know," the guy said. "Maaloe, the guy your buddy was asking about, hangs out down here, and they've been doing some construction."

"What kind of construction?"

"Excavating. At night they've been bringing dirt out in burlap bags."

"For how long?"

"Weeks. Maybe a couple months. I'm not sure."

The stairwell opened up into a sophisticated control room done all in white and black. Mainframe computers ranged the walls. Three desks sat in various corners of the room, all with desk computers.

The other corner held a door with lettering that sent a chill up Lyons's spine: Warning! Hazardous Biochemical Materials! Keep Locked! Almost hypnotized by the words, he walked forward and looked through the reinforced glass. Steel and glass tubes filled the room, twisting and running in all directions, hooked up to metal coffin-size boxes.

"What the hell is that?" Blancanales asked. He'd taken possession of the prisoner while Schwarz sat in front of one of the computers and lifted the modem.

"Looks like a storage room," Schwarz said. "But those tubes look like some kind of pneumatic delivery system."

"A delivery system?" Lyons echoed. Then he remembered their prisoner's comments about the dirt being taken out of the lower level. "Jesus. Breckenridge said it was only a mile or so to Lake Itasca."

"That's about the distance," Blancanales agreed.

Lyons looked back in the storage room. "What if they've got it set up so this stuff can be dumped into the lake? Hell, they might not even have to dump it into the lake if they can just get it into the groundwater."

"That's exactly what it is," Schwarz said.

Lyons turned to look at his teammate. Schematics showed on the monitor. With only a little effort, he could see that an underground line had been run from Flair Subsidiaries to Lake Itasca.

"And the delivery system's already been activated," Schwarz said grimly. "I've got Aaron working on it, but he can't get inside the system yet."

"How long have we got?" Lyons asked, moving over to the row of lockers.

"Six and a half minutes."

Lyons opened the lockers and found a "clean" suit inside. It was one piece and designed to be impenetrable to any sort of contaminants that spread by physical touch, whether in solid, liquid or gaseous form. He was familiar with it from bomb squads he'd worked with on his days with the LAPD. He shed his gear and pulled it on, adding the gloves and boots, then using the quickseal tabs to close them securely.

"Where are you going?" Blancanales asked.

"To find out where those pipes go," Lyons answered, taking the C-4 he carried in his gear. "Looking through that door, the tunnel looks big enough for me to walk through. At least for a ways. Let me have your plastic explosives."

Schwarz and Blancanales quickly passed over their C-4.

"If I close that pipe down," Lyons said, "cause it to collapse, that virus will have no place to go. It can be cleaned up later if it's buried. But if it reaches the lake, we're screwed."

"Good luck, amigo," Blancanales said, clapping him on the shoulder, his face grim.

"How are you going to get out?" Schwarz asked.

Lyons paused at the door. "I'm hoping they have some kind of maintenance entrance. If they don't and Aaron can't stop the system and I have to blow the tunnel, bring a shovel. How much time do I have?"

"Four minutes and forty seconds," Schwarz answered.

"Used to do a mile in under that." Lyons gave them a salute and met their eyes, knowing either of them would have gone in his place. But he figured he could cover the distance faster, and he wasn't as good on the computer as Schwarz or as willing to network things with the marshals as Blancanales.

He slid through the maze of pipes and wished he could simply blow up the room. But he had no way of knowing if these pipes were the only ones going to the lake. Others might join in along the way.

Once in the tunnel, he had to stoop, but he could move at a quick jog. "Count me down," he said into the headset.

"Three minutes," Schwarz replied.

It was hard to breathe through the mask he wore, and the air inside the tunnel seemed thin. He switched on the flashlight he'd brought with him, and the beam flashed out bright and hard against the metal sides of the tunnel.

"Two minutes."

Lyons heard the beating of his own heart, magnified a thousandfold by adrenaline and the enclosed space. God, he'd been claustrophobic as a kid. Now it was all coming back to him. The tunnel had to have an opening somewhere. He didn't want to be buried alive. His back ached from carrying the C-4 in front of him and having to run bent over.

"One minute."

Breath rasping, Lyons tried to figure out how far he could have gotten. The radio communication was still clear.

"The marshals caught Maaloe outside the building getting into one of the cars," Blancanales said.

"Forty-five seconds," Schwarz announced. "Carl, set those explosives and get down that tunnel as far as you can. We'll be right there."

Lyons knew he had to set the C-4. And it was too far to go back once he did. The virus would be blown back that way. He worked it into a line along one side, angling it so the concussion might weaken the steel pipe and let the earth overhead collapse inward. Damn, he hoped there was enough of the C-4. He didn't know if he would even be able to outrun the blast, much less the virus.

"Thirty seconds."

He slapped a remote control detonator into the C-4 and started to run. His lungs were threatening to collapse without enough oxygen. He felt like he was underwater, straining to breathe but getting nowhere.

"Twenty seconds."

Lyons swept the tunnel with the light. "Fifteen. Carl, dammit, are you clear?"

"Clear," he said.

"Is there a way out?"

"No. Don't hold back when you get those shovels, guys. I don't like it down here now." Then he spotted the ladder rungs leading up just ahead of him. "Wait! I see something.' He was gasping when he reached the ladder and looked upward with the flashlight. A smaller tunnel, maybe even his size, led up to an access door. "It's a door."

"Ten seconds. Move your ass."

Lyons's hand slipped off the rung, then he pulled himself up and tried the door. The lock was stiff, but it moved.

"Five seconds. Four, three..."

Lyons hauled himself out of the access hole, then slammed the lid shut behind him, touching the remote control. Explosions shook the ground, and less than forty yards away he saw a huge amount of the wooded landscape suddenly sink, leaving a hole in the snow cover.

"You did it, Ironman," Schwarz called out over the headset. "The explosion shut down the delivery system to the lake. Computer's going wild saying it can't fulfill the request."

"Terrific."

"We got a bonus, too, amigo," Blancanales said. "Kurtzman got the antidote for the virus from Maaloe's files."

Lyons leaned against a tree and inhaled deeply. "If you guys don't mind, I'm going to take my time getting back. Catch my breath." The forest looked serene, relaxed, and he suddenly realized he'd never seen brighter stars.

"You do that, Ironman. We'll be here."

"Yeah." Lyons started walking. Wilhelmus Kamer's operation was shut down in America, but he had to wonder how things were going for Striker and Phoenix Force.

The Mpunga River, Walukagi
7:10 a.m.

"HAVE YOU FOUND HER YET?" Wilhelmus Kamer asked as he walked into the small house Masiga had assigned him. It was Spartan in furnishings, and no place he wanted to be at all.

At the computer, Vanscoyoc shook his head. "Not on any airlines or trains or buses that I can find. Unless she's driving across Africa, she must have had another name we didn't know about."

Kamer poured himself a drink from the whiskey
they'd brought. Memory of Sonnet Quaid's naked and
lovely body taunted him. There'd been very few things
denied to him for a long time now.

He sipped his drink and stared out over the fortification. Few of Masiga's men were awake at the time.
Most of them were exhausted from the fruitless search
for the special forces people who'd escaped the attack
on the train. Above the palisade walls, the sky was dark
and overcast. It was raining now, and it looked like it
might rain forever.

"You don't know why she left?" Vanscoyoc asked.

"No."

"She took nothing?"

Kamer shook his head. "All my accounts, all my
business is fine."

"What are you going to do when you find her?"

"Kill her," Kamer said without hesitation. "If she
chose cowardice over loyalty, that's all she deserves. If
she did steal from me in some way that I don't know
about, then a sudden death is too generous for her."

Vanscoyoc nodded.

"But that can wait." Kamer looked at the satellite
telephone by the desk holding the computer. "The
Americans should be calling sometime soon."

Then the phone rang.

Kamer smiled and raised his glass to the Dutchman.
"A toast to victory and a long future of riches."

Vanscoyoc lifted the phone, then a graveness appeared on his face that confused Kamer.

"The Flair Subsidiaries complex is under attack," the
Dutchman said. He took the telephone from his ear.
"The line just went dead."

Dread swept over Kamer. "That doesn't make sense.
How could they know about Flair?"

"They did," Vanscoyoc said as he gathered up a pair of binoculars. "That's the part you need to deal with right now. If they have Flair, they may have the antidote. And if they have the antidote, they don't need us."

Kamer followed the Dutchman out of the house and up the steps beside it. An observation walk had been constructed on top.

Vanscoyoc looked through the binoculars, then back at Kamer. "We're under attack, too."

Taking the binoculars, Kamer focused on the Mpunga River. There, just above the lip of the palisade fence, was a ship in full sail. An American flag flew from the mast. "Shit," the White Tiger Investments CEO said. He reached for the pistol at his side and fired through the whole clip, alerting Masiga's sleeping troops.

The Mpunga River, Walukagi
7:12 a.m.

"GUNNER!" MACK BOLAN yelled as he heard the flat crack of the shots and saw the stronghold suddenly galvanize into movement.

"Sir!" the two 76 mm cannon men yelled in response.

"Take down your targets."

"Yes, sir."

"Helmsman," Bolan said, bringing up his binoculars. He felt the rhythm of the sloop beneath him. The *One-Eyed Jack* had been constructed for fast engagements.

"Sir."

"Take us in. Full speed."

"Aye, sir." Henry handled the craft with a deftness that would have made an onlooker think he'd been running pirate ships all his life. He called out orders to the men handling the sails, getting the most out of them.

A bend of the Mpunga River dodged in under one wall of the fortification and came out the other, providing a constant source of fresh water. The river was used as a waterway, too, because gates were closed on both sides. Small docks held outboards and canoes tethered to pilings.

Water splashed up before and behind the sloop in ten-foot-tall eruptions as cannon fire struck the river within yards of it. The dulled booms followed on the heels of the explosions. When the 76 mm guns returned fire, the sloop shivered from the recoil.

Bolan put the binoculars away and hung on to the bow railing, the wind blowing through his hair and shuffling through his clothing and equipment. Spray from the river dampened his skin. He held the Franchi SPAS 15 in his hard right hand. The exhaustion from the past few days was forgotten. He had his target in his sights, and the doomsday numbers were playing his song.

A cheer went up from the sloop's crew as the 76 mm guns took out two cannons along the palisade walls. Small-arms fire joined the cannon now as the *One-Eyed Jack* pulled within two hundred yards.

The machine gunners aboard the sloop opened fire on Katz's command and started taking down Masiga's men from the palisades. With the stores they'd rescued from the *Seahorse Moon,* they were well provisioned with ammo. Brass tumbled across the deck.

Kissinger stood nearby, the sniper rifle in his hands speaking decisively. The armorer was calm and measured.

The distance decreased to a hundred yards, and the sloop took its first hit in the stern. Timber flew, and a dozen holes were rent in the rearward canvas. Chief Henry never lost his bearing.

"Gary," the Executioner called.

"Yeah."

"Drop the gates." The *One-Eyed Jack* was seventy yards from the entrance to the stronghold, closing fast.

In response, explosions rose in quick succession along the gates, shearing first the upper supports, then the lower ones. Cut free, the gates first fell toward each other, then dropped into the water.

"Gunners," Bolan said.

"Yes, sir."

"Rake that shoreline."

"Yes, sir."

The 76 mm cannon and the machine guns went to work at once, blitzing across the muddy ground near the uneven wooden pier. Masiga's men went down like dominoes. Craters opened up in the ground as the 76 mm warheads struck.

Another cannon shot from the stronghold hit the sloop's mast and broke the top third of it away. The huge timber hung in the rigging and in the sails and came tumbling down, creating a moment of confusion. No one was hurt, but they had to free themselves from the ropes and the canvas.

Chief Henry held her steady, easily cruising between the blown gates, the hull scraping against at least one of them. Her prow was aimed at the shattered wooden pier. Two more cannon positions went down to a 76 mm gun and Kissinger.

"Gary," Bolan said.

"Ready for the back wall?"

"Do it."

A line of explosions ripped through the timbers along the eastern wall, knocking them down like straw. Katz and Bolan had agreed that if Masiga's men were given an option between staying and fighting or running, they could be convinced to do the latter.

It didn't take long for many of them to make up their minds. A mass exodus started for the back wall.

Then the sloop was on top of the pilings. Wood broke and splintered with sharp reports that sounded like bones snapping. Bolan held on tightly, trying to stay with the railing. A number of the crew aboard the ship went down.

With the sloop still moving forward, though considerably slowed, he leapt from the railing and landed ankle deep in the mud. Two hardmen taking cover behind a low shed that had survived the impact turned toward him, guns in their fists.

The Executioner brought up the combat shotgun and loosed two rounds. Both charges of double-aught buckshot caught their targets and spilled them into the river.

Lifting his boots from the mud, ignoring the extra weight, the warrior broke into a jog. Huts decorated the hillside leading down to the river. Most of them were on stilts to avoid flooding.

A few gunners were hiding in the one to his left. The line of autofire drove him to cover behind the rusted husk of an automobile of indeterminate origin. Bullets ripped into the fragile metal.

"Striker, stay down. I've got you covered."

Bolan looked back and saw Jack Grimaldi lift his M-16/M-203 to his shoulder. A 40 mm warhead leapt from the grenade launcher's muzzle, then blew the stilt house back into sticks and straw.

Bolan waved his thanks, then got back to his feet. The stilt houses made a maze, but he took his bearings from the mountains behind them. The muddy ground made maneuvering hard, but he wouldn't give in. Rain dripped down from the gray sky and blurred his vision at times. Behind him, the 76 mm guns continued to crack with measured authority.

Coming around a corner, he had to duck to avoid an Uzi-carrying hardman who'd been almost too quick on the trigger. He threw himself to the ground and raised the shotgun. One shot blew the man through the straw wall of a barn where goats and chickens were kept. The animals were mad with terror and bleated and cackled unrelentingly as they scattered.

He ran on. Skirting more stilt houses, he saw Grimaldi and three blacksuits hot on his heels. Behind them, farther down the steep incline, the *One-Eyed Jack* was listing badly in the water. Outnumbered at least twelve to one, the Stony Man forces were gradually turning the battle around, going more and more on the offensive.

"Car pool's going up," McCarter called in a laconic voice. "At least the ones that haven't already been used to evacuate the less patriotic troops."

A drumroll of explosions followed. To Bolan's right, where he placed the car pool from earlier recon, a sheet of flame sprayed skyward, defying the rain.

Slogging through the heavy mud, Bolan reached the house they believed belonged to Masiga. Katz and Grimaldi joined him there, providing cover.

"Masiga was here a moment ago," the Israeli said.

Bolan stood on the uneven porch and looked at the partially open door.

"So were Kamer and Vanscoyoc," Grimaldi added. "Spotted them both, and didn't get a shot at either one."

"They must have chosen to fight again another day," Katz said.

"Kamer may not know Able Team shut down his operation in Minnesota," Bolan said. "Some of his associates may get away, but for Kamer, there's no getting away. There's not going to be another day for him."

They went through the house by the numbers, covering each other. At the back door, only a few yards away, they found a wood-and-rope suspension bridge that led up the steep side of the mountain. Mud on the wooden slats let Bolan know someone had passed that way recently. Besides the imprint of human feet, there were also muddy paw prints from a big cat.

He tapped the headset's transmit button. "Striker to Phoenix Two."

"Go, Striker. You have Phoenix Two." McCarter sounded calm, ready.

"You've got the field, guy." The warrior told him what they'd found.

"Carry on, mate. We're aces here."

Looking over the battlefield, Bolan believed it. The fighting was dying down, and the bodies that were spread over the muddy hellzone belonged to Masiga's men.

Taking the lead, Bolan raced up the hanging bridge. Mud fell from his boots as they hit the wooden slats with hollow thunks.

The suspension bridge rose at a steady and deliberate angle, vanishing over the top of the sheer ridge forty yards away. The ground was now about eighty feet straight down. Slightly winded from the exertion, Bo-

Ian pressed on. As he crested the ridge, movement alerted him.

"They're in the trees," he warned, going to ground. Grimaldi and Katz took cover, as well. The bridge shivered under the impact of bullets. Several of the worn slats shattered.

Bolan aimed and shot one of the gunners out of the tree overhanging the sheer cliff face. The man screamed and clawed the air as he began the long descent. The scream ended abruptly, before the echo of the shots died away.

"We can't stay here," Bolan said.

"What do you suggest?" Grimaldi asked.

"Cut the suspension ropes," Katz answered. "That will drop us below their line of fire and allow us to climb up."

Bolan nodded and reached for his knife. It was the only way.

"Shit," Grimaldi said, looking down. "When I'm this high up, I figure I should have wings."

"You let go when this bridge slams into that cliff face," Bolan said, "maybe you will."

"Thanks."

With quick strokes, the Executioner sliced through the ropes. At first the bridge twisted like a live thing, as if it were trying to get rid of them. Then, when the last rope was cut, it plummeted.

Bolan hung on, watching the cliff face swing toward them. The impact numbed his shoulder and jarred the breath out of him, nearly making the Franchi SPAS 15 slip from his shoulder.

After making sure Grimaldi and Katz were still with him, he began the sixty-foot climb. Thirty feet from the top, a hardman stuck his head over the edge, then brought around his AK-47.

Bolan lifted the combat shotgun and fired one-handed. The recoil almost tore him from his precarious hold, but he held on. The corpse dropped so near him he could have reached out and touched it as it fell past.

At the top, he pushed himself into a standing position, scanning the jungle terrain. He dumped the nearly empty magazine from the shotgun and put in a fresh one.

Suddenly the sound of arriving aircraft filled the sky. Bolan looked up, seeing planes and helicopters coming from the east.

"They're ours," Grimaldi stated. "McCarter's about to have all the help he can handle."

"Able Team must have been successful," Katz said.

Bolan nodded and took a firmer grip on the shotgun. "Let's see if we can flush our quarry." He started down the steep cliff, heading into the jungle. His combat senses searched the foliage around him, at home in an environment similar to the one where the Executioner had been born as a warrior.

"Down!" Grimaldi yelled, diving.

Bolan went to ground, rolling to one side of the trail while Katz rolled to the other. Both of them came up on their knees. Bullets ripped through the branches of the tree Grimaldi used for cover, raining twigs and leaves to the ground.

Focusing on the sounds, Bolan searched the jungle, using his peripheral vision because it picked up motion quicker than regular line of sight.

"Do you see him?" Katz asked.

Bolan shook his head. The land continued out for almost eighty yards. "Cover me."

Katz and Grimaldi gave him tight nods.

The warrior moved at a sprint, staying low. His skin tightened, expecting to feel the sharp bite of a bullet. A rifle banged again, but instead of going for Bolan, the sniper aimed at Grimaldi.

Bolan had twin impressions of Grimaldi going down and Jakob Vanscoyoc partially revealed behind a tree almost fifty yards away, just out of range of the Franchi SPAS 15. Moving smoothly, keeping the Dutchman in his sight, the Executioner hooked the Desert Eagle .44 from his hip holster and brought it up.

Vanscoyoc was pulling back, intending on playing hide-and-seek in the jungle.

Leading his target, holding the big pistol in one hand, Bolan fired. The 240-grain hollowpoint drilled across the intervening space and took Vanscoyoc between the eyes just as the man sensed Bolan and turned to face him. The Dutchman's body pitched backward.

Falling back, the Desert Eagle up, Bolan returned to Katz and Grimaldi.

The Israeli had dragged the pilot to shelter behind a large boulder. "Lung's punctured," Katz said, taking a field dressing from his chest pouch. He cradled Grimaldi's head in his lap. "Bullet slipped behind the body armor and bounced. Someone's going to have to stay with him."

Bolan nodded. He sealed himself off from the emotions that assailed him. Grimaldi looked pale and weak already, a line of bright blood bubbling from the corner of his mouth.

"Katz has got me, Sarge," Grimaldi said, his speech labored.

"Make sure you're still here when I get back," Bolan told him.

"No prob." Grimaldi closed his eyes.

Katz was already in radio communication with Calvin James, Phoenix Force's medic, and with the special forces captain running the air insertion.

"Take care of him, Yakov. He's been a friend for a long time."

"He'll be okay," Katz said. "I just need to be here in case that lung collapses and causes more problems. Calvin's on his way, and they've got a med-evac coming." He looked at the jungle. "You got the Dutchman?"

"Yeah."

"Be careful out there. Masiga and Kamer won't hesitate about killing you."

Bolan nodded and moved out. He pushed thoughts of Grimaldi from his mind, becoming as much a part of the jungle as the other predators who hunted the grounds. He leapt over Vanscoyoc's corpse, jogging now because Kamer and Masiga wouldn't have time to waste. They'd know the American and British forces were converging on the stronghold.

Birds darted through the branches ahead of him, brilliant splotches of color that resembled aerial heartbeats. Monkeys shrilled, interfering with his hearing. He spotted Masiga at the same time the big man saw him.

They were ten yards apart, running in the same direction. Masiga carried Colt .45s in both fists. He changed directions and rushed at Bolan, firing both pistols as he came, screaming.

Bolan stood his ground, the Desert Eagle hard and sure in his fist. It bucked against his palm three times, and tore away the lower part of Masiga's face in a spray of blood. Two of the .45 bullets had smashed into Bolan's body armor at his abdomen with stunning force but didn't penetrate.

Masiga collapsed in front of the Executioner, stopping only a few feet away, dead before he stopped moving. Bolan sheathed the .44 and ran on, figuring Kamer would have been heading in the same direction as Masiga. There was enough jungle to hide the man, and Kamer knew how to use it.

Emerging from the tree line, he saw the White Tiger Investments CEO at the edge of a cliff only twenty yards away. To the left, Bolan could see helicopters descending on the other side of the ridge.

"Kamer," Bolan called in a graveyard voice. He leveled the shotgun.

Turning, Kamer stared at him. He held a Detonics Scoremaster in his right hand. "You."

"Yeah," Bolan said, walking forward easily.

"What do you want with these people?" Kamer demanded. "Why would you want to protect them? Men like you and I, we're meant to take the things we want from life. These kaffirs aren't worth one drop of your blood."

"I don't see it that way."

"Then you're an altruist." Kamer kept his hold on the pistol and spared a glance over his shoulder. "These people are ignorant savages. They exist hand-to-mouth. Europeans came here and tried to make something of this land, tried to give them civilization. They spit on it, spit on everything that's been done for them."

"They already had civilization," Bolan said, coming to a stop ten feet away. "They didn't need someone else's idea of civilization rammed down their throats. And you're not talking about enhancing a culture, you're talking about greed, pure and simple. There's a difference between being a savage and being primitive. This land is primitive, true, and death is a constant companion of everyone here until they learn to get past war and disease. I think it will happen, under the right circumstances.''

''You fucking bleeding hearts get to me. Given the chance, these people will kill each other.''

The Executioner's voice was flat and hard. ''You're the savage here, Kamer. You would have sacrificed a city to achieve your own ends, maybe even more. Life is hard and lean in its own right. Like the man said, no one gets out alive. I fight people like you so that the innocents who can see beyond greed and the need to dominate others will have the chance to build better lives for themselves and those who come after them.''

''You make yourself sound so noble.'' Kamer forced a laugh. ''And how many people have you killed today?''

''The way I look at it,'' the Executioner said, ''I'm still one short.''

''Sharde!'' Kamer said in a loud voice, ''kill!'' Then he brought up the pistol.

Remembering the tracks of the big cat on the suspension bridge, the warrior turned toward the faint rush of noise behind him. Uncoiling, the leopard yowled with bloodcurdling intensity and leapt.

A bullet slammed into Bolan's back, stopped by the body armor. There was no time to bring the shotgun around and fire. Stepping to one side, he buttstroked the big cat, feeling the meaty impact of the SPAS 15 strike against the massive shoulders.

Yowling again, this time in pain, the leopard landed on the ground and immediately set itself for another leap, its face split in fang-baring bloodlust.

Bolan dived to one side as the leopard leapt. Still rolling, only inches from its claws, he shoved the shotgun's barrel into its face and pulled the trigger. The double-aught buckshot turned the black and gold fur into bloody ruin. Bullets from Kamer's weapon chopped a ragged line of holes in the wet ground behind the warrior.

From almost twenty feet out, the Executioner brought up the SPAS 15 and pointed it at Kamer. A bullet burned his cheek as he pulled the trigger.

The tight pattern caught Kamer in the neck, almost taking his head off. The force staggered him backward, knocking him over the cliff's edge.

Bolan pushed himself to his feet. He felt warm blood trickling down his cheek, and the flesh was already turning numb. At the edge of the cliff he looked down and saw Kamer's broken body lying amid a jumble of rocks.

"Striker."

He tapped the headset frequency. "Go, Yakov."

"Jack's been stabilized. The med-evac left just a few minutes ago. How is everything there?"

Bolan stood at the cliff edge of a primitive country whose freedom had been paid for with the blood of many brave men, and stared down at the body of the man who would have taken its future away. Some of Kamer's words held merit. He was a warrior, part of the savagery that would have to give way for true civilization to take root. When that time came, he knew he'd gladly lay down his arms. But until then, he was going to fight the cannibals with everything he had.

He tapped the headset. "We're done here." And for a time he stood in the crisp, cool rain and let it wash away the blood, knowing that this was only a brief respite between battles. His War Everlasting would find another front, and he wouldn't shirk the call.

When all is lost there is always the future

JAMES AXLER

Crossways

In CROSSWAYS, Ryan Cawdor and his companions emerge from a gateway into the familiar, but ravaged world of the Rockies. But this is not a happy homecoming for Ryan and Krysty Wroth as the past becomes a trap, and old debts may have to be repaid.

Hope died in the Deathlands, but the will to live goes on.